Who Shall Sleep, Who Shall Die?

She drifted in and out of sleep while listening to Bolan's even breathing, thinking what a comforting sound it was. During one of the "out" periods she'd gotten herself worked up with a little light sleepytime fantasy and raised to an elbow to lightly brush his lips with hers, thinking him to be safely asleep. But even as their lips touched she saw that his eyes were slitted. He lunged away from that light encounter with the big silver pistol rising up between them.

"Sorry!" she gasped.

"My apology," he muttered, in a flash totally relaxed again, those remarkable eyes retreating behind the slitted lids.

She'd known, then, how frighteningly close she'd been to death—and she'd gained another important insight into this unusual man. He slept with his eyes open and a gun at instant access. How terrible!—how horribly grim for any human being to be forever cocked and ready, poised at the edge of the abyss of death, unwilling to let go even in sleep. And she understood, however imperfectly, the terrible price this man was paying to pursue his "impossible" war.

He'd told her, later, "Sure, I sleep. But it's a trick I learned on the Ho Chi Minh Trail. I guess it's a form of divided consciousness. The part that needs to sleep, sleeps. The part that needs to remain aware, doesn't. It's like the mind posting its own sentry. I call it combat sleep."

* * *

Within hours the battle would be underway and the man who never slept, never closed his eyes to the world he watched, would once again visit death and destruction on the enemy, on those who also watched and struck at a society too often asleep or oblivious to their sinister activities.

The Executioner would wake them all, and decide on who should reap the sleep of the dead.

THE EXECUTIONER SERIES

the EXECUTIONER #34

TERRIBLE TUESDAY

by Don Pendleton

PINNACLE BOOKS • LOS ANGELES

EXECUTIONER #34: TERRIBLE TUESDAY

An original Pinnacle Books edition, published for the first time anywhere.

First printing, January 1979

ISBN: 0-523-40334-8

Cover illustration by Gil Cohen

Printed in the United States of America

PINNACLE BOOKS, INC.
2029 Century Park East
Los Angeles, California 90067

For my mother, who raised me to be
a gentle man—and nearly succeeded;

For my wife, who took over the terrible
task—and led me to the typewriter;

For my daughters, who make gentility
not only desirable but mandatory;

For all, because they remind me that
gentle is not soft, and that a man's
treasures are worth protecting.

It is a common prejudice advanced by the intelligentsia of every age that soldiering is a mindless profession undeserving of any moral respect, as though somehow the preservation of the estate of mankind is a minor effort to be left in the hands of fools and brutes.

—Don Pendleton (unpublished memoir)

Away with those that shall affirm learning to surpass arms; for I will say unto them ... they know not what they say.

—Miguel de Cervantes (*Don Quixote*)

Not all scholars are soldiers. But I have never known a good soldier who is not also a constant scholar.

—Mack Bolan (from his journal)

TERRIBLE TUESDAY

PROLOGUE

"You've done your mile in hell," Brognola told him. "Now it's time to end it. More important work awaits you."

Hal Brognola was the nation's number one cop in the official war on organized crime. He was also the President's chief advisor on internal security matters. Curiously enough, he was also among Mack Bolan's closest friends and supporters—in a covert sense. Bolan was an outlaw. He was wanted by the police in virtually every major city in the country and in various foreign capitals, as well. He was at the top of the FBI's "most wanted" list. If he were to be tried in each court having jurisdiction over his various "crimes," he would die of old age long before the final charge could be heard.

Except that Bolan had always known that he would never die of old age, nor would he ever stand that first day at the bar of justice. Because others sought Mack Bolan and his day of "atonement" with much more fervor and determination than all the police agencies combined. He would not survive the first night behind bars—and Bolan had forever known that. Those "others" were the Mafia—and Mack Bolan was their mortal enemy. From the first clash of arms in his unofficial war against the Mafia, Bolan had been fully aware that he had embarked upon that "last mile" of the condemned man. There was no turning back, no reversal of the inexorable law of the jungle to which he had consigned his destiny.

An ancient sage had observed: "A man's character is his fate." Bolan understood that. And accepted it. He'd been a deathmaster in Vietnam—"the best of the best," as described by a former commanding officer—but it seems that the Bolan character had been rather well formed even before the Vietnam experience.

In an early Vietnam journal, the young soldier had written: "I am beginning to understand this enemy. I am in Quai Tho—or what is left of Quai Tho after the VC withdrew. It numbs the mind. Compared to these guys, even napalm seems merciful. If they do this to their own people, what would they do to *my* people if they had the chance. Yes, I understand them now, I think—but there is no hatred in that understanding. This is the twentieth century, and civilized men will not hate the savages. But we cannot allow them to have their way. I believe I understand why I am here, even if most of the world does not. The savages cannot be allowed to inherit the earth. I try to picture

2

them sweeping into Pittsfield the way they swept Quai Tho. The very image stuns the mind. I am glad we are fighting them here, not there. I don't claim to be a scholar, but I have studied military history and I know that the story of mankind has forever been a contest between negative and positive—the barbarians versus civilization. And I guess that is why I am here, today, in the ruins of Quai Tho."

A couple of Vietnam tours later, back home now in Pittsfield, that same warrior would write: "Why defend a front line eight thousand miles away when the real enemy is chewing up everything you love at home?"

The real enemy . . . this was Mack Bolan's awakening to the understanding that human savagery knows no geographical boundaries. Mack Bolan had met the Mafia . . . and now he could understand this enemy, as well.

"A man's character is his fate," said Heraclitus.

"I have seen the enemy," said Mack Bolan, "and I cannot turn away."

Heroes may be made in heaven, but they are realized only in hell.

Which is, perhaps, why the offer from Washington was so difficult to refuse.

"End it," urged Brognola, following Bolan's 32nd devastating campaign against that enemy at home. "You've beat them . . . in every practical sense. There's nothing left now but the mop-up—and others can handle that as well or better than you. We need you in Washington. You'll be given full amnesty—a new identity, a new life, a whole new reason for living. Can't you accept the obvious? You've won! You beat that damnable last mile! Your time in hell is finished!"

But Bolan was not so sure. The military mind did not see the situation in precisely the same terms as the police mind.

He had to be sure.

"I'd like to come in, Hal. I want to. I really do. I am sick to death of this whole business. Please tell the President that I am flattered and warmed by his offer. But I have to set my own timetable. I have to do it my own way . . . in my own time."

It had something to do with character.

"You've just got to do that second mile, eh?" Brognola replied, already resigned to the idea.

"If that's what you want to call it," Bolan quietly told his friend. "All I need, though, is six days."

Remarkable. The guy wanted six days, during which he intended to finally sweep the country clean of the remaining strongest pockets of Mafia infestation.

Impossible!

But Hal Brognola had learned long ago that—for Mack Bolan—the impossible was merely a way of life. Of course, it could also quickly become a way of death—and that was the line which Mack Bolan had trod throughout his Mafia wars.

But the President wanted the guy—wanted him in the worst way, to head up the country's official but covert response to the threat of world terrorism and militant anarchy. He was prepared to give Bolan everything that had been taken away by the Mafia wars—and it was a second chance, which no sane man would lightly spurn. Brognola had known how difficult it was for Bolan to make his decision. The "six days" thing was a salve to the Bolan conscience. After all he'd been through, the remarkable warrior still felt uncomfortable with any thought that he may be turning away from a commitment. So he had to go that second mile. And Brognola could respect that. So could the President.

"Give him his six days, then," said the chief. "But, Hal—I want you to make this your personal responsibility—I want to see the man here, alive and well, at the end of that six days. I want you to see to that. He is to have every support possible."

Which was a hell of a laugh. There was no way to support Mack Bolan—not in any meaningful sense. The guy played his own game, his own way. Direct support was out of the question. It would also be illegal . . . and terribly dangerous for any government officer. Bolan did not read a victim his rights before he blew him away. So there was really no way to offer direct support as long as the guy was blitzing the domestic theater. The best Brognola could do, anyway, was to pace the edge of the war zone and hope for the best. The first leg of the six day blitz had gone okay. Bolan had taken on the new Midwestern kingpins and walked away with their heads. Literally. And that took care of "Monday's Mob."

But now it was Tuesday. And the man from blood was descending on the West Coast for the second leg of his own version of the Six Day War. He would find a vastly different setup here in California. Much of the Mafia

5

power left in the country was now being consolidated in the western branches of the organization—brokered by a shadowy coalition of once minor hoods under the intriguing banner of the California Concept.

No one in the straight world had yet been able to gain any understanding of what was happening in California, these days. All of Brognola's intelligence wires had been broken at about the same time that the whispers had begun about the California Concept. Not even Bolan had been able to gather any meaningful pre-intelligence from his usually productive sources.

Brognola was feeling very jittery about the whole undertaking.

And all he could do was pace the edges of the war zone and hope for the best. And maybe that would not be enough . . . not for Tuesday, Terrible Tuesday.

CHAPTER 1

THE START

Both were naked. He was a hairy guy of maybe thirty years, lean and well-muscled. She was hardly more than a kid, with silky brown hair all mussed and tangled, the pretty face frozen now in an expressionless mold while the awakening eyes tried to understand what was happening.

The water bed sloshed and undulated as the guy made an angry lunge for the covers.

Bolan shoved him back with a foot on the bare chest and a cold caution. "Huh uh. Stay."

The guy growled a menacing, unintelligible response and glanced nervously at the girl.

He was Terry Fortune—*nee* Tanto Fortinelli—once apprenticed to primo hitman, Jersey Jake Natti—recently rumored to be a freelance contractor available to any with cash enough—mean as a snake and twice as dangerous.

She was, Bolan hoped, one Darlene McCullough—daughter of a wealthy and politically influential Southern California businessman with strong underworld connections.

The girl was giving Bolan a long, appraising look—apparently unruffled by her exposure to his cold gaze—the eyes dwelling and expanding upon the wicked black Beretta with oversized snout that seemed carved into his big fist.

He instructed her: "Go to the bathroom and get your clothes on."

"Why?" she asked sleepily, still staring at the Beretta.

"Then don't," Bolan said. "I just thought you'd rather not share a bed with a dead man."

The guy shifted his weight uneasily, sending more strong ripples across the surface of the waterbed, worried eyes beginning to search the corners of the room for a solace that was nowhere to be found. "Who sent you?" he inquired in a choked voice.

The girl said, "This isn't necessary."

"We can work it out," the guy quickly added.

"No way," Bolan said quietly as he sent a nine millimeter hole to sprout and gush between Terry Fortune's shocked eyes.

The girl let out a horrified yelp and tumbled from the bed. Bits and pieces of Terry's unfortunate remains had splashed onto her. She was shuddering and gasping, nearly hysterical in her attempts to rid herself of the organic muck.

Bolan picked her up and carried her to the bathroom. He shoved her into the shower and wet her down good, then pulled her out and toweled her off. The eyes were large and rounded but uncomplaining as he fitted her into blue jeans and blouse. She left the Sunset District apartment at his side, without comment and without looking back, and got into his car with a resigned sigh.

As he started the engine and put that place behind them, she slouched into the far corner of the seat and muttered, "You're a real bastard, aren't you?"

"I guess I am," he quietly replied.

Sure. That went without saying. And Tuesday had only just begun.

"McCullough is scared to death of Terry Fortune," Leo Turrin had reported to Bolan. Turrin was a longtime friend and ally. Thanks in large part to Bolan's efforts, he was now privy to the secrets of *La Commissione*, the Mafia ruling council. He was also a federal cop. "He doesn't want the kid playing around with the guy, but at the same time he's afraid to make an issue of it. Terry knows damned well that the old man don't like it, but he's just that kind of guy—and that may be the only reason he's interested in the kid. Whatever, it's a potentially explosive situation out there—so I think it's as good a place as any for you to make your start."

"How'd you get onto it," Bolan had wondered.

"Hell, McCullough sent word. He wants someone to take Terry Fortune off his back—or out of his kid's crotch."

9

"You mean he actually sent a complaint? Through channels?"

"Not through official channels, no. See, it's very chaotic out there right now. Nobody knows who's calling the plays."

"Who's their man on the commission, now?"

"Willy Nick—but he's just a figurehead, a mouth. We get the idea they're pulling out—setting up their own thing—or at least getting ready to. But, see, McCullough is just an *amici d'amicu*—a friend of the friends. He's got no standing so he can't really make much noise. And apparently he couldn't find anyone in the local shed who was willing to handle his complaint."

"This complaint came to you through Willy Nick?"

"No. It came via a guy in Jersey. The guy calls me and says, 'Look, Leo, our friend McCullough has done us a lot of favors out there. Now he's calling the tab. We owe him. Let's get that guy off his back.' That's about the gist of it."

"So who'd you send?"

"We sent nobody, yet," Turrin replied. "They're still kicking it around. They worry a lot, lately, you know."

Yes, Bolan knew about the shaky men of *La Commissione* and their recent worries.

"Also, they're trying to figure a way to make it pay. You know?"

Yes, Bolan could understand that consideration, also. When a territory as large and important as California seemed to be breaking away from the national cartel, then the men back east would quite naturally be looking for some handle to keep the thing cozy.

"Send the word back through your man in Jersey," Bolan requested. "Make it a very quiet word."

"Okay." Turrin understood perfectly. "No names mentioned."

"No names, right," Bolan said. "Just tell him that a friend will be looking in on the problem."

It was a good enough place to start, sure.

So now it was started.

It was not quite dawn when the "friend" delivered an errant daughter to the worried father.

The girl evaded a fatherly hug and flounced up the stairs without a word.

McCullough was a large man with thick gray hair and deeply suntanned skin. Maybe fifty, maybe not quite. He'd made a fortune in land speculation and development but not without the right friends in the right places.

He fiddled nervously with his dressing gown as he watched his daughter disappear up the stairs—then he turned to Bolan with an embarrassed grin and warmly clasped his hand.

"You fellows work fast," he said admiringly. "I just got the word a few hours ago that they were sending someone."

Bolan did not return the smile. "I know nothing about that," he replied soberly. "I ran across the kid and I brought her home. That's all there is to it."

McCullough winked knowingly and said, "Sure. I understand. Look—I want to go up and have a few words with Darlene. Can

11

you—would you like some coffee? I'll only be a few minutes."

Bolan allowed himself to be persuaded to stay awhile. He was shown to a breakfast room from where he could watch the sun rise over the Santa Monica mountains while the host went upstairs for a parley with the rebellious daughter. A silent little man in a white coat brought coffee and a tray of breakfast pastries. Bolan's trained eye noted the presence of a small revolver concealed beneath the white coat.

"Things are tense," Bolan said quietly as he accepted the coffee.

"Yes sir, very tense," the little guy replied. He returned to the kitchen without adding to that brief conversation.

Bolan sipped the coffee and tried to cast his mind into the mood and atmosphere of that brooding home, reaching for an understanding of the forces at work there beneath the surface. He'd been alone for perhaps a minute when a divine creature in flowing silk breezed in and took a chair opposite him at the table. She was too young to be the mother, too old for a sister—and far too beautiful for that hour of the morning.

Bolan showed her a solemn smile and said, "Hello."

She wasted no time on pleasantries. "I'm told you brought Darlene home." It was a gentle, melodious voice—neither warm nor cold.

Bolan cocked his head and took his time lighting a cigarette. Then he said, "That's right."

"Why?"

He tasted the coffee as he replied, "Who's asking?"

"Mrs. McCullough is asking."

"Then you should be asking Mr. McCullough," Bolan told her.

"Are you a private detective?"

He grinned. "Not hardly."

"Why doesn't everyone just leave her alone? She's an adult, perfectly capable of choosing her own friends and—"

"And her own poison?"

The woman lowered her gaze, took a deep breath, and asked, "Where did you find her?"

Bolan said, "Not even her daddy asked me that."

"I'm not her daddy."

"Obviously." His eyes roamed that lovely face as he added, "Nor her mommy."

"I'm the only mother the child has known," she replied calmly.

"You just said she was an adult," Bolan reminded her, tiring of the little sparring match. He smiled suddenly and asked, "Have I seen you in the movies?"

"Fat chance," Mrs. McCullough told him in that same melodious voice, neither warm nor cold. She rose gracefully and breezed back out of there.

Bolan's mind had barely uncoiled from that interchange when a shriek from the kitchen sent him whirling to his feet, the Beretta unsheathed and seeking direction.

But the "direction" was all too obvious.

Several handguns were sounding off simultaneously from behind the swinging door to the kitchen.

That door bounded open as the little guy in the white coat toppled through and slid into the breakfast room on his own blood.

Another guy with gun in hand came charging through and was met there smack in the doorway by a sizzling round from the Beretta. It punched him back into the kitchen and the door swung closed behind the falling body.

Bolan gave it a beat to see what else might try it via the swinging door, then he whirled to the window and kicked his way outside, getting there in time to spot another guy sprinting across the grounds in fast retreat. He quickly released the sound suppressor and hoisted the Belle into target stance, squeezing off a single round that caught the guy in mid-stride at about sixty yards out. The guy did a flinging cartwheel and stayed there. Instantly a car, somewhere down the street, roared into motion with tires squealing in frantic getaway.

The guy on the lawn was dead and carried no identification. Likewise, the one on the kitchen floor. An elderly woman, obviously the cook, had died with a bullet in the belly. The little man in the white coat had taken two hits in the chest, which had killed him instantly.

McCullough was huddled with his ladies in the library.

"I've called the police," he told Bolan.

"Then I'll be leaving," Bolan told him. "I wasn't sent here to start a war, anyway."

"You didn't start it," the guy told him. "But you saved our lives, and we're grateful."

No doubt about that, no. This one bore all

14

the signs of a classic hit. A dawn raid. If those guys had gotten their way, they would have left nothing but dead bodies strewn from kitchen to bedrooms. And this could have had nothing to do with the hit on Terry Fortune; there had been no time for such retaliation.

"You're in big trouble, McCullough," Bolan needlessly pointed out.

"Yes. I know."

"Can you handle it?"

"I can handle the police question. I don't know about the rest."

The cold Bolan gaze flicked to the women. It met hostility in the young one, apology from the other.

"Get your women out of here as quick as you can," he suggested. "Send them some place cool and keep them there until I say different."

The McCullough face showed instant relief. "Does that mean you'll be staying in town for awhile?"

Bolan gave him a sober smile as he replied, "That's what it means. Play it careful. I'll be in touch."

He gave the women a final, cool inspection then went out of there. The cops would be responding very quickly, in this exclusive neighborhood. He wished to be well clear before their arrival.

The sun was just beginning to show over the hills.

Tuesday, Terrible Tuesday. Already it had claimed the lives of five people in Mack Bolan's shadow.

And yeah, Leo—it was a hell of an inspired starting place.

15

CHAPTER 2

CLOSURE

During his New Orleans campaign, Bolan had acquired a twenty-six-foot GMC motor home, or RV (recreational vehicle), which—with the assistance of aerospace engineers who rallied to the cause—became the Warwagon, a rolling dreadnought with advanced electronics systems that had added significant new dimensions to his war effort.

Besides massive and sophisticated firepower, the big cruiser also provided the highest reach in electronic surveillance and intelligence gathering capabilities. The rolling laboratory and gunship had also been "home" to the warrior ever since New Orleans, providing the perfect cover beneath her innocuous RV exterior and allowing the man to move freely about the continent within his own little world, thus avoiding many dangers of detection and entrapment.

But the big vehicle had posed a special problem for this second mile effort. A six-day nationwide blitz could be mounted only with air transportation. Bolan had felt that his effort would be severely diminished if he were to leave the gunship behind. Therefore his single request of Brognola was for air support—an airlift operation to keep man and machine together along that second mile.

Brognola gladly complied, placing a C-135 aircraft with military crew at Bolan's disposal and further providing a "trusted technician" to pilot and safeguard the gunship for the airlift operations.

The "trusted technician" turned out to be a female operative out of Brognola's own Washington headshed with the unlikely name of April Rose and the dazzling beauty of a Hollywood starlet. The lady was an engineer and physicist with a specially developed background in computer technology and communications. She was a whiz kid—and a gutsy one, at that.

"The lady has it all together," Brognola had assured his friend, the warrior. "She can be a lot of comfort and you're a damned fool if you don't utilize her talents to the fullest."

"Just what are her talents?" Bolan had wished to know.

"She can run that bloodmobile for you, I'll guarantee that. The lady could write the book on that Buck Rogers gear you have in there. That's mainly why she was selected. I was afraid to turn just anybody loose with that stuff. But she's a lot more than a babysitter for computers. Believe it."

Bolan had learned to believe it; the lady had proven her guts and had come through quite well under fire during their initial operation in Indiana. But there had been frictions early on, fueled perhaps by the inevitable male-female chemical reactions flowing between these two exceptional poles of human excellence. Bolan naturally resisted the idea of placing that lovely life in the jeopardy of his savage world. April herself had trouble reconciling Bolan's *modus operandi* with her own deeply ingrained concepts of justice under the law. The frictions were still there, just below the surface of the association—and that was natural, also. Even though time expands and relationships mature rapidly in the heat of high adventure, the fact remained that these two had known each other for barely more than twenty-four hours.

Still, frictions and all, the two had reached a certain level of understanding and accommodation in a remarkably short time. They had made war together and they had made a sort of love together. More than anything else, they had made peace together. April Rose was now fully "on board," and she was providing essential services to the six day war—so much so, in fact, that Bolan would soon be forced to acknowledge that he could not swing it without her.

She was "on board" that Tuesday morning, also.

Bolan established radio communications with his "rolling base" immediately upon departure from the McCullough home.

"Blackjack to base, hello."

Instantly, cool and calm: "Go ahead, Blackjack."

"What's your situation?"

"A lot quicker than you led me to believe. I hardly had time to get set."

"You're on it, then."

"You bet I'm on it, General. We're heading west on Mulholland—about, uh, two miles east of Topanga Canyon Boulevard."

"Great. Play it loose. Don't try to close. Is it wired good?"

"Affirm, the wires are good and I am playing it loose."

"Maintain track. I am closing."

"Roger."

She was sharp, yeah. There had been no thought that the game would erupt so soon. She'd arrived in the McCullough neighborhood just behind Bolan to begin the stake-out. Then, according to her report, she'd hardly settled in when the shooting began. Now she was on that getaway car, trailing loose with an electronic lock to minimize the chance of discovery.

It could be a useless exercise, of course. There was no certainty that the hired killers would provide any sort of useful link to the new conspiracy in California. But Bolan was forced to grab for straws. His own understanding of the situation was entirely nebulous—and although he knew the identity of many of the players, he did not know precisely where all of the diverse connections came together, where each of the particular players fit, nor even if he had the leaders identified. Most discouraging, he did not understand the new logic. What was this proudly whispered California Concept? How did it differ from the standard logic of the Mafia world? Which areas of the straight society were being manipulated and shaped to fit the criminal need?

Each of these were highly important considerations if the blitz was to be effectively targeted.

A large element in Bolan's success at crimebusting was his understanding of the enemy. It was a game of tactics and strategy, movement and countermovement, a complicated and sensitive game of wits. He did not merely charge in with weapons blazing—although this may appear to be the case to casual observers. The man was much more than a killer, though. He was a soldier—a one-man army in every sense of the term—and he played the game that soldiers had invented: warfare. It was a science and it was an art. Mack Bolan was perhaps the supreme artist in this area of human accomplishment. The big turnabout in the Washington attitude toward this man was a recognition of that expertise. The U.S. government had not extended an official embrace to a psychopathic killer, but to a dedicated and highly accomplished military strategist and tactician.

The Bolan game was not a simple game, no—but, at the moment, it had been reduced to an elemental level of action-reaction. He had hoped to apply pressure that would topple dominoes all along the action-reaction sequence, straight to the heart of the California question, and he had set up William McCullough as the trigger domino. But there was the time factor which Bolan considered inflexible for his six day war, coupled with the principle of uncertainty inherent in any such approach. He had to make a start then run with the developments, relying upon his own fine instincts to seize the proper moment and run the true course.

The hit on McCullough seemed to provide one such moment—and one that held much more dramatic possibilities than the original plan. So Bolan was "playing the ear"—which, simply translated, meant that he was following finely developed instincts and hoping for the best.

Instinct can take the warrior only so far, though. The rest must come from that combination of science, art, and heart that produces the superior warrior—and Bolan was aware of that fact, also.

So it was not a psychopath filled with bloodlust who tracked that hit car into the Topanga Canyon wilds on Terrible Tuesday. It was a scientist and artist with a warrior's heart, sallying forth to bait the dragon in its lair.

The hell of it was that he did not even know what the dragon looked like.

CHAPTER 3

MISTY

The track had swung south at the upper western edge of Los Angeles, following Topànga Canyon Boulevard, a rugged arterial connecting the San Fernando Valley to the coast above Santa Monica. A pea-soup fog was laying in from the sea to drape the mountains and seep along the canyon toward the valley, clinging in turgid pockets of ground-based clouds to the hollows and depressions of that tangled landscape.

For miles, now, the visibility had been fluctuating rapidly from fifty feet to zero in an unpredictable pattern, at times producing a vertigo-like sensation as the big vehicle crept through the twists and turns of the tortuous route. At one early point, April had to remind herself that she was still within the city of Los

Angeles—a curious fact, considering the wild isolation through which she was moving.

The tracking would have been impossible without the aid of the Warwagon's sophisticated systems—and perhaps it was this very circumstance that was producing the occasional vertigo. She was navigating as much by instruments as by direct reference to the road, dividing her attention between the roadway and the terrain-reference monitor of the navigation console, upon which was displayed a road-sector map overlying the grid of the computer-fed electronic vectoring system. It was a fabulous device, embodying the most advanced state-of-the-art concepts of modern technology, a delight that was not lost on the engineering mind of April Rose. She had told Bolan, at their first meeting: "I'd like to meet the person who designed these systems." More than that, though, April would savor the opportunity to dig into the computer heart that integrated all those diverse electronic subsystems, combining radar-following, microwave radio, lasers, infrareds, and magnetic field detectors into a single display function to provide, at once, target tracking, track orientation, and terrain-route orientation. The result, as translated to the monitor-viewscreen, provided a visual display similar to a roadmap upon which three tiny, pulsing lights revealed the positions of the target vehicle, the Warwagon, and the chase car bearing Mack Bolan. The three were creeping south along the canyon, spaced about two hundred yards apart—and they had been running in this attitude for more than twenty minutes when the monitor signaled a change of track.

April immediately reported the development to Bolan. "Deviation."

"Roger. Is it a charted road?"

"Negative. This could be end of track. Stand by."

A moment later the pulse from the target vehicle changed color from amber to red. "Engine shutdown," she reported.

"Where away?" Bolan radioed back.

"One hundred yards south of my position, fifty yards east."

"Stand down," he instructed. "I am coming aboard."

She found a broad shoulder and pulled the cruiser off the road, immediately activating the audio scans and bringing them on line. The headlights of Bolan's car swung in behind her a moment later and the big man came aboard.

He threw her a quick smile and two clipped words—"Good work"—and went straight to the rear. He was removing his clothes—and she knew what that meant. With a guy like Bolan it meant war, not romance. Never romance, damnit. It appeared that such never quite fit into his timetable. Or maybe it was just some anachronism called chivalry that stayed the romantic beast. Whatever, her initial misgivings about their close association had borne no fruit whatever. Within minutes after their first meeting, he was ordering her to undress. For war, naturally. Chivalry or whatever, it sort of hurt a girl's self-image to have a man stare right through her nudity and think of only war. And even when the war was over, for awhile, he had lain down with her nudity to gently touch and console the hurts and bruises thereon with no attempt whatever to capitalize upon the moment.

"What are you?" she'd asked him whimsically, last night, as they lay closely touching, but not really, during the flight from Indiana. "Some sort of monk?"

And she'd known he was smiling, though she could not see his face as he quietly replied, "Some sort of tired. You too, soldier."

She was, of course. Damaged, too—though, she thought, not visibly. A madman had played kickball with her pubes, among other indignities. There was no way she could have accommodated any sort of romantic involvement with that area of her anatomy. Maybe the general knew that, or guessed it. But at least he could have *tried*.

"Catch you later, then," she'd murmured, feeling all warm and good and secure in the strength of his presence. She'd drifted in and out of sleep while listening to his even breathing, and thinking what a comforting sound it was. During one of the "out" periods she'd gotten herself worked up with a little light sleepytime fantasy and raised to an elbow to lightly brush his lips with hers, thinking him to be safely asleep. But even as their lips touched she saw that his eyes were slitted. He lunged away from that light encounter with the big silver pistol rising up between them.

"Sorry!" she gasped.

"My apology," he muttered, in a flash totally relaxed again and those remarkable eyes retreating behind the slitted lids.

25

She'd known, then, how frighteningly close she'd been to death—and she'd gained another important insight into this unusual man. He slept with his eyes open and a gun at instant access. How terrible! How horribly grim for any human being to be forever cocked and ready, poised at the edge of the abyss of death, unwilling to let go even in sleep. And she understood, however imperfectly, the terrible price this man was paying to pursue his "impossible" war.

He'd told her later, "Sure, I sleep. But it's a trick I learned on the Ho Chi Minh Trail. It's a balancing act, sort of. I guess it's a form of divided consciousness. The part that needs to sleep, sleeps. The part that needs to remain aware, doesn't. It's like the mind posting its own sentry. I call it combat sleep."

A terrible price, yes. And now the man who warred even as he slept was back there in the war room changing the costumes of unending warfare. He was getting into the "blacksuit"—a form-fitting nylon affair, which resembled a surfer's wetsuit but had been designed for far grimmer purposes. Strategically placed slit pockets on arms and legs provided quick and easy access to various small tools and lethal devices—some as old as mankind, others as new as Moonshot and Surveyor. The suit itself had to be regarded also as a weapon of war, if only for the psychological implications, but she knew that Bolan also placed great store in the outfit for the values supplied toward ease of movement, convenience, and concealment. During periods of darkness, the suit rendered him practically invisible.

He was now drawing on the "combat rig"—a system of belts and devices for carrying guns, grenades, ammunition, and other necessities of war. Earlier that same morning April had experimentally tried to get into that rig and found it almost too heavy to lift. She could not imagine packing it around on her person. Bolan hardly seemed to notice the burden as he easily slipped it on and cinched it down.

"Looks as though you're going for a heavy score," she commented, eyeing the formidable figure of the warrior as he touch-checked the weaponry.

That granite face was poised between a scowl and a smile as he replied, "The boy scouts say you should be prepared. I try to be."

"What's troubling you?"

"Nothing," he replied coldly. "You ready to truck?"

She nodded her head in mute response, knowing what was troubling the big softy. He still did not like the idea of sending her into jeopardy.

He instructed her, "Give me two minutes. Then you take a recorder pack and find the telephone feeder. Get the wires on and get back here without delay. Then haul it out of here and wait for me a thousand yards south." He pushed past her and stepped forward to set the mission clock. "If I'm not back in thirty minutes . . ."

He did not complete the instruction, nor did he need to do so. April understood.

"Be careful," she said quietly.

"Always," he replied, lying in his teeth.

Impossibly, it seemed, the big man had been with her for less than a minute. He was no dawdler—and moments like these sometimes seemed to expand infinitely. The audio sensors were just beginning to growl into a lock-on. April quickly manipulated a control at the console to refine the fix. Deep-well rumbles began issuing from the monitor: a metallic click and thump, as though a door or iron gate had been opened and closed; a snarling whine, definitely canine; ghostly mutterings of male voices in unreadable conversation.

"I can't clarify that," she told Bolan.

"Fog refraction," he explained. "Or terrain factors. Maybe both. Did you hear a dog?"

She jerked her head in a curt nod. "Definitely a dog."

He sighed and went aft again to select another weapon from the armory—and then, without a word, he was out the door and lost in the mists.

April fought a lump in her throat as she set the timer and began preparing for her own EVA. The emotions inside that vehicle had been as thick as the fog outside—yet out he went without a word. But she was beginning to understand that facet of the relationship, also. It had something to do with "staying hard." Like sleeping with the eyes open. Like loving without touching. *Economy!* That was the word! Mack Bolan was a very economical man—in everything but war. He could not afford the emotional seepage; he needed it all where the moment was poised between life and death.

Sure. April understood. And she was weeping silently without tears as she watched the spot where the man of her dreams had entered the mists. What a hell of a waste.

"Live large, big fella," she murmured to the mists. She understood that one, too. In Mack Bolan's game, it was the only alternative to dying small.

. . . . to . . . . . to . . . .
. . . . to the . . . .

CHAPTER 4

PORTENTS

The fog was as much a hindrance as a help.
Even though it cloaked Bolan in virtual invisibility, the heavy atmosphere also precluded any
realistic reconnaissance except by touch and
feel. The graveled private drive angled into
what appeared to be a shallow box canyon less
than a hundred yards removed from the main
road. Beyond a chainlink fence with a pad-
locked vehicle gate loomed the ghostly outlines
of a house in low profile. Apparently every
light in the place was turned on, but only a
pale luminescence seeped through the windows
into the enshrouding mists. A security flood-
light mounted on a high mast added very little
to the visibility factor, imparting only a muted
glow to the saturated air immediately surrounding it.

Bolan delicately probed the fence for electrical currents and sensors, then quickly scaled it and dropped lightly to the ground inside, Tran-Gun in hand and ready. The dog appeared immediately, lunging at him from the mists with fangs bared and snarling into the attack.

He met the charge with an upraised foot to the breast and, rolling with it, sent the dog hard against the fence. The impact dazed the animal momentarily. He lay there whimpering and trying to get his legs synchronized for another charge. The air pistol sneezed quietly, imbedding its knockout dart into the fur just below the throat. It was like throwing a switch; the animal instantly curled into a furry ball and drifted peacefully toward doggy dreamland.

Bolan gingerly retrieved the small hypodermic and went on. Two cars were parked abreast on the drive at the side of the house. The one that had brought him here yielded no meaningful identification, but the other was registered to a James Portillo with a San Francisco address. The name touched an elusive little coder in Bolan's mental mugfile but it would not surface. Even so, the San Francisco connection was interesting enough.

He continued on to the house, a smallish frame structure nestled into the hillside. A patio window yielded quickly to his touch. Too quickly, maybe. He left it and went on around in a cautious recon, checking windows and peering into the lighted interior for a reading of the situation there. The reading was "temporary camp." There were no curtains or blinds. Walls and floors were bare. Furnishings were minimal and simple. Each of the three bedrooms contained an air mattress and an open suitcase. One boasted a folding camp chair. A single large room served as living room, dining area, kitchen. It held only a portable TV resting on a wooden box, a couple of chairs and a small table. The kitchen appliances were built in. Two men stood at the stove, conversing with great animation. And instantly Bolan had his make on "James Portillo."

He returned immediately to the patio window and entered the house through a bedroom. Three steps along a narrow hallway took him to the living room. The guys were still going at it, both talking at once with raised voices and heated words.

Bolan moved on in with the big silver Auto-Mag leading the way and was halfway across the room before his presence there was noted.

A pregnant silence descended abruptly as two disturbed faces turned to an inspection of the warrior.

Portillo was a big beefy guy with graying hair and cherubic face, maybe forty, smooth-looking—a politician type. He'd come up in the Cleveland Mob and gone west with the flow of black bucks from that area, figuring prominently for a number of years as Cleveland's liaison man with the burgeoning western empires. The dapper front man had disappeared from public view at about the same time as Bolan's San Francisco campaign. Rumors from both sides had him either dead or retired in Central America. But the name kept popping up in intelligence reports. Bolan had heard it mentioned in a contemporary reference as recently as the Arizona adventure.

In Mob parlance, Portillo was known as a "grease merchant"—a man with important connections into the business and political sectors.

The other guy was a nonentity. About twenty-five, maybe Sicilian and maybe not, tightly kinked hair worn in a neat Afro style, mean eyes.

The differing reactions to the Bolan presence told the tale of contrasting types. Portillo met the threat with a tentative smile and hands raised limply to shoulder level. Mean-eyes was not quite so intelligent. He made a break for gunleather and tried a spinout. Neither move bought him more than a couple of ticks of the heart. The AutoMag thundered once to dispatch 240 grains of splattering death whistling up the guy's nose. The top of his head exploded and sprayed fragments onto the wall behind, the body falling back into the startled arms of the grease merchant.

Portillo shuddered and withdrew support from that gruesome horror, dancing clear while hastily showing that his hands were high and unencumbered.

"Jesus!" he groaned, eyes glazing on the big silver pistol.

"Kiss it goodbye, Jimmy," Bolan said coldly.

"Why?" the guy pleaded. "What've I done to offend you?"

"You exist. That's offense enough."

"Wait! Hold it!" Jimmy the Grease was coming apart rapidly, from the inside. "I know you! I know who you are!"

33

"Congratulations," said ice-eyes. "So you know why."

"But you've got it wrong! I'm clean! I'm retired!"

"Tell it to McCullough," Bolan said.

Portillo's frantic gaze bounced hopelessly off the walls for several seconds, then he muttered, "Who? I don't . . ."

The AutoMag thundered again. The lobe of the guy's left ear disappeared. He howled and fell to his knees, frantically pinching at the wound to halt the flow of blood.

Bolan calmly told him. "The next one takes the lip. So you better use it while you can."

"I swear I didn't send them!" Portillo howled. "You should know better! You know I'm not into that kind of stuff!"

"What are you into these days?" Bolan inquired, the tone almost conversational.

"Nothing! I told you I'm . . ." Reality had suddenly grabbed hold of the guy. Bolan could see it settling into the eyes, even before that shaking voice continued. "Okay—no—you're right. It's no time for word games, is it? I swear I don't know why I'm here. I was told to come and wait. I would be told when to make my move."

"What move?"

"I wasn't told that, either. But you're right. It had something to do with McCullough."

"But you don't know what."

"That's right. I don't know what. I'd tell you if—"

"A guy with your brains can put it together. Put it together for me, Jimmy, while you've got brains to put with."

34

"I guess—I guess it has something to do with—political, I guess."

"Uh huh."

"Probably, yeah. That's my specialty, of course. I spread the grease, ease the slide."

"You can't spread it for McCullough if he's dead."

"You've got it. That's right. So I guess I—after—after McCullough."

"After he's dead."

"I think so."

"Who's taking him over?"

"God I don't know. I don't know, Bolan."

"Who sent you?"

The guy's eyes were starting to bounce off the walls again. He was in a hell of a predicament. "I don't know," he whispered.

Bolan sent some quick reinforcement to the sagging memory. Another thundering round blew from the ventilated silver barrel and buried itself in the floor between fat knees. Samples of scorched fabric and shrieking skin went with it.

Portillo screamed and fell onto his side, both hands shakingly exploring for damages. He shuddered and very quietly reported in. "Arthur Bloom sent me." He took a deep, shuddering breath. "Arthur called and said they wanted me to come here and wait."

"Who is Arthur Bloom?" Bolan asked, just as quietly.

"He's in Sacramento."

"Doing what?"

"Same as me. But he's a registered lobbyist. Lawyer. Represents many interests."

"Mob interests," Bolan said flatly.

35

The guy sighed. "Them too, yes."

"So Arthur Bloom sent you."

"Well it was—message, messenger, he just passed the message along."

"From who?"

"From . . . *them.*"

Bolan coldly inquired. "Would you like one square through the knee, Jimmy?"

No, Jimmy certainly did not want that. Very quickly he replied, "It's the new bunch—the new—I don't—you busted California all to hell, you know. Wasn't much left after Frisco. Hell. These guys just moved it in, slick and easy. Nobody knows for sure who they are."

"From back east?"

"I doubt that. No. That's why I—see, I got no connections now—I mean *family.* That's all gone. Has no meaning now. Know what I mean? I mean, not like the old days. It's all new. All changed. Well, mostly. Mostly new."

"So now you just jump to any fingersnap, eh?"

Portillo gave him a hurt look. "Well no, not—leave me some dignity, huh? I know who sent me. But I don't have any *names* for you. See, that's uh, it's the new concept."

Bolan felt the hair rising along his neck. "The California Concept," he said quietly.

"Right. Nobody knows nobody and nobody knows nothing. Like invisible, but it's there just the same and everybody is watching his own ass. That's the way it is now. They say do it and you better damn well do it. 'Cause you really don't know where it's coming from. You do it or you get a bullet and a burial at sea."

"We're still talking about the boys, Jimmy."

"Sure, it's still the boys. But *which* boys? That's the kicker, see. Listen, they don't have to worry about *omerta* anymore 'cause there's nobody to *omerta* for. Tell you the truth, Bolan, it's better this way. You can't talk if you don't know what to say. Right?"

"Wrong," Bolan said. "You're talking fine. Keep on."

"I don't know what else to say."

"McCullough."

Portillo sighed. "McCullough is doomed. They missed once. They may even miss twice. But sooner or later they—how'd you get onto this?"

Bolan ignored the question. "Why is he doomed?"

"I swear I don't know that. Except he obviously has something *they* want. That's why I'm here. Not to take it but to grease the slide for *them* when they take it over." He sighed again, the sigh ending as a faint sneer. "But *these* guys—these *punks* . . ." His gaze slid to the dead triggerman, then bounced quickly back. "They know even less than me. Like that trained dog out there. Say *hit* and he hits. He doesn't ask why and he doesn't care who. Same with these punks. No more than guided missiles. Do you know, I don't even know this poor boy's name? They called him Junior. Supposed to be a hotshot driver. That's all I know. It's all I wanted to know. I'm not one of these, Bolan. You should know that. I never killed a man in my whole life."

Bolan could believe that. But killing was not necessarily the worst of crimes.

He took a small first-aid box from his belt

37

and dropped it onto Portillo's thigh. "You bought yourself some time," he told the guy. "Spend it wisely."

"I'm dead if I do and dead if I don't," Portillo replied quietly.

"You've been dead all your life," Bolan said disgustedly.

He went out of there, returning to the mists.

The fog, he knew, was almost portentous of the Terrible Tuesday he was going to find in California.

He had an inkling, now, of what this new "concept" was all about.

It meant fog—ultra-concealment—invisibility—a truly "secret society" of thugs getting set to plunder and loot the great Golden State.

And Mack Bolan himself was still enveloped in the mists. But maybe not for long.

CHAPTER 5

ECHOES

Bolan knew this territory well. Very well. He had come here early in his war to visit death and destruction through hill and dale, from shore to desert, in a titanic struggle to shake down the bloated empire of Julian "Deej" Di-George, then undisputed boss of everything west. Despite what had gone before, in Pittsfield, the battle for Los Angeles and environs had marked the moment when Mack Bolan's homefront effort truly attained the stature of all-out warfare. It also marked a point of maturity for the warrior himself. He had come to Los Angeles with little more than a hope and a prayer, the hounds of hell hot on his scent and closing for the kill. He'd taken his baptism in hell there, emerging a much stronger and far wiser warrior—seeing clearly for the first time the true dimensions of the task he'd set for himself. Undaunted by that vision of hell everlasting, he'd gone on from the Southern California victory to slash at other tentacles of the Mafia octopus, which was strangling the world—never once daring to believe that a final victory would be his, or even possible.

Yes, the warrior had matured here. In a sense, he had died here. It was hallowed ground for Mack Bolan.

And Portillo's sensing of the changes in the California Mafia was just a bit awry. The knockout punch had been delivered not in San Francisco but in Los Angeles. The later operations to the north, as well as south in San Diego, had been mere peripheral actions when viewed in the total context of the California problem. The real battle had been fought here. And there had been no truly effective Mob movements in the area since the fall of Julian DiGeorge. Until now. And . . . now . . . well, now it seemed that someone had found a new handle and was busily rebuilding the crime machine. Bolan's immediate task—to be accomplished in a matter of mere *hours*—was to find that handle, tear it loose, and dismantle the new machine. It was not an enviable task . . . but it was the one at hand, the only game in town for Mack Bolan.

He had made a start.

Now he could do little more than hope for a positive reaction from the other side . . . and to be there when it came. For that, he was depending upon the technical abilities of April Rose.

She was tense and fidgeting at the communications console when Bolan returned to the cruiser. "How'd it go?" she asked, the voice barely more than a husky whisper.

"You'll have to tell me that," he replied, immediately stepping aft to shed himself of the combat rig.

"You were gone so long," she complained. "I counted three shots and—I wish you'd carry a radio."

Bolan smiled and said, "Okay. Next time I'll try to find room for one. What have you got?"

She waited until he came forward before replying. "So far, not a thing. But the patch is good. I know it's good."

"If the guy was leveling with me," Bolan mused, "he could have nothing to move with. He could decide to just hot it out of there. So let's watch for that, too."

The lady tried and failed to make it sound like a casual inquiry: "What's happening, Mack? What are we doing?"

"Don't ask," he replied quietly.

"But I am asking. Don't you think I should? . . ."

He sighed as he dropped into the command chair and lit a cigarette. "You're right, April. Sorry. Sure you need to know. Guess I've forgotten how to work with a partner."

"Am I a partner?" she asked, those great eyes flashing at him from the midships console.

He chuckled and replied, "Junior partner, sure. The guy you wired is Jimmy Portillo. He came west on the heels of the big postwar wave from the eastern families. This was open territory, then—from the Rockies to the Pacific. No one family had domain. DiGeorge was just get-

41

ting his hooks into Southern California. *Don* DeMarco was quietly mining the San Francisco area. Bugsy Siegel had opened Las Vegas and was moving in on the movie industry. Then comes Portillo. The guy had no rank, no visible power base. But he probably did more than any single man to organize the west and to consolidate most of the power under DiGeorge. DeMarco managed to hang onto his little empire up north, but everything else belonged to Deej. Thanks largely to that guy in there, Jimmy the Grease. When things went to hell around here, though, Jimmy quietly dropped out of the picture. He's a politician, not a fighter. And his party was out of power. I believe they're trying to get it back. That would make Portillo a very important man again." Bolan grinned at the lady. "And we lucked onto him. Your wires, m'lady, could save the day."

"You believe he's trying to reconstruct the old organization?"

Bolan shook his head as he replied, "A new one. Maybe larger than the original. Maybe a hell of a lot more dangerous. Whatever, Portillo would be the logical architect. The guy knows the territory."

"How would he go about it?"

Bolan sighed. "Via the imperfectibility of man," he replied quietly.

"What?"

"A *Mafioso*," he explained, "is a very cynical man. He operates on the oldest vices of mankind. Every man has his price, see—or so the logic goes. A *Mafioso* religiously believes that. It's the only thing that makes his world function. Jimmy the Grease could have invented the idea. He's a genius at buying and selling men's souls. That's where any crime syndicate gets its power. And, yeah, *Mafiosi* are very cynical men. With damn good reason."

"Are you a cynic?" the lady asked softly.

He grinned and seemed to be thinking about that, then replied, "I'm a spot cynic."

"What is that?"

"I believe in the imperfectibility of some men."

"I see," she said soberly. "Which explains your distrust of our criminal justice system."

"It explains nothing," he said tiredly, unwilling to be drawn into another debate on those grounds. "I am not involved in quote unquote justice. I am conducting a war. So let's not—"

There would be no unwanted debate. As he spoke, the monitor at the surveillance console came alive. Portillo was making a telephone call. The decoder "read" the tone-dial signals and visually displayed the number being called. It was a local area number. April recorded it and cocked a quizzical eye at Bolan as the call went through.

He nodded and muttered, "This could be it."

It was.

The guy had probably been pulling himself together and tending the minor wounds, trying to decide a course of action—or maybe the delay was natural caution. Whatever, some ten minutes had elapsed since his encounter with Mack Bolan—and the guy was sounding cool and together.

"Yes. Who is it?"

"Hi, this is Jimmy. I have unhappy news."

43

"Just a minute."

There was a brief silence, then another voice came into the connection: "What is it, Jimmy?"

Something was very familiar about that voice.

"Hi. Trouble, I'm afraid. It fizzled."

"Why?"

"Somebody was sitting and waiting for them. They walked into a lot of unhappiness. The last one. All of them."

A long silence, then, *"All* of them?"

"I'm afraid so. All but Junior. And he really pulled a dumb one."

Muttered curses, then, "What'd he do?"

"Beat it straight back here, that's what. And brought the heat with him. Can you beat that?"

"What kind of heat?"

"The worst kind. I was just giving him hell about it when this guy walks in on us out of the fog. Right past the damn dog."

"What guy?" sneered the familiar voice from somewhere in the past.

"You won't like this," said Portillo. "Prepare yourself."

"Don't say any names right out."

"I wasn't going to. No need to. You know what happened to Deej. Well, it's trying to happen all over again. The guy is back."

A loud groan preceded the quick response from the far side of that connection. "Are you sure?"

"No way to mistake it. We stood eyeball to eyeball for five minutes or more. He leaned on me pretty hard. Listen. The guy is all they say he is, and more. Listen. I'm a lucky S.O.B. And don't I know it."

Portillo was becoming emotional. The other voice was growing colder.

"What'd you have to sell him, Jimmy?"

"You don't *sell* that boy, Charlie." *Charlie! Of course!* "You just doubletalk all you think you can and you pray a lot. Don't worry. I gave him nothing. He shot me twice and left."

"He *shot* you! What?..."

"Nothing serious, I'm okay. I played dead. Poor Junior didn't have to play. We'll have to put him away in a bucket. I don't know exactly what he told our friend but it sure didn't buy him any pity, whatever it was."

"Wait a minute," said Charlie. "Let me see if I understand this. You say Junior was—"

"He was talking, yeah. That's all I know. Guess I was unconscious for a little while so I don't know exactly what was said. When I came to, Junior was pleading for his life and saying the guy should keep his end of the deal. Hey, I was hit—twice. I just laid there. Damn quick, Junior was just laying there, too, only not so lucky. So I don't really know what was said and what wasn't. I guess it all depends on what Junior knew. I don't know what he knew, I leave that to you. But listen, that guy went roaring out of here with blood in his eye, so you better—"

"This was when?"

"Just now. Just this minute."

"Okay. How's the fog up there?"

"It's murder."

"Okay. What can I do for you?"

"I don't know, Charlie. Right now, nothing, I

45

guess. But I'm very nervous about this whole turn of events. And I'm worried about—well, you better pass the word. It's big trouble, Charlie."

"I know it is," agreed the voice from Mack Bolan's past. "Okay. Thanks. Do you need a doctor?"

"Naw. I'll take care of it. You just take care of *them.*"

"I better tell them. And let them decide . . ."

"Oh sure," Portillo quickly agreed. "Tell them. And be careful. You know how this guy operates. He's hell on wheels."

"Yeah. Okay. Thanks. Let's keep in touch. Where will you be?"

"I'm checking into a hotel, Charlie. I'll call you."

"Do that."

A deeply troubled man terminated the connection at the far side. An audible sigh from Jimmy the Grease accompanied the final hang-up.

Bolan already had the engine fired and was directing the cruiser through the mists in the return trip to town. The other vehicle had served its purpose; this was as good a place as any to leave it.

April was staring morosely at the dead monitor.

Bolan said, "Good work. Keep the wires on. Did you get that number?"

"I got it," she grumped.

"Fine. I'll want you to translate it into name and address. You can use your credentials if you need to. Just get me the fix."

"I'll get your fix," she assured him, the voice small and distant. "Was he telling the truth?"

"Who?"

"Him. Portillo. Is that the way it happened?"

"What do you think?" Bolan growled.

"I think you're conducting an imperfectible war," she replied softly.

Maybe so. Yeah, maybe so—regardless of the *modus*. At any rate, it was no time for a moral defense of the self—and Bolan was beginning to resent the girl's constant plucking at his methods. He squelched that, though. A war, imperfectible or not, was building rapidly to a white heat. He needed to get the lady to the telephone office. The rest would take care of the rest.

But Bolan did not really need a *name*.

He had recognized the reedy voice at the other side of Portillo's call. An echo from the past, yeah—a very unhappy past.

It was the voice of Charlie Rickert, once known and respected as "the twenty-four-hour cop."

The rest, yes, would take care of even the past.

CHAPTER 6

CHANNELS

There had been a time when Mack Bolan was the hottest "fugitive" in the country—when police of all the various jurisdictional levels kept close tabs on his known movements, reacting swiftly, cooperatively and massively wherever his presence was noted. Tim Braddock, as the first big city cop to head a "get Bolan" effort, had become something of a celebrity in the national law enforcement community and had spent considerable time and energy tracking the fugitive around the country, working with other departments as an expert consultant on the Bolan problem.

Through all that, Braddock had secretly hoped that the Bolan "problem" would never go away—that the guy would go on to success after success and finally achieve his stated desire to rid the world of the Mafia cancer. Nobody gave him much of a chance to do that, of course, but obviously Braddock was not the only cop to secretly wish he could.

A lot of the steam had gone out of the "get Bolan" movement as more and more the law enforcement agencies of the nation began to see the fantastic effect of the guy on the underworld power structures. The federal hunt had fizzled out a long time ago, for all practical purposes. It was even difficult, now, to gain access to the federal files on Mack Bolan. Rumors within the police community had grown to the virtual conviction that Harold Brognola himself was covertly supporting the Bolan crusade. A congressional oversight committee had recently leaked a new rumor that the White House was working up an amnesty package in an effort to bring the crimebuster into official government service.

Braddock had followed all such developments with great interest. He had always admired the guy, even from the very beginning during a time when the hue and cry was hottest for Mack Bolan's blood—before, even, that climactic moment when Braddock lay dying from Mafia guns and would have bled to death but for the intervention of the "fugitive."

Yeah. Those had been days hard on the conscience of a good cop. They'd branded the guy with a "mad dog" label and the orders were to "shoot on sight—shoot to kill."

True, the guy had committed just about every crime in the book. But as the matter began to sift itself into all the neat little police compartments, it became more and more obvious that the only "victims" of Mack Bolan's war were professional criminals themselves—of the worst kind. Braddock had even been privileged to observe at first hand Mack Bolan's most outrageous rampage—the one in Boston, when he thought the Mob had snatched and snuffed the ladylove and the kid brother. That had been *something else!* But even then, with all that mental agony, the guy had not lost his perspective. He had shed no innocent blood during that "kill orgy."

Big Tim Braddock simply could not read Mack Bolan as a common criminal. Not even as a criminal. The guy was a true hero, in every sense of the word. He deserved a ticker tape parade through every city in the land. He should have schools and boulevards named after him. At the least, at the very least, his name should be stricken from the wanted lists everywhere and carved in granite somewhere as a symbol of rare human courage and commitment.

But the name had not been stricken from the wanted lists. Right here in L.A. there was a whole book of charges against the guy. And, whatever he might feel in his heart, Tim Braddock was still a cop and Mack Bolan was still a fugitive. So it was with no great surge of police spirit that he received the tip that Bolan was back in town. Even less did he like the tipster.

"I don't want to talk to you, Rickert," he growled into the telephone.

"That's your loss, Tim," said the disgraced ex-cop. "I'm doing you a favor."

"Do it to someone else," Braddock said quietly and was about to hang up when the guy said the magic words.

"Bolan's back in town."

Braddock paused to light a cigarette and gather his thoughts. Rickert had been a crooked cop, sure, but he was no looneytune. And, of course, the guy held Mack Bolan personally responsible for his downfall. In his own twisted mind, he had plenty of cause for hate.

"Where'd you get that?" Braddock asked him.

"Oh, you know me," the ex-friend replied breezily. "I still get around. You can take it as gospel. He's here."

"For what?"

"What else? You could look into a disturbance at Bill McCullough's house this morning. Also—you got a pencil handy? I'll give you an address in Topanga Canyon. It's out of your jurisdiction, but—"

"I have a pencil," Braddock said heavily.

Rickert supplied the address, then said: "I haven't seen the guy personally, but I know a reliable subject who did. And it's got his tracks all over it. I thought you'd want to know."

"You ready to produce that witness?" Braddock inquired.

It was purely a rhetorical question. Rickert laughed it away and said, "The guy doesn't leave many of those, does he? I thought you'd want to get set for the fireworks."

Braddock sighed into the telephone. "I don't have to tell you that it's against the law to give a false report. I hope to hell it's false, Rickert."

The renegade laughed lightly at that one, too. "Perish the thought. I wouldn't even spit on the sidewalk these days, if I thought you were watching. What is it with you, Tim? Don't you think I suffered enough? The D.A. thought so. After all, I lost my job, my pension, my good name—all on the word of a psychopath."

"Bolan is not a psychopath," Braddock said tiredly, "and you lost nothing. You spent it, guy, you spent it all yourself. And if I had my way, yeah, you'd be in the joint right now. The mere mention of your name is enough to stink up the halls around here. And, Rickert—don't call me again."

He hung it up and pushed the pad around the desk for a moment, glaring at the telephone.

Damnit. Damnit.

The wrong guy was the fugitive.

He sighed, then, and again picked up the phone.

"Get me a hot line to Washington," he ordered. "Don't use the WATS line. I want Harold Brognola, Department of Justice. I don't want an aide. I want the man himself. Give this the red flag. I'll sit here until you get him. Get him."

The newest deputy chief at LAPD knew full well that he was "sitting here" on a time bomb.

But . . . he had to know. Dammit—he had to know for sure.

The building was one of those new Sunset Boulevard highrise developments, which serve both business and residential needs. Judging by its ground floor office space, *SecuriCom* was a large and thriving company. It provided security services not only to this building but to a number of industrial and business clients in the area, as well. The record would reveal that many of those—perhaps all—were owned or controlled by William McCullough's *California Investors Limited*. Which made for a nice twist to the villainy now afoot within that empire.

Bolan's Mafia threads and tinted glasses apparently passed the cold scrutiny of the television camera. The door buzzed and opened to his touch. A guy in a snazzy uniform sat at a small turret-console just inside the huge outer office of *SecuriCom*. He was surrounded by banks of CCTV monitors and other electronic devices. Two more uniformed men sat at desks toward the rear; another was working at a computer.

The guy in the turret shoved an open book toward the visitor. Bolan signed the register "D'Anglia" and shoved it back. The guard half smiled as he asked, "Who'd you want, sir?"

"Rickert should be expecting me," Bolan said as he gave the place another quick look.

The guy wrote something in the book, then told the visitor, "I guess you know your way."

He did, yeah. He'd just spotted the door with the gilt lettering: CHIEF INVESTIGATOR. And, beneath that, in smaller print: Charles J. Rickert.

It seemed, on the surface of things, a rather painless exile for a kinky cop.

Bolan's visual memory of the guy was clouded and tinged with emotion. His one personal encounter with then Lieutenant Rickert had come at an anticlimactic moment, at a time when Bolan was both physically and emotionally exhausted—and Rickert himself had seemed half demented. It was beneath the cliffs of Balboa on a dark and tragic night. Rickert was about to gun down a fellow officer—none other than Carl Lyons, later a federal under-cover cop whose friendly path would cross Bo-lan's at many points along the wipeout trail. It seemed unlikely that Rickert had ever actually laid eyes on Bolan—and even if he had, his memory would be of a face that no longer ex-isted. Shortly after that encounter, Doc Brantzen had worked his plastic wonders at Palm Desert to fashion the *battle mask* behind which the warrior had lived ever since. Police sketches of the new face had never really cap-tured it and few living *Mafiosi* could summon forth a reliable image other than vague refer-ences to "them damned eyes" or "cold, man, cold."

So Bolan felt no great identity risk inside the enemy's lines. He was also a master at role camouflage—the ability to take on almost any identity of his choosing.

At the moment, he chose to be a Mafia tor-pedo. And Charlie Rickert, ex-twenty-four-hour cop, seemed to be buying him right from the top.

A television monitor stood beside Rickert's desk and there was a small console through which apparently he could select any of many closed circuits for display. At the moment, the monitor was displaying the reception area just outside. The guy had obviously seen him com-ing in.

Rickert did not look up from his desk and there was no exchange of greetings. Bolan went to the window, lit a cigarette, and stood there smoking with his back to the desk.

"There's big trouble," he said quietly.

"Don't I know it," Rickert muttered. "I hope you didn't come here to *tell* me that."

The voice fit, yeah. A man's physical parts can change quickly—especially so at Rickert's age. He was in his late forties, maybe early fifties. The hair was mostly white, now, with little tufts of black here and there, worn short and bristly. Bolan had not remembered that particular feature. And the guy was heavier than he'd seemed that first time around. But it was the same guy.

Bolan turned from the window with a tight smile and said, "Some people worry."

"As well they should," Rickert replied, looking at him directly for the first time.

"How about you?"

"Sure. I worry, too. It's my job to worry."

Bolan turned back to the window and fiddled with the blinds for a moment, then he moved across the room and took a seat atop the desk.

Rickert growled, "Get your ass off my desk!"

"Put it off," Bolan-D'Anglia invited.

"Let's understand it, up front!" Rickert snapped. "I don't take petty shit! So next time you come, leave the games at the door!"

Bolan chuckled. He said, "You're okay, Rickert."

"Get your ass off my okay desk, then."

Bolan chuckled again and moved away to casually prowl the room. "Let's not get off on the wrong foot," he suggested, softening the voice. "If we're going to work together on this, then we should—"

Rickert snapped him off. "Who says we're working together?"

"Five bills a day say it."

The guy was mad as hell. "They didn't say anything about—"

"*They* don't have the say. Someone else has a lot more to lose."

"Someone *else?*"

"With a lot more to lose," Bolan repeated.

Rickert understood it, that time. His face flushed angrily and he lunged toward the telephone. "What's that name again?"

"What's in a name?" Bolan responded casually. "Just tell them that Crusher has arrived. They'll report directly to me until this little matter is cleared up. To *me!* That's important. All other lines are closed, as of now."

The guy glared at him for a long moment, then woodenly asked, "How do they reach you?"

"They reach me here," said Bolan-D'Anglia-Crusher.

Rickert was frowning, his hand poised above the telephone. "That's not such a swell idea," he said. "We shouldn't be mobbing up. Not at a time like this."

Bolan was damn glad to hear that. He went to the desk and scribbled a telephone number on Rickert's pad. "You're right," he said. "Give them this. It's a hard phone. They shouldn't worry about it."

The ex-cop was still frowning worriedly. "You want them to contact you?"

"Only if the need is great," Bolan replied. He was instructing the guy, now. He had very deftly taken charge. "That doesn't apply to you, though. You keep me informed. I want to hear every footstep."

He was moving toward the door.

"Hold it!" Rickert cried.

Bolan went on to the door before again showing the guy his face. "What?"

"What are we supposed to—what's the—?"

"What've you done, so far?"

Rickert was giving him the fish eye. He rose to his feet and said, "I got the whole force mobilized. I've staked out all the hot spots. And I tipped the cops."

"To what?"

"To what's going down. I figure they can keep some heat on the guy." He grinned slyly. "It's their duty, right? To protect the citizens from maniacs?"

"Just so it doesn't boomerang," Bolan said, showing the guy a sour grin.

"What's to boomerang? We're covered completely. There's no way to—I even had to put out some dummy targets for the guy to give him something to hit. I'm on top of it. And you can report that to your man. What I want to know is where *you* fit."

"I *told* you where I fit," Bolan replied coldly. "Now *you* tell *them.*"

Rickert's gaze wavered. He said, "Sure. What I meant was—"

Bolan growled, "Like I said, you're okay. Just keep on top of it. You'll know when I need you. Keep me informed."

He went on out, left a pleasant word with the guy in the turret, and put that place behind.

It had been a very soft game. Not too soft,

hopefully, but strong enough to seize the enemy's greatest strength and turn it into his own.

And to hell with the "dummy targets."

Very soon, now, the Executioner should be hearing from *them*.

CHAPTER 7

UNWIRED

It had been an entirely successful penetration. He had located and invaded what appeared to be the nerve center of the Los Angeles operation, conned the security boss, and left wires all over the joint. Totally successful, yes. So why did he feel so uneasy about the whole thing? It had been a textbook operation. The equipment used was the latest, most sophisticated stuff available for electronic surveillance. A small recorder-transceiver and power pack were neatly tucked away in a wall crevice at the third floor level. Micro-pickups with fantastic sensitivity were emplaced at the reception desk, in the window in Rickert's office and under his desktop. The confidence act had gone without apparent hitch; Rickert had bought him as a security envoy from the man up high. To all appearances, Bolan had breached the security apparatus of the men he'd come to defeat.

So why the uneasiness?

He'd left the Warwagon stashed two streets over in a residential neighborhood. With all the cautious footwork required to assure his own security, it had taken about ten minutes to return to the cruiser and to initiate contact with his Bell connection. And he still was entertaining that uneasy mental atmosphere as her familiar voice sang through the mobile phone: "Special operator."

"It's set," he reported tersely. "How 'bout you?"

"We're already cooking," she replied, restrained excitement filling that good voice. "He's talking to someone right now and we're running the fix. I'll put it in your collector so keep a watch. How'd the interior decorating go?"

An inexplicable chill traversed the Bolan spine. He shook it away, reminding himself that he was getting too damned emotionally involved with the lady, dismissing the chill as a formless fear. "It went fine. I guess we're cooking everywhere. You sure it's okay there?"

"Sure I'm sure," she said pertly. But then some altered quality of Bolan's voice in the inquiry must have penetrated. Some of the perkiness dropped away as she added, "Why shouldn't it be okay?"

"I had a shiver," he explained. "Combat jitters, probably. Sometimes I can smell the big one coming long before the rest of me knows about it. Uh, listen, these guys are not clowns. They probably have damned good counterintelligence. I want you to play it close to the breast. I'll call you home as soon as possible. And when I say the word, I want you to come running."

She gave him a very subdued, "Okay"— remembering, perhaps, the tribulations of yesterday.

Bolan terminated the contact and quickly went to work at the surveillance console. He poked in a computer program, then remoted the whole show to the command console. Then he went forward and immediately set the cruiser adrift.

The "drift" was a planned cruising pattern of the streets surrounding the *Investors* building and the mission was audio surveillance. The little transceiver, which he had mounted on the outer wall at the third level, was good for about a mile under optimum conditions, but probably would range no more than two or three city blocks in this area of high buildings. With all its limitations, it was a very nice little package. The power pack would allow several hours of continuous operation. The recorder was sound-actuated, though, so continuous operation would be an unlikely circumstance. Actually, days of recorded surveillance could usually be packed into the little machine. Even that capability had never been tested in the sort of operations Bolan conducted. He could command the tiny unit from the surveillance console in the Warwagon to change the mode from *Record* to *Continuous Broadcast* or he could trigger "collections" of the stored recordings for high speed playback and tone transmission to the onboard recorders.

As one of the limitations, the remote unit could not record and broadcast at the same time. This normally posed no special problems to Bolan's surveillance efforts, but this time it did. He would prefer a continuous "live" program from the offices of *SecuriCom* but he also needed to know what had transpired in there during the fifteen minutes since the recorder began operating.

He opted for a quick collection, a "drain" of stored moments in the recent lift of one Charlie Rickert. The remote unit responded instantly to the summons. A two-second tone sounded in the monitor. The console went into automatic processing while Bolan's mind fidgeted over the implications of the two-second transmission. There could not be a hell of a lot on there. High speed recovery, sure, but still the ratio figured at about sixty to one—a one-second tone for each full minute of recorded data.

The console was flashing *Proceed* at him. He gave it the countersign and was immediately greeted by his own voice echoing dully through the audio monitor.

"Some people worry."

Rickert, then, distantly responding in muffled and indistinct tones, *"As well they should."*

Bolan poked in a fast advance, moving well forward of the moment when the second bug began picking up.

It was Rickert's voice, close and clear now: *"Sure. What I meant was—"*

Bolan again, himself now distant and a bit garbled: *"Like I said, you're okay. Just keep on top of it. You'll know when I need you. Keep me informed."*

A dead zone followed—then muffled undertones of quiet male voices—a door sound—footsteps—suddenly this, from Rickert: *"Did you get a good look?"*

Another voice, unfamiliar: *"Not very good, no. But I know I never saw that guy before."*

Rickert: *"What about the name?"*

"What? Crusher? No, I think that's a—"

"Sure it is. That's a—he signed his name D'Anglia."

"There's a family back east that—"

"Right, right! I know who you mean! They're—"

"He's an import, Charlie. A classic if ever I saw one. A guy like that has only one purpose in life. I wonder what this means."

"It means—it couldn't have come at a worse time. But I know for damned sure, hey, he didn't come all the way from the east just this morning!"

"You're right exactly. I'd give a nickel to know who's sponsoring him. Hey, I think the guy knows it all."

"Sure he knows it all. What the hell you think he came for? He's the insurance man. Someone way up is paying his freight. I wonder how long he's been. . .?"

"Forever, probably. I told you my people don't take much on faith. I bet they've got us under a microscope. I told you—"

Rickert, greatly perturbed: *"Jesus Christ!"*

"What is it?"

The sound track became very noisy at that point. When Rickert's voice came again, it was obviously via a more distant pickup—faint, barely readable. "There may be more. I'll shake it down. You get in there and—is he still on the damn phone? Tell him to—no!—wait!— activate the—yeah!—yeah!"

A door slammed in the distance.

End of recording. And the two-second drain was explained. Sly Charlie had discovered Mack Bolan's ears.

But what about April's?

The combat spine had known, sure. And Bolan would forever ponder such inexplicable capabilities of the human mechanism. But it was no time, now, for mind puzzles.

He grabbed the phone and summoned his lady. "Get out of there!" he commanded, the instant the line opened. "Now! Run one block west, one block south. I'll pick you up. Go *now!*"

The lady was very confused by all that. Because it was the wrong lady. "What is this!" cried the strange voice. "What's going on?"

Bolan snarled back, "This is agent Striker! Where's my special operator?"

"Some men just came and took her away!" the lady wailed.

The Bolan heart was already frozen in place. "Calm down," he said, talking for his own benefit, perhaps, as much as for the lady's. "Just take it easy and tell me about it."

"They came in waving guns. I'm the supervisor. They showed me badges. They said—I told them she was—I thought they were part of—I showed them, and they took her away."

"When was this?" Bolan asked numbly.

"Just now. Just this instant."

Sure. The spine had known. The rest of the man should have known, as well. Bolan was not the only guy in town with access to sophisticated equipment.

For every action, a reaction—sure. The art of electronic countermeasures had grown proportionately with the development of electronic snooping. The guys at *SecuriCom* evidently were experts at the game.

So . . .

It was a forlorn hope . . . but the only one at hand.

At their last contact, only a few minutes earlier, April had told him, "He's talking to someone now and we're running the fix. I'll put it in your collector."

The collector was a recorder drop in the communications computer, fed by a mobile phone loop, used primarily as a means of receiving messages while Bolan was out of the vehicle.

And yes, she'd made a deposit there.

"Striker. A call at 10:17 went to a Jay Leonard at 3040 Silverlake Boulevard in Hollywood. They're still talking. I'll deposit the conversation when it is complete, but I want to get you this information up front. We started getting a peculiar ultrasonic pulse on that line a couple of minutes ago. The sine wave reveals a possible ECM characteristic. Also it appears only on the hot side of our patch. I'm afraid it's a tap detector. I'll abort as soon as—uh oh—cheese it—looks like a flying squad descending here. Could be cops. Don't worry, I'll stonewall. Good luck, Striker."

Good luck, indeed.

Well . . . maybe they were cops. It was worth hoping for, anyway. But he could not rest with mere hope. Still . . . it seemed highly unlikely that Rickert could have reacted that quickly—in a matter of minutes—to locate the tap and put a squad of men down at the source.

He could not rest with unlikelies, either.

And, of course, in the world of electronics, time and space had little meaning. If the guy had the gear to do it, sure, he could have flushed that tap in a split-second and—yeah, yeah, he could do the rest, too. He'd told Bolan-Crusher that he had "mobilized the entire force"—which could mean, among other things, roving squads of security cops blanketing the city with quick-reaction capability. Rickert had been trained by one of the best police departments in the nation. And how many "cops" did *SecuriCom* employ? No matter about that. He could have lucked into it with a squad in the vicinity of the telephone exchange where April had set up shop. A couple of minutes? Sure. Blind luck or not, the result would be the same for April. So there was damn little hope with the unlikelies.

Bolan had to play it where it lay. Whatever and whomever, the detectives had been detected. Bolan had to take the assumption that April Rose was in enemy hands.

They would not be particularly tender hands.

"Good luck, Striker."

She was contemplating a stonewall while wishing *him* luck. Some kind of plucky lady. And, yes, Bolan had to admit the truth: he was very strongly emotionally involved with the lady.

66

If it was cops . . . then okay . . . no problem
. . . no problem.

If not . . . well, the Striker knew and the
lady knew that there was no stonewalling those
other people. They could bust the mind wide
open and empty everything from it in mere
minutes. Nor would they hesitate to do so.
Some of them would even enjoy doing it, necessary or not. And there would be no return for
April Rose from such an adventure.

Luck, April?

Mack Bolan knew that he and the lady would
need much more than luck. They both would
need a miracle. And sometimes, a guy simply
had to make his own.

He needed to get their attention—their full
attention—and to give them something much
larger than April Rose to think about. Or else
he had to snatch the lady back, damned quick
—and that could be the toughest task of all.

Luck, okay. He'd take all he could get. And
he'd take one of those miracles, too, thanks.

He'd take whatever the hell he could get.

CHAPTER 8

A QUESTION OF TIME

The question was entirely one of *time*—and Bolan was not convinced that there was enough of that left in all the world for April Rose.

He left the cruiser idling in the alley and went in via the service entrance.

The naked eye of a television camera ogled him as he stepped through from the receiving docks to the interior passageway.

He was carrying a special cutdown version of the M-79 beneath his coat and the bulge must have been obvious but there was no challenge as he proceeded on toward the nerve center.

Another camera watched him into the short hallway leading to *SecuriCom*. The one mounted above the security door had little time to read him. He unleashed the '79 from twenty paces out, sending forty flaming millimeters of HE thundering into that door and obscuring the hall with puffing clouds of smoke.

The heavy steel door was buckled inward by the blast, hinges sprung and askew, still standing but a bit cockeyed and open to entry.

Some crazy people behind the smoke were firing handguns at phantoms of their own imaginations. Bolan moved inside with the smoke and immediately dispatched another round toward the back wall. The two crazies back there had already opted for cover, but not quite soon enough. The blast caught them both in mid-dive and flung them on into a row of filing cabinets with battering force. These were simple concussion rounds, no shrapnel or other dispersal materials other than the flame and smoke unleashed by the blast itself and super-energized molecules of air. Even so, they could knock a man silly from ten yards—and a contained blast could flatten the walls and drop the roof of a small building.

The guy at the console up near the door had gotten his bell rung by the first blast. He was lolling in his chair about half conscious, blood oozing from both nostrils, not giving a carefree damn about the alarms erupting from his equipment.

Bolan turned into the little anteroom and sent another charge into the door at Rickert's private office. That one broke into two pieces and hurled itself on into the room. He thumbed in another round as he moved in behind the blast. At that same moment, a trick panel in the wall to his left swung open and a guy in civilian dress came charging out, pistol in hand, wild-eyed and grunting. The charge became a sliding halt in the confrontation with the gaping barrel of the '79. The pistol kept on moving across the room as the guy's hands flew quickly overhead.

"What the *hell!*" he muttered.

This guy was a brother of the blood, for sure. And Bolan had heard the voice minutes earlier, in the taped conversation with Charlie Rickert.

"You tell me what the hell," Bolan growled. He punched the weapon into the guy's belly and shoved him against Rickert's desk. "Where's the man?"

"H-he not here! Gone—he left!"

The still smoking muzzle dug deeper. "Know what happens if I let fly right now, *amici?* They'll be sucking your intestines off the blinds with a vacuum cleaner."

The guy had no heart for this sort of thing. Instant sweat appeared on the forehead and the eyes rolled as he yelled, "I swear he left! What can I—what do you—"

Bolan plugged that attempt with another vicious jab into the belly. The guy sucked it in and turned deathly pale. Bolan could see the mind inside buckling. He maintained the pressure and said, "Make me happy."

"Okay, okay," the guy replied quietly. He was trying to pull it together and also reaching for a bit of dignity. And Bolan was willing to give him that. "He said he was going to Burbank."

"What's so great about Burbank?"

"We got a plant there, a facility. By the airport. We got this problem."

70

"You've got a problem right here, bud."

"I know but . . . this broad, see—we caught a broad. She had a court order, see, which we think is a phony. ID, too, you know—federal, federal ID, also probably phony. It's a hell of a sweat. See, we—"

"You know who I am?" Bolan growled.

"Sure. You're D'Anglia. I was here when you—I was in the back room."

"I don't know who you are, friend."

"I'm Lambert. I'm the auditor."

"The hell you're Lambert."

"Oh, well, of course, changed from Lamamammamamma . . ."

The guy's tape was stuck. Bolan said, "Changed from what?"

"Lamamammafria. You can see why I changed."

"What do you audit?"

"I audit the—you know—I audit this account . . . for *them*."

"What account?"

"*SecuriCom*. I keep an eye on Rickert and his boys."

"You stink, Lamamamma."

"What? I don't—what did I? . . ."

"Some auditor. These guys walking away with the whole thing and you never tumbled to it? You want me to believe that?"

"I don't understand—I didn't know . . ."

"That *broad* works for *me*, guy."

"Well, we didn't—I didn't know! Rickert said—and I figured—I didn't know what to you saying the guy is kinky?"

"You know damned well he's kinky!"

"No, I—listen—please—don't pull that trigger!" The dignity had gone to hell. "I'm sorry about the lady! They're taking her up to Burbank. Rickert's meeting them there! I swear—now I *swear* that's all I know about it! But if you say he's kinky then he's kinky. By god. I'm sorry. I really didn't—"

Bolan pulled the '79 out of the guy's belly and slapped him across the temple with it. He fell onto the desk and slid to the floor, apparently unconscious.

So far, so good.

Time consumed: about a minute, maybe two.

He explored the back room—a plush little inner sanctum without windows—and found another way out.

Ten seconds later he was in the battle cruiser and pointing her nose toward Burbank.

As he eased onto the street, he could see throngs of curious folk on the sidewalk in front of the building and a couple of police cruisers at the curb with lights flashing. Far down the boulevard, a procession of fire vehicles were approaching the scene.

Bolan had cut it pretty damn close, yeah. But he was now much closer to April Rose—and that had suddenly become the new game in town. Rickert could not have more than a ten minute lead on him. And maybe he could even reduce those numbers just a bit in the chase to Burbank.

The firemen could relax—there were no fires to fight in that joint.

Most of the fire was in Bolan's belly and it was building by the moment. He'd damned sure better find that girl alive and well. Otherwise, Sly Charlie was going to discover the true meaning of holocaust. And there would be no place in time or space to avoid that reckoning.

Bolan was in love with the lady, for sure.

That, too, was a reckoning to be met—even if it occurred beyond space and outside of time.

CHAPTER 9

THE TURNING

"They've located Mr. Brognola, Chief. They're patching you through, now."

About damned time. He'd only been waiting for—

"Brognola here."

"Tim Braddock, Hal."

"So they told me," sighed the familiar voice. "It's the only reason I'm here. What brings you to my table? Long time no see. By the way, I did hear about your new appointment. Congratulations."

"Thanks." But he had not called for back-slapping. "Where are you?"

"I'm, uh, not in Washington at the moment."

"I didn't ask you where you're not, Hal."

The guy was not about to tell him, either. "What's the problem?"

"I'm hoping you can tell me. I received a

rather reliable tip awhile ago. Concerns you, I believe."

"Uh huh."

"I think so, yeah. It says a certain subject is operating in my town again. I thought you could confirm that for me."

"A certain subject? Can't you do better than that?"

"I'd rather not. We both know who I'm talking about. Let's leave it that way. Is it true or not true?"

The fed sighed then chuckled lightly into the connection. "How would you rather have it?"

"Not true."

"Then it's not true."

"Damnit!" Braddock snapped. "Don't play games with me! I don't want—"

"Have a cigar, Tim."

The son of a bitch. How did you stay mad at a...? "I gave up smoking when I made deputy chief," Braddock said sourly. "Public image and all that. I'd sort of like to keep the image. You know. No smoke around my head."

The federal voice was sober and calm as it told him, "I know how you feel. If an apology would help..."

"It wouldn't. Call the guy out, Hal."

"I didn't send him in, Chief. How could I call him out?"

"But you knew about it."

"I won't confirm or deny that, either. I'll say this: there will be a public announcement early next week. From very high. And you will find no smoke about your head. That's the best I can give you, for now."

It was true, then—the new rumor. It could

75

be very strange, thought Braddock, the way the world sometimes turned. That other time, back near the beginning of Braddock's involvement with this "certain subject," the world had been a far different place. The subject was just another kid from 'Nam, gone haywire and running amuck in the civil society. Tim Braddock was just beginning to move up in the administrative ranks. Harold Brognola was leading a local federal task force on organized crime. A different world, yeah. Then the world had turned. Mack Bolan became the symbol of red-blooded American heroism and the absolute scourge of the Mafia conspiracy. Tim Braddock was turned into a deputy chief of one of the most respected police departments in the world. And Brognola had become head honcho of federal law enforcement everywhere, advisor to presidents and a consultant to *Interpol*.

Yes, the three B's—Bolan, Braddock, Brognola—intertwined by fate and circumstance— or perhaps by parallel destinies, if you could add a touch of romanticism to the strange ways this old world had turned.

"It's a clean phone, Hal," he said quietly. "What's going down?"

"You don't really want to know that," was the calm response.

"Okay, maybe I don't. But tell me, anyway. Is it true what I've been hearing from Washington?"

"About our subject?"

"Same subject, yes."

"Yes, Tim. It's true."

Well damn! He could not keep the quiet elation out of his voice. "Okay, I'll ratify that—

smoke on the head or not. It should have come long ago."

"We tried to send it long ago. The guy wouldn't accept it. I'm not altogether certain he's going to accept it this time."

"What do you mean?"

"He's given us a conditional go, that's all."

"What's the condition?"

Brognola gave a long, tired sigh. "He's insisting on a second mile."

"A second what?"

"Mile. Like the condemned man, back in the age of romance. The last mile, you know. The guy did his, and then some. Now he says he's got to do it again."

Braddock did not fully understand. "You mean the whole damned? ..."

"Once around lightly, this time . . . or so he says. He calls it a mop-up. I call it insanity. Did you hear about yesterday?"

To be sure. "I heard, yeah. But I didn't get all the—"

"We didn't release it all. I can tell you, though, between buddies, that the heartland of the nation has been thoroughly pacified, to use a military term. It will be a long time before they can gather the pieces for another try. And we'll be there, bet on it, to fit some pieces of our own into the picture. So ..." Another deep sigh. "So I really can't argue with the man. He's doing a hell of a job on these people."

"Yes, I've seen a few of his jobs," Braddock murmured. "I can't see what he's going for here, though, this time. I haven't found any pieces forming a fit of any magnitude since he did it here the first time."

"There have been, uh, movements, Tim."

"Gee, thanks for telling me. When did you—"

"I didn't. He did."

It was Braddock's turn for the deep sigh routine. "So he's taking it apart again, eh?"

"I hope so, yes. That's the general idea. Hey. Don't fault me, buddy. I have no control over this subject. Hell, I just trot along behind and try to pick up the broken pieces."

"Is that what you're doing now?"

"Huh?"

"Huh hell. You heard what I said. Is this a round-robin telephone connection, Hal? Are you in L.A.?"

The fed chuckled. "Relax. We're trying to cover the guy, that's all. I've got my orders straight from—well, no, let's not politicize it. No room for that. I understand, though, they got a full bipartisan okay from Capitol Hill. The thing is set. It's going to work. If we can just keep him alive for five more damn days."

"Did you say five *days*?"

"Counting this one, right. He said six days. Yesterday was day one. Listen to me, Tim . . ." The guy was becoming emotional—a rare scene, for that one. "It would be the most terrible—it would be—if this subject should fall to *police* guns, for God's sake—why, I just don't think—it would be a national calamity. Talk about politics—the good citizens of this nation would rise up in their wrath to behead us all. And we'd deserve it. We can't let—"

"You don't have to sell me," Braddock

78

growled. "On the theory, anyway. I have to live with the realities, though. We still have wants on the guy and some of them are yours."

"Yeah, but—"

"And I'll tell you something, Mister Fed. A good L.A. cop does *not* play politics. He doesn't play national opinion polls, either. He plays good guys and bad guys. As of this moment, our subject has been rather thoroughly identified as a bad guy. I can't call twenty thousand cops in here and tell them to look the other way when a certain bad guy lopes past waving a gun and hurling grenades. Wouldn't do it if I could. If they can do it for one, then they could decide when and where to do it for any—all on their own. We can't run a department that way. The law is the law—and that's the way it has to stay. So what are you suggesting to me, *Federale?*"

Brognola very quietly replied, "Hey, Chief, it's your nickel. I'm suggesting nothing. Can I go now?"

"You don't suck me away that easy, mister. I think you'd better come in. We need to—"

"Nothing doing, Tim—sorry. I really can't. If the subject is right, we'll only be around for a few hours, anyway. Suffer us to that extent. I'll make you a promise. If it goes beyond nightfall, I'll come in and we'll put the heads together. How's that?"

"That's awful," Braddock replied, but he knew it was the best he was going to get. He laughed lightly and added, "But I'll expect you for dinner."

"Deal," Brognola said quickly. "Now you promise me."

"Promise you what?"

"You won't react to wild tips and rumors of war. You won't throw up a damned Maginot line like the last time."

"Haven't you heard?" Braddock replied lightly, "the taxpayers are growing restless over irresponsible spending. We can't squander the manpower on *rumors* of war. However . . ." The tone became heavier as he continued. "When the shooting starts, Hal, you know damned well what our reaction has to be."

Brognola growled, "Yeah, I know that. Okay. I'm saying goodbye for now."

"One more thing, old pal."

"Okay, hit me."

"Are you carting a federal judge around with you?"

"Where would you get such an idea?"

"A piece of police routine that hit my desk this morning. It says that this special judge has been magically appointed and transported overnight to alleviate some of the overload in this district. I was just thinking how convenient that could be for a—"

"Okay, you got me. He's mine. It's one hundred percent legal, strike force authority, so don't let—"

"Say goodbye, Hal. I believe the shooting has started."

"Literally?"

"Literally, yes. Goodbye, Hal."

He put the phone down and turned troubled eyes to the uniformed cop who was fidgeting in the open doorway. "What've you got, Johnny?"

"You said you wanted to be alerted to any reports of paramilitary activity or the like."

80

The shooting had started, yeah. He'd seen it in Johnny's eyes even while he talked to Brognola. "Let's have it."

"Offices of a security outfit on Sunset Boulevard, Chief. Explosions and gunfire. Street cops on the scene say it looks like a war zone."

The deputy chief did not need an on-the-scene assessment. His gut already knew, and the scene was clearly imaged in his mind.

Charlie Rickert worked for a "security outfit" on Sunset. And Rickert had longtime associations with certain criminal elements of the community.

"No more rumors," Braddock muttered.

"Sir?"

"We'll have to sound an area alert. Advise Communications to stand by for—no, cancel that. We'll await confirmation. Send Hallowell and his experts to the scene. Tell him I need solid evidence to justify a *Hardcase Two.*"

The cop's eyes flared at that one. He'd been around during the original Hardcase—several damned turns of the world ago. "Well bullll shit," he said softly, forgetting himself for the moment.

"It's not applesauce, Johnny," Big Tim growled, perhaps too quietly for the officer to hear.

And indeed it was not. It was the most unpleasant task ever to burden a law enforcement official. He had to do his damndest to catch or kill a man whom nobody really wanted caught or killed. Except the Charlie Rickerts of the world . . . and their rotten-ass compatriots.

"Wait, Johnny, I—"

Too late. Johnny had already quietly closed the door and departed on his assignment.

Too late, yes.

The world keeps turning, Bolan. Get off, man—get off while you can!

But he knew the guy would not. *That* guy would only be *carried* off.

So be it, then. So be it.

CHAPTER 10

CONNECTIONS

That tight coagulation of districts, communities and municipalities loosely referred to as Los Angeles could be a nightmare for the unwary visiting motorist, who had been conditioned to believe that some methodology of rhyme or reason should accompany the laying out of a city's streets and thoroughfares. Even the highly vaunted freeway system, which serves more vehicles per capita than anywhere else in the world, could bring a lump to the throat and a quiver to the heart at bumper to bumper speeds of 60 mph and more, with vehicles often hurtling along five or six abreast into dead men's curves, offramps, onramps, upramps, downramps, spirals and cloverleafs—not to mention the bewildering complexity of instructional signboards flashing past faster than the mind can comprehend or even assimilate.

Bolan had to guess that the energy consumed on those freeways each day could probably heat the homes of the entire rest of the nation.

And this was midday traffic. Shudder the mind to even contemplate the peak hours of this madness.

The city of Burbank borders the Los Angeles districts of Hollywood and North Hollywood.

It should be a simple matter, then—shouldn't it?—to journey from Sunset Boulevard in Hollywood to the Hollywood-Burbank airport.

Wrong.

It seems that Griffith Park, Forest Lawn, Warner Brothers, Universal Studios and the Hollywood Hills form the natural boundary between Hollywood and Burbank. If a guy was determined to stick to the freeways, he could journey east along Sunset to the Hollywood Freeway, then cut back northwest for several miles to North Hollywood, then onto the Ventura Freeway running due east again for a long run to the Golden State Freeway for another jog northwesterly for five miles or so to San Fernando Boulevard and the airport.

Or . . . he could take the Hollywood to Barham Boulevard then take his chances on the arterials all the way through the city of Burbank in a full south to north transit.

He could also go on up to Universal City and take Lankershim and Vineland . . . or . . .

Or, of course, if he was fortunate enough to be driving a vehicle with an onboard navigational computer, he could simply turn the whole problem over to the electronic brain.

The computer advised Bolan to proceed north on Highland for an interchange with the freeway near the Hollywood Bowl, then off at Barham and on to Hollywood Way, which would take him to the southeast corner of the airport and the terminal access. So much for freeways, which figured into that route for only a mile or two.

He accepted that route and gave the thing its head, turning his own mind onto more substantive matters.

He could not dwell upon the present predicament and possible fate of his lady fed. So the mind turned naturally to an assessment of the overall situation now confronting him across this tangled landscape.

Fact: a new "thing" was a building in the Golden State.

Fact: the principals so far encountered were a diverse lot of personalities, such as:

(a) A rich but kinky businessman, whose troubles with a rebellious daughter now seemed remote and unimportant;

(b) a kinky ex-cop who now commanded a private police force of unknown but probably impressive size, which was probably financed by (a) above;

(c) A holdover Mafia master architect from the old order who had direct involvement with:

(d) A nameless team of hitmen who had unsuccessfully tried to snuff (a) above, and also had some connection with (b) above;

(e) A Mafia "auditor" set as a watchdog over (b) on behalf of:

(f) An unidentified "them" who appeared to

be the budding bosses of the reconstituted Los Angeles Mob.

Sub-fact, with a question mark:

This new "thing" was being structured along an unusual pattern called the California Concept, which probably meant, in this early analysis:

(a) A combination of Mafia and non-Mafia elements joined together for mutual comfort and assistance,

(b) Welded into a supertight, superquiet organization with:

(c) more lateral than vertical lines of responsibility and activity; and

(d) invisible lines of authority.

In other words, a "Mob" that was not really a Mob, structured along some new "concept," which did not reveal visible connections between the layers. In simple, it did not appear to be a "crime family" operation.

The traditional Mafia pattern in America was a pyramidal structure with the boss at the apex. He would franchise "territories," which could be set up geographically or categorically or both, and which would be ruled by subbosses who, in turn, would franchise smaller subdivisions to their lieutenants who then would sublet various enterprises to their individual soldiers.

The soldiers were in business for themselves, running their little scams and operations with almost total autonomy so long as they remained within their licenses and in good standing with the "family."

Just as any individual business that operates under a large corporate umbrella, the bottom level mobsters benefitted from the total power of the full organization without themselves being required to worry about legal services, investment capital, political influence, and so forth. On the other hand, they were merely operating business franchises. The lieutenants took a cut from the soldier's profits. The sub-bosses took a cut from the lieutenants. And, of course, the boss always got his.

From such a pyramid, the cash flow upward from all the soldiers of a vast empire was astronomical. And, of course, the guy at the top of the pyramid was the guy who grew fat and rich from other people's labors.

It was an inverted pyramid, of course, tapering back like a mirror-image from its base in the straight world to layer after smaller layer, deeper and deeper into the underworld. Still, it was an almost perfect model of the structure for corporate capitalism—and, being free of upperworld restraints, infinitely more profitable per dollar investment.

Bolan had to wonder, now, what had replaced it. Or had it been replaced, at all, in this California Concept?

Were *they* or *them* a group with fully delegated powers to direct the criminal activities in a newly consecrated territory? Were they directors, then, of a new criminal corporation that was trying to build upon the ruins of the DiGeorge empire?

If so, did the fictitious Crusher draw his authority, so presumed and accepted by the boss of the war committee, from the Chairman of the Board himself? Or did such an entity even exist in the real world?

Lamamamma had said to Rickert, in that taped conversation, "I told you my people don't take much on faith. I bet they've got us under a microscope."

Were "my people" a generalization or did it refer to actual persons behind the scenes of the Los Angeles push?

That same guy had told Bolan-Crusher: "I audit this account for *them*. I keep an eye on Rickert and his boys."

Back to *them*, again. *My people*?

As opposed to *whose* people?

McCullough, Rickert, the hit team—not *my people*, no. McCullough, Rickert—outsiders. Not brothers of the blood. Not in any sense . . . but a curious relationship. McCullough owned *California Investors*, which owned, in turn, *SecuriCom*, which employed Rickert. Yet Rickert's boys—also not "brothers"—had been sent to snuff Bill McCullough who had appealed to eastern "brothers" for help in his own front yard.

Curious, yeah.

Was McCullough *really* all that torn up over his daughter's liaisons—or had that merely been a cover story to involve east with west?

And who was "Jay Leonard"—the recipient of the heavy telephone call that soured the day for April Rose? A call that Bolan had hoped would lead him to the mysterious *them*. Maybe it had. Or it could, still. Bolan had not lost interest in Mr. Leonard; the interest had simply given way to an overriding priority. But . . . *was* Leonard one of them?

It was all very tangled . . . but not hopelessly so. The confusion was not at all surprising or demoralizing. Bolan had not expected a cakewalk in Los Angeles. If the city's streets could be nightmarish to the visiting motorist, then certainly the coagulations of underworld power in such an awesome setting could be just as confusing and unwieldy for a visiting crimebuster.

A federal task force of legal experts and methodical investigators would need months and perhaps years to untangle all the diverse interconnections of cause and effect in such an organization. Even then, the legal evidence to effectively prosecute the perpetrators of a criminal conspiracy could be doubly elusive. Meanwhile the shit machine would run on virtually unchecked until it gained such financial strength and political clout that all the good cops in the country could not hope to contain it, let alone dismantle it.

Mack Bolan was not confined to the rules of that sacred game.

All he needed was a chink in the walls, a toehold from which to launch an attack with no holds barred—and, yes, with a bit of luck and a mind that dared, he could dismantle that shit machine in a single day. Let the constitutional lawyers and professional liberals agonize and handwring the loss of the sacred game that made the dungheaps possible in the first place. Bolan was waging a war . . . without convention . . . and without respect for dumb rules that insured victory to the enemy. He claimed no holiness for his own game, either. There was no mantle of righteousness cloaking Mack Bolan's war. If his government could catch him at his illegal game—then okay—he'd suffer the consequences without bitterness or complaint—and he would tolerate no battery of lawyers trying to establish his holiness, either.

But that was all theoretical garbage.

If Bolan lost this game, it would be to the enemy—not to the soldiers of the same side. It was not that the cops *could not* or *would not* catch him; it was simply that all the odds were with the other side. If he was going to fall, then he knew where that fall would come. His head would end up in a paper sack carried by some gloating geek who . . .

Ah well. Sufficient unto the day was the evil thereof.

For the moment, Bolan had job enough simply trying to save the day for April Rose.

And if that were not possible?

Well . . . if that were not possible . . . then for sure it was going to be one hell of a terrible and nightmarish day for the visiting crimebuster.

And perhaps for this awesome city, as well.

CHAPTER 11

WOW TIME

It looked like a *SecuriCom* convention. Uniformed men were milling about in the light rain outside and more could be seen inside the office through the open doorway. The building was set on airport property at the south perimeter. It was a warehouse or maintenance garage—or both—with loading docks and overhead doors running the whole length of maybe a hundred yards. There was no fence nor a hell of a lot of tarmac between road and docks. The office occupied the east end. A half dozen cars with company decals were grouped in the small parking area near the office door. Two large vans and a smaller one were backed into loading position at the docks. One of the overhead doors was open and more uniformed people could be seen moving around just inside.

The fog had lifted some time earlier but the

cloud base was hovering just overhead—perhaps at a thousand feet or so—and a steady light rain had been falling through most of the journey up from Hollywood. Rickert had arrived just ahead of Bolan and was met outside by two men in street dress. They were standing outside the office jawing in the rain as Bolan cruised by.

A car rental terminal abutted the facility to the west. He pulled into there and parked amidst the U-drives while the combat mind coolly clicked through the various possibilities of approach.

He was not here to thump the chest and announce his rage. He was here to get that girl back, whole and healthy. Suicidal urges would serve no useful purpose toward that goal. He could blast his way in, sure—and maybe he could even blast his way out. But the chance would be about one in a hundred that he would emerge with April Rose all in one piece.

He could go in softly—and maybe even come out the same way. But could he bring the girl with him? Rickert was no clown—and Bolan's masquerades would perhaps not stand the test of time. Even saying that he could pull it off again, there was no assurance and perhaps only a fifty-fifty probability that Rickert would continue to accept the "authority" of D'Anglia the Crusher. And, of course, it was entirely possible that Sly Charlie had already put the pieces together and come up with Bolan-D'Anglia.

It was no simple decision.

These kinds never were.

In the end, though, it always came down to

the simple imperative. Bolan would simply have to seize the moment and run with it. Play the ear. The moment was about as favorable as could be expected. Rickert had just arrived on the scene and was being briefed by his lieutenants. Judging by the pace of other activities there, the thing with April Rose was hardly more than a footnote to the larger endeavor. Obviously the "force" was assembling and preparing for some sort of aggressive action.

So it was a moment out of balance—and Bolan knew that he had to put that moment to work. He had to run with it.

He brought the fire control system to the con and centered the rangemarks on a vehicle in that congregation parked outside the office, poked in target acquisition, set up a one-two automatic program and selected another target for the follow-on, then enabled the rocketry and cycled the system into standby for EVA-Remote.

Bolan was setting up a contingency only; he hoped that he would not have to use it. Other business structures were nearby and a residential neighborhood was just a stone's throw. He had no wish to spill his war into innocent laps. But he did need that backup. He was going in rigged for light combat. He selected the Auto-Mag as head weapon—a .44 Magnum autoloader, the big stainless steel pistol that Bolan had dubbed "Big Thunder"—and rigged it about the waist. The silent Beretta in shoulder harness remained in place. A variety of small ordnance items—flares, smokers, boomers —went onto the waist rig. Finally he clipped the tiny remote fire control device—the "black box"—onto the readybelt and donned a black slicker to cover it all.

The Executioner was ready to go a'hunting.

The rain was coming much heavier. A personnel door at the west end of the building was covered by one of those damnable television eyes. He warily skirted that hazard at safe range and came in along the loading docks. The guys at the far end, near the office, at least had sense enough to come in out of the rain. They were moving to cover beneath the eaves. The visibility was definitely worsening. With all the movement down there, it was impossible to spot Rickert or even to distinguish clothing in that group.

Bolan went on to the parked vans for a quick inspection of their contents. The larger two were personnel carriers—confirming a gut feeling he'd had about those vehicles. Upholstered benches lined each side, equipment racks filling the center aisle. The small van was outfitted like a plush camper, with much of the rear area devoted to wall-to-wall bedspace. The bedding was mussed. Near the door, Bolan discovered a lady's slipper. A familiar one, sure. When last seen, that slipper was on the dainty foot of a lady fed.

He moved on inside the party van and across the bed to the rear doors. Tinted portholes looked out onto the dock and beyond into the busy interior of the building. It was a warehouse, yeah—or had been. Now it looked like the staging area for a military operation. Shotguns and riot gear were stacking up just inside. Deeper inside could be seen row upon row of what appeared to be ammunition boxes.

Several men wearing *SecuriCom* uniforms were moving vigorously about—lugging boxes, sorting, stacking.

Outfitting a war party? Probably, yes.

It was beginning to look like a hell of a hard mission. Too hard, perhaps, considering its nature. A hundred armed men or more—alerted, maybe, and simply awaiting the appearance of an undesirable alien in their midst.

Or maybe not.

There was one simple, direct way to find out. Bolan opened the van, gathered the slicker about him, and stepped onto the dock.

A uniformed guy in the doorway gave him a startled look, then cast a curious gaze toward the van from which he had just emerged.

Before the guy could have too much time to wonder about it, Bolan growled at him: "Great day for the ducks."

The guy looked at the sky as he growled back: "Yeah. We can sure pick 'em."

"We almost ready? The boss is here."

"I saw 'im. We're about ready, yeah. You in charge of the? . . ."

The guy let it hang but Bolan assured him that he was indeed in charge of whatever.

"Yeah." He tossed April's slipper into the air and caught it with the other hand. "Where's Cinderella?"

The private cop chuckled as he jerked his head toward the interior of the building. "She's in the safe." He leered. "Didn't you get enough?"

"Not nearly," Bolan replied soberly. He stepped past the guy and went inside. Another uniform was standing with hands on hips, staring quietly in his direction. The eyes dropped as Bolan approached and the guy turned busily toward the ammo boxes. "Quick it up," Bolan growled as he walked past that one.

"Yessir," the guy muttered.

There was strength in numbers, yeah—the other guy's numbers, when they grew too great for ready recognition.

No one, now, was paying him the slightest attention though he was virtually surrounded by spiffy blue uniforms. And he was about twenty paces inside when he spotted April Rose.

The "safe" was a glass cubicle at the far wall of the building. It was crammed with electronic panels and other gear. A turret similar to the one noted in the Hollywood office, but much larger, dominated the enclosure. It took two men back to back to man it—and both looked busy as hell. It was quite an operation.

April sat on a high stool in a corner of the cubicle. She looked okay except that her clothing was torn and disheveled. Two guys in civilian clothes seemed to be interrogating her—but no hands were upon her.

Rickert was present, also. He was speaking with great animation and a lot of handwaving into a telephone.

It was a "safe," yeah. Soundproof—bulletproof, too, no doubt. Not glass, after all, but some heavy plastic material. The combat mind instinctively scanned for support systems even while the greater consciousness was zeroing on the mission goal. It was an old building, but obviously a spanking new control center. That meant a lot of extra power requirements far beyond the original scope of the aged building—plus some heavy air conditioning to keep all those electronics at proper temperature.

And, yes, a fragment of the consciousness had spotted the trunklines coming down the back wall from the attic, numerous air vents in the ceiling—telltale evidence of new wine in old bottles.

But perhaps all of that was in the realm of useless information.

Rickert had spotted Bolan, also—and the displeasure was obvious in that unhappy face. Not alarm, though—just displeasure. The guy was scowling at D'Anglia-Crusher, not at Bolan-D'Anglia. The way things had gone since their last meeting, though, one identity could be about as hazardous as the other.

So which way did the ear turn?

What the hell. He placed his lips close to the door intercom and growled, "Open it, Rickert."

One of the guys at the turret-console looked up quickly, then back to Rickert. The latter appeared frozen for a moment, the phone still at the ear but drooping away as interest focused elsewhere. Then Bolan saw those tight lips move in a terse command. The door opened. Bolan stepped inside.

April Rose was staring at him with suddenly horrified eyes.

The two guys with her did not notice the reaction; they, too, were giving full attention to the new arrival.

But all of Bolan-D'Anglia's angered attention was being directed to the unhappy man at the telephone. "You damned idiot!" he said savagely, raising the voice in a clear carry to bounce from all the plastic walls.

It was a good enough approach.

Rickert put the phone down and said woodenly, "I know. I was just talking to Jack Lambert. He says we made a little mistake."

"*Little* mistake!" Bolan snorted.

Rickert's voice was ruffled and tense but placating. "You didn't have to tear up our goddam offices." His eyes went to the slipper in Bolan's hand. "How the hell were we to know she was yours? Her goddam stuff all checks out solid. Even the warrant. How the hell were we to know?"

"You didn't think she was a fed when you grabbed her!" Bolan raged. "Where do you get off disrupting a—?"

"Of course not, we didn't know what—how the hell?—hey, it was *my* goddam phones under the tap! You think I hold still for that kind of shit? I warned you before that I—"

Bolan reached the guy in two long strides and caught him flat-footed with a vicious open-hand blow to the face. The guy took off like a whirling dervish, hitting the floor on hands and knees. "You warned me *hell*!" Bolan said, giving a convincing demonstration of outraged authority. The rage part was easy, requiring no acting whatever.

None of the other four men present moved a muscle or even twitched. Rickert was shaking his head, trying to get the silly out.

Bolan looked at the girl and asked, "You okay?"

"I'm fine," she said, the voice soft and controlled.

"Lucky for them." He tossed her the slipper and she caught it. "Let's go, we're trucking."

Rickert pulled himself onto a chair. The left side of his face was beet red and pulsing. "You're crazy, D'Anglia," he wheezed.

"Not as crazy as you," Bolan-D'Anglia replied coldly. "You don't even know who your enemies are. You're supposed to be going after *Bolan*, damnit, not—and you screwed up a heavy—we weren't earing *you*, dummy. We were going for the fink."

"What fink?" Rickert muttered.

"What fink," Bolan said disgustedly. "You think the guy is psychic or something? How do you think he got onto?—how'd you ever get this goddam job in the first place?"

"We're going after him," Rickert replied, smarting under the abuse. "We'll get him, too, hot ass. And then—well, you and me are going to have it out, D'Anglia."

Bolan-D'Anglia snorted derisively, took his lady by the hand, and went out of there.

Too heavy? Maybe. Maybe a shade too heavy.

"Wow," April said quietly as they moved into the warehouse.

"Don't wow it yet," Bolan muttered. "We're a long way from clear."

A long way, yeah. Rickert and the two other men in civvies came out of the safe room behind them and were tagging along about ten paces to the rear.

No—it was not wow time, yet.

Bolan's hand moved inside the slicker and found the command button on the black box.

He sighed and summoned the fire, calling forth the rocketry program.

Three seconds to raise, another three to lock, one more to fire.

He was counting silently from one-thousand-one and had reached one-thousand-four when Rickert called out to him.

"D'Anglia!"

Bolan muttered to the girl, "Get clear." Then he halted and turned back. "Yeah?"

April kept on moving toward the large open doorway of the loading dock.

"You, too, little lady. Hold it a minute."

... *thousand-seven* ...

"Go to hell, Rickert!" Bolan snarled. "You've had your—"

The bird came slamming home, rattling the ears and twitching the eyeballs as it plowed into the tight assemblage of vehicles at the east end.

Rickert and his two boys went rigid for a moment, then came unstuck and raced toward the dock as gasoline secondaries began cutting loose. Bolan stepped casually aside and let them pass, taking his lady once again by the hand and moving her on.

The second bird came home just as Rickert reached the loading dock. It blew away the whole northeast corner of the building. The whole structure quivered, puffing flames and smoke back into the warehouse area.

One of the guys with Rickert gasped, "What the *hell*!"

"Looks like you've found your boy," Bolan said as he moved past them. "Let's see you take 'im."

The private force was running around like ants at a fire when Bolan stepped down from the dock. He swept his lady into his arms and moved west, into the rain and away from all that hell. As Bolan and the lady moved out of earshot, Rickert was yelling for fire extinguishers and warning his troops about the explosives stored in the warehouse.

"Wow!" said April Rose, looking back at the leaping flames and utter confusion behind them. "Or is it still too soon for wow?"

No. It was time for wow. Bolan sent a silent one, himself, toward the heavens and clasped the lady closer.

But he knew that he had not seen the last of Charlie Rickert and his private army. What he had seen of those guys, so far, was barely the beginning.

CHAPTER 12

LINKAGE

April went directly to the bath for hot water and cosmetic repairs while Bolan moved the cruiser back along the service road past the combat zone. Airport emergency vehicles were responding and people were running in on foot from every direction. He wished to get clear—but not entirely—while traffic still could move through the area.

All six of the *SecuriCom* cars at the east end were tumbled together in a common pyre and the flames were roaring high into the rain-soaked heavens. That end of the building was also engulfed in the action and blue-suited men were scampering about in apparent rescue operations.

Others for whom no rescue was possible were being laid out on the tarmac.

Bolan idly wondered how many men he'd

killed with his robot rockets, but knew without attempting a guess that it had not been nearly enough.

SecuriCom was beginning to look like some kind of fantastic setup—so fantastic that Bolan was starting to rethink his logic model for the so-called California Concept.

He cleared the combat zone and went on to the airport terminal where he wheeled about and parked with a clear if distant view of the disaster scene. April emerged from the toilet wearing nothing but panties and bra. She tossed her hips immodestly and called forward, "How do I look?"

"Edible," he replied, watching her in the mirror.

"Promises, promises," she grumbled, and went to find fresh clothing.

Two Burbank city police cars screamed past, followed closely by ambulances and a fire department medical unit. A jumble of sirens could be heard approaching in the distance.

When April came forward to the con, she was clad in faded denims and a knit top. She told Bolan, "Your pants are soaked from the knees down. Take 'em off."

He just grinned at her and continued the surveillance.

She apparently became aware just then that the vehicle was parked. "Where've I been?" she asked, with wonder in the voice. "I thought we—what're we doing here?"

Bolan knew where she'd "been." Stress and its sudden release can do strange things to the mind—giddy things. He told her, "Sit down and pull it together, soldier. Our day has just begun."

"*Your* day," she corrected him. "I just had my soldierly adventure."

"You retiring?"

"I'm thinking about it," she replied quietly.

He said, just as quietly, "Well . . . at least a picture is emerging. Your soldierly adventure was a godsend, kiddo. I think I know, now, what these guys are doing."

He was thinking about that "safe" with its electronic marvels. The plastic fishbowl.

Apparently April Rose was thinking about something else. "You are really some kind of terrific, you know," she softly told him. "It's such a damn waste, Mack . . . such a waste. You could make it big in almost anything you'd like to try. You're intelligent, articulate . . . so wise and so . . . so . . ."

"So pretty?" he asked, smiling faintly.

"I'm trying to be serious."

"So am I." He fired up the optics and tried for a fine resolution through the rain, bringing a hundred feet of service road into the con with them. "Those people want to eat your world, April. It's been done before. It could happen again. So where's the waste?"

She did not respond to that.

"You're the expert," he said, sighing. "And you were in there longer than me. What did you see?"

She shrugged daintily and crossed her legs. "I saw about a zillion dollars worth of sophisticated equipment. It's the new standard technology. All the large security outfits these days use that gear, or variations. They could be a legitimate outfit, you know."

Bolan grinned sourly. "All the large security outfits are not owned lock, stock and body count by the organized underworld. This one is. It's not just Rickert that's kinky. It's the whole damned outfit."

She said, very softly, "Take me to the Riviera, Mack. Or to Rio. I'll settle for Acapulco. I don't want to weep over your broken body. I want to laugh and love and make babies."

He replied, just as softly, "So do I, April."

She sighed and went aft, returning a moment later with pad and pencil. Then she sketched as she recalled the contents of that command center. "I saw about a dozen closed circuit systems under constant video monitor. Several banks of video recorders, also—so they're getting hard copy. And computer terminals—three of them. If they have access, they can hook in anywhere—Washington, Sacramento, city hall. And, uh, telephone relays with audio recorders. What else?—let's see—oh yeah, I think a microwave system—some sort of telemetry. Miscellaneous scanners, bleepers, radio dispatch systems." She tossed her head. "It's a bunch."

Yes. It was a bunch. But even that was not all.

He asked the lady, "Would you say there are other fishbowls lurking about?"

"Very probably," she replied quietly. "They're on some sort of sophisticated linkage."

Some sort of linkage, yeah.

That was the way Bolan had read it in his

once-over-quickly. Which meant maybe a whole damned network of "fishbowls."

And God only knew what kind of linkage.

They came out as he'd expected them to—three vans, threading their cautious way through the confusion of emergency vehicles and disaster workers, making a run for daylight. Rickert would not wish to have his war party detained by the inevitable police investigation of the incident. He probably would have left only a few men behind to satisfy police curiosity. The rest would be packed into those two personnel carriers. Each of those would normally transport twenty-five to thirty men with full equipment; so, yes, there could be a lot of hell moving out of there—perhaps even headed toward a rendezvous with elements from other facilities in the area.

A lot of hell, yes. And Bolan doubted very strongly that all this force was being deployed solely for his apprehension. Something else, something large, had been set into motion coincidental with Bolan's arrival on the scene. Something that large required much planning and preparation. And if it were a highly elaborate something, then it probably would not or could not be called off simply because a complication had arisen.

Actually, the rumbles had been moving along Bolan's intelligence grapevine for quite awhile —since shortly after his command strike at New York. And he'd had this area on his revisitation schedule even before the recent decision for a six day national blitz.

So it was not entirely coincidence that placed

him smack in the middle of this fevered situation in California. Bolan had long ago lost respect for coincidence. Too often had he felt the force of offstage hands manipulating the human actors on this stage called life. Not that he gave much credence to the various theories of predestination and fated lives. But he was a man strongly attuned to "fine" influences; every combatman is—and every successful commander in the field is as much psychic as soldier, winning by hunches and sudden inspirations, which unknowing men call genius.

Military genius, Bolan knew, was no more than the fine art of reading subtle influences and reacting in the proper direction at the proper time.

Influences or whatever had brought him here at this place and time. He would not presume to question the why or the how of that. He was here, that was enough. The enemy was moving massively—and that was too much.

"Linkage," he muttered as he locked the electronic track on the rear personnel carrier and joined the procession.

"What'd you say?" April Rose inquired.

"Some sort of linkage," he said, repeating her earlier statement.

"There are all kinds," she said dreamily. "How 'bout boy-girl, for starters?"

He showed her a sober smile and said, "Sounds great. Let's keep it on the agenda."

"But not for starters, eh?" she said drily.

Not for starters, no. Another sort of linkage had taken the field—the kind that binds man to event, and event to life, and life to the world.

Survival.

Of what? Of the fittest?

No.

Survival of all the things that make life a beautiful event in a meaningful world. Boy-girl linkage insured only a portion of that. Man-event linkage would have to supply the rest.

And Mack Bolan felt unequivocally linked to the large event that was shaping up for this beautiful city.

He took the lady's hand and squeezed it with all the passions that were his at that moment. He wanted to live, sure. He wanted to love and laugh and sing and dance. He did not want to kill and destroy and hate and weep.

She felt his unspoken anguish. "I'm sorry," she whispered.

"Me, too," he replied quietly, and meant it.

Sure he meant it. He was sorry for all the broken dreams and broken hearts and broken lives—everywhere. He was especially sorry for April Rose.

Maybe one day he would take her to the Riviera . . . and to Rio . . . Acapulco . . . and all the other warm places of the world.

Then again, maybe he would not.

CHAPTER 13

FAVORS

The track was running north into the San Fernando Valley and the rain was beginning to slacken a bit. Bolan had just settled into a comfortable pace along the Golden State Freeway when the coder clanged into his mobile phone terminal. He punched the button and said, "Go."

"Striker, this is Alice."

"Alice" was Hal Brognola, so coded because of his adventures in Washington, Wonderland by the Potomac.

Bolan's clouded gaze dwelled momentarily on the lady beside him before he responded. "Are you local?"

"Yes, I'm local." That good federal voice had a bit of emotion in it. Which was not exactly strange but at least notable. "Can you get to a laundry line?"

He desired a clean telephone contact.

Bolan replied, "Not without missing a play. Can the laundryman wait?"

"I guess not," said that troubled voice. "Let's risk the dirt. Where is the babysitter?"

He was worried about April. Apparently Brognola had learned of her misadventure.

"The babysitter is whole and healthy," Bolan assured the chief fed. He grinned solemnly at the lady as he added, "Sends love and kisses."

The relief at that news came through clear and clean. "That's wonderful. I was hoping you were on top of it. I suppose that explains Burbank."

He'd heard about that, too, already. Bolan told him, "That explains it, yes. You have quick ears."

"I'm not the only one," Brognola said worriedly. "An area plan is going down. I think you know what I mean."

Bolan knew, yes. A police plan. The L.A. area contained dozens of police jurisdictions, but the many agencies could function as one under an "area plan" when the need was there. And these guys had about the best cooperative record going.

"I didn't expect a cakewalk," Bolan told his friend, the fed.

"I know you didn't. I was talking to our hardcase friend awhile ago. The heart is there, Striker—but the fist extends from the mind, not the heart. You get my meaning."

Bolan got it, sure. And he did not fault those in the police establishment who took their duties seriously. "Everyone does his job, Alice," he said quietly. "That's what makes the world go round."

"Yeah. Well. Wanted you to know. Step carefully."

"Sure," Bolan said.

"Uh, say, we picked up the babysitter's crumbs. Not much there. Meaningless conversation. And you can forget about that Silverlake address. It's a punchout."

Meaning that there was no "Jay Leonard." Not unless you wanted to give a name to a robot telephone relay. The intelligence game was getting trickier all the time. It was becoming a game for magicians.

Bolan hid his disappointment as he replied to that. "Too bad. Guess I've struck out with all the cutesies. Punchout, eh? Is there any way you can follow it down?"

"We followed it to Sacramento. Blind punchout there."

"Blind?"

"Blind, yeah. It self-destructed minutes before we reached it. No way to bridge that gap, now. So write it off."

"Maybe not," Bolan said. "I'm going to give you an open send, Alice."

Meaning he was going to speak plainly.

"If you think it's worth it, okay. Go."

"I think it's worth it. The pace is getting too hot for cuteness, anyway. Here's a Sacramento name. Try to plug it into that open gap. Arthur Bloom. Like what the flowers do. He's connected. Via Jimmy Portillo."

Brognola whistled at that one. "I've been hearing that guy in various ports of call," he said quietly.

"He was local at dawn today," Bolan said.

"That's very interesting."

"I thought so, too. When I left him, he was hurting mildly and heading for a hole at the Hollywood Hilton."

"You sure of that?"

"No," Bolan replied. "But I know he called there for a room."

"Okay, I'll look into it," Brognola said. "As long as we're getting reckless, what's happened to McCullough?"

"It broke too fast," Bolan explained. "I was running with the play and had to leave the guy to his own devices. I suggested he find a hole and stay there."

"I guess he found one," Brognola mused. "The whole family has vanished. Who called on 'im, Striker?"

"The word I get, it came via that connection I was telling you about. But there's a lot more we'd better save for the laundry line."

"Uh huh, okay. Will you file a report at your earliest convenience?"

The guy wanted a braindrain on the day's activities. It was a reasonable request and not at all premature. Both men knew that Bolan was living on the heartbeat. If he should not survive the day's activities, then at least there should be a hard record of his findings.

And, yes, there was quite a bit of material already that deserved preservation.

Bolan told him, "The babysitter is working on one right now. We'll drop it in the Z file." The Z file was a special computer bank in Washington, to which Bolan had access from the Warwagon.

"Do that," Brognola said heavily. Then, a bit more on the upbeat: "Watch the swinger, pal."

"Always," Bolan replied, chuckling, and terminated the contact.

April commented, "He sounded worried."

"He's a realist," Bolan told her. "I think he's worried more about the L.A. cops than anything else. Probably trying to run some interference and they snapped his tail off."

"No, he said he wasn't . . ." Her eyes said she'd blown it. "Damnit, Mack. Don't look at me like that."

"You knew he was in town, eh," he said, very quietly.

"Not exact—well, sure, I knew he was close by."

"Why didn't I know it?"

"I guess it just never came up," she replied innocently.

"Who's with him?"

"Oh . . . I guess . . . a bunch."

A bunch, sure. Brognola usually traveled with a strong mobile strike force of federal marshals, whom he generally preferred over the usually stiff-necked FBI agents.

"How close, April?"

"Don't worry about it," she said, a bit irritably. "They're not going to crowd you. Mr. Brognola knows that you like plenty of room."

But he did worry about it. Bolan was always very much concerned about the identity of those whom he may encounter in the combat zone. It was problem enough keeping friends and innocents out of the heat even when he knew whom and where.

"Get him back," he requested.

"Get who back?"

"Brognola."

"What makes you think I know—"

"Get him!" Bolan insisted.

The girl sighed, made a face, and got him back via mobile phone connection.

"Whose nickel?" asked the familiar voice.

"Guess," Bolan growled.

"Okay. Okay." Honestly defensive. "Try to do a friend a favor and all you receive in turn is hostility."

Bolan said, "You've got me wired. Right?"

"You don't really believe that."

"Sure I do," Bolan replied coldly. "You're standing on my shadow, friend. It hurts. What's the separation?"

There was resignation in that responding voice. "Call it two minutes. Now how the hell could that hurt?"

"You want to do favors, eh?"

"At your service, sir."

Bolan said, "Okay. I'll be dropping the baby-sitter in precisely one minute. Mark it. One minute. I want you to pick her up."

April cried, "That's not fair!"

Brognola said, "That's easy. Do I get a reason?"

April yelled, "Damn you!"

Bolan said, "She'll explain it to you. And, Alice—another request—get off my shadow."

April flounced about in her seat, turning her back to him.

Brognola said, "Don't be so touchy. We are remaining physically clear of your territory."

"Physically?"

114

"Yeah. Physically. But don't ask us to turn the heart off, guy."

That was genuine and moving. Bolan's voice was warm in the reply. "Okay. Just be advised. I will not be looking for friends in the bushes."

"We are so advised," Brognola replied.

Bolan said, "Thanks," and terminated.

April turned a woebegone face his way and said, "That's the lousiest . . ."

He growled, "Knock it off, April. I have a job for you. Damned important so forget the sillies. I want you to query every government computer you can find. I want a complete package on McCullough—all of it—his investments, his connections, his marriages, all the troubles with his kid, everything. And I want—"

"But I can do that from here!" she protested. "Can't I?"

"No you can't," he replied firmly. "It would tie up the equipment at a crucial time. Besides, I'd rather you work it on a clean line. Brognola can help with that. Also he can help with the accesses. Several federal agencies have had McCullough under scrutiny off and on for the past couple of years. Hal will know what I need. Be sure you understand completely—then, damnit, get me a full package."

Her expression had softened. "Then it really is an assignment? You're not just . . ."

"Of course it's an assignment," he said brusquely. "And I expect you to work your tail off on this. I want the package within an hour or two. Bank it in the Z file for me and send a hit to the floater when it's ready."

"Then I can come back?"

"Soon as possible. Sure. Why not?"

"I thought you were . . . upset with me. Because of . . ."

He said, "Sure I'm upset. But not enough to slap your ears down. Anyway, we're partners. Right?"

Her eyes were revealing a certain confusion but she replied, "Okay. I guess I understand what you want."

"Get ready for the drop," he said.

She was at the door ten seconds later when the cruiser pulled to the shoulder.

He blew her a kiss.

She caught it and stuffed it down her blouse as she disembarked.

Her image in the rearview mirror as he pulled away looked small and vulnerable. Yeah, especially vulnerable.

She *could* have used the onboard computer, sure. And Bolan really did want that package. Even more, however, he'd wanted that girl cleared to the safe zones.

The combat spine had been sending new messages.

A hell of a fight was shaping up. And damn quick.

CHAPTER 14

COMING TOGETHER

The track continued past the city of San Fernando and began to climb toward the high mountains beyond. When it swung abruptly northeastward at State Route 14, pulling toward Soledad Pass, the Bolan spine was at full shiver. He was being drawn into very rugged countryside, into the San Gabriel Mountains and the Angeles National Forest. On the other side lay Palmdale and the Mojave Desert. Edwards Air Force Base was up that way—also China Lake, site of a Naval Weapons Center. Also a junction with U.S. 395, the main route between Southern California and Sierra Nevada country. Or a guy could link up with Interstate Route 15, the mainline to Las Vegas.

Where the hell were they headed? It was not comforting to contemplate the possibility that they were headed nowhere—that he was being sucked into the boonies and away from where the real action was going down. But that did not seem to fit the circumstances.

Just when the shivers were beginning to spill into the gut, his floater beeped the announcement of an incoming call.

Bolan intercepted the call at the recorder and routed it to the con.

It was Leo Turrin, his inside friend in New York.

"I'm here," Bolan announced. "What's on?"

"Can you get to a landline?"

"Not unless it's a matter of life or death," Bolan told his closest friend.

"Well, maybe it is," the little guy replied worriedly. "How far have you gone with that blind date I sent you?"

"All the way," Bolan said. "She was easy."

"Yeah, well, maybe that's what's bothering me. *Too* easy, if you know what I mean. I think maybe she's infected. I need to talk to you about that."

"If it's safe on your end, go ahead. I can't EVA right now—maybe not for quite awhile."

Turrin sighed and thought about it for a couple of beats, then said, "It's okay on my end, sure. I'm downstairs. Listen. The whole place has been going bananas all afternoon." Meaning the headquarters operation for *La Commissione*. "They are in executive session right now. It all has to do with your blind date. They had me doing the hot squat for thirty minutes or more. The guy in Jersey denies everything. Says he never heard of your man and that he hasn't seen or talked to me for over two weeks.

118

Said that right in my face at council. It stinks, Striker. I think it's a setup. I think—"

Bolan said, "Wait, let me get it straight. Do they know you sent word west for an intrusion?"

"Hell no. That never even came up. I told you before, you know, that they were still considering the request. Well, suddenly it seems to be very hot, after laying cold all this time. I don't know what caused the heat. I just know it got suddenly hot. They called in the guy from Jersey. He played it dumb. Said I must have talked to some other guy. And, of course, said nothing about the word I sent him last night. So I didn't, either—naturally. But the whole think stinks like—"

Bolan interrupted to inquire, "Where does all this leave you standing, buddy?"

"I'm okay," Leo growled. "You know me. I always land on my feet. We sent the guy back to Jersey and I told the men the whole thing stinks. I recommended we pretend no word was received, forget the whole thing."

"How did that go down?"

"They said okay, sure, forget it. But they didn't. They're still up there—making phonecalls by the dozen and sending for this guy and that. They're still working it, Striker."

"Those phonecalls—local calls?"

"Not all, no. One to Vegas, a couple to Los Angeles, one to Palm Springs."

"Who's in Palm Springs?"

"Bunny Cerrito."

Cerrito was an elder statesman who'd retired years ago. Bolan said, "Uh huh. Is Bunny keeping a hand in, here and there?"

"Not that I've ever seen," Leo replied. "Hell, he's about eighty. But you know these old guys, Sarge. They're never completely out of it until they're in the grave. I believe Bunny still does diplomatic work, now and then. You know—a call here, a word there."

Bolan said, "Yeah." He was trying to fit the pieces. None of it worked. He told his old friend, "I think you're right. Something's out of joint. Could you disappear, gracefully, for the rest of the day?"

"Sure," was the wry reply. "If you think I really should."

"I think so, yeah," Bolan said. "And don't go back into the water until you've tested it thoroughly. Right?"

"Right," said Turrin. "Well, it's past four o'clock here. How's Tuesday shaping up for you?"

"Terrible," Bolan replied.

"Anything I can? . . ."

"Where do the San Gabriel Mountains grab you?"

"Nowhere."

"China Lake?"

"What's that?"

"How about the Mojave Desert?"

"Big graveyard *a la* DiGeorge. That's all it ever meant to me."

Bolan sighed tiredly and said, "You're no damn help at all, buddy." He was getting a deviation signal from the navigation console. The quarry had abandoned Route 14 at North Oaks to swing south again. "Got to go. Drop off, Striker. Play it cool 'til you hear from me or Hal."

"Right, gotcha. Stay hard, guy."

Bolan deactivated the communicator and turned full attention to the track.

The back of his mind, though, was playing with the realization that the radio signal feeding the mobile phone had grown steadily stronger throughout that conversation. It should have been growing weaker, if anything, since the linkage was via Los Angeles Bell and the track had been moving steadily away from Los Angeles. Maybe it was the increased elevation that was helping the signal. Or maybe Bell's transmission towers were . . .

That last thought froze into the gray matter.

Linkage. Microwave relays—transmission towers . . .

Hell! Something was coming together!

It had to do with space age technology and the communications revolution—with magicians playing wondrous tricks with ultra-sophisticated equipment—linkage!

The California Concept?

Maybe.

And maybe Mack Bolan had stumbled onto the caper of the century.

CHAPTER 15

FACES

It was a new asphalt road, unmarked except
for notations to the effect that it was private
and closed to unauthorized traffic. It ran
straight and level for only about two hundred
yards, then began a twisting climb with numerous S-curves and switchbacks. Bolan had
penetrated for approximately a mile some of
the roughest terrain in recent memory when he
began receiving disturbing wave patterns on
the telemetry. He quickly killed the radar
sweep and all other electronic systems and
pulled off the road at the first hospitable point.

A cautious EVA exploration confirmed all
suspicions.

High fencing and a heavily guarded vehicle
gate stood just around the next curve. Worse, a
strangely configured antenna system was
mounted on the roof of the guard house and

was sweeping the approaches—a weird double-dish affair that looked a bit like radar and a bit like microwave, but not really like either. Two men in *SecuriCom* uniforms manned the gate. Two more sat in a landrover parked nearby. All were packing automatic weapons.

The obvious goal lay about a mile inside that fence—and perhaps a thousand feet above it—visible now and then through the mists only as twinkling red lights atop a nude mountain peak.

Yes, April . . . linkage.

A large medallion on the vehicle gate was in the shape of two worlds in close conjunction and banded by the inscription:

FACES

Bolan returned immediately to his cruiser and fired up the communications channel to Brognola. It was a necessary risk. He did not want that task force blundering in and setting off alarms. "Keep it short and quick," he cautioned the chief fed. "Are you still on me?"

"Yeah," was the quick response. "Sort of. Where's the party?"

"Top of the world," Bolan told him. "It's called FACES. I believe that's an acronym. It's hot-wired so stand down right where you are. Turn off all electronic gear."

"What's the gig?"

"Ask the babysitter. Tell her it looks like the master link. Shut down everything that radiates. Radios, engines, everything! I'm gone, bye bye."

Bolan terminated the contact and quickly began preparations for heavy EVA. He chose blacksuit, heavy boots, binoculars, ordnance chestpack, utility backpack—the AutoMag at the right hip—M-16 over'n-under slung to the rear—Ingram "room-broom" dangling to the waist on a neck cord—various other light utilities and weapons—and, finally, as a promised concession to April Rose, a small radio transceiver.

It was quite a load. The ordnance alone weighed forty pounds. But he knew that he had to make the first trip count. There was no way to know what he may encounter inside that fenced area. Only one thing was certain: a long cross-country trek up a mountainside awaited him. He had to be prepared for most anything once he penetrated and made contact. So he EVA'd as a pack mule, leaving the cruiser in good cover and approaching the fenceline well south of the road.

The weather was perfectly miserable. Light rain, patches of fog, chilly. Not much to cheer about if a guy was looking for animal comforts. Bolan was not looking for that—and he gladly accepted the weather conditions as a comforting ally.

He approached warily and made contact at the south corner of the barrier. It was heavy chainlink topped with six strands of barbed wire. And it was instrumented. It was also electrified—and bore warning signs to that effect. Fairly new, too. The fenceline through the rough terrain had been cleared very recently—apparently with mechanized equipment. Tread marks left by a bulldozer were evident

124

and the earth was raw in a six-foot clearance to either side of the fence.

The rain had caused some minor washouts in the steeper spots along that line. This circumstance appeared to offer the best hope for a quiet penetration. Bolan followed the fence westerly, looking for a severe washout. The search was rewarded some ten minutes later where the fence crossed a steep gulley. Tons of rock and dirt had been dumped along the fence line to build up the eroded area and provide a suitable base for the fencing. The attempt had not been entirely successful. New erosions had carried away several yards of fresh dirt from beneath the fence, leaving only the rock and shallow gaps at several points.

Bolan lay his burdens aside and went to work at the most favorable spot, removing rocks and forming a burrow beneath the fence. Five patient minutes of this labor produced a passage large enough for safe entry.

He tied garrotes to his gear and pulled it through then concealed it in bushes inside the compound, proceeding from that point some eighty pounds lighter with only the AutoMag and the Ingram for company.

There was still a hell of a long way to go—and the return trip could seem even longer with all of *SecuriCom* on his back.

But he needed some visibility.

He needed to know what was here, and who was here—and why any of it was.

Deep in his gut, though, he knew that he had found the California Concept. It was large, and it was heavy, and it was scary as hell—whatever it was.

Apparently Rickert had brought in reinforcements. To protect what? From whom?

Faces.

What the hell could it mean?

Bolan damned sure intended to find out—before he committed himself to open combat on this enemy turf.

A guy at least liked to know what he was dying for.

CHAPTER 16

EPITAPH FOR TWO

The two big tour buses had proceeded on beyond the exit to the private road and were now idling in a small roadside park a quarter-mile or so farther on. Both were outfitted with tinted, one-way glass and bore legends of a sightseeing tour. But the occupants were not tourists and none were particularly interested in the views of this scenic area.

One of the buses was largely given over to electronic equipment. The driver was a federal marshal. Besides Harold Brognola and April Rose, it carried as a standard complement six project technicians with backgrounds similar to April's.

The other bus was comfortably loaded with heavily armed marshals, stoic professionals who knew how to play the waiting game and did not mind it a bit.

Brognola had thoroughly debriefed his female operative regarding the "master-link" cryptogram supplied by Bolan in that most recent radiophone contact. And he was liking none of it. They had, of course, blanked all systems in response to Bolan's request for a total electronic shutdown, but the technicians had continued to monitor and measure the electromagnetic emissions of the area with their sensitive devices. They had not assured the chief that their present position was well clear of the disturbance area, which had so alarmed Bolan.

"I am sure," April told him, "that Striker encountered much stronger levels of the radiation pattern as he approached the source. He probably suspects an intrusion detection system—and, of course, all such systems have strongly defined parameters."

Another technician reported, "I would guess it to be some kind of microwave pulse emission—but it has other elements accompanying it. We would need a very detailed wave analysis before we could even contemplate countering it."

The consensus from all the experts agreed with that. One other ventured the further opinion that the emissions were "movement sensing patterns in the microwave spectrum"—and, again, "with something else included."

"Could they sense the movement of a single man?" Brognola wondered.

"Such a system could sense the movement of a single bird," was the response. "But such close parameters would defeat the intent. In an area like this, with all the wildlife, you would want to set a threshold that is responsive only to objects of significant mass—such as automobiles and aircraft."

"Also, electronic surveillance radiants," April added pointedly.

"That could explain the *something else*," said the project leader. "It could mean an electromagnetic field sensor."

"Which would necessarily be severely localized," added another.

"But entirely effective," said the leader.

Entirely effective, sure. And that was bothering hell out of Hal Brognola.

He put April to work on the FACES cryptogram. She scored on the first query. The UC data bank spit the answer right back at them.

FACES: FACILITY FOR ASTRAL CALCULATION
OF ELECTROMAGNETIC
SYNCHRONISMS.
SAN FERNANDO CA 91302

"What the hell is that?" Brognola muttered disgustedly.

But the answer was already being supplied at the computer terminal.

SPATIAL ENERGY RESEARCH.
STUDIES OF STELLAR ELECTROMAGNETIC
PHENOMENA AND THEIR
RELATIONSHIPS TO TERRESTRIAL EVENTS.

"Give that to me in five cent words," Brognola growled.

"It could mean many things," April explained. "Stellar electromagnetic phenomena are simply the natural byproducts of processes occurring within stars and star systems. Like pulsars and quasars . . . black holes . . . or even sunspots. Any radio engineer can tell you about the terrestrial effects of sunspots. It's their biggest headache. Sunspots can even cause power blackouts over wide areas."

"So it could be a legitimate study."

"Sure. That's a valid research area."

"And it could cover a lot of sins," Brognola decided.

"Electronic sins, sure," April said. "It's a perfect cover."

"Check out this FACES thing all the way," Brognola instructed his star neophyte. "Mesh it in with the stuff you're developing for Striker."

It was getting hairy. Too hairy, maybe. What the *hell* was going down, here? Who could *afford* to bankroll an operation like this? Who would even want to? Where was the profit?

He went to his desk and picked up the telephone. The chief fed was worried. *Damn* worried. Not just for the sake of Mack Bolan, either. Brognola was worried, too, about . . .

He wanted to consult with the National Security Advisor. And maybe the CIA should take a look, also.

"This is Justice Two," he told the voice in the telephone. "I'm going to give you an NSC coder prefix then I want you to clear me to a scramble alert wire. Do you understand the request?"

"I understand the request, sir," was the quick reply. "One moment, please, while I set up the crypto responder."

But Brognola begrudged the guy that one moment. Bolan was out there somewhere all alone, going single-handedly against God knew what.

FACES?

It was more than an acronym. It could become an epitaph.

The telephone conference consumed about ten minutes of Brognola's time and attention—and left him feeling none the better. At least he'd alerted the top security brass to the possible international overtones and the Washington machinery was firing up. There would be damned little application to the immediate problem, however.

Worse, yet, April Rose was nowhere to be seen.

The project leader told Brognola that the girl had "received a program package. She put a pistol on her hip and went outside without a word to anyone."

The "program package" was nowhere in evidence.

And Hal Brognola's star pupil was nowhere in view outside. Doubledamn! She was taking the package to . . .

"Make that," Brognola growled to the world at large, "an epitaph for two."

CHAPTER 17

WAY STATION

The reconnaissance was revealing a much larger problem than Bolan had anticipated. The last few hundred yards of terrain to the top had no ground cover whatever except that being provided by the weather. He still could not see clearly the top of the mountain. The impression received through the mists was one of a sizable facility with several large buildings and numerous antenna installations—but that was only an impression and could not be relied upon as hard intelligence. The whole thing was nestled in the clouds and—as another impression—seemed to be the highest ground around. On a good day, it might command a view covering hundreds of square miles including the entire Los Angeles basin and perhaps some seven or eight million inhabitants.

Apparently the security force was relying upon the electronic safeguards to keep away unwanted visitors. Bolan had not encountered another human presence since the penetration, nor even a hint that this mountaintop was inhabited. But he knew that it was. And he suspected the presence of another security line encircling the peak—some type of electronic surveillance. The problem was to get across the nude zone and into the encampment without detection. If only he knew what *type* of detectors...

He was remembering the other *SecuriCom* "facilities" and their love affair with CCTV. Video systems could be damned effective, of course, along controlled access routes. But they had their limitations as terrain scanners—especially in weather like this. If the love affair extended into the application here...

Naked-eye visibility out here on this rainy, fogbound, windswept mountainside was rapidly variable from one hundred feet to momentary eclipses of zero feet. Occasionally a tunnel would open to allow brief glimpses along defined corridors penetrating for as much as a hundred yards through the wet atmosphere, but these were extremely veiled glimpses—and a guy could see all sorts of shapes and patterns that existed primarily in his own mind. So there could definitely be a chance against TV scanners.

It was his only prayer and he knew it.

The gut was telling him to chance it. About the worse that could happen would be a firefight out here on this slope—and all the conditions were weighted in Bolan's favor if that should occur. It would be his kind of fight. Even so, it would be a Pyrrhic victory, indeed, to win a minor skirmish and thereby lose the opportunity for the full rout he had in mind.

Also, the possibility remained that the whole thing was a large suck play, designed solely to lure him into an inescapable position. Rickert could be a wily and dangerous adversary. If he'd had Bolan "wired" all the way . . .

He had to let that idea go. It simply did not seem to fit the pattern of events that had brought him here—and further worries along that line could be self-defeating. Bolan had to play the hand he held.

So, the gut said go, even while the warrior mind was descending into a sort of melancholy. Maybe it was the weather—or the situation—or a combination of both. Probably, though, it was a matter of sheer fatigue coupled with the certain knowledge that the chances were now considerably less than fifty-fifty that he would live to see the beginning of another day. Or maybe it was simply the accumulation of "impossible" missions, which had been weighting his days for such a very long time.

Whatever, Mack Bolan suddenly felt very alone and very tired and very vulnerable. If Hal Brognola were to chance along at that very moment and suggest that they chuck it all and just truck on over to Washington, this instant—well, he just might do that.

But Brognola was too many heartbeats away . . . and Washington was too many lifetimes ahead . . . and Mack Bolan was no more alone now than he'd always been since that fated day in Pittsfield when he picked up a Marlin .444 and declared his war against the Mob.

The Mob is still here, guy.

Yeah. Make book on that. Right up there on that mountaintop, a scant two hundred yards through driving rain and scudding clouds.

They're still trying to eat everything you hold decent and lovely, soldier.

They were doing it, too. A bite at a time.

Who's going to stop them, guy?

Bolan sighed and got to his feet and went back down the mountain. It took him ten minutes to reach his "stash" and another twenty to return to the edge of the nude zone with his equipment. There, he took it all apart and methodically laid it out in the rain and began reassembling the combat pack.

He ate a chunk of cheese and a chocolate bar and downed half a canteen of water as he reworked the rig. Twenty pounds dropped from the load would mean about two strides quicker in a twenty-yard dash. It was life and death being weighed in that rearrangement.

Satisfied that he'd reached an optimum balance, he strapped on the rig and took a long look up that ghostly, cloud-draped hillside. The view reminded him of a painting he'd seen once, an artist's idea of a way-station between life and afterlife.

Bolan had no firm commitment to any concept of an afterlife. Heaven and hell could be one and the same place—or perhaps only differing states of consciousness. And maybe the same could be said for life and death.

But hell . . .

135

It was not the mission that was bothering him. It was not the weather . . . or the fatigue . . . or any fear of Charlie Rickert.

It was April Rose.

He wanted to go on living . . . for her . . . with her.

Well, maybe he would. And, then again, maybe he would not.

The next few minutes would tell the tale.

CHAPTER 18

OF HEAVY COUNTENANCE

April had run all the way to the last known fix on Bolan's vehicle, visions of his torn and lifeless body driving her on and enveloping her in a living nightmare, not stopping once until she rounded the bend in the road and saw the shimmering outlines of the guard house looming in the mists. She instinctively tumbled to the ground, then, and rolled into the bushes beside the road—and it was here that reality and reason began reestablishing command of her thought processes while she lay there panting and fighting her body for control. Her legs were suddenly so much trembling rubber and she could hear her own heart pounding the pulses as she got to hands and knees and crawled back along the roadway toward better concealment. Her stomach hurt and her sides felt like knives were piercing them. Any moment, she knew, she may throw up—and she was sure that the men at the FACES gate could hear her thundering heart.

It thunders for thee, Striker.

Oh God! Please let him be okay!

Steady! Steady, girl! Think like him!

She thought like him—and wore his mind to the place where the Warwagon left the road and buried itself in the forest. And she had no trouble locating the hidden interlocks to defeat the cruiser's security systems. But she felt like death itself as she stepped into that emptiness and tried to read the vibrations left there by the man she loved.

There were no vibrations.

And perhaps there was no man, by now.

She sank onto the chair in the war room and lay the alarming package of intelligence on the plot table, gazing around expectantly as though he were about to emerge from some trick panel and lay one of those soft smiles on her. He would give her holy hell for being here—and she would remind him that he'd told her she could return upon completing her assignment. He'd forgive her and she'd forgive him—and they'd call off the damned war and go to bed for crazy, crying love—and he'd . . .

Where was he, damnit?

Steady. Okay. He's on recon. He's scouting the enemy camp. Like a cat. He walks like a cat. He wouldn't go barging in there on a hard EVA without . . .

Yes he would. He didn't have *the package*!

She checked the con for a note or a message and found nothing—then went aft to the "quarters" looking for some nameless comfort.

He was really a most fastidious man. A place for everything and everything in its place. Precise, methodical . . . everything so proper, so together.

She smiled faintly at the precision emptiness. The military mind. Was there a bit of a sneer in that realization? Could she still have *that* hangup? What was wrong with the military mind? Why make fun of it? Physical excellence—discipline, duty, honor. What made them stale concepts? Had the world gone so wacky as to . . . ?

The neat row of books above the bunk caught her eye. She had not noticed them before. Some surprising titles, there. She pulled down a worn and well thumbed volume of *Don Quixote*—the novel by Miguel de Cervantes. Vibrations there, yes. She could almost feel the hand that had turned those pages. It was not exactly light reading, but the sort of thing one might find on required reading lists at school. April had dodged this one. Now the darned thing was vibrating in her hand.

A faded inscription in a feminine hand was on the inside front cover:

Mack honey—sorry it took so long. Had to search every book store in town. Also I read a couple of chapters and got hooked —had to finish it. Too bad you don't have this guy in 'Nam with you.

Love forever—Cindy

So! And who was "love forever—Cindy"?

Probably the girl he left at home. Where was she now?

That's it. Settle the mind on something it can grasp, April. Stop acting like a jerk!

A bookmark was placed at a discourse by the Knight of the Woeful Countenance and several long paragraphs were marked by marginal brackets. She read the discourse all the way through, then returned to read a particular passage twice again. Quixote was speaking:

Away with those that shall affirm learning to surpass arms; for I will say unto them, be they what they list, that they know not what they say; for the reason which such men do most urge, and to which they do most rely, is, that the travails of the spirit do far exceed those of the body; and that the use of arms are only exercised by the body, as if it were an office fit for porters, for which nothing were requisite but bodily forces; or as if in that which we that profess it do call arms, were not included the acts of fortitude which require deep understanding to execute them; or as if the warrior's mind did not labour as well as his body, who had a great army to lead and command, or the defense of a besieged city. If not, see if he can arrive by his corporal strength to know or sound the intent of his enemy, the designs, stratagems, and difficulties, how to prevent imminent dangers, all these being operations of the understanding wherein the body hath no meddling at all.

Vibrations, sure. The book had all but leapt
into her hand. She looked up, half expecting
Bolan to be standing there and smiling at her
perplexity. The passage so fit her own thoughts,
moments before she even saw that darned book.

And there was more, all having to do with a
comparison between students and warriors—
which also touched a nerve from April's not-
distant past.

... peace is the true end of war, for arms
and war are one and the selfsame things.
This truth being therefore presupposed,
that the end of war is peace, and that
herein it doth excel the end of learning, let
us descend to the corporal labours of the
scholar, and to those of him which pro-
fesseth arms, and consider which of them
are more toilsome.

... the pains of the student are com-
monly these: principally poverty (not that
I would maintain that all students are
poor, but that I may put the case in
greatest extremity it can have), and by
saying that he may be poor, methinks
there may be no greater aggravation of
his misery, for he that is poor is destitute
of every good thing; and this poverty is
suffered by him sundry ways, sometimes
by hunger, other times by cold or nakedness, and many times by all of them together; yet it is never so extreme but that
he doth eat, although it be somewhat later
than the custom, or of the scraps and re-
version of the rich man, and the greatest
misery of the student is that which they

term to live by sops and pottage: and though they want fire of their own, yet may they have recourse to their neighbour's chimney, which if it do not warm, yet will it weaken the cold: and finally, they sleep at night under a roof.

... By this way, which I have deciphered so rough and difficult ... they attain the degree which they have desired so much, which many having compassed, as we have seen, which having passed through these difficulties, they command and govern all the world from a chair, turning their hunger into satiety, their nakedness into pomp, and their sleeping on a mat into a sweet repose among hollands and damask—a reward justly merited by their virtue. But their labours, confronted and compared to those of the militant soldier, remain very far behind, as I will presently declare.

The soldier suffers as the student; however:

Let after all this the day and hour arrive wherein he is to receive the degree of his profession—let, I say, a day of battle arrive, for there they will set on his head the cap of his dignity, made of lint to cure the wound of some bullet that hath passed through and through his temples, or hath maimed an arm or a leg. And when this doth not befall, but that Heaven doth piously keep and preserve him whole and sound, he shall perhaps abide still in the same poverty wherein he was at the first, and that it be requisite that one and another battle do succeed, and he come off ever a victor, to the end that he may prosper and be at the last advanced. But such miracles are but few times wrought; and say, good sirs, if you have noted it, how few are those which the wars reward, in respect of the others that it hath destroyed?

. . . That one may become eminent in learning, it costs him time, watchings, hunger, nakedness, headaches, rawness of stomach, and other such inconveniences as I have partly mentioned already; but that one may arrive by true terms to be a good soldier, it costs him all that it costs the student, in so exceeding a degree as admits no comparison, for he is at every step in jeopardy to lose his life. And what fear of necessity or poverty may befall or molest a student so fiercely as it doth a soldier, who, seeing himself at the siege of some impregnable place, and standing sentinel in some ravelin or half-moon, feels the enemies undermining near to the place where he is, and yet dares not to depart or abandon his stand, upon any occasion whatsoever, or shun the danger which so nearly threatens him? But that which he only may do, is to advise his captain of that which passeth, to the end he may remedy it by some countermine, whilst he must stand still, fearing and expecting when he shall suddenly fly up to the clouds without wings, and after descend to the depths against his will. And if this appear to be but a small danger, let us weigh whether the grappling of two galleys, the one with the other in the midst of the spacious main, may be compared, or do surpass it, the which nailed and grappled fast the one to the other, the soldier hath no more room in them than two foot broad of a plank in the battlings, and notwithstanding, although he clearly see laid before him so many ministers of death, for all the pieces of artillery that from his body the length of a lance, and seeing that if he slipped ever so little aside, he should fall into the deeps, doth yet nevertheless, with undaunted heart, borne away on the wings of honor, which spurreth him onward, oppose himself as a mark to all their shot, and strives to pass by that so narrow a way into the enemy's vessel. And what is most to be admired is to behold how scarce is one fallen into that place, from whence he shall never after arise until the world's end, when another takes possession of the same place; and if he do likewise tumble into the sea, which gapes like an enemy for him also, another and another will succeed unto him, without giving any respite to the times of their death, valour, and boldness, which is the greatest that may be found among all the trances of warfare . . .

April shivered and put the book back on the shelf. The Knight of the Woeful Countenance, yes. Her man. Why fault him for that heavy countenance? He wore it honestly.

She drifted into the armory, still searching for some nameless comfort. Everything in its place...

But everything here was not in its place. A great lot of it was missing. He was not merely scouting, then. He'd gone out rigged for heavy combat. Her heart lurched. How could he *hope* to...?

The rocket pod had been rearmed—four wicked little firebirds nested there in a fresh bracket. A grenade launcher was missing... a submachine gun ... the EVA ordnance pack—heavy combat, yes.

She smiled faintly, noting the absence also of one of a pair of miniature transceivers. She went quickly to the con and switched on the UHF monitors then turned her thoughts back to the timeworn *Don Quixote* purely as an occupation for her idling mind.

Yes, the world had gone so wacky. That novel was a product of the Middle Ages—somewhere around the 16th century. It had been around a long time. And yet the world had gone wacky. It had been very fashionable for April's college generation to speak of one world, one people—peace and love and the brotherhood of man—while at the same time very *de rigueur* to accept the "fact" that all cops are pigs and all voluntary soldiers are blockheads. What had become of "undaunted hearts, borne away on the wings of honor."

Someone had ripped off April's generation. Or maybe they'd ripped off themselves. Such confusion, such hypocrisy. "Marching to a different drummer"—all of them, each of them— yet all, it seemed, marched to the same drummer and none thought to inquire where *he* found *his* cadence.

Harold Brognola was not a pig.

Mack Bolan was anything but a blockhead.

Cervantes declared that peace was the end of war—the reason for it. Mack had told her that the meek shall never inherit a savage earth. Who was Mack Bolan's drummer?

She thought she knew, now. And she knew, now, that she would never find that "nameless comfort" for which she had been searching. There was none, for those who love warriors. And it was *not* all for nothing. It counted, it mattered. It was not a "waste"—even if she never saw his heavy countenance again.

Her own countenance was growing heavier by the moment. It weighted the eyes and pulled at the little muscles of the lips.

Each woman since time immemorial had sat stolidly and awaited news of her warrior.

Not April, damnit. Not April.

She had waited long enough.

CHAPTER 19

THEM

His hunch had been right. A battery of television cameras were emplaced in a circle around the bald knob of the mountain, set into low-profile concrete housings at ground level—most inconspicuous. Apparently they were meshed into a sequenced scan with a slight overlap to provide constant 360-degree surveillance of the approaches. Normal range would provide coverage of the entire nude zone; today, the cameras were having the same visibility problems as any other eyes.

Bolan could not be certain that he had not been spotted already. There could be a ring of steel awaiting his arrival at the top of the hill. But he had to play the hand he held. The best approach would be through the center of a particular scan—avoiding overlaps. That way, he could play to a single eye and double the chances for a successful penetration.

If he could not clearly see the eye, then it should also hold that the eye could not clearly see Bolan. He had to time the charge to coincide with a blind moment—and more, he had to pick a moment that would hopefully extend to the back side of the camera pit.

The moment came—borne by the puffy, ragged edge of a cloud scudding along the slope—and Bolan ran with it, lunging to his feet in a full upright, all-out sprint.

Twenty yards, *hell*! Make it thirty, with also about a thirty degree upward slope—and momentary vertigo, with the feet pounding the uneven and muddy terrain in an absolutely blind charge.

He overran the pit and tumbled past it, sprawling flat in an exhausted heap. But he'd made it. The trailing edge of the friendly cloud was just then clearing the camera eye. Beyond and just above lay pay dirt, less than fifty yards away . . . and no ring of steel awaiting. He could see the installation clearly now, moment to moment as the weather would allow.

It looked like a moon base.

Domed buildings were scattered all about with huge antennae of diverse configurations protruding from the domes—also two large towers lifting hundreds of feet higher with twinkling warning lights for aircraft and bearing other antennae—a long, low building that looked like a warehouse—many large house trailers parked all in a row at the far side.

Those latter would be personnel quarters, no doubt—for the guard force, and perhaps even for the technical crews. The two vans that Bolan had followed here were parked in that area. Other vehicles were scattered about. But there was no sign of human activity. Apparently his presence had gone unnoted and none felt a need to venture into the inhospitable weather. Bolan could hardly blame them. They had plenty of reason for confidence in their robot defenses—and it was a chilling, penetrating downpour. Bolan himself was soaked to the bones.

He pulled himself to his feet and walked on to the top of the slope—feeling almost nonchalant, now, inside the security circle. None came forth to challenge him as he ambled past the domed buildings and went on to the tower area. There, he removed the chest pack and began molding explosive strips and applying them to critical stress points at the bases of the towers. Seven minutes later he was walking casually among the house trailers, peering into windows and taking their numbers, dropping here and there beneath the wheeled structures small canisters of chemical smoke and timed explosive devices.

Toward the end of that stroll, he rounded the end of a trailer and came up eyeball to eyeball with a guy in a rainslicker carrying a six-pack of beer. The guy was wearing civvies under that slicker and the face was definitely *Mafia*, though Bolan's mental file registered no definite make. Those startled eyes had a definite make on Bolan, though—instantaneously —and the beer went flying as panicked hands sought a fast way inside the slicker.

There was no way that fast. A lightning

chop to the throat and a piston-quick knee to the gut, delivered simultaneously, brought a swift end to panic and dropped the guy without a sound or hardly a pause in Bolan's forward motion. He pushed the falling body on beneath the trailer and kept moving.

Five minutes and counting.

The first domed building to receive his scrutiny contained no personnel. It was only about twenty-five feet in diameter with no interior partitions—crammed with electronics, all busily humming and clicking with robot chores under the orchestration of a central computer. The function was beyond Bolan's limited understanding; even an engineer may have found it too much for quick comprehension. He left an incendiary with a four-minute fuse and went back outside. All of the domes but one were that same size; all were remote-robot installations, probably feeding a central data control in the remaining dome, a huge structure of, perhaps, a hundred-foot diameter. Bolan was headed toward the large one when alarms began shrieking all over the place. He immediately went down on one knee and brought the combo around in the firing ready, squinting through the swirling mists in an effort to determine from which quarter the attack would come.

It came from the big central dome—but not toward Bolan. A platoon of uniformed guards charged out of there and ran off toward the far perimeter—the side from which Bolan had made his penetration.

The horns were making a hell of a racket, squawking lustily from various points around the compound. Trailer doors were beginning to open and carbon-arc searchlights mounted high on the towers sprang into mist-muted brilliance.

Bolan was wondering what the hell was going down, but he did not have long to wonder. The little transceiver, which he carried in a shoulder pocket, beeped at him. The first thought to touch his mind was that the feds had begun a premature movement. But that thought quickly fled as he inserted the ear plug and growled a quiet "Go!" toward his shoulder.

It was April.

"Striker, thank God! Where are you?"

His heart was frozen. "Me, hell!" he hissed at the offending shoulder. "Where are *you*!"

"I'm under the south tower!" she replied in a breathless rush. "Guess I tripped an alarm!"

He guessed she hadn't been as patient with the cameras as she should have been—or maybe she just hadn't been as lucky.

He calmly instructed the shoulder: "Hit the dirt. A war party is searching for you. If they spot you, throw up the hands and surrender immediately. Roger that."

"I roger that," was the faint response.

Then it hit him. He glanced at his chronometer and delayed that instruction. "Forget it! That tower falls in two minutes! Get clear. Walk due west. Roger it!"

"Roger, I am walking due west."

Bolan raised the combo and let fly a hot one toward the east perimeter to divert the search, then quickly repeated fifteen degrees left. The tandem explosions briefly lit the heavy atmosphere over there and brought raised voices in immediate reaction.

"East rim! Cover it!"

"Spread out, spread out!"

He then sent a couple into the trailers to discourage any hasty movements from that quarter—then went looking for his lady. He found her with the help of leaping flames from a burning trailer and calmly took her hand and led her to safer ground. She was terribly embarrassed and more than a little frightened—but her only words were in anticipation of a harsh rebuke for blundering in where only seasoned professionals belong.

"I'm an idiot," she said softly.

But there was no rebuke in him.

"We all are, one time or another," he told her.

It was a moment separated from time and space. The Klaxon horns were still squawking. Flustered footfalls were pounding this way and that across the cloudbound mountaintop while excited voices screamed out instructions and warnings from every quarter.

But this moment belonged to Mack Bolan and his lady. He understood her anguish—and he had never felt closer to another human being.

"I'm sorry," she whispered.

"Me, too," he said. "We should have gone to Rio."

She quietly giggled and replied, "I'll settle for Disneyland."

"I'd settle for a dry bunk," he said, chuckling.

A moment carved free from time and space,

yeah. But only a moment. He kissed her softly on the lips, then patted her bottom as he told her, "You picked a hell of a time to come calling, lady. I'm busy as hell."

"So I see," she murmured. "Is this what they call 'the Bolan effect'?"

The moment was gone.

He asked, "Why, April?"

"Had to. I got that package you ordered. Thought you'd like to know what's in it. This is the mother lode, partner. For you, it's a powder keg. I-I thought . . . I mean, I was afraid you didn't know what you were walking into."

He dropped to one knee and pulled her down beside him. *One minute and counting.* "I didn't," he admitted.

"Your Mister Big is William McCullough. He owns all this—or controls it, anyway."

Bolan sighed. "It figures. The ants found a new picnic. Why not take it over?"

"Do you know what this place is?" she asked him.

"Vaguely," he replied. "Looks like a moon base, doesn't it?"

"That's what it's supposed to look like. FACES is in the book as a center for cosmic studies. I'm betting their studies are strictly terrestrial. Did you read *1984*?"

The novel by George Orwell. Yes, he'd read it. "The Big Brother routine, eh?"

"Yes, but with a private enterprise slant. I have a two page list of supposedly legitimate corporations who are 'contributors' to this foundation. They're buying eyes and ears, Mack. And the price tag is enormous so you know the profit potential must be, too."

It was all together, now. Almost.

Twenty seconds and counting.

"How do you read these antennae, April?"

"It's an intercept system. With the right computers, they can tap the secrets of the world. Anything that moves by radio or long distance telephone. Even ComSat."

"Not for long," he murmured.

Five, four . . .

"Mack, McCullough is—"

. . . ignition!

"Moon Base" lifted off.

Both tall towers flung their bases aside and came crashing down. A walking line of explosions in the trailer area sent brilliant streamers of fire trumpeting skyward to overwhelm the heavy atmosphere, diverting even the clouds and sucking them briefly off the mountaintop in a hot vertical vacuum.

The power station arced and sputtered, then lent itself wholeheartedly to the festivities, sending horizontal lightning bolts crackling across that tortured landscape before finally escalating into full self-destruct and flinging itself to the four winds.

House trailers leapt and staggered, great rents opening along thin metal walls and disgorging contents and flames and howling men in a cacophony of doom.

It was pandemonium time at Mafia Heights.

April's eyes were wide pools of awe. Bolan pushed her flat to the ground—commanded, "Stay!"—and went off to join the party.

Most of the activity seemed to be centered around the trailer area. People were yelling and scampering around that disaster zone in total confusion. But that was not the party Bolan had in mind.

Another wild scene was amid the wreckage of the south tower. Apparently the "war party," which had gone baying after April Rose had recovered their offensive just in time to greet the falling tower. But Bolan's interest was not there, either.

People were spilling in panic from the large central dome—a mixed group of uniformed guards, white-coated technicians—and, leading the pack, a tight-knit cluster of excited men in business suits, five of them. Charlie Rickert was one. The others rang no bells in Bolan's memory banks—but this was the party he was seeking, for sure.

A limousine with all four headlights blazing lurched across the tarmac and screeched to a halt across the path of the fleeing group. The civilian party melted into the vehicle and it surged forward even before all the doors were closed. Bolan had a fleeting image of Rickert standing behind, with hands on hips and watching the departure with a twisted smile; but this was not Rickert's moment.

The tall figure in rain-soaked executioner black stepped onto the roadway in the path of the fleeing vehicle, the combo weapon at the hip, headlamps framing him there in the swirling mists for that split-second of doom. Then the muzzle of the M-16 came aglow with stabbing darts of lightning, which reached out and seized that hurtling mass; and shredded it; and shattered it; and sent it reeling back across the tarmac under a dead-man's throttle in a closing circle to the starting point. It plowed head-on into the central dome and punched through the steel wall, burying itself to the windshield. And then the gas tank joined the celebration, whoofing into a spectacular finish for that aborted flight.

When Bolan got there, Charlie Rickert was lying on the sidelines in a stupor, a Chief's Special .38 held loosely in an outflung hand. There was no sign of the whitecoats and only two *SecuriComs* remained in close focus. Both of those hurriedly threw up the hands and gladly accepted Bolan's scowling invitation to lose themselves.

He kicked the .38 out of Rickert's hand and touched the hot muzzle of the '16 to the guy's pulsing throat. Those eyes rolled for a moment, then focused on the heavy countenance above the weapon. Confusion showed there, for a moment, in that searching gaze—then resignation as recognition dawned and the split identities of D'Anglia-Crusher-Bolan merged into one.

"Suckered me again, didn't you," Rickert declared weakly.

"You suckered yourself, guy," Bolan told him. The cold gaze shifted briefly to the burning vehicle. "Them, too. You sold them security, Rickert. You delivered nothing but a flaming coffin."

"Fuck 'em," Rickert growled.

Not exactly King's English—but it was the answer that Bolan sought. He'd found them—and buried them in the same moment.

"You did," he assured the security boss.

So much for "them."

All that remained, now, was to find "him."

156

CHAPTER 20

ACES A PAIR

The entire mountaintop was in flames when the marshals arrived on the scene—and the total image was straight out of *War and Peace*. Dazed and damaged men wandered aimlessly in the rain or sat in the mud with heads bowed in absolute defeat. Others, not so fortunate, lay about the tumbled landscape in lifeless lumps. Vehicles had been demolished, buildings gutted and everywhere was ruin.

Hell had visited the heights that day, and all who'd been there knew it.

The marshals disembarked from their vehicles and stood in silent awe for a moment before moving on in their grim duties. Brognola and a big, square-jawed man stepped into the rain and quietly contemplated the devastation.

"Jesus Christ," the head fed commented in a choked voice.

157

"Not so pretty, is it?" said the other.

"Prettier now than before," replied the fed.

"Say it again, Sam. It gave me chills just *thinking* of this joint. How could we ever have touched it?"

"Think of some others, then," Brognola suggested. "Nothing says this is the only one." His gaze flicked to a gutted limousine, which was partially buried in a burning building. "If there's anything left to identify, I'm sure you'll find brothers of the blood in that car. That means cancer cells, pal, and they already could have spread everywhere. What a nightmare. We've got to—"

"Not in my territory, I hope."

"Naw, I'd think not."

"That's not what's clawing your guts, Hal."

"No—you're right—I guess I—"

Two marshals, who were coming down out of the bus behind Brognola, were now gazing past him and grinning with unabashed admiration at a tall figure in dripping black who was walking in. The guy was braced from head to foot with every gadget and artifice of warfare old and new. One had to wonder how he could even move under all that load. He was pushing a limping, battered man ahead of him and a soggy young lady was hurrying along at his side.

Double jubilation, sure. And let the gut claw for something else. The epitaphs were for the other side.

"That's Charlie Rickert," growled Brognola's companion.

The chief fed snapped eyes at the marshals,

who immediately moved forward to take charge of the prisoner.

"Handle with care," said the tall man as he turned Rickert over. "We made a deal."

The marshals hustled the silent prisoner away while square-jaw snapped, "What kind of deal?"

The tall man was giving the guy a searching look, as though trying to place the face.

Brognola harrumphed and quickly leapt into that breach. "Striker, this is Tim Braddock."

Recognition showed, then. "*Captain* Braddock," Bolan said.

"Chief, now," Brognola corrected him.

"*Deputy* chief," said Braddock. A faint smile was setting into the chiseled features as he stretched forth a hand to the man in black. "This is, uh, quite a way outside my jurisdiction, though. I have no official status here. As a private citizen, I'd like to shake your hand, Mr. Striker."

The protocol was perfect.

Bolan took the hand and gripped it, solemnly replying, "My pleasure." He then presented the young lady. "Mr. Braddock—my partner, Miss Beautiful."

"Miss Mischief is what he really means," the girl said, eyes a'sparkle despite her soggy condition.

"Can't we get out of the rain?" Brognola suggested.

Bolan's sharp gaze flicked to the bus. "Who's inside?"

"Just my driver."

"Same guy?"

"Same guy, sure."

Bolan decided, "You can take us down the hill and drop us."

All four moved inside. Brognola gave the driver instructions and escorted his guests to the lounge area.

"Drink?" he inquired of all at once.

"Coffee, if it's handy," Bolan said.

"Me, too," said April Rose, the teeth beginning to chatter just a bit.

Brognola draped a blanket over the sodden figure and grinned inside. She was sticking damned close to Bolan. He'd been wondering about those two. Now it was patently obvious. A bit sad, though, too—considering their chances.

The bus got slowly underway as the head fed handed out the coffee.

Braddock gave the blitzer time for a tentative sip of the hot liquid, then repeated his earlier question. "What kind of deal, Striker?"

Bolan smiled faintly as he replied, "I gave him life."

"What'd he give you?"

"Information."

Brognola injected himself at that point. "I guess he'll tell us about it, Tim."

"Not yet," said the big cold man. "You wouldn't want it until I've checked it out."

Sure. Brognola knew how this guy checked things out. The evidence was all about them. He'd been "checking out" FACES. Look at it now. But the head fed had no complaints.

Braddock was saying, "If my presence is cramping your style—"

"Not at all," Bolan assured him. "Maybe you

160

can tell me something. Do you know of any official surveillance on Bunny Cerrito?"

The big cop winced and grunted, "Who?" He recovered before a response could come and amended it with: "Never mind, I heard you. Yes, our OrgCrime Unit gets Palm Springs advisories on his movements."

Brognola growled, "What's with Cerrito? I've had no rumbles on him since, uh . . ."

"Since DiGeorge," Bolan finished it. "Right. But—"

"He enjoys elder statesman status," said Braddock. "That's all we've noticed since— come to think of it, though, he has been coming into our town quite often, of late."

"Is he connected to McCullough?" Bolan inquired.

Braddock's face fell.

Brognola said, "Well there's a—it's what brought Tim out . . ."

Braddock picked it up with a sigh. McCullough is dead."

Bolan said, "Do tell."

"And his wife and daughter. We found them hacked to pieces in the basement of their home—and the pieces floating in an acid bath."

Some indefinable emotion tugged at the stoic Bolan features but it quickly vanished. "When was this?" he asked quietly.

The bus was approaching the gate area.

Brognola went forward to instruct the driver while Braddock handled the inquest.

"We discovered them about noon," the cop explained. "They'd been in the acid for several hours. Luckily, it was a fairly mild solution.

161

There was still enough left to distinguish the bits and pieces."

April shuddered.

Bolan asked, "Enough left to positively identify?"

"The ID is tentative, but it will probably stand," the cop replied. "It's already fairly solid on the daughter. Had a nasty accident a couple of years ago, lot of broken bones. Forensics found some convincing matches with X-rays from her medical files."

"The others?"

"Evidence enough," Braddock sighed, "that the coroner is fairly convinced."

Bolan said, "Damn!"

He was looking at his lady as though seeing another in her place.

Brognola returned to the group in time to catch the eye signals between the two. He said to April, "I suppose you'll want to be toddling along with the man."

"Better believe it," she murmured.

Bolan said, "Well, maybe—"

"Damnit, no!" she said, quietly defiant.

"What's going on?" Brognola demanded.

Bolan told him what was going on. "It isn't done, Hal. I need to check something out. Do us all a favor, though—stay off my shadow. I'll keep you informed."

"Do that," the fed said gruffly. "There's enough here to keep me busy the rest of the day, anyway." He looked at his watch. "Which isn't saying a hell of a lot, anyway."

The time was five o'clock.

Plenty of time left, though, for that damn guy to burn down a few more mountaintops.

Bolan and the lady were on their feet. Braddock was looking pained, apologetic and a bit flustered all at once. He said to the blitzer, "I never thanked you properly."

The big guy grinned at him and said, "Sure you did. I like your force, Chief. It's a hot team."

He always had a way of passing it back. And now he turned to Brognola and almost casually inquired, "Did you get a wire on Jimmy the Grease?"

Casual, hell. "Yeah," the fed grunted. "Left his hotel at three o'clock in a rented car. He's wired."

"Where'd he go?"

"North on Pacific Coast Highway. Why?"

"Playing on the spine, Hal," the damn guy explained while explaining nothing at all. "Get me a fix on him and pass it to me, earliest possible. I'll be rolling on his track."

April Rose smiled sweetly, and triumphantly, over her shoulder at Brognola as she and her man made their exit, hand in hand.

They disappeared almost instantly into the surrounding forest.

"Quite a pair," said Braddock, sighing. "It's almost cute, isn't it?"

Cute, hell.

It was damned well murderous.

CHAPTER 21

HIM

It was over, really. The whole ambitious empire had been buried atop that mountain overlooking the sprawling metropolis of Los Angeles. What remained of the empire, in incidental fragments, would be summarily tracked down and expunged by the collective police efforts of those two good men he'd left back there at the gravesite. And the intelligence package so adroitly gathered by the computer tactics of Miss April the Beautiful would go a long way toward seeing to it that all involved in the intended rape of the public's privacy would find their just receipts at the hands of the law.

It had been one grand scheme, all right—and it could have worked beautifully except that someone had become just a bit too cute while trying to insure the outcome.

One William the Cute McCullough, by name.

The guy must have thought the world was stocked with dummies—especially those who stood to do him in. He did not trust the mob who had made him and enriched him far beyond any concept of a just reward—nor any of those individual "brothers" who both served and governed him—and he certainly did not trust the law, whose finer nuances he had habitually disregarded and trod upon and crapped upon throughout a long and blemished business career.

He did not trust even his wife of five years, the former Eva Lynn Whitley—ex-beauty-queen and widow of a pioneer electronics developer and manufacturer—nor Eva Lynn's daughter, Darlene, the comely but wild heiress to the Whitley patents, whom he had legally adopted shortly after the marriage.

He had not trusted even his pals in Sacramento and Washington who'd worked so diligently to bring the pieces home, even to the point of obtaining government grants and blessings for the bogus "spatial energy" studies.

No. He'd trusted none of them. And he thought the world was full of dummies just like himself.

So he got too cute.

It was very likely that McCullough himself had engineered the "problem" between his adopted daughter and Tanto Fortinelli, the hitman—or, perhaps, it was just one of those circumstances that inspire fated moments. Whatever, he'd used that entanglement as a too-cute invitation for an East Coast hitman to cruise over and hit a West Coast hitman. But the men back east were not such dummies. They sat on the request and chewed it, then spit it back out—suspicious, perhaps, that someone was trying to create a problem where no problem should exist. And they were right. McCullough would have loved to get them *all* out of his hair . . . forever. The "boys" had never been too understanding about letting go of a good thing—and Bill McCullough had been an extremely good thing for a very long time—in a completely symbiotic relationship with the whole crime structure.

No. They would not let go gracefully.

So McCullough was not entirely a *dummy*. He was greedy, as well—and a very devious, crafty dude. He would engineer a shooting war—then finger them all one by one, side against side, until finally he had the whole magnificent Big Brother operation all to himself. He intended to share it with no one.

That, probably, was the California Concept in a nutshell.

And certainly there were riches a'plenty to be harvested via the clandestine supersnoop operation. Handled properly—and not too greedily—a mere handful of strategically oriented corporations could manipulate at will the most sensitive business operations that held the world industrial community together: stock markets, commodities, currency exchanges, vital materials, the whole wide range of buying and selling and trading the dwindling resources of a troubled world. And that meant looting, raping, pillaging and sacking on a world scale never before experienced or even attempted.

And, hell, it wouldn't have stopped there.

They would have soon been into the closets and under the beds of world leaders everywhere—in every sensitive area of human interchange and perhaps in even the most common areas of day-to-day humanity: the teachers, the bakers, the candlestick makers and all the mundane activities that provide the glue for men to live together responsibly.

But Bill McCullough got too cute, too greedy, and perhaps a bit too careless.

He sent to the east for a hitman. Any hitman.

And he got Mack Bolan.

April said, "I don't understand. Who was trying to take him over? Who sent the gun crew to his house?"

"He sent them," Bolan said.

"*Who* sent them?"

"Him. McCullough. It was a set-up. They'd probably been on twenty-four-hour alert for weeks, just waiting the call. And not far away. He sent for them while I was in the house. And sent his beauty pageant wife down to entertain me and keep me there. Poor lady. She never had a prayer."

"But I still don't . . ."

"I was supposed to die there, April."

"Oh! I see! No I don't see. Why?"

"The lady was to die. The kid was to die. All the house people were to die. And an East Coast hitman would be left behind as proof positive of treachery and villainy from the east."

167

"Oh!"

"Enter, then, Jimmy the Grease. Via the good offices of someone greatly respected—someone like old Bunny Cerrito, who must be getting senile—a retaliatory force would be gathered and sent east to return the favor."

April sniffed and said, "That sounds like burning the house to warm the bed."

Bolan chuckled grimly and told her, "Oh, it's a lot cuter than that, even. McCullough was to die, too, you see."

"Mack, you're talking in riddles," she complained. "It's giving me a headache."

He kissed that dear head to ease the ache and said, "Have faith, dear friend, and all shall be revealed to you."

"*Don Quixote*," she muttered.

He gave her a sharp look and replied, "No, I think it's more like rough *New Testament*."

"Close enough," she said lightly, backing gracefully out of that one.

But he was not so easily put off. "You've been into my library," he noted.

"Is it sacred territory?"

"No."

"Then I've been into it." She took his hand and gave it a warm squeeze. "And I love it."

"I love you," he muttered.

"What did you say?"

"I have to say it twice, eh?"

"Endlessly," she whispered.

"Okay. April, Miss Mischief, I love you endlessly. But you pull another damn stunt like you pulled today and an end may come a lot sooner than either of us desire. Do I make myself perfectly clear?"

"Yes, sir," she said meekly.

"I could have killed you, myself. Why do you think I demand firm separation from Hal and his people? There's no place to hold hands in the hellgrounds, April."

"I know," she said contritely. "I'm sorry. It shall not happen again. I promise. I understand. Have you ever boarded a galley?"

He showed her a silly grin and said, "What?"

"You know—with those ministers of death scarce a lance's length away, and the terrible sea yawning two broad feet to either side of that narrow way?"

He chuckled and said, "Damnit, April."

"Well I have to say something to alter that heavy old countenance. I mean, after all, there's more to life than *arms*."

True. Very true. And this very able and admirable young lady had already added an important new dimension to the life of Mack Bolan.

"Just keep me on my toes, pretty lady," he growled.

"I'd like to get you on your back, first. Or on my back. I mean . . ."

She'd turned a fiery red and was sputtering in embarrassed confusion.

"You know what I mean!"

"I'll let you show me," he offered, grinning.

"When? Damnit, when?"

"Soon," he replied. "Very soon."

And he sincerely meant that.

But first a final item of business in the California sweepstakes awaited his attention. Not much. It was over, mostly. All that remained was almost a personal item.

Yeah.

But a very important item.

CHAPTER 22

HER

The weather had broken. The ragged trailing edge of the system could be seen a mile or so offshore and there were blue skies beyond.

Bolan accepted that as a portent.

Terrible Tuesday was all but finished.

It had been a long and tiring day—fourteen hours, so far, with hardly a break in the galloping pace. But it was ending, now, and none beneath that emerging blue heaven would find more acceptance of that ending than Mack Bolan.

The second lap of the second mile.

The Warwagon was pulled atop a rocky bluff overlooking the cold Pacific. On another jutting finger of rock one hundred and seventy yards south of their position stood a large mansion-by-the-sea. It had a small beach a hundred feet below and a steel ladder descending the rock

171

face of the bluff. To the rear was a swimming pool and a rather large patio with hanging lanterns and other frivolous adornments. Three men sat at a table in that area, talking animatedly over tall drinks. Another three prowled the beach below and another walked lone patrol along the north periphery of the bluff. Very probably others also wandered hither and yon across that property, insuring privacy and tranquility to the three at the patio.

Bolan had those three in the con with him, though, in fine resolution.

April asked, "Who are they?"

"The old hood on the right is Bunny Cerrito," Bolan explained. "He retired from the business when I was a little boy. Too bad. He should have taken his retirement seriously. I guess someone made him an offer he couldn't refuse."

"Which one is Portillo?"

"The one facing Cerrito. He's been sort of retired, too—or so it has been said. Jimmy helped put together the original California kingdom. I had it figured that he was helping to build another. Now I wonder."

"What do you wonder, mine general?"

Bolan sighed. "I think maybe he's been doing just the reverse."

"Working for McCullough," she said.

"Yeah."

"But I thought he was part of the plot to take over McCullough."

Bolan sighed again. "So did I. The guy had me convinced. I guess that's why he's called Jimmy the Grease. He's slippery as hell, that guy."

172

"But how do you know he wasn't?" she persisted.

Bolan muttered, "Because that third man over there is none other than Cute Bill McCullough."

"Are you sure?" April gasped. "That's *him*?"

Him, yeah. "The one and only," Bolan assured the lady. "The *him* I've been looking for these fourteen hours. Isn't it a blast?"

"You *knew* it already!" she cried. "And you've been letting me get headaches with your damn puzzles! Rickert told you!"

"I guess Rickert didn't know, either," he replied. "He was lowly security muscle. He may have guessed—but he didn't know for sure the identity of the man at the top. I was guessing, too, April. I had to see it to know it, for sure. Monsters like that one don't drift by every day."

April caught her breath and let out a little moan, the full significance of the thing finally descending. "The bodies in the acid!—they—for real? His wife and daughter?"

"You heard Braddock," Bolan growled. "The daughter for sure. That means the other is for sure, too. And a stand-in for himself. Damnit, April, adopted or not—a daughter is a daughter! I've never known a real brother of the blood anywhere to get himself that bloody. That guy is . . ."

"You already said it," she whispered. "A monster. But why? I mean, why the women?"

"I guess it was expedient."

"*What* expedient!"

"He arranged his own death, April. You're the one who pulled the package—everything he

173

had was set up in trust. Guess who's going to be administering that trust. He wanted the Mob off his back and the law off his tail. The women would have been a constant danger to his new identity. I'll bet he already has a plastic surgeon stashed and waiting somewhere to deliver him a new face."

"Do you think he knows?"

Bolan was programming the fire, now, bringing the system on line. "Knows what?"

"That he's already lost his other FACE. Acronym-wise, that is."

Bolan growled, "Whether he knows it or not, April, he's lost all the face he can ever get."

Glowing rangemarks became superimposed over the image of the patio table. Bolan commanded the *Raise and Lock* sequence and an instant later the console flashed compliance. He commanded *Fire Enable*. The console enabled the fire and the rock-press foot control slid into view beside his foot.

April's lower lip was beginning to tremble.

He warned her, "Get aft, if you'd rather. I'm going to erase a terrible human mistake. Three of them."

"I'm staying," she told him. "But it really isn't necessary, is it? Not now."

"It's necessary, yeah," he assured her.

"But..."

"You told me yesterday that you revere life," he reminded her, turning to face her squarely. "Let's get this all settled between us, once and for all."

"Of course I revere life," she replied, very agitated. "That is why I... why..."

"Then don't put such a damned cheap value

174

on it," he said savagely. "Turn your back on guys like those . . . turn your guts off, too, and call for a cop then look the other way . . . for God's sake, April! These people are eating your world. And they're eating *people* by the score. Get hard, damnit! Eat back. Don't let the damned cannibals swagger away and pick their teeth with your bones! If you revere life, by God you'll demand an eye for an eye and a tooth for a tooth and you'll stare the damned savages back into their holes, even if all the hounds of hell are baying at your heels!"

It was quite an emotional speech, for the likes of Mack Bolan. His face had gone white—and she'd never seen it that way, not under any circumstances. And she'd caught a glimpse of his drummer, yes.

"Get up," she softly commanded.

"What?"

"I'm taking the con. Show me how to work that gadget."

His anger was gone, replaced now by wary concern. He told her, "I'm not sure you're ready for that, April."

"Don't tell me when I'm ready," she said, the voice very soft. "I'll tell you when I'm ready. I'm ready. Put my hand where your mouth is, Striker. Get up."

Bolan solemnly swung away from there and yielded the con to his partner. He stood behind her, then, and instructed her in the fine art of getting hard.

"Right foot in the pedal. Keep the plane steady. Rock forward on the toe for vertical depression, backward on the hell for upward correction. The pedal is controlling the image,

175

now. It swivels left and right for horizontal control. Center the rangemarks on your target—that's it. Hold it there, hold it centered, even after you fire. The bird will travel straight down the visual envelope."

"How do I fire it?"

"Your fire will equal downward pressure on the pedal. The entire plane of the foot must travel together. If the toe dips a bit, so will your trajectory. So keep the foot stiff when you're ready to fire, ankle directly below the knee. Then just pound the knee."

"Pound it?"

"Sharply, yeah, with the ball of the fist." He sighed. "Are you sure this is what you want, April?"

For reply she raised the tiny balled fist high and viciously pounded the knee.

The firebird rustled away from its rooftop nest and flashed overhead on a tail of flame and smoke.

The security people over there had already become curious about the presence of the motor home and were now running in full alarm toward the house.

But the men on the patio had other things on the mind.

World-eating things.

The scope changed colors rapidly as the missile closed on the target, then the optics flared out bright white as one hundred and seventy yards away a mansion-by-the-sea's patio did suddenly "fly up to the clouds without wings" —carrying all that had been there with it.

April's face was white and taut, but she was already "correcting right" and acquiring a new target: the house itself. Again she drove the knee home and again a firebird rustled away in its "ministry of death."

"Eat that, damn you," she said to the scope in a shaky voice. And, to Bolan, "Is that hard enough for you, partner?"

That house over there had just gone to hell.

"Give me another target, damnit!"

He said, "Enough, April."

"I'll give them, by God, two board feet to stand on!"

She was sobbing and going to hell fast, herself.

Bolan dragged her out of the con and clasped her close for a brief moment—a very close moment—then set her gently in the other seat. He took the con and took them away from there in a sedate withdrawal.

Tuesday, thank God, was done.

But April Rose, by God, was just getting started.

EPILOGUE

Bolan sent his report to Brognola and arranged for a midnight rendezvous with the transport plane.

Then he called Leo Turrin and assured the undercover fed that all loose ends had been neatly snipped.

Tomorrow would find another hellground—and another lap along that bloody second mile.

Tonight was for tonight.

He pulled the cruiser onto a deserted stretch of beach and parked in the shadow of a sheer rock wall and took his love to bed.

And, yes, that girl was just getting started.

Dear Reader,

I'm an Arizona girl, and I live out by a mountain. Every summer, we have wildfires in our state, and the past couple of summers I grieved as I watched the smoke rising over the mountain. I fear for the wildlife and for the teams of hotshot firefighters who risk their lives every day to save lives. I've seen the flames. And I've seen the damage they leave. This past spring, as I was out hiking, I met a team of hotshot firefighters and this book sprang to life through them.

I also started my writing career as a journalist—I was a stringer for the *Dayton Daily News* in Ohio and even had a byline once or twice.

So...meet Shelby, a journalist, and Luke, a hotshot firefighter, who are fighting for their lives as they tackle the unknown in the world around them and in their hearts and minds, as well. I love this book on so many levels and hated typing *The End*. I hope that you give me the chance to bring you along on the journey.

Happy reading! If you take nothing else from this book, my message would be: never give up hope!

Dana Taylor

A FIREFIGHTER'S HIDDEN TRUTH

Tara Taylor Quinn

HARLEQUIN

ROMANTIC
SUSPENSE

HARLEQUIN®
ROMANTIC SUSPENSE™

Recycling programs
for this product may
not exist in your area.

ISBN-13: 978-1-335-59372-6

A Firefighter's Hidden Truth

Copyright © 2023 by TTQ Books LLC

For questions and comments about the quality of this book, please contact us at CustomerService@Harlequin.com.

Harlequin Enterprises ULC
22 Adelaide St. West, 41st Floor
Toronto, Ontario M5H 4E3, Canada
www.Harlequin.com

Printed in U.S.A.

A *USA TODAY* bestselling author of over a hundred novels in twenty languages, **Tara Taylor Quinn** has sold more than seven million copies. Known for her intense emotional fiction, Ms. Quinn's novels have received critical acclaim in the UK and most recently from Harvard. She is the recipient of the Readers' Choice Award and has appeared often on local and national TV, including *CBS Sunday Morning*.

For TTQ offers, news and contests, visit www.tarataylorquinn.com!

Books by Tara Taylor Quinn

Harlequin Romantic Suspense

Sierra's Web

Tracking His Secret Child
Cold Case Sheriff
The Bounty Hunter's Baby Search
On the Run with His Bodyguard
Not Without Her Child
A Firefighter's Hidden Truth

The Coltons of Colorado

Colton Countdown

Where Secrets are Safe

Her Detective's Secret Intent
Shielded in the Shadows
Falling for His Suspect

The Coltons of New York

Protecting Colton's Baby

Visit the Author Profile page at Harlequin.com for more titles.

To all of the many teams of hotshot firefighters in Arizona and across the US who risk so much and spend so much time away from loved ones for not nearly enough pay. You are known and so very much appreciated.

Chapter 1

It had been almost five years since he'd had sex with her, paid her off and walked out of her life. Like she'd been nothing more than a prostitute instead of the partner in a whirlwind, weeklong romance she'd dreamed up in her head. An overactive imagination—while professionally lucrative—had its downfalls.

There was nothing imaginary about the man's face. Even with an oxygen tube, hair that needed a wash, a blank gaze in those unforgettable vivid blue eyes and his head on the pillow of his bed, she knew him.

"His name is Luke Dennison." Shelby turned to walk out of the hospital room, leaving the police to deal with their problem.

"You know me?" The voice—the timbre of it sending an unwanted wash of desire over her—stopped her in her tracks. As angry as she still was nearly five years later, there was something else going on inside her, something she wouldn't allow herself to explore. Something to do with the fact that the man's four-year-old son was currently at home with his babysitter.

And the hotshot firefighter sounded so...needy. As though he'd start begging if she didn't turn around.

She'd heard her father beg after breaking her mother's heart. Too many times to count.

"Yes, unfortunately, I know you," she said, turning back around but stepping no closer. The door was her immediate destination.

The man in the bed frowned as though he was in pain. And maybe he was. He'd been found out in the desert, would have died in the fire he'd seemingly been attempting to contain on his own when he'd slid, falling backward. The police had surmised—based on the crime scene and the location of the rock that had slammed into the back of his head, rendering him unconscious—that he was only alive because the wind had shifted, changing the course of the blaze. "I'm sorry, have I done something to upset you?" He looked truly perplexed.

Which pissed her off.

And she'd learned long ago that it was more to her advantage not to let that show.

"Come on, Luke, why would I be upset with you?" The question was pure sarcasm. Her smile and tone of voice made that obvious.

"I'm guessing if you weren't before, you're going to be now," he said then, shaking his head. "Because I have to ask, who are you?"

If he'd been in his right mind, the irony would have been too much to bear. Shelby took a deep breath, giving herself time to determine her next course of action. Did she walk out the door and thankfully bid good riddance to the man once and for all?

Or did she listen to the softer part of herself, the one who looked for the human-interest stories a lot of reporters didn't bother to find, and give the man another chance?

Why don't I have a daddy like Jason does? A replay of Carter's tear-filled, heartbreaking question flashed through her mind. From when Carter's little friend Jason got to go fishing for the weekend.

And immediate answers became clear. She had to buy herself time. "I'm a reporter," she told the man, the only part of their truth she was willing to let him know. The police had said his memory loss was complete. Meaning he wouldn't remember that she'd gone to his home to tell him that she was pregnant.

And wouldn't remember the way he'd accused her of lying, telling her the kid couldn't possibly be his.

Dare she hope, for Carter's sake, that he'd matured in the past five years?

That the great, self-sacrificing part of the man she'd interviewed back then had gained the upper hand over the womanizing snake in him?

"I did a human-interest story on you five years ago," she said, walking closer to the bed as the detective who'd brought her to the room for identification stood by. "For a digital forestry publication." She'd moved up in the world dramatically since then.

Made enough per story, freelancing to top digital venues, to be able to pick and choose what, where and when she worked.

Not that she'd tell him, but the story she'd done on him had been what had jump-started her career. The managing editor of *The Custodian*, one of the largest digital news publishers in the world, had read that story. And had offered her one chance to prove herself.

Pregnant and alone aside from her mother, who was also alone and on a fixed income, she'd given her all to that opportunity.

And had succeeded.

Luke Dennison's eyes opened wider, showing a true interest. And perhaps a bit of desperation as well. That's what her intuitive eye saw, anyway. Not that, in her current situation, she was open to trusting that special gift of hers.

It had almost ruined her life the first time she'd met the man.

Except that she'd persevered. Had wanted her baby even if he hadn't.

"Would you mind…if… Do you have the time…to sit with me a few minutes? To fill me in?" He glanced toward the detective, who shrugged and left it to Shelby to answer the victim.

She wished she hadn't insisted on driving separately from the law enforcement investigator who'd walked her in. She had wanted an immediate escape route. It was turning into a trap.

"I can stay for a few minutes," she heard herself say, even over the loud internal groan in her head.

Detective Johnson nodded, excused himself and left.

The warmth, the gratitude in Luke's gaze as he kept his eyes glued in her direction—even when she moved— touched her empathy nerve.

And she knew she'd made a big mistake.

Only one person in the world seemed to know who he was, and she was clearly not fond of him. Didn't bode well.

What had he done before he'd been found nearly dead by the local fire department?

Did he really want to know?

She'd written an article for a digital forestry publication? On him?

The great-looking mystery woman didn't sit. She stood there in her black-and-white sundress and black flip-flops, with her wavy, long blond hair almost a shield around her, and seemed about ready to bolt.

"How old am I?" Not as ancient as he felt, although his hair wasn't gray.

But how many years had he screwed up? How many decades left to fix it all?

Or…God forbid, what if he found out he couldn't fix it all? What if he found out that he'd done things he needed to forget?

"You're thirty-two." Her answer took a while to arrive. Leaving questions in its wake.

Did she really know?

"Why are you so hesitant to talk to me?" he asked, figuring it was what he needed to know most. But with the meds keeping his aching head from exploding, he wasn't sure he could trust his own judgment.

Having your memory check out on you did that to a guy.

"When I did that story on you almost five years ago, our association ended rudely."

That was it? He'd been rude?

Sheesh.

Still didn't explain why he'd been in the hospital for two days and no one had reported him missing or come forth to claim him.

What had he done to make no one want him? Was he on the run?

Didn't feel right, him a runner.

But nearly dying in a small desert fire didn't sit right with him, either.

"Why did you do a story on me?"

"Because of what you do for a living." She came a little closer, sat on the edge of a plastic chair along the wall several feet to the side of his bed. "I'd read about the Bodell fire. Everyone was writing about the hotshot-crew lives that were lost, and there you were, the one lifesaver, with only a brief mention—and not only a trained hotshot but a smoke jumper with EMT certification as well…"

"Wait." He sat up straight, nearly pulling off the oxygen tube he no longer needed. "You're telling me I'm a hotshot firefighter?"

He knew what that was. Did everyone?

She nodded.

"And an EMT?" He definitely knew what that was.

Another nod. Holy hell!

He was a good guy.

"Am I married? Do I have family? What about parents? Where was I born?" Suddenly, he couldn't get enough. Kept lobbing questions even as she shook her head.

"Detective Johnson said the doctor told him that it's likely you'll start remembering things fairly soon."

Yeah, he'd been given the same information. He could expect the return to take a couple of weeks at most. But if something she told him could trigger even a slight peek…

Seeming to have made a decision, the woman nodded, opened her mouth to speak, but he blurted out, "What's your name?"

"Shelby Harrington."

He searched his massive blank spaces. Found not even the slightest recognition of her.

"I have no idea if you're married. You told me back when I interviewed you that your schedule precluded any kind of partnership or relationship. You said a lot of guys make it work, but you didn't want to put a woman through constant, unexpected absences for sometimes weeks on end, with the risk that you might not ever come back. Your mother died when you were a teenager, and her loss had something to do with your decision."

"I told you that?" Didn't seem like something he'd say.

"No, I asked if that was the case, and, after thinking about it, you acknowledged that it was. That's it—you just said yes."

Had she asked for personal or professional reasons? The question intrigued him. A lot. But considering how little he had rattling around in his brain, her small details pretty much had the place to themselves.

His mother was dead. The knowledge brought sadness.

Because he remembered her? Even a little?

Or just because it was a sad thing?

He looked for any flashes of a funeral. Of a smile. Or a reprimand.

Came up blank.

"What about my father?"

When she glanced down at her hands, his gut sank.

"He died last year in a car accident."

Luke jerked. His entire body stiffened. And then... nothing.

"Now that you know who you are, you can look all this up."

"If I knew what to look up," he said, still feeling the shock of his father's passing. Feeling it for real?

He was pretty sure he was. And he had a flash of a watch. His watch that had survived the fire. Had his father given it to him?

"My guess would be that your hotshot team will know more than anyone else. You probably want to contact them when you can," she said, and he stared at her. Why hadn't he thought of that?

He had a team?

"Detective Johnson said they were called to a fire in northern Arizona the afternoon you were brought in. It's zero percent contained, so they might be there awhile. He said as soon as I made the formal ID this morning, he'd be getting in touch with the forestry department…"

Zero containment. He knew what that meant. Nearby population had to be assessed, evacuation orders established, containment lines determined. But when he tried to stay with the orders in his head, to see more, he ran into nothingness.

Still, adrenaline coursed through him. For a second there, he'd felt like someone who knew exactly how to fight a wildfire.

He had a team!

And a reason no one had come to identify him. A few short minutes, and two days of frustration and growing anxiety were easing dramatically.

There'd been nothing to indicate that his memory loss was permanent. To the contrary. He just had to be patient…

Patience didn't feel like a familiar companion to him.

Was he remembering that, too? Or was he just highly impatient with his current situation?

"Where do I live?"

"I've had nothing to do with you for nearly five years."

Funny how easily he recognized a prevarication. "Did you know where I lived then?" Made sense. The interview could have been in his home.

"You were working out of the San Diego area, and you had a temporary apartment there. You owned a cabin here in Arizona. North of Phoenix."

An apartment. Didn't resonate. The cabin sounded right, though.

Shelby stood up, and he sat up straight again. "Don't go." She was his lifeline…

"I have to go," she told him. She didn't elaborate.

"Will you come back?"

"Anything I'd have to tell you is in the article I wrote. Just google both our names, and it will come up." She was walking to the door as she spoke.

Clearly done with him. Eager to get away.

Which didn't sit well, for more than just his selfish need to be with someone who knew things about him.

"I'm sorry."

"For what?"

"Whatever I did that was rude."

Nearly at the door, she shrugged. Didn't even turn back.

"What was it?" he blurted out before she could reach for the handle to let herself out.

She stopped. Stood there, her back to him.

"Probably best if you get your memory back before we go there," she finally said, glancing at him over her shoulder.

"Does that mean I'll see you again? When my head's back in shape?"

She shrugged once more.

"I guess that's up to you. I'm easy to find. Always have been."

And yet…

He'd apparently never gone looking.

Luke wanted to know why.

What had he done to her?

As he sat there alone, watching the closed door she'd left behind, he had a lot of questions. But none that he wanted answered more than that one.

Chapter 2

Shelby's brisk walk from the hospital took effort. She wanted to run. To get away from the man who'd rocked her more than any other, in so many ways.

Because, just as strongly as her urge to run, she'd felt compelled to pull that damned hard-plastic chair up to his bed and spend the day doing what she could to help him.

She'd admired the heck out of him even before she met him. All the research she'd done on his team, on the forestry-technician hotshot crews in general, had left her mostly in awe. She'd been prepared to be at least a little disappointed in the real thing. He was, after all, just a human being like everyone else in the world. Instead, she'd been mesmerized. He'd been decent to the core. And had a sixth sense about him: seeing things in people or situations that others might miss. She'd always been that way—looking at people and seeing what wasn't being shown, hearing what wasn't being said. Luke Dennison had been the first person she'd ever met who could inhabit that world with her. She'd only known him a week and actually thought she'd met her soul mate.

And then she'd woken alone the morning after they'd made the most incredible love, and had picked up the envelope he'd had delivered with the breakfast he'd ordered for her. She'd opened it and found a thousand dollars in the thank-you card...

She'd seen him one other time. She'd looked up his address and had driven up to his cabin in Payson to tell him that she was pregnant, figuring she'd leave him a note if he was—as she'd hoped—out at a fire. Or still in San Diego. Not that she'd wanted a fire anywhere; she'd just hoped he would be gone for a few days.

So she could have more time to get over her own shock and figure out a new plan for her life.

He'd been home. Had come outside to speak with her, pulling the door closed quickly behind him, but she'd still heard the woman inside, calling out to him to come back to bed. And when she told him that the baby was his, he'd said she was lying. Had firmly denied the possibility since they'd used a condom, and then stepped back inside and shut the door in her face.

And then, nearly five years later, she saw his picture on the local Phoenix news, depicting a guy who'd been pulled unconscious from the desert just north of the city and had awoken without knowledge of who he was. At first, she'd turned away. Waited for someone else to tell authorities who he was. But by the second day, with the fact that his father had died nagging in the back of her mind, that he had no other family to her knowledge, he didn't live in Phoenix, and his hotshot team could likely be out on a fire, she'd called the police. And had reluctantly agreed to see the man to positively identify him.

She'd told herself she was doing her duty as a good citizen, but that part of her brain that she tried not to listen to when it came to adult men in her life—the part that loved the good in them even when she knew full well that the bad outweighed the good—had perked up, too.

Three times Carter had come to her, asking why he didn't have a daddy.

And she didn't even have a grandpa or an uncle to give him.

So what if, like her own father, Luke turned out to be a good dad—while sucking at being a faithful or trustworthy romantic partner?

And what if, when the man regained his memory, he turned out to be as awful at fatherhood as he'd been at even considering the possibility that he might be a father?

She'd planned a full day's work after leaving the hospital, stopping by various places, including a dance cooperative, looking for her next story. An entire file of potentials hung out on her computer; she read all the requests but only in case something in them triggered her nerve.

Otherwise, she kept her eyes, heart and ears open and pursued anything that spoke to her.

Nothing was going to speak to her that Wednesday morning. And there was only one place she wanted to be. One person with whom she wanted to be—Carter. Turning toward the home she'd purchased the previous year, she couldn't stop her mind from going right back to where it had been. Grinding out thoughts, the same ones over and over, faster than she could process them.

She was in a quandary, unable to land on whether or not she was going to attempt to see Luke again while knowing that, for Carter, she couldn't just walk away.

Not if there was even a slight possibility that the man would be a good dad.

But no way was she exposing Carter to him until she knew more.

That's where she was.

For the first time in years, she actually toyed with the idea of trying to find herself a husband. After Luke, who wasn't her first disastrous romantic relationship, she'd figured she was one of those women who were attracted to men like their fathers, and she had made a very clear, rational and contented choice to be done.

With a baby on the way, she just hadn't been able to risk being her mother.

Couldn't take any chances that a child of hers would grow up like she had.

Still, there were a lot of great guys out there. She turned down dates as often as many people mowed their grass—partially because, with her job, she was always meeting new people.

Maybe trying to find a good man would be the lesser of two evils. Instead of giving Luke Dennison even one more thought, maybe she should try to find a father for her son…

The fact that the hotshot firefighter's face had shown up twice on her television set, just as she happened to be watching, didn't have to be an omen. It could have been a coincidence.

Some people said there were no coincidences, but the word existed for a reason, right?

Turning the corner into her neighborhood, she slowed down to take the dirt-and-rock shoulder she was being forced onto due to road-widening construction, hating that she had to put her pretty new blue SUV through the abuse every time she came and went. Knowing that most people just powered right on over the shoulder at normal speed, she checked her rearview mirror to make certain that there wasn't someone barreling down on top of her.

She saw the delivery truck approaching quickly just as there was a bump, a loud noise, and her car jerked hard to the left, like someone had taken control of her steering wheel. She didn't let go. She saw the truck about to rear-end her again and pulled so hard to the right a muscle in her upper arm popped, throwing the vehicle over a slight incline and then down into a ditch.

After being smacked in the face by her airbag, Shelby had no idea what had just happened, and with shaking hands and few wits about her, found her phone and dialed 911.

Luke hadn't expected to see Detective Johnson again. He was just an amnesia patient now, no longer a missing person. Figuring the guy was just being nice when he knocked on Luke's hospital-room door and stuck his head in, asking if he could talk to Luke for a second, Luke readily waved him in.

He'd never imagined how quickly a guy could go stir crazy with so little in his brain. Watching television was boring to him. He couldn't relate because he had no memories to pull from to make anything personal. He'd found out he had a cabin in Payson, an hour and a half northish of East Valley, so he would have a place to go when he was released from the hospital. His phone had burned up in the fire, he'd been wearing an old watch that had survived, and Johnson had already called late that morning to let him know he had bank accounts and credit cards in his name.

He'd readily given the detective permission to access any and all information, including expenditures, to help him start to put his pieces back together and had discovered that his finances were being handled by a personal banker, Gerard Michaels.

A call to Mr. Michaels had filled in many blanks in his life details, like the fact that he was quite well-off, having earned his own money by taking dangerous side jobs when he wasn't out fighting fires; he had a trust fund left by his mother; and he'd also inherited a sizable chunk when his father had died the year before.

The man had also told him, when he'd asked, that his old watch had been his father's. He'd known.

That meant a lot.

He'd requested a laptop and new phone ASAP, and both had been delivered earlier that afternoon. He could look himself up.

And look up Shelby Harrington, too.

Which he'd done first. And had only just started clicking on links when Johnson showed up.

"I wanted to let you know a couple of things," the detective said, pulling up the chair that Shelby had left by the wall that morning. "But first—you're feeling okay?"

Luke, sitting up in bed with a T-shirt on, figured that one was obvious—no way a guy who couldn't remember anything about himself was feeling okay—but nodded anyway. "Smoke inhalation can be a problem in the days to come, but for now, I'm clear. Breathing is fine. I'm not hoarse. The burns were all superficial—nothing I can't handle. And if tomorrow's tests on my head come back okay, I'll be released. Doctors say I'm one lucky son of… Well, you get the point." He didn't feel lucky.

He felt…angry.

And then some. If he was some hotshot firefighter, putting out blazes that covered hundreds or thousands of acres, and climbing up mountains that reached the clouds, how in the hell had a forty-acre desert fire gotten the better of him?

A first-year rookie in the Phoenix fire department could have handled that one.

And how did he know that?

"Glad to hear it," Johnson said, but the man didn't look glad. His frown could have been due to fatigue or borne from some personal problem, but watching him, Luke didn't think so. The man seemed...perplexed.

Concerned.

And he was staring straight at Luke.

"What?" he asked. Had the good detective found out something else about him? Something not so good?

Like what heinous thing he'd supposedly done to make Shelby Harrington uneasy even being in the same room with him?

"A couple of things," Johnson said.

And clearly, they weren't just wishing him well and having a good life type stuff.

"First, there's clear evidence that the fire you were found near was human caused."

"A four-wheeler sparks in that dry brush and..."

How did he know that? He wasn't even finished with his internal wondering before Johnson shook his head.

"It was set deliberately. There was a trail of gasoline leading right up to where we found you. If the wind hadn't changed course, you—and all evidence of how the fire started—would have burned."

Staring in horror, Luke felt completely helpless. Someone had set a fire and, what? Had dared him to put it out on his own? Who would do that to him?

And how in the hell would anyone even put together a suspect list if he couldn't come up with anyone who knew him? Or anyone, other than Shelby, that he'd pissed off?

"There's more."

With dread in his gut, he waited.

"The bash to the back of your head... It happened before the fire started. Forensics came back on the rock. Your blood was on it prior to the smoke."

"I didn't fall and hit my head?"

"From what Forensics tells me, the rock hit your head from a different angle, clearly knocking you out, and then was placed under your head. Blood splatter and blood pooling were pretty clear on that one."

So not only would he be dead, if not for the grace of fate, but also whoever wanted him that way had taken extreme measures to make certain it happened.

And he couldn't remember a damned thing to help himself.

The detective wasn't asking what Luke assumed would have been the usual questions: Did he know of anyone who had a beef with him? Anyone he'd angered? Someone, maybe, whose woman he'd slept with?

Or stolen something else from?

"I'm not in debt," he said.

Johnson nodded. "I know."

Of course he did. Luke had given the man access to his own financials. Johnson had seen them first.

"I've never been married," he said, laying out another fact Johnson had told him. No ex-spouse wanting him dead for his money. Or nearly ex.

But that didn't rule out a girlfriend.

He had to get up to Payson. Ask around about himself. Talk to someone in the hotshot crew he'd been told he was part of.

"There's one other thing," Johnson said then, and Luke stared, chin jutted forward. Would the guy just please get it all said so Luke could at least figure out what he couldn't figure out?

"Shelby Harrington…"

He sat up straighter. Ready. He needed to know what he'd done to the woman,

"After she left here, she was in an accident…"

The detective's frown touched Luke's nerve endings, putting every one of them on alert.

"Shelby's hurt?"

The shrug was better than a shake.

"She's bruised. And shaken but okay," Johnson said. "Thing is, she had a tire blow on a brand-new vehicle…"

"Tires don't blow on new vehicles," Luke said. "Even if you run over something, you get a slow leak…"

So he knew about tires.

"On rare occasions, there could be a manufacturer defect."

Right. Possible. But about as likely as winning the lottery.

"But that's not what happened here. The sidewall had been cut, a thin line that didn't go all the way through. Just far enough that when she hit a big bump, or bumpy patch, the tire would blow."

"You're saying someone deliberately tried to kill her, too?"

Because of what he'd done to her?

"I'm not saying that. At all." Johnson's head shake wasn't as convincing as his words. "I do think that it's strange that someone wants you dead, and the person who comes forward to identify you ends up in life-threatening trouble right after being here, where you are."

Right. Made a hell of a lot more sense than a very brief five-year-old connection.

"Shelby says that there was a delivery truck coming

up fast behind her when her tire blew. If she hadn't been able to wrench the SUV over an incline and into a ditch, she'd be dead."

Growing cold and angrier, frustrated and confused, Luke shook his head. "Did you find the driver of the delivery truck?"

"No. And she's certain which company the truck was from, and they had no deliveries in the area this afternoon."

"Someone could have paid an off-duty driver..."

"There are protocols, but sometimes trucks do go places other than their assigned routes... For enough money, I imagine someone with knowhow could dismantle any Global Positioning System or tracking the company puts on their trucks to make a little side trip."

Okay, but...wait...

"How could that person have known right when her tire would have blown?"

Johnson's nod, that worried look on his face, snatched any of the relief Luke might have felt before he even had a chance to get to it.

"The road right outside her neighborhood is under construction." Everyone who was familiar with Phoenix knew about the never-ending road construction.

Great. He had useless tidbits but nothing that could save a life?

"Cars are forced onto a rocky shoulder. Anyone knowing where she lived would know that it would be as sure a tire blow as you could get. All he'd have had to do was follow her and bump her as she hit the rough patch. Tire blow, fender bender, and off she goes."

"But...how would anyone know she'd been coming here?"

"That's what we have to figure out." Johnson stood,

then added, "And maybe the two incidents aren't related at all."

But the man didn't sound convinced of that.

And neither was Luke.

If Shelby Harrington felt that she had reason to hate him for what happened in the past, this turn of events sure as hell wasn't going to change her mind.

Chapter 3

The first thing Shelby did once she had driven herself home in a rental car after being checked out at the hospital was hug her son. The second was pay the babysitter, see her off and then dead bolt herself and Carter inside the home she'd made for them.

And then, while her son played in the family room set up like a kid's haven, she called her mom, packed a bag for Carter and drove her little boy down to Tucson, an hour and a half away from the near-death experience she'd just had.

If Carter had been in the car with her...

Sylvia Harrington begged Shelby to stay the night. The only reason she did so was because Carter was tired and had asked her if she could please not leave for work until breakfast time. Her son was used to having days at his grandmother's. He never complained. Sylvia adored him, doted on him, and Shelby always felt guilty leaving him there. Every time.

Except that one.

As she left her mother's home the next morning, she was comforted by the fact that Carter would be safe there until she could figure out what in the hell was going on.

Detective Johnson and his team were investigating, of course, but she knew enough to realize that cases like her crash could go unsolved for eternity.

Their only real lead was what, to her, seemed an absolute obvious link, not just a suspicion: Luke Dennison.

Which was why she typed the address to the hospital into her map app before she even pulled out of her mother's driveway.

The man already had so much to answer for. Knowing him for one week had changed her entire life, shaped her future, forever. And he'd sent her off to deal with it all alone. No way he was going to skate on this one.

Her knocking on his hospital room door was more of an announcement that she was entering than a request to come in. So much so that the power of her knock caused the slightly ajar door to swing inward, revealing a man standing in a pair of tan shorts, pulling a short-sleeved white shirt over his head.

Her gaze went straight to the chest. After five years, she'd been certain she'd embellished her memories. With a displeased gulp, she realized that she hadn't.

How could the mere sight of a chest she'd kissed all over—she recalled the feeling of his moans vibrating against her lips—melt her insides?

"Luke..." she said, starting right in, ready to tell the man he had no right to implode her life, when he stuck his head out of the collar of his shirt and stared.

"Shelby! Thank God. Seriously. I've been trying to reach you. Johnson wouldn't give me your number, and it's not listed on any internet people-finder, either."

She was a mother with a vulnerable young son to protect. And a very public job. "I'm on the national registry to keep my number private."

Detective Johnson had asked for her permission to share her information with Luke at Luke's request. She'd declined. And hadn't explained herself to Luke, either.

Nor did any of that make sense with her telling him, at the end of their first meeting, that if he wanted to find her, he could.

"First, regardless of Johnson's need to keep an open mind while he looks at all the evidence, I'm taking full responsibility for your car crash yesterday. Johnson said the vehicle was new, and I'm going to see that you get another, brand-new one, rather than having yours fixed."

She opened her mouth to protest. Because her independence gave her strength... But then he said, "A car with an accident report on it loses value."

He was right.

And really, when you looked at four years' worth of child support... Yeah, he could buy her a car. But... "I didn't own it free and clear," she told him. "I'd settle for whatever the difference is from the insurance payoff or trade-in to what I owe. I hadn't even made my first payment."

She wasn't out to make him finance more than his share. She needed to know if he'd be a good father, and then she'd have to find out if he'd consider changing his mind about having a son.

All of which had to wait until he got his memory back. He could hardly explain what he didn't remember.

"Okay, on to the tough stuff," he said then, standing there with his hands on his hips, facing her like he had complete control of his world.

Something she recognized from the past. One of the

many things she'd admired about him—his ability to just take on whatever was before him—until he'd thought he could pay her off and then shut the door in her face.

"I've hired a firm I've done some work for from time to time," he told her. "Sierra's Web—they're out of Phoenix. You know of them?"

She did. Had actually covered a couple of cases the nationally renowned firm had taken on. After the fact. But... "The private firm that provides experts in pretty much any field, yes. I didn't know you worked for them." She was shocked. Felt betrayed.

And recognized she was being asinine.

His shrug was a bit embarrassed, but his composure and confidence didn't seem to suffer much as he said, "I actually didn't know, either, until last evening." Throwing up a hand, he told her how he'd followed his own financials, seen that the firm had paid him, and looked them up and given them a call. "I'm trained for many different kinds of dangerous, emergent situations, and apparently the firm was involved with child-trauma management during a fire I commanded three years ago. We hooked up from there."

She wanted to close her heart to his words. Knew her and Carter's well-being depended on her ability to maintain objectivity. And yet the part of her that had sought Luke out five years before to tell his story recognized the selflessness of his work life.

And admired him all over again.

Just like she'd always been drawn to the good qualities in men with major ethical failures.

"Here's what I'd like to see happen," he said. "Hear me out first, and then see what you think."

Did he remember that she waited to reserve judgment until she'd heard the whole story? Remember part of her?

Would she get her answers sooner rather than later and be able to walk away?

While her mind fought its usual battles when it came to men, she nodded.

"One of the big immediate questions is how someone knew, before you were here at the hospital yesterday, that you were coming. Your tire had to have been slashed in the parking lot here because Johnson said you drove here straight from home, and you had to drive over that bumpy stretch of shoulder to do that."

Having her tire slashed at the hospital was the most likely conclusion. She'd already reached it herself the night before.

"So how did someone know you were coming? And why?"

Was he actually standing there and accusing her of putting herself in danger by telling someone about her mission the morning before?

"I didn't say a word to anyone," she told him, not even blinking as she looked him straight in the eye. "Only my babysitter knew I was gone, and she thought I was doing research for a couple of potential stories, which I had also planned to do."

His nod seemed appreciative. She warmed to it.

Stop it.

"It's more likely that someone here at the hospital or within the police department had been approached when I turned up alive, and that person was subsequently paid off. Johnson has had a crew outside my door since yesterday afternoon."

She'd seen the uniforms five or six feet on either side of his door. Had nodded at them.

"That being said, the plan is for Sierra's Web to get us safely into hiding. We'll have bodyguards at all times, and no one but the firm, and Johnson, will know where we are. All expenses will be paid through the firm, and I'll reimburse them…"

No way was she going into hiding with him.

"…a team of experts is already being pulled together to work on every aspect of my life. I've apparently worked with the IT guy before. Then there's finance, a medical expert and a PI looking into my private life. There will be overlap, but we need this done as quickly as possible."

She was not going into hiding with him.

"As far as our safety is concerned, we can have two separate and distant places. That is not advised, however, as you and I need to be able to converse, and we won't be able to do so if we aren't together. We both have to cease use of all electronics and cell phones. At least until we get a better handle on what we're dealing with."

"I can't be without my cell phone." Carter. Done deal.

"If we're looking at someone with police connections being paid to make sure I don't escape again, the second you use a phone, you're putting a target on your head."

Wow. No intuitive understanding there.

Or maybe there had been.

He didn't know…

"I have a child," she said.

"You're married?"

Yeah, right, uh-huh. The father of her baby wanted to be her husband.

"When it became clear to me that I had no desire to ever marry, I chose to have a baby and raise him on my own."

Eyes narrowing, he homed in on her. "How old is this kid?"

Heart pounding, mouth dry, she knew she had to be more careful. No way could she let him know yet.

If ever.

She needed his answers first.

Ones he didn't yet have.

But he had a firm of experts who would most probably find out.

Because she'd become one of his targets.

Damn. Why was it that any time the man showed up, she had to suffer?

"He's four." But his birth certificate, his exact birth date, was private. She'd call Johnson and make sure it stayed that way. Even if it meant telling the detective why.

Luke's glance intensified. She prepared herself for the truth to fly out long before it was supposed to. Before she was anywhere near ready to deal with his response.

No matter what it was.

"And you interviewed me five years ago."

The article was dated. He'd surely already looked it up. From what she remembered about him, he probably had the whole damned thing memorized.

She nodded.

His shoulders dropped. His entire countenance diminished as his gaze fell to the floor. When he raised his head, his expression was filled with regret.

Which didn't mean a whole lot when he didn't know the facts—didn't remember slamming the door in her face when she'd brought him the news of Carter's conception.

She hadn't told him where Carter was. Could put in a call to her mother to take Carter and leave the state until further notice. Just the mention of the possibility of Carter's father's advent into their lives would ensure that she'd keep the boy safe. If there was one thing Sylvia had perfected, it was keeping kids from their snake fathers.

If anyone knew about Carter's parentage, if they wanted to get at Luke, they'd...

Her breath caught. Surely, Luke would see that it was best if...

"It was me, wasn't it?"

Feeling the blood drain from her face, she just stared.

"Whatever it is I did to you, it's the reason you decided you never wanted to marry. I drove you into a life of single motherhood."

Relief making her almost giddy, she maintained her stance.

Unable to believe her luck.

Wow. He couldn't have walked into that one any better.

She told him the absolute truth: "Yes, you did drive me into single motherhood."

Looking him straight, belligerently, in the eye.

"Tell me what I did."

She shook her head. "No way. You don't get to start building up different justifications in your head to cloud real memories with fiction."

His brows raised, he studied her another second or two. Nodded. "Fair enough."

She thought they were done. Until he said, "But it was so bad that you were pregnant within three months?"

More truth burst out of her in an attempt to hide the one thing he couldn't know—for Carter's own safety, she now realized.

"It wasn't just you." She'd already made her choice to never marry before she'd interviewed Luke. Which was why her consequent behavior had been such a shock to her. Had opened her eyes to her complete inability to discern male character when she got involved with them. "I won't bore you with details, but I'm drawn to men who have great qualities but who make immoral choices in their personal lives. A therapist I saw suggested that it leads back to my father. After getting hurt three different times, I decided to be kind to myself and stop."

"So it wasn't me?"

For a second there, she wanted to keep the hope that she saw in his eyes alive. She could almost feel how desperately he needed to be able to cling to that hope.

"Oh, it was most definitely you," she said. He'd been her fall off her own addictive wagon. The one that had straightened her up for life. "You just weren't solely responsible."

He nodded again. Shrugged. "If it means anything at all, I'm sorry about it now."

"If you remembered the way it went down and said that, it would mean something." Her response wasn't kind. Not to him. She was being kind to herself.

So why didn't she feel good about it?

The response came to her—because she wasn't like him. And that did ring true. A major moment. A reminder.

She would not become bitter like her mother. While Sylvia was fabulous with Carter, there was no man involved in his life.

At some point, Carter was going to be a man. And would need one as an example.

"I'm done."

Shaking her head, shrugging, she looked at Luke. Done with her? With talking about her past?

"I asked you to hear me out. You've done so."

He was waiting for her response. "I want two separate bedrooms," she said.

"Two rooms? You plan to bring your child?"

Oh Lord. Of course not.

"Why on earth would I put him in danger like that?

Someone only wants me because I can identify you, and while I have no idea why that matters, I'm confident that my son is of no use to them."

Unless as a way to get to her? "But," she went on, "if you wouldn't mind getting a bodyguard to an address I don't wish to specify to you, I would very much appreciate it."

"Done."

Good. At times, he was a really decent man. Times when others' lives were at stake. He'd risked his own countless times to save someone else.

That mattered.

"I meant two bedrooms, at the very least, in the safe house."

Eyes pointing intently at her, he said, "You're agreeing to one safe house."

"I am. But I need a burner phone or some way to communicate with my son."

"If you're in agreement, I'd like to leave those details up to Sierra's Web."

She was. She nodded.

And she soon found herself being whisked away, down into the bowels of the hospital, through a bunker of sorts and out another way, with Luke hurrying right behind her.

Watching her back.

Chapter 4

They set up shop in a hotel suite. As though his existence wasn't surreal enough at the moment, they'd been transported in the back of a windowless van, on side seats, like prisoners. Luke had had no idea what Shelby was thinking about it all. She sat, mostly expressionless, watching out the front window as they drove.

Taking stock of where they were going, he figured.

He didn't ask. Didn't want to push his luck with her.

Bruce, one of their two bodyguards, had been concerned that they were being followed for several minutes there.

If they'd had a tail, he never got close enough for a description of the driver, and Bruce, with some quick turns and doubling back, had lost him. There'd been no front license plate—it wasn't law in Arizona—but Bruce had called in a description of the vehicle to Johnson.

The suite—in a luxury hotel in the middle of a ritzy

part of Phoenix—was spacious. The open living and conference area was easily the size of his entire cabin.

A flash hit.

Home.

Dropping to the sofa he'd walked past on the way to his room, he closed his eyes. Clinging to the image. With all his might, he tried to hold on, but it slid away, leaving emptiness as though that's all there had ever been.

But he'd seen something in his mind's eye. He remembered having the memory.

Bruce and Lorraine, the female bodyguard assigned to Shelby, were plugging in electronics at the conference table, their noise bringing him back when he didn't want to be there.

His cabin. Not big.

Hand on his forehead, he pushed.

Come on, damn it.

And...there... Another flash.

He took a mental picture that time.

Brown corduroy couch. Ceramic-tile floors.

Tile didn't burn like wood did.

The cabin had had solid wood floors when he'd purchased it...

When had that been?

He pushed. Looked.

And saw gray again.

"Is your head hurting?" Shelby's voice was close. Jerking his hand down from his head and opening his eyes, Luke saw her standing, still in the shorts and tank top she'd had on when she showed up in his hospital room that morning, just a couple of feet away.

Her frown of concern, while kind, left him feeling

weak. Not in any good sense. Weak as in helpless. Not strong.

A bit warmed, too, and not in a bad way. Which was bad.

Glancing over at the bodyguards and an IT expert, who'd be working from the suite, setting up across the huge room, he kept his voice low.

"No," he told her, sitting back with a sigh of resignation. His condition, the memory block that was taking his life from him, was absolutely no fault of hers.

"The gash, the stitches…" She was keeping their conversation between the two of them, too. A small thing to notice. And not of any import. Except that when you were drawing mostly blanks, small things could take up a lot of space.

And look bigger.

"It felt like my head was going to bust open the first day or so," he admitted.

He hadn't actually seen the back of his head but knew that some of his hair had been shaved for the fifteen stitches that were due to come out in another three days. Bruce had received instruction on wound care, but Shelby had been standing by at the time and would have heard it all, too.

"I don't even notice the stitches," he told her. "Until I'm lying on them. That's not pleasant and something I try to avoid." Small talk. He wasn't good at it. Not a memory—just something he seemed to know. "I need one of those cushions with a hole in the middle for my head at night," he said, making matters worse. The only such cushion coming to mind was one used for sitting after hemorrhoid surgery.

He was trying to make light of the untenable situation he'd unknowingly pulled this woman into. Had to get to work—to do, not just sit—and find a way to solve the problem.

She wasn't smiling. And he noticed the tablet she held in her hand and glanced at it pointedly. She said, "I was just coming out to show you this."

She handed him the ten-inch white device.

He read, growing colder with each word. A daily online report for a small-town police department said that police had been called by a neighbor to a home on Willoughby Lake at noon on a Sunday dated not quite four years before. The private rental vacation residence had been the site of a weekend party and was trashed. The person who'd rented the home and thrown the party was Luke Dennison. Mr. Dennison had made full and immediate restitution, and no charges were filed.

"I have no memory of this." He said the words like they held some weight. Like the fact that he didn't remember actually held credibility. But...

"I know my cabin has tile floors because wood burns too easily," he told her, handing back the tablet, as if that somehow mattered. "And that I'm not good at small talk. I'm gaining back a sense of who I am, and this doesn't compute. At all."

He heard himself trying to convince her, trying to gain credibility for his words, and from the outside in, he even failed to convince himself.

"You should share that information with the team," he said then.

"I already did."

Right, of course she had. Sent his information to strangers before giving him a heads-up. He was looking to get his life back and be alive to live it. She just wanted safely out of there.

And then it occurred to him... They'd just arrived at the suite. The tablet was brand new. As were the clothes and incidentals that had been waiting in their individual rooms for them. How had she happened to access that small snippet from years ago so quickly? And had already had time to pass it on?

Concerned now for their safety, he asked, "You aren't accessing any of your professional investigative databases, are you? Depending on how good this guy is, he could already have a trace on your personal log-ins." More particularly, if their mole was in the police department.

Hugging her tablet to her, she shook her head. "I'd already sent the file to Sierra's Web from the hospital."

And the firm was somehow routing things over a series of networks to a room several floors down and then using a private mobile network within the firm to transfer information back and forth from their suite upstairs. He was an emergency guy, not a techie.

But...

"You already sent the file?"

She nodded.

"You just happened to find a completely innocuous police report overnight?" And what else might she have found to turn her against him further?

All activities of which he knew nothing and so could therefore not only not defend himself but couldn't anticipate, either.

No way to prepare himself.

And why in the hell, with all that he was facing, did he give a damn what she thought about him?

He needed her safe.

And then they'd go their separate ways.

She hadn't answered him. Glancing up at her, he was

surprised to see Shelby looking somewhat uncomfortable. As though she'd actually done something less than perfect. For once.

"I didn't mean just the police file," she told him. And then stood there in front of him, still holding her tablet with both arms to her stomach, and admitted, "After you were…rude to me… I'd already written the article, had been writing it over a course of a few days' worth of interviews, and before I saw who you really were, I'd sold the article and had turned it in. I'd already queried the publication, and they'd agreed to buy it if they liked the finished product."

What her dissertation had to do with the police file, he had no idea, but he found himself listening like a dehydrated man crawling toward a pond.

Significant pieces fell into line in his head. The interview had taken place over a few days. They'd met more than once.

He hadn't done whatever he'd done until later.

How much later?

"Anyway, after…everything…I started to worry that the article was going to hurt my professional reputation because I'd originally seen you as a really good guy, and I depicted you that way…"

He'd read the article earlier that day. Though he hadn't remembered anything included therein, he'd felt as though he aligned with it.

Had been holding on to hope that the man she'd seen, the man about whom she'd written so eloquently, was who he really was.

But he also wasn't perfect, and he'd somehow managed to offend her. He did tend to say things up front to get right to the point.

In his line of business, there wasn't time for nuance.

Most often, his mind was busy assessing. People, danger, weather, wind strength and direction, height of blaze, natural accelerants, distance to communities, in which directions, predictions of speed of blaze travel, crews, personalities, needs…

The information was just there. Pouring through him. He let it settle over him. *In* him.

And was surprised at first when she said, "So I did periodic searches, intending to fix what I'd written earlier if need be. I couldn't have my article be something that was used to make you look better than you were to cover up who you were."

Just that fast, he was back with her. Right smack in the middle of his private hell. He knew, without remembering a damned thing, that he'd rather be out fighting a Level 5 fire than be sitting in that suite right then.

Level 5. The highest level of wildfire.

He was coming back. Just as the doctor had predicted. But how in the hell could he speed up this process? Get what he needed rather than bits and pieces that didn't help at all? Tile floor wasn't going to find a potential killer.

"And you kept a file of everything you found," he said, finally catching up with her.

She nodded.

"I'd like to see it."

Lifting her tablet, she tapped and slid her finger along the screen and then turned it to him.

As badly as Luke needed to see what she'd collected, he dreaded looking just as much. Chances were good—based on Shelby's continued and obvious low opinion of him—he wasn't going to like what he saw.

She'd intended to give him the tablet and head back to her room. To let the various professionals do all their digging and pray that they solved the case that day. To be available for any and all conversation pursuant to her.

To try to clear her mind and find a way to be objective about Luke Dennison. Because even when they caught whoever was trying to kill him—and her, too, apparently, for identifying him—she still had a real dilemma staring her in the face.

The questions consuming her.

Could the man be a good father to her son?

To his son?

But before she'd turned to head back to her room, Luke said, "Would you mind staying?"

Yeah. She was looking for a polite way to express the response when he added, "Sit, please? Whatever is in this file, you have background on. A frame of reference as to where something took place or what other events were going on at the time, things I won't have."

His request was fair. The research was hers. She knew how she'd come about every piece of information.

And the man had no memory.

Helping him rediscover his past might help him remember…everything.

And he could try and explain to her why he'd done what he'd done. Depending on that answer, she could start making better decisions of her own.

He'd only been reading a minute or two when something else occurred to her.

"Don't you find it odd that someone tried to kill me after I'd already identified you? It wasn't like if I were dead, authorities would suddenly forget who you were. Once they had your name, the rest would be kind of by the book."

She'd been wondering the same since the night before…peripherally. Mostly, she'd been rattled by her near-death experience and afraid that someone would try again.

That Carter would be hurt.

"From what Johnson said, it's possible someone thought my identity would still be in question for some reason. Or thought that authorities wouldn't be able to identify me conclusively and would need to rely on you in case of a battle for my estate."

Johnson hadn't bothered sharing that tidbit with her.

"I don't have fingerprints on file in the system," Luke said. "No family."

"So who gets your estate?"

He shrugged. "No one has found a will on file for me. Gerard, my personal banker, isn't aware of one. Or aware of any bills paid to an estate attorney."

For all Shelby knew, there could be an ex-wife in the picture. She hadn't gone as far as keeping track of marriage and divorce records. His choice to take a partner didn't reflect poorly on what she'd written. And as far as Carter went...

Maybe she hadn't wanted to know.

Maybe he had other children.

Her stomach tightened. Children who knew him as a father, while Carter cried because he didn't have one?

"Think about it," he said. "Everyone who's confirmed my existence is just doing so based on your confirmation and then showing my driver's license photo from that identification to others. For all we really know, I'm not Luke Dennison. Maybe I'm just someone who looks a lot like him."

He sounded so lost...so powerless...her heart lurched. The man she'd known, even in creep mode, exuded strength. Confidence.

She'd just been starting out, and his high levels of energy had spilled over to her, giving her confidence in herself. That man had believed there was nothing he couldn't do to save a life.

And had run into fires over and over again, willing to die trying to save them.

"Dorian, the Sierra's Web medical expert, will have medical records soon."

"Unless I've got some artificial joint with a serial number on it or a scar I don't see that proves some surgery, the only things those records are going to do in terms of proving identity is confirm my picture or social security number, which is what she's using to access them."

True. She knew that. Just...

Wasn't thinking as clearly as she needed to be.

Mostly was thinking that she had a way to prove his identity with a simple DNA test—Luke's compared to her son's.

Unless something happened to suddenly question the validity of his identity, she was absolutely not going to offer that source.

No one was questioning who he was except for Luke.

Because he was playing without a memory bank. She sympathized. But no way was she going to sacrifice her son just to give Luke Dennison peace of mind.

As much as her heart yearned to help him.

Chapter 5

The second he got up off the couch, Luke called Bruce into his room and asked him to get an urgent message to someone to get up to his supposed cabin in Payson and find out what kind of floors it had.

His lack of memory was making him vulnerable to everyone.

And he had a killer after him.

The next thing he did was look through the flash drive of financials Johnson had brought him, going specifically to the date on the police report Shelby had shown him.

And there it was. A large, stupidly wasteful payment to a private vacation-rental broker.

He didn't feel like a partier. He felt like the guy who'd rather live in a cabin in Payson than have a place in Phoenix. Or any other big city.

But what did he know?

There'd been other things in the file Shelby had given

him. Fires he'd fought, lots and lots of them. As though she'd been gathering information to support her article, too, in case there was future backlash based on his lesser self. Not just looking for reasons to possibly write an addendum to her article, acknowledging that while he did some heroic acts, she didn't support his other life choices. Because that's where she'd really been going with all that.

But the worst thing she'd found...

He'd read it once. Had almost lost the contents of his stomach. A report of disturbance in a hotel room. Loud noise. Possibly someone hurt.

The police had been called, but it turned out to be a happy threesome, role-playing. While there'd been alcohol present, no one was drunk. And all had acted responsibly when speaking with members of the hotel staff. There'd been no damage to the hotel, and the threesome chose to leave then and there, of their own accord.

Nothing illegal about it.

He wasn't even sure how Shelby had managed to get hold of that report. Didn't seem like something that would show up on a public police activity log, but the "how" of the situation hardly mattered. She was a damned good investigative reporter. Fine. He got that.

But the rest of it...

If someone asked him right then, right there, if he'd ever even thought about taking part in a threesome, he'd have adamantly denied it. He liked his women focused solely on him and liked to focus solely on them as well.

As in, one at a time.

Not as in, one woman—the only woman—all the time.

Or he thought he did. Apparently not.

So was anything that was coming to him real? The doctor had said his memory could come back in flashes or all at once. The fire-assessment flashback he'd had earlier…he'd known…could feel himself running through the mental process… That had to have been real, right?

Unless he had a strangely vivid imagination, and the things that had come to him weren't legitimate parts of the process?

He went for his new tablet to look up training for the forestry technician hotshot crew and…

Had no internet access. Of course.

Sticking his head out the door, he made another request to the team at the dining table and had the information on his screen within minutes.

He perused information that was like taking a shower; it was that much a part of him. He'd taught the stuff…

Oh.

He'd been an instructor, too?

Please let that one be real.

Leaving his room, he strode across the space to Shelby's, knocked briefly and opened the door, intent on his mission—and realized, too late, that he should have waited for a "come in," as he read her shocked expression.

She was fully dressed, if you called shorts that showed off those gorgeous legs and a tank top that showed him more shape than it concealed fully dressed. She was sitting at the table for two just down from her dresser, in the corner of her room opposite the couch and coffee-table conversation area. The room was identical to his. He knew its layout.

But concentrating on such inane details reeled in the thoughts he most definitely should not have been having. That moment was critically not the time to get his libido back.

Or to be sexually aware of a woman who kept a report about his threesome and his partying, and who already apparently had personal reasons to disrespect him.

"I apologize," he said, bowing his head. Then: "May I come in?"

"Yeah."

Breathing relief at her non-defensive tone, he stepped just inside the door.

"I just had a memory of teaching a hotshot class. Am I an instructor? It didn't say so in the article you wrote, and I didn't see anything about it in the follow-up collection." Thinking of the threesome—horrified that she knew that about him—he stood there looking for some kind of redemption.

Not wholly for the man he'd been; there was good there. But for some of the things that man had done.

Not that teaching made up for being offensive.

Or offending Shelby Harrington, at any rate.

"I don't know," she said, giving him the dissatisfying answer. "You didn't mention it during our talks. And nothing about it came up in article searches."

She'd been searching the internet for dirt on him.

Whatever he'd done had stuck with her. Didn't bode well for him finding out whether he could live with it.

He needed to go. Had obtained the answer for which he'd come.

She wasn't asking him to leave. Instead, she was looking at him like she expected more conversation.

Or needed more from him?

She could join the club on that one, getting in line behind him. Once he had his answers, he'd give her absolutely everything he had.

She'd risked whatever ill he'd done to her—something bad enough to solidify her decision to be off men for life—to come identify him.

Really, that was all he needed to know about her.

But he wanted more. So much more.

He was looking at her. She was looking right back. Someone had to say something. Or he had to go.

"How did you find out about the threesome?" The words fell out. He cringed. And felt as though he'd done so countless times before. He wanted to know what she'd accessed for information that wouldn't have been in an article. And the last thing he wanted on her mind was that damned hotel fiasco.

"Police records are public in Arizona."

She'd gone that far. She hadn't just happened on the party-house police log through an internet search. Whatever he'd done had made her fear he'd be in trouble with the law?

Wishing he didn't feel so drawn to her that he didn't want to stay and talk, he pulled the door closed.

Praying that his acute attraction to her had only to do with the fact that she was the one person around who could give him personal insights into the life he didn't remember.

"Luke?" Shelby called out to the closed door more loudly than she meant. She'd been looking for a way to tell him what she'd just found. Feeling like she needed to talk it over with him, as next of kin, before saying anything to anyone else.

As a courtesy—nothing more.

"Yeah?" The door opened immediately and there he was, attentive and all hers.

For the moment, she reminded herself.

One of the things she remembered most about Luke Dennison was the mesmerizing way he could make a woman feel like she was the only person in the world he wanted to be with. She'd been younger then. Still falling for stupid—her own brand of stupid, that is.

She'd seen what she'd wanted to see. Or rather, hadn't seen what she hadn't wanted to see.

Because while she'd been what he wanted, and he'd been all in with her the one night they'd spent together, he'd made it very clear afterward that she was nothing at all in his life after that night.

He'd told her—in the interview, when he'd talked about his unmarried status—she just hadn't listened.

"You did just call out to me, didn't you?" he asked then, frowning, and looked as though he might retreat.

"I did." They had to find a way to be together without tripping over every word. Just while they were sharing bodyguards, at the very least. She nodded toward the other chair at the table where she sat.

And warmed inside when he took the chair as though he owned it. Another thing that had drawn her to the man: the way he owned his space.

Even without conscious memory of who he was, he walked with confidence. As though he was certain he could handle whatever came next.

She wasn't so sure.

"I've been doing some research of my own," she said, hearing words spill out much more haphazardly than she'd heard them in her head. "I know you've hired the best, and I'm not purporting to be anywhere near their standards. It's just that…I look for the story behind the story, within the story—the story that no one else sees in a situation… That's my brand…and…"

She was pretty sure he didn't give a damn about her digital publishing brand.

"I started thinking about everything that's happened, and one thing that came up a couple of times was your father's car accident."

His brows raised in clear surprise. Like he'd been preparing himself to hear something else entirely.

Because heretofore, in his memory of knowing her, she'd been nothing but the bearer of bad news. Once she'd gotten past the part of giving him back his identity.

"I've been following you for so long. You were my first big story, and your father dying... Something about it just spoke to me. So last night, I asked Johnson to send me the police report for the accident, which he did. I just opened it a little bit ago."

His jaw clenched. She knew that meant he was emotionally moved. Hated that she still seemed to remember every nuance about the man. And then, keeping her gaze away from him—as though she could shield herself from his reaction—she said, "I'm not sure it was an accident. Actually, I'm fairly certain it wasn't."

She turned her tablet around, showing him the report.

"I've purposely stayed away from looking up the accident," he told her, drawing in her gaze despite her decision to remain distanced. "I wanted to wait until I remembered my father before reading about his death."

So he wasn't going to look?

He didn't have to. She was ready to show her findings to the team out in the dining room and let them either investigate for themselves or get the information to Johnson.

After looking her in the eye for what seemed like forever, Luke lowered his gaze to the tablet.

And then, eyes wide, stared at her again. This time with the intensity she'd noticed in the past. "The accident was put down to a faulty tire."

Yep. He'd seen the same thing she had. Circumstances of the two crashes were different, of course. There was another car involved with his father's.

Her theory might be wrong.

"This can't be a coincidence," Luke said.

Which gave her the impetus to tell him what else she was thinking. "They haven't found the delivery vehicle I saw in my rearview mirror, but if this is some version of the same stunt—and it might not be, with the fact that your father hit the other car... But if it's the same, we know the car and the owner of that one."

"We might have our first real lead to the killer," Luke said, standing and heading toward the door with her tablet.

Just like that.

He'd been with her, and then—taking her possession with him without even acknowledging her presence or participation in the situation—he was gone.

He'd wanted to hug her. Luke couldn't believe the temptation he'd felt. Overwhelming to the point of not recognizing himself.

And he caught the irony in that thought with absolutely no sense of humor.

It had to be that he was identifying so strongly with her because she'd identified him. Because she'd known him. He kept telling himself, reassuring himself. But as Sierra's Web investigators got to work on his father's car accident, partnering with Johnson, he holed himself up in his room, where he wouldn't chance a run-in with the far-too-sexy reporter.

He spent the time poring over hundreds of pages of his own financials, hoping that something would spark a memory and, in the meantime, learning more about his life.

Still on his first pass through it all, continuing where he'd left off the day before—when he'd been interrupted with the news of Shelby's accident—he was only skimming accounts, payees, amounts, looking for anything that jumped out at him, but he intended to go back and check the items line by line. It wasn't like he had anything else to do.

And he had to keep his thoughts focused so they didn't slide back over to Shelby. If he just knew what he'd done to offend her, maybe then he could get past her.

He wanted to think so.

There was a knock on his door, and his head jerked guiltily toward the sound. As though just thoughts of her had conjured her up.

Having her in his room, her scent lingering behind, wasn't a good idea. Whatever they had to discuss could happen in the living room, he determined as he strode over and pulled open the door.

Bruce stood there, with the rest of the Sierra's Web team behind him, still seated at the table. But all five experts were watching him intently.

Like he was a donkey getting its tail pinned again and again.

"What?"

Was he some kind of criminal? Going to be arrested in moments?

Hudson Warner spoke. "We just heard from the off-duty officer we hired to drive up and check out what type of floor you had in your cabin."

Okay, so they all thought he was making less-than-stellar choices by paying to have someone drive an hour and a half to look at his floor. He'd apparently done much worse.

"Was it tile?" he asked, needing a nod in the worst way. Needing to trust the little bits and pieces that were coming to him.

"The place burned down, Luke," Bruce said, his tone man-to-man but with a definite hint of compassion, too.

He suddenly understood all the looks.

He didn't want anyone's damned sympathy.

But...

Come again?

He had no idea what he'd lost...

He finally found a way to inject himself back into the conversation. "When?"

"The day you were found in the desert."

Feeling the blood drain from his face, he stepped out into the great room. Sat in one of the three vacant chairs at the table. Next to Hudson Warner, the IT partner at the firm, who was also running the team of experts on his case.

"I don't get it. The same day?" he asked the table in general.

"The fire in Payson was set after the desert fire," Hudson told him. "The authorities in Payson tried to reach you, but your phone just went to voice mail."

"This guy doesn't just want me dead—he wants all traces of me to disappear." Even for a man with no past to lose, the thought was too much to comprehend.

What atrocious thing had he done to make someone hate him that much?

With no answers, he homed in on the first question he'd had.

"Was the floor tile?" So it wouldn't burn. No humor there, either.

"It was," Bruce said.

And Luke almost wept.

Chapter 6

With her door open, Shelby could hear the drone of conversation taking place at the conference table in the suite's large living area.

Other than their bodyguards, the rest of the Sierra's Web team were only there for the day. They'd each be returning to their homes, or the firm's headquarters, or wherever else they did their actual work after this initial first meeting.

Which would, feasibly, leave her time to be alone with Luke. Time to talk to him, to try to figure out her own next moves. Once the killer was caught.

She'd thought she would have to wait until he had his memory back, could explain his earlier actions to her, but maybe she was missing the opportunity she had right in front of her. Wouldn't his current state more likely reveal the real man inside Luke Dennison, the motives and heart that drove him, more clearly than when those same traits were muddied with memories and outside perceptions?

After Luke left with her tablet, she'd gone through and put away the new clothes and essentials that were waiting in her bedroom when she first arrived at the suite. Without her tablet, she had little else to do.

The trauma of the accident the morning before—the soreness, meeting with Johnson, driving to Tucson, sitting up and watching her son sleep, the early-morning drive back, and then being whisked off to protective custody—had caught up to her. Closing her door, she tried to use the time to rest, dozed on and off for a bit, but eventually gave up.

Watching television didn't appeal.

Starting to feel trapped, she opened her door again.

She wasn't going to be able to handle too much of the current situation. There were three changes of clothes in the shopping bags she'd emptied. Three days of being cooped up in a room?

As opposed to, say…being dead?

Luke's voice joined the conversation, and she was envious. Because he had something to do other than sit?

Because the Sierra's Web team got to spend time with him?

Had the accident rattled her brain more than anyone had thought?

The conversation outside her room seemed to get a bit louder all of a sudden, and she tensed.

Had they found something?

More bad news about Luke's past?

Something current?

When she heard the word *fire*, she stood, went to the door. She was just walking out when she caught the tail end of Hudson, the team leader, saying, "The cabin fire is clearly a sign that someone wants all evidence of Luke gone. Why? We need to know *why* to better find out *who*."

What cabin fire?

When?

Luke's back was to her. No one else seemed to care that she'd ventured out, and she sat on the couch, listening to the ensuing discussion.

"What if I had something stored there?" Luke's distinctive voice reached her. "Some kind of evidence of something?"

"Or some contraband," the investigator, Will, said.

Shelby's heart lurched. Painfully.

Wait.

Cabin.

Luke's home was a cabin.

Oh, God. Had the man's entire life burned down without him even knowing what he'd lost?

Tears filled her eyes. She quickly blinked them away, feeling ridiculous and young and not at all herself.

Yeah, the man was in a horrible situation at this moment, and he'd made some pretty horrendous choices in life, too.

But criminal ones?

Why else would someone attempt to kill him and then burn down his home?

"Maybe to make certain that no will could be found."

She said the words aloud, turning her head to look toward the table. All eyes were trained on her.

"What if someone believes he or she is an heir to Luke's estate?" She'd asked him earlier about a will. Not because she wanted anything for her son. At all.

But maybe someone else did.

Another "her" out there. Someone else he'd impregnated and shut the door on...

She'd been burning up for a second there as she considered telling the team the truth about herself, telling them about Carter. She needed them all to turn back around. To leave her alone.

They'd have to put her on the suspect list.

She should have kept her mouth shut.

Always the nosy one, feeling around for what's not being said in a situation.

Except she wouldn't have tried to kill herself.

As conversation started up again beside her and she started to breathe once more, Shelby realized that there was no way anyone would think she'd identify Luke and try to kill herself if she wanted him dead.

And beyond that, she had no reason to tell a soul about Carter. No one, absolutely no one, knew that Carter was Luke's son except herself.

And Luke, if he'd chosen to store that in the memory bank that was yet to open.

Not her doctor, not her mother, not one single person knew who'd fathered her son. Which meant Carter being Luke's son couldn't possibly be an issue in the case.

But…if he'd denied her pregnancy, Luke could most certainly have done the same to someone else.

"She has a point," Hudson was saying. "We got nothing on a marriage- or divorce-record check, but we need to get to someone on his team and have someone up in Payson ask around, find out who Luke's seen in the past ten years, if you can get back that far. Check birth records for Arizona and California, see if his name pops up…"

She turned toward the sound of Hudson's voice, saw the back of his head; then she saw Luke stand, his back ramrod straight, and leave the table.

He couldn't refute the theory that he'd fathered children who could legally attach to his estate if he were gone.

Though he didn't know it, she could give proof to the validity of that very real possibility.

* * *

Unless someone died because of him, Luke was pretty sure the day couldn't get any worse. It was horrifying enough to wake up without a life—but to doubt whether or not you ever wanted it back, to fear what you were going to hear about yourself next, was worse.

The fact that Shelby Harrington was present to hear it all, that the reporter who'd spent a whole bunch of time researching his life was actually coming up with viable theories about who could be after them, was horrifying him.

For no good reason.

What did he care what she thought about him?

She'd identified him. He wasn't even sure anymore if that had been a favor or a curse—and yet he yearned for her good opinion.

When had he ever cared what someone thought about him?

Other than his parents and himself, of course.

Oh.

Something new.

He'd cared what his parents thought of him.

Which meant…he must have grieved his father's death. And maybe the incredible sadness and untenable weight of responsibility he'd been experiencing in waves since finding out his father's accident looked suspicious were borne out of emotional memory.

Starting with the watch. He'd put it on as soon as it was given back to him at the hospital. There was nothing fancy about it. It did nothing but tell time, and not even digitally—but at the moment, it was worth more than gold to him.

His bond with his father had mattered to him.

That piece of information, he'd take.

And be grateful for.

To know that he'd cared deeply for someone other than himself…

He'd been back in his room, desperately searching for himself in his spending habits for about an hour when Hudson knocked on his door, asked him back to the table.

He looked for Shelby first as he exited his space, saw her on the couch, pursuing something on the tablet Hudson must have returned to her. Only one night had passed since she'd identified him, and yet he felt drawn to her as though he'd known her for years.

He *had* known her for years.

And wanted to know her a whole lot better. In very detailed ways a decent man wouldn't think about a woman who'd never given him a signal that she shared his desire.

Who'd never told him yes to a request for…

"We've got something you need to know about," Hudson started in, and Luke's gut sank even lower. He'd already seen those looks around the table too many times that day.

He sat in his chair next to Hudson, determined to take it on—whatever *it* was.

Amazing, really, that one guy could have so many possibilities for people wanting him dead and still be alive.

Should he count himself lucky?

"There's this charity account," Hudson said, and Luke glanced across the table to Jeremy, the finance professional handpicked by the firm's financial expert, Winchester.

"I know. I've seen the regular deposits to it," Luke said, glad to have a reason for some enthusiasm in his tone for once. He'd been called to the table for good news after all.

Glad, then, that Shelby was listening behind him, he

continued, "Bodell Charitable Society. More than ten percent of my income goes there."

The 10 percent was significant. Somewhere in his brain, he had the idea that 10 percent was a decent charitable contribution.

He did good stuff.

A lot of it.

There was proof.

Jeremy's nod did not contain any sort of matching enthusiasm. And when Luke glanced at Hudson beside him, the team lead's expression was equally grim.

"The Bodell fire is..."

"I know it," he interrupted. When all eyes he could see grew wide, he shook his head. And heard movement behind him.

"It's how I first met Luke," Shelby said, taking an empty seat directly across from him. She was there for her own safety but also as someone who knew him personally and who knew a lot about him prior to the day before.

"I read the article she wrote about my part in that fire," Luke finished, holding Shelby's gaze.

Regardless of what she might think, and what he might wish he thought, he was extremely glad she was there.

Beyond just being grateful.

Strangely enough, considering her low opinion of him, Shelby's presence gave him the one brief light of hope he could see at the moment.

"I looked up any and all charities associated with the fire," Jeremy said then, drawing Luke's gaze and attention back to what was really happening around him. "I was hoping to find someone who knew you, thinking you give them so much money that maybe you do more, make appearances at fundraisers or something..."

Yeah. Good. He'd like it if he'd done that.

"Turns out, Bodell Charitable Society is not a charity that provides any monies to any known fund or program assisting with anything to do with the aftermath of the Bodell fire. No family members who lost hotshot firefighters that day have ever heard of it. None of the rebuilding funds have ever heard of it…"

He got the idea. "What's that mean?" he asked, getting to the point and focusing only on the man with the information at the moment.

"It means it made me suspicious enough to ask our finance partner to dig deeper, and he found out that there is no such registered charity in the United States—not national, not state. In fact, the Bodell Charitable Society is the name of a shell company attached to an asset that is housed in the Cayman Islands."

Good God.

Just when he'd thought it couldn't get any worse.

What in the hell had he done?

"What am I involved in?" he asked, pretty sure he'd reached the lowest point in his life. Wondering why he'd fought hard enough to survive to get back to face this moment.

Jeremy's shrug was almost too much. Luke sat there, every muscle and nerve clenched, and waited for the moment to pass.

Hudson took over. "Winchester has been in touch with Gerard."

His personal banker. Good.

"The first concern—to a finance mind, anyway—was whether or not you'd be charged with tax fraud," the man continued. "I guess fake charities are a means to avoid paying income tax…"

Luke felt himself freeze, from the inside out.

"Pay whatever is owed. Now."

Hudson shook his head. "You didn't take the tax cut."

Luke's gaze shot over to Shelby then, the first time he'd looked her way since hearing the latest bad news on his record. Her expression changed as soon as she caught him looking... But for a second there, he'd seen warmth.

Compassion.

No sympathy. Just...like she understood what he was going through. Like she...knew.

Like he wasn't stranded out in the middle of nowhere, sinking in black turbulent waters, all alone.

Being alone in danger, getting out of it alone, was his thing.

No, wait. He had a team.

"According to Gerard, you opened the account shortly after the Marnell fire."

Shelby's gasp drew his attention back to her. He made a quick mental check through all he'd read and learned in the past thirty-some hours and remembered...the Marnell fire had happened right after she interviewed him.

And, he was presuming, right after he'd done whatever atrocious thing he'd done to her.

Please, God, knock me dead now if I laid a wrong hand on that woman. If I so much as tried to kiss those lips without permission...

She was no longer meeting his gaze.

He tuned back in to hear most of what Hudson was telling him. "...said you just gave him the account number, told him how much money to put into it, and when asked about using it for a charitable contribution, you told him to pay whatever taxes were called for."

"So how do we trace an account in the Cayman Islands?" Luke asked.

"That's just it. We can't. But Gerard said that this

month's automatic deposit was returned due to account closure."

"The account's been closed?"

Nods from the partners were all he saw.

"I closed it?" Had he hidden the money in his cabin? Had someone trashed the place, found it and then burned it down?

"Or someone you were involved with—someone who wants you dead, for instance—did so."

"So where's the money?"

No one had any answers to that one.

Chapter 7

The man who'd spent the majority of his time risking his life to save others was in agony. He sat alone in the suite's living area, at a room service table set for two, holding a fork and staring at the chicken fricassee he had yet to taste.

Shelby's own plate of Asian chicken salad in hand, she turned away from her bedroom door and made her way to the far-back corner of the room—in front of a window overlooking the Phoenix valley—and put her dish down on the white linen tablecloth.

The Sierra's Web team was dining together at the conference table; some working, some in quiet conversation. Once the experts left that night, she likely wouldn't see them again.

If they solved their case, she wouldn't have reason to see Luke again, either. Her son needed her to spend time with the man while she could. She'd already sent messages, via Lorraine, to her mother and heard back that

Carter was doing fine. And that they'd been assigned a bodyguard, a Charlie Dresden, as well.

That news was a big reason she was back at the table.

Luke was looking at her, watched her pull the metal lid off her plate, saying nothing.

"Thank you for arranging protection for my son."

He shook his head. "Wasn't my idea. The Sierra's Web team and Johnson were all concerned that it would be easy for the killer to find out about him and then use him to get to you."

Because of Luke.

It all came back to that. Every time.

Good and bad.

"All I did was pay for it, and that's a no-brainer," he said. He picked up his glass and finally took a sip of wine, followed by a bite of chicken.

He wasn't eating because of her, but it kind of felt like it, and she was gratified. Tried to tell herself it was for Carter's sake. That Luke having an emotional core that could be reached was a good thing. As long as Carter reached it.

Or something…

It just felt good sitting across the table from him again. Facing him. Feeling like he was glad she was there.

And it shouldn't.

Because she knew—with Luke, with any man who attracted her—where it would lead.

But *oh*. He'd been the one. Physically, for sure, but much more than that, too. For those few good days…

He was eating like he was really hungry but was also watching her over his glass as he sipped. And she knew that he had something to tell her even before he opened his mouth to speak to her.

"I've been remembering some things." Fork midair, he swallowed, his look was intent.

And it hooked her. Just as it had five years before.

As though they were speaking without words. They both were able to assess and see what others missed...

She couldn't fall back...

She couldn't turn away, either.

"Like what?" she asked. That his cabin had had tile floor, apparently.

More of the same?

"I feel like I've kissed you before."

Her fork slipped. She caught it before it banged against the china and set it down. Glanced across to the far end of the room, where the team was working and talking, engrossed in their own business.

Not watching Luke and Shelby.

A definite separation of employee and employer.

Or so it felt to her.

"I haven't told anyone else," he added, as though her glance across the room had denoted worry that others knew.

If only *he* knew.

Their kisses were the least of her worries where he was concerned. She needed him to remember past that.

To the money he'd paid her.

And the door he'd slammed in her face.

But...she didn't feel ready for that, either. She needed to know more about the man's personal life than the fact that he was a snake with women.

She needed to know if the Sierra's Web team's search had come up with other women, children, who'd want a part of him.

See how he reacted to them.

She licked her lips. Had a split-second thought about

a quickie while in isolation, no hearts involved, and gave herself a strong mental shake.

"I can do the math," he said then. While she'd been having a meltdown, he'd resumed his dinner.

Jerking as he delivered his statement, right as she'd been reaching for her wineglass, she'd have toppled the rose liquid if not for his fingers on the stem as well. Steadying her.

His warmth...

It was like they were naked again, and his hand was sliding over her stomach on its way to...

She stared at him.

The math?

What exactly had he remembered?

"I'm the last man. The one who tipped you over the edge. You're off men because of me," he said. "At least, I'm the solidifier in a stew that was already boiling," he added. "That means that whatever I did to offend you was on a personal man-to-woman level. And while I could theorize that you'd come on to me and I rudely turned you down—thus humiliating you, which would be offensive...that's not what happened, was it?"

She didn't break eye contact.

Or move any other muscle in her body, either. He was theorizing.

He didn't remember anything but a sense of having kissed her.

Pulling her wineglass free from his grasp, she lifted it to her lips. And an orneriness she didn't know she had pushed her to lick her lips once more when she lowered the goblet.

Not in a sexy come-on way.

She wouldn't be that bold.

But she was human enough to take a moment of satisfaction when she saw him glance at her lips. And then get back to his food.

Suddenly hungry herself, she dove into her own dinner with a lot more gusto. Enjoying the bursts of taste with every bite. Feeling more alive than she had all day.

"I remember the feeling of needing to kiss you."

She glanced up again. He was frowning.

Serious.

Not at all trying to give her a hard time.

Probably hadn't been since he'd started the conversation. She was the one who was all over the place. But then, she had a lot more ground to cover when traveling back over their past than he did.

"I wanted it. Intensely. In a way I'd never wanted another woman."

What in the hell was the man playing at? Anger spiked up in her, and she set her fork down in the middle of her plate, preparing to take it—and her wine—to her room, as originally planned.

She should have known better than to let any softer feelings she'd experienced toward Luke take center stage.

Even for a meal while he appeared to be struggling.

"Shelby."

The one word, the serious tone, gave her pause and brought her gaze up to his.

"Please don't go. I'm not trying to make you uncomfortable."

Her hands still on the sides of her plate, she sat there, staring at him. Hard. He was going to have to do better than that.

"I'm trying to let you know that whatever awful thing I did in the end, it didn't start out that way. You weren't just another woman to me."

God, she wanted to believe that.

So, so, so badly.

Even with the way it had ended, if she could at least know that the night her son was conceived had meant something special...

"Think about it," he said, leaning in as he spoke, his voice low and yet burning with energy, too. "What have I got to gain from you? You've already identified me. You're here, helping us find my killer... I already did whatever I did—you aren't going to forget it even if I never remember. And even I'm not jerk enough to hit on you under our current circumstances..."

Relaxing back in her seat, she let her hands drop to her lap as she held his gaze.

And then she nodded.

She had to.

It felt completely right.

As did the gift he'd just given her.

The week they'd shared that had resulted in her son... She hadn't imagined the power in it.

He'd had to tell her. It seemed wrong to walk around with the feelings these brief snatches of memory of her gave him, without her knowledge.

She'd feasibly been attracted to him at one point. Or else how could anything he'd done hurt her?

Unless he'd forced himself on her.

Not likely that she would have bothered to come forward to identify him without saying so, if that were the case.

He could have hit on her, though. And taken her rejection badly?

"This whole thing—you, me, the past you know and I don't—it's driving me nuts."

There. It was out.

Pressure eased in his chest.

Even as his gut clenched, ready for her to actually vacate the table that time. He'd managed to keep her with him once. And had to go and push harder.

Obviously, he was a danger-zone junkie.

"I'm not trying to be mean by withholding what happened," she said, surprising him with the warmth in her tone, the compassion he read in her gaze. "I just don't want to have you dreaming up possible reasons to justify your actions before you actually remember the real ones."

Made sense. Though why any justification mattered to her at this point, he didn't know. Still, he owed her... over and over.

"But I also know that you're struggling to know if what's occurring to you is real or just imagination... And I know how desperate you are to have signs that you're getting your memory back and to be able to trust what you're getting..."

Something inside rejected her hitting him so on target. "You got all that from me saying I feel like we kissed?"

"No, I got it from your reaction to finding out that you had tile floors in your cabin."

Oh.

Right.

He eyed her with what felt like new respect—admiration, even. She could see what others overlooked...

Did he know that now? Or from back then?

Was that why he'd done the interview with her?

Wanting to be interviewed didn't really seem like him.

"We did kiss," she told him then.

And he had to ask, "Did I force it in any way?" And held his breath.

"No."

His sigh was so loud he was sure it could be heard

across the room. No one looked over, so it probably hadn't been that loud, but...

"Thank God."

She was watching him, assessing him.

He smiled.

She smiled back.

And he wanted to kiss her again. Right then. Right there.

Strangely enough, he was pretty sure she wanted it, too.

"More wine?" he asked, lifting the bottle from the iced decanter beside him, half expecting her to shake her head. Half thinking she should, too.

"Thank you." She held out her glass, no longer smiling or looking at him but...still there.

There was more between them. More she remembered and he didn't—besides his fall from grace. It sat there on the table between them. Lingered in the air they were breathing.

And thrummed through his body.

Was it beating in hers, too?

"You want to know if we did more than kiss," she said, glancing down, up at him, at her wineglass, back at him.

"I'd rather be prepared than suddenly be sitting at the conference table and be hit with an image of how gorgeous your breasts look naked in the moonlight."

Lightning crackled. Tingled his skin.

His damned mouth.

Eyes wide, horrified, he stared at her.

And she watched him.

As though waiting.

"That was a memory, wasn't it?" he asked. "I told you your breasts look gorgeous in the moonlight."

Lips pursed—in a jut, not a sexual tease—she nodded.

"They were naked at the time." *God, bring that visual back to me.*

No. Don't. It would be torture.

But what sweet torture…

"Yes."

"You've seen me that way as well."

"Yes."

Had he been as hard as he was growing right there in that chair, his lack of restraint free for her to see rather than as it was now, hidden by the table and its expensive cloth covering?

"Was it good?"

What in the hell was he doing?

More importantly, why was he doing it? He didn't feel like fun and games. Or a night of casual sexual innuendo.

Truth was, he didn't feel like casual anything with her.

She didn't blush. Flinch. Or smile, either.

"For me, it was." She could have been talking about a movie she'd watched or a song she'd heard, for all the emotion in her response.

Something had gone wrong.

They'd already established she wasn't going to tell him what.

But… "I told you it wasn't good for me?"

Being blunt, that sounded like him. But not enjoying sex with her? No way in hell could he see that one. Not with the way he was feeling, without a single memory of the act to spur him on.

"No."

"Then why did you say it like that?"

"I can only speak for myself." She leaned forward. "I'm not going to feed you my impression of what you felt," she said. "Nor am I going to repeat what you said.

Either of which could taint your perception of what really happened."

Damn.

She was right.

Didn't make him any less frustrated.

"I'm guessing this isn't what you want—me sitting here, having flashes of intimate memory, with more back there, waiting in line to show itself to me."

She shrugged.

"I keep trying to distract myself from the feelings… They're not making it easy."

"You want me to stay in my room?"

If he thought it would help…

"I'm getting them while alone in my room, too, not just out here with you…"

Her chin jutted that time as she nodded. And took a rather large swallow of wine. Maybe he should snag another bottle from the refrigerator behind the wet bar.

But…considering that alcohol had a tendency to enhance libido…maybe not.

"Look, don't worry about me," she told him, meeting his gaze, but the intensity he'd read earlier was gone.

Banked, at least.

Well banked.

Before he could come up with a response to that, she continued, "The second I chose to make those memories with you, I was giving up any right I had to keep them from you…"

Sitting back, Luke stared at her, impressed all over again.

The woman had a way of looking at life, at the world, that cut right to the quick of the matter.

As his words had a tendency to do.

"So that just leaves me with one more question on the

subject," he said. One question he was willing to ask, at any rate.

"What's that?"

"Do you want to know?"

"Know what? The question?"

"Do you want to know what I remember, when I remember?"

She blinked. Sipped.

Took a deep breath.

Studied him.

And said, "Yes."

Chapter 8

She had to know. Which meant she wanted to know.

But oh, she so did not want to know that Luke was having flashes of her bare breasts. When she thought about the other things they'd done that incredible night they'd spent together...

They were painful enough, arousing enough, as distant memory. But for him, they'd be brand new.

In the moment.

And without her step back of pain to unsweeten them. He hadn't been hurt. Humiliated. Devastated.

He'd been the hurter. Not the hurtee.

Things had ended at his bidding. Just as he'd wanted them to.

As she relived those moments with him, she had to remember all of it. Not just how it had begun but also how it had ended.

She had to keep her mind on her own course.

They'd finished dinner, but neither left the table. They sipped their wine. She couldn't say why he didn't walk away.

"Have you remembered a lot of things today?" she asked. She knew about the tile. And now her breasts. How much more was there? At what rate were things coming back to him?

Not that one day was anything to go by. He could wake in the morning with full memory.

Or never get it all back, though doctors had thought that unlikely.

When he shrugged, there she was, noticing the shoulders again. Reacting to the timbre in his voice. "I'm getting things constantly, I think, but mostly impressions of things I know or who I am."

"Who you are?" That's all she needed. *Just tell me who you really are.*

Or which part of you is most dominant.

In her father, the untrustworthy philanderer had been a fifty-fifty thing. If he had shown up as he'd said he would, he would have been the perfect dad.

And if he wasn't in hot pursuit of some new woman, he'd almost always shown up.

"I'm not good at conversational nuances."

"No. You were blunt. But from what I could determine, you're honest, and that matters more. At least someone knows where they stand with you."

In the moment. Problem is, you had no warning when the moment was going to change.

"I know what I know, and I think I expect others to listen and follow."

She almost smiled at that one. "True. But it's because you do know what you know. You're an expert in your field. And lives are saved when your orders are followed."

"What about in my personal life? Do I order people around?" His look intensified. "Did I order you around?"

"No." She had to give him that. "You were quite respectful." Until...

"You never tried to sway or direct my interview, or anything else about me," she continued, trying not to let her own prejudice interfere with the truth.

"And if we had differing views?" he prodded, giving her the suspicion that he was trying, in a roundabout way, to find out what he'd done wrong with her.

"You didn't try to change my mind. You just spoke your own truth and left it at that."

He studied her. Sipped his wine. And said, "For what it's worth, I'm sorry."

She could only shrug at that.

"You don't believe me."

"How can you be sorry for something you don't remember?"

"I'm sorry that I did something to hurt you."

Didn't matter.

"You don't believe me."

He wasn't working at full speed. "I believe the part of you you're in touch with right now means what you're saying. The rest of whatever lives inside you that prompts other reactions isn't here right now."

But he'd be back. As the Sierra's Web team pushed their dirty dishes to the end of the table and seemed to be convening, she glanced back at Luke. There was more she needed.

"Do you get the sense that you and your father were close?" He'd said he had a plethora of impressions. She needed them.

"Yeah. I know we were. I can't remember any specific conversations—or even, for sure, what he looked like—but I know I trusted him with my life. And stayed in touch with him. Crazy, huh? Why do I know that but couldn't tell you what he looked like?"

"Maybe you're remembering what matters most to you first?"

She froze as soon as those words were out of her mouth.

Was she implying that her naked breasts held one of the top honors?

She knew for a fact they hadn't. He'd paid for the use of them...

"Hold it!" The abrupt command came loudly from the other side of the room; Shelby's gaze jerked quickly in the direction from which it came.

Bruce stood, his moving glance taking in every person in the room. "Pack up, we're moving out," he said. "Now."

Before the words were even completed, Lorraine was by Shelby's side, ushering her to her room, while Bruce took charge of Luke. There was a brief sense of commotion as the Sierra's Web team gathered everything off the table, and then her door was shut and she and her bodyguard were closed off from the rest of the suite. Five minutes later, after dumping her brand-new possessions—other than the completely offline tablet she was holding—down a trash chute, Shelby kept her head lowered and let Lorraine lead her down a flight of stairs.

Heart thudding in her chest, she prayed that Luke was okay.

And that she would make it home to her son.

They'd had an exit plan from the time they arrived. Luke learned of it when Bruce told him to gather up everything in his room in preparation for trashing it. His bodyguard then led him up a flight of stairs reserved for staff, through a ceiling panel and down a ladder-like thing in the walls—built as a means to service the cargo elevator, he presumed.

He didn't ask.

They weren't talking.

He thrived on the physical exertion, was working with Bruce to determine their quickest route to the ground. If it hadn't been for the knowledge that Shelby was some-where near, possibly in life-threatening danger, he'd have been in his element.

Fighting the physical environment to save lives was his thing.

Fighting it to save his own life, while someone else remained in danger…was not.

He didn't breathe easy again until he exited into a basement, where he was hustled into the back of a differ-ent van—smaller, red instead of white—and saw Shelby already there.

Was that worry he'd seen in her eyes when the door opened? Followed by relief when she saw him?

He took the seat directly beside her, strapped him-self in as the van pulled up a ramp and out into the now-darkened night.

That morning, he'd been seated across from her. She'd never looked at him. Turning his head now, he expected to see her staring out the front window.

She was looking right at him.

And when she didn't turn away, Luke held on—his gaze and hers. Touching.

"The dessert tray had arrived outside our door. Bruce pulled up the feed on the hotel security camera for our floor and saw a glass of milk instead of a sealed carton, which had been established protocol. He put us in mo-tion then. Lorraine has since received confirmation—

because it all happened so swiftly and employees were still all on shift—that a member of the staff was paid a thousand dollars to switch out the carton for the glass. They're assuming the milk was laced with something but won't know until it goes through Forensics," he told her.

They'd been made. In less than twenty-four hours, in the middle of a huge city and buried in one of many mammoth luxury hotels. Whether the milk itself had been tainted or it was only a test, no one paid a thousand bucks to switch a glass for a carton just for kicks.

"Sierra's Web is good," Shelby said, still watching him.

"They're the best." He wanted to take her hands. They lay in her lap, her thumbs worrying back and forth across each other. "I'm doing everything in my power to keep you safe," he told her instead.

She nodded. "I know."

Everything in his power, and then he'd left her alone with someone who wasn't him, who might not have his extreme level of tolerance for danger when he was saving a life. Memory or no memory, that trek he'd just taken with Bruce—climbing through plumbing and hanging from rafters... He'd seen each step before the next.

Hadn't hesitated a single second.

Shelby deserved that level of dedication. Of adrenaline.

"You have a son waiting for your return," he told her. "I swear to you, I will be by your side, fighting whatever comes our way, until I can get you back to him."

The words were said in almost a whisper, and when he heard them, he figured they sounded almost laughable.

And yet...

She wasn't laughing.

Her eyes were moist as she stared at him.

A long time.

And then, with a tremulous smile, she nodded.

What was she doing?

Breaking eye contact with Luke, Shelby couldn't quite make herself move away from him. Or quit absorbing his energy.

He was right: he was the guy you wanted around when you were in danger.

And he'd just promised to get her home to Carter.

He'd put her son front and center.

Something a parent would do.

They ended up in a shack off a dirt road out in the middle of a barren desert—someplace up north, she guessed, based on the temperature gauge on the dash. It had dropped from a typical hundred-and-five to eighty-two degrees.

They approached with the headlights off. She and Luke were told to stay down when the vehicle stopped, which Luke did not do. She saw him keeping watch as Bruce jumped out, and then, minutes later, Lorraine gave the direction to head inside. Shaking, completely sure she didn't want to exit the van, Shelby climbed down as she was told, but she caught up to Luke before they'd even entered the place.

"I'm not staying here."

"It's just for the night," Bruce said from in front of them. "We're on a private ranch. The owner owed me one, and I'd already arranged this in the event we had to move quickly."

After shoving them inside, he left, closing the door behind him. She heard the van start up almost immediately and drive off.

"There's a bunker close by where he's hiding the van,"

Lorraine said, as though someone had asked. She'd already lowered the room-darkening shade in spite of the shutters that were down over the outside of the one window.

"You think someone followed us out here?" Shelby asked, shivering. Luke, looking focused, was busy opening every cupboard, checking under the one bed, then up, beneath the mattress, and on to the couch cushions across the small space. The plastic-topped table and two chairs were the only furniture he left untouched.

"It's our job to prepare for every eventuality," the female bodyguard said, standing at attention by the door. "We believed the hotel was secure…"

Right.

You never knew.

Hands on her shoulders, Shelby just stood there. Feeling useless. And afraid. Two things she'd promised herself, after Carter's birth, she'd never feel again.

She wasn't a prisoner. She was free to go.

To walk out, demand a ride back to the city, and take on any and all possibilities that whoever was after Luke, whoever had tried to kill her, was no longer interested in her.

To take him on by herself—if he did indeed still want her dead.

He *or* she… If some woman had been pushed too far and was after Luke's money to support the child he'd had with her…

"What can I do to help?" she asked.

And Luke, apparently satisfied with the furnishings, moved over to the table. "Come sit with me," he said.

"We've got a briefing for you as soon as Bruce gets back," Lorraine told them both. "He and I will be trading off sleeping on a cot out in a lean-to at the side of the shack, and standing guard tonight."

"You don't have to sleep outside," Shelby blurted out because… Well… It seemed… One bed…the couch… the small room…her…Luke.

"We're outside so that we're the first to know if we've been compromised," the bodyguard clarified. And pointed out the door Luke had already opened and shut, leading into a space only large enough to hold the toilet and sink that jutted right next to it. "You hide in there if you hear anything," Lorraine said. "There are two dead bolt locks on the inside."

"This place is built for security," Luke said. "The walls are reinforced steel."

"Yeah."

"Who is this guy? Who's the owner?"

"I have no idea."

Shelby wasn't sure Luke believed the bodyguard, but Shelby did. Lorraine was doing her job. Doing it well and with composure.

Still, Shelby had a feeling that the woman was uneasy.

Which made her want to crawl in and cram herself beside the toilet, under the sink, and just stay there.

With Lorraine and Bruce outside and Luke guarding the door. She was a human-interest reporter. Not an adrenaline seeker.

A mother. A daughter.

Luke reached for her hand. She let him hold on to it.

A woman who most definitely fell for the wrong kind of man…

"I promised you," he said softly, holding her gaze.

And the panic inside her settled back down to lie in wait.

Chapter 9

The place was built to withstand fire—gunfire included. It was the closest thing he'd seen to an underground bunker that was above ground.

Luke's thoughts stalled as yet another fact revealed itself to him; he had no way of knowing if it had come from his own knowledgebase or was just something that his bored brain had put together from his imagination.

Had he been in an underground bunker at some point? No confirmation presented.

Bruce came in, his face all business beneath the light of the one overhead bulb. Feeling Shelby's foot bump against his as she jumped, Luke would have liked to have kept hold of her hand, and almost grabbed it again as Lorraine slid out the door before Bruce closed it behind her.

"I've got the team's rundown to distribute," the six-foot-two, two-hundred-and-twenty-pounder said, maintaining his post by the door. "I'll have radio connection tonight, and we'll regroup in the morning. The team's planning to have people on this all night and are hoping to have the identity of the killer by morning. No guarantees on that one, of course."

Luke nodded. Sierra's Web employees were experts; they weren't superhuman. "I appreciate everything all of you are doing," he said, antsy to get the report and know what else he had to deal with. What else Shelby was going to know about him that he had no means to explain.

Again, why her opinion mattered so much rankled him. Why didn't he care what Bruce or Lorraine thought of him?

If he could remember other women in his life, would Shelby still matter as much?

All questions added to the other million for which he had no answers.

"Financial report. They're looking more closely at your personal banker. The Cayman Islands account is a concern, and Gerard Michaels's explanation fell short. Detective Johnson is getting a warrant to look into Michaels's financials," Bruce said, looking directly at Luke, reciting from memory. The man was impressive. Someone he'd want on his team. If Bruce had fire training…

With a blink, Luke brought his thoughts back in focus.

"IT has found the same screen name on a few adult sites, all paid for by the Cayman account. And they're following up on some apparent associations established on common social media sites with the same screen name."

"I don't do social media. And I don't do porn." There was no arguing that one with him.

But what credibility did he—a man without a memory—have to offer?

Jaw tight, he couldn't look at Shelby. And was glad he

was no longer holding her hand. Saved him from having to feel it slide away.

"If Michaels is somehow involved in this, it could be him using the screen name, sir," Bruce said, then shook his head as though he'd been speaking out of turn.

Right. Good.

Well, not good that the man he'd trusted with his entire financial life might be screwing him over and wanting him dead. But at least there was a possibility that Luke wasn't a slimeball he didn't want to remember.

Although he *was* something of one. He knew that.

Shelby's initial reaction to him, her continued distrust of him, was proof of that fact.

"Sierra's Web investigators have spoken to a member of your hotshot team, Randy Miles, who relayed that they were devastated to hear about your near death but glad to know why you hadn't shown up at work. Apparently, that was a first. Randy would like to speak with you."

The name meant nothing to him. "I'd like someone to get word to him, and the rest of the team, that I'll be in touch as soon as I can."

Bruce nodded. Luke felt confident that the message was as good as sent.

"Our investigators—there are two experts on your payroll as of now—are also looking into any other relationships you've had. They're using financials to trace where you might have entertained. There is a list of names of women, if you want it, but none of them that have so far been approached seem to have any beef with you. Mostly, they wish you well."

"Are there any with kids?" Shelby piped up, and Luke was cut by the edge in her tone. The woman's low opinion of him was getting more difficult to digest.

He had to make amends.

But how do you fix what you don't know?

"Not that I've been told." Bruce looked at Shelby as he spoke. The bodyguard didn't seem to notice anything amiss, and Luke swallowed his frustration as the report continued.

"Johnson has reported that the department has re-opened your father's death, looking at it as suspicious rather than accidental. Based on photos, the tire of your father's vehicle was slit in exactly the same way as the one on Ms. Harrington's SUV."

"Shelby. Please." Shelby's voice was surprisingly strong, drawing Luke's gaze to her. Her attention, of course, was focused all on the bodyguard, but Luke saw renewed strength in her expression.

"Shelby." Bruce nodded, then said, "In reconstructing the photos from the accident, they were able to determine that the tire blew, causing your father's car to ram into the vehicle in front of him. They suspect that the vehicle was stopped, positioned to block him from going forward when he hit the bumps and forcing him to hit the cement embankment…"

"Made to look like an accident." Shelby nodded as she spoke.

"You were right," Luke told her, impressed. And grateful.

The glance she sent his way was more a "let's get on with things" than any kind of self-aggrandizement. "Let's just hope it leads us someplace."

She wanted to get out of there. Had a life waiting.

The reminder was important.

He was living in a no-man's-land. He wanted her around.

She didn't want to be there.

"Also pursuant to investigative work," Bruce continued, his tone unchanged, "police got a description of the guy who paid a thousand dollars to switch out the carton of milk for the glass. He was six feet tall, white, was wearing a blue hoodie…"

"A hoodie in one-hundred-five-degree heat?" Shelby blurted out.

Bruce's shrug seemed to concur with her questioning the man's choice—or rather, why others hadn't noticed it. But maybe they had.

"He had tattoos on his face," Bruce continued. "Leaves scrolling down one side, a snake on the other. They're looking for any gang or other affiliations there might be to them."

"I'm guessing he was also on someone's payroll," Luke said. His father's death, getting away with it, setting two fires, causing Shelby's accident and not getting caught or even noticed…probably not looking at a perp with ink scrolling his face.

"They're scouring cameras, both inside the hotel and out," Bruce added.

Luke asked the question that mattered most to him at the moment: "And no one has any idea how we got made?"

"None. IT has been over our secure server, looked at the network we had set up, and nothing was hacked."

"So we were followed this morning like you first thought?"

Had it only been that morning? Seemed to Luke like they'd been in that hotel suite for days. They hadn't spent one night there.

Bruce, shaking his head, looked to Shelby. "That's the obvious conclusion, but I find it highly doubtful. Both Lorraine and I are trained to know when we're being followed. We're certain we lost the one vehicle that made us both uncomfortable, and there was nothing else suspicious…"

And yet, as the bodyguard had pointed out, it was the obvious conclusion.

Just like figuring he watched porn, threw wild parties, had fake charity accounts tied to the Cayman Islands, had a threesome in a hotel room and had seen Shelby naked, after which he'd offended her so horrendously she'd sworn off men forever.

Of all of it, the only thing that rang true was seeing Shelby naked.

She'd even confirmed his impression to be correct.

But he didn't get to choose which parts of himself he wanted to claim. Whatever he'd done, he'd done. Including offending Shelby, which she'd also stated as fact.

He had to live with his past.

Could only make better choices in the future.

"And the medical report," Bruce said, pausing as he glanced from Luke to Shelby. "We can do this privately, if you prefer."

Luke shook his head. "Go ahead."

She had some reason not to trust him, but he trusted her. And figured—considering the circumstances her good deed on his behalf had put her in—she had a right to any and all information at the moment.

"Aside from everything you heard when you left the hospital this morning, something potentially important has come up. You were injured in a fire five years ago, the Marnell fire—"

Shelby's gasp came right in line with his own recognition. He looked at her, saw her glance at him and then away.

Did he dare hope that he hadn't meant to offend

her? That maybe it was all a big misunderstanding? He glanced back at Bruce. "Hurt how?"

"A head injury," Bruce said. "You lost your memory then, too, briefly."

"'Briefly?'" How brief was *brief*?

"A couple of days," Bruce said. "The pertinent thing here is that your current memory loss could be related to that one. Or could have been triggered by it. Your doctor will want to do another series of tests as soon as we determine you're out of danger here..."

Fine. Whatever. His gaze was glued to Shelby. Had the news made a difference to her? Could he hope that he hadn't knowingly hurt the woman as badly as she'd thought?

Health laws wouldn't have let his medical information go any further than his care team...

She wasn't looking at him. As Bruce gave them instructions for getting his or Lorraine's attention, reiterating what Lorraine had already told them about protocols for the night, Shelby stood, facing the bodyguard, her back to Luke.

He stood, too, because it seemed the decent thing to do, wanted Bruce to hurry up and get out of there, and prayed that when Shelby turned back around, he'd find forgiveness in her gaze.

She couldn't look at Luke. She needed time to assimilate. There'd been no report of injuries during the Marnell fire. Not that she'd seen.

Didn't mean there hadn't been one. Medical records rarely lied. Just meant the injury didn't make it to a fire-incident report. The memory loss would have come after Luke was no longer servicing the fire. Maybe the supervisor thought he'd had a minor concussion and was fine...

Which, ultimately—in just days—he had been.

She clung to factual thoughts as long as she could to distract herself from the importance of the news of earlier memory loss.

If any.

Bruce had said that, after the injury, Luke had lost his memory, which would have included the week before the fire. If he hadn't remembered having sex with her, one could possibly understand why he'd accused her of lying. He'd gained memory back right away, he'd thought, but who'd have known if memories of her were still missing? No one knew about them but Luke and her.

But...to just shut the door in her face. Most particularly if he'd suffered from memory loss. He'd have known that there could be a chance she was telling the truth, and he hadn't even engaged in conversation.

And the Marnell-fire memory loss had no bearing on the fact that he'd paid her off. He'd done that before he'd left to go to the fire that morning.

Before he'd been hurt.

What he'd done to her was reprehensible.

Still.

Staring at the door Bruce had closed, she felt trapped. Had nowhere to go that didn't also contain Luke Dennison.

And that was kind of as it had been for the past five years. Every time she looked into her son's blue eyes, she knew that Luke was there. Part of her and Carter.

Even as determined and single-minded as he was, he couldn't wipe out his biology.

And apparently, even a woman as in the know and forewarned and devastated as she was couldn't stem the flow of awareness, of compassion, of...bonding she felt with the man who'd treated her so heartlessly.

Because she felt his heart.

In the actions he'd performed over and over again, running headfirst into danger to save lives. In the way he'd seemed to listen to her feelings as well as her words during the week they'd spent together.

In the way he was giving everything he had to keep her out of danger.

Taking responsibility for a past he didn't remember.

And caring about a future he couldn't yet see.

Luke didn't seem angry or entitled. He was clearly eating himself up inside with regret for things he didn't remember doing.

Disliking the man he'd been when he'd done them.

But what happened when he remembered...

"You going to stand there staring at the door all night?"

She'd been there a long time. Way too long. And still didn't turn around to face him. The room was too small.

Her emotions too huge. And raw.

She'd had to tell her son good night, to tell him that she loved him, via prerecorded video before dinner, to be taken by the team back to Sierra's Web headquarters when they'd left the hotel that evening.

Prior to the whole bugout thing.

She was used to being gone overnight. Carter was used to having her gone. But she always told him good night and heard his "I love you, too, Mama."

Every night.

"Do you believe a person can change?"

Luke's question, clearly loaded, shot through her. They were going to be sharing the small space until daylight. She couldn't stand frozen, staring at the door until then.

Turning, she saw him seated where he'd been earlier,

on one side of the small table. Her empty chair seemed glaring in the little vignette.

It called to her.

Better that than the couch.

And most definitely not the bed. If they slept at all, he could do it there.

She would not lie down on another mattress with him in the room.

A flash of her on the bed, with Luke waking up and joining her—quietly, tenderly—sent liquid fire through her veins of such a magnitude that she had to move.

Or melt.

She put her butt in the chair and, as though they were strangers discussing philosophy, said, "I think that we all change, all the time. We learn by experience and by the accumulation of knowledge, both conscious and unconscious, and the collective then shapes our perceptions and choices."

He was watching her. The hint of…something pleasant in his expression unhinged her a bit. Made her blurt out, "But I also think that we have certain character traits that will be with us our entire lives." Her father just couldn't stop himself from liking women. Different kinds, different shapes, but always in the plural. He was libido driven, not family driven.

But he wanted to be part of a family, too. He wanted the time. It just came second. He was who he was.

And Luke was who he was, too.

Mark, her relationship just prior to Luke, had simply been a self-centered, egotistical smooth talker.

And Josh, before that, had sucked her in with how much he'd needed her. Only problem was, he couldn't be there when she needed him back. He knew how to drain her emotions but didn't get that, in a healthy relationship, he also had to do his share of filling up the well.

"I can't speak to what I did to you." Luke's voice broke into her thoughts—the tone, the sincerity shining from his gaze, hooking her. "But I have to believe that I can make amends."

Luke didn't lie. The memory came to her. When he was being rude, he did it right to your face, just as when he'd been talking about saving lives.

Telling her about his mother's death.

And letting her know how drawn to her he'd been. Her body, yes, but her thoughts, too. They'd spent an afternoon on a couch just talking, about all kinds of things, and neither of them had wanted the time to end...

"I can promise you, as the man who sits before you right now, that I will do everything in my power to make it up to you."

Those blue eyes, they glistened with the power of his message.

Reminding her of Carter's big blue eyes filled with tears as he asked her why he didn't have a daddy.

"There are some things that aren't that simple," she said. She wasn't the only one his callousness had hurt.

Question was, even if he couldn't make it up to her, could he be there for Carter?

In some capacity?

She made the mistake of meeting his gaze, and Luke, hands together on the table, leaned forward as though reaching out to her, but he stopped before actually touching her.

"I don't care how high the mountain I might be facing turns out to be," he said. "I will climb it."

Oh, God, was the man trying to break her heart?

Was she wrong to hold a grudge against him? Was she

letting her own feelings get in the way of a relationship her son desperately needed?

Luke was close with his team. They all admired him. He was there for them. So many examples from past conversations came to mind. The way he'd been there for a guy who'd come home to find his wife in bed with someone else. The time he'd helped build a memorial after a female team member's father had died.

And, extremely telling—his closeness with his own father.

She'd known about that five years before.

Had the knowledge been what had kept Luke on her mind, and in her investigations, ever since? Subconsciously, had she known this day had to come? Assuming Luke matured and was interested in being a father...

Would she trade having known her own father if it meant she hadn't had to be the rope in her parents' tug-of-war?

Did it matter if Luke remembered what he'd done to her before she told him about Carter? Would it ever matter?

What had happened between her parents...they'd brought it to her—or rather, her mother had used her as a sounding board for her own very real and understandable pain—but Shelby had grown up knowing that both of her parents loved her.

"I don't have much of a past right now to shape my present," he told her, not sounding at all needy, just plain factual. "All I know is the bottom line of who I'm sitting here with, inside me. All I've got is who I'm left with. And I have memories of you...of being drawn to you... And I know, down to my core, that I don't want to go through the rest of my life without making this right."

He had to stop.

There was nowhere for her to run, to get away from him.

And while he couldn't help not knowing his less-than-likable side, she did know that guy. Far too well.

"Haven't I already done enough for you?" her broken heart cried out. To him and to the others who'd wanted her to keep giving, over and over, to keep understanding. And forgiving.

And then she froze. Was she turning into her mother? Putting her own pain above that of her son? Her own peace of mind over his emotional wealth?

She wasn't here for herself—well, other than staying alive, of course. But she'd been following Luke Dennison's life for Carter's sake. After identifying him, she'd made the choice to pursue the possibility of Luke being in his son's life.

With all the DNA options available—and she'd have to assume they'd be even more prevalent as Carter got older—her son would likely discover his father on his own at some point...

Luke had pulled back from the table. Was sitting there, nodding, his gaze open. As though he was about to tell her that she was right. That he'd respect her wishes and leave her alone.

That she'd never hear from him again once their lives were out of danger.

She was afraid that that was what he was about to tell her.

And before she could form another thought, the words ripped out of her.

"Carter is your son."

Chapter 10

He didn't believe her. Of all the horrible things he'd imagined he'd done to harden her against him...

"I told you about him..."

"I would never turn my back on my own child." Point-blank.

There was no arguing that one. Didn't matter how much memory he did or did not have. No way anyone would ever convince him that he'd do such a thing.

She'd said that she'd gotten pregnant a few months after knowing him. Because of him. That she'd done so knowingly, wanting a child, but not a man in her life.

She was the liar.

He stared her down. Didn't care if he was coming off like a high-handed moron. She didn't flinch.

He admired that about her. The ability to stand her ground.

But not when she was trespassing on his.

"You can get as strong and fierce and determined and

adamant as you want," she said then, her chin jutting. "Biology doesn't lie. I'll provide Carter's DNA, you provide your own."

"Well, we're damned well going to do that," he said, fire burning through every inch of him. Inside and out. "I'll get Sierra's Web on it right now."

He stood up and strode over to the door, knocked once to let Bruce know they were okay. He waited for the knock back and then pulled open the door. Stepped outside.

He explained to his bodyguard what he needed, went back inside and shut the door.

If she thought she was going to...

He'd just call her bluff...

If he had a four-year-old boy in the world, he'd have been coaching T-ball or soccer or dance or swimming or...just sitting and watching cartoons. Just as his father had done with him.

He'd hated them all—except the swimming. Then his dad had taken him rock climbing...

Oh. Another memory. One that would have to wait.

Still on his mission to walk forcefully, to stand for himself, he made it back to the table. Sat. Ready to find out why the woman he'd thought he'd felt such a pull for would try to mess with his head in such a despicable way...

He didn't look at her. But as he sat, another thought hit him. Hard.

Had he pulled something similar on her? Lied to her in a way that had changed her whole life? And she was trying to show him why he couldn't just waltz in here and tell her he'd make it up to her?

Giving him a taste of his own medicine because he didn't remember having dished it out to her?

Taking a deep breath, calming for a second, he looked over, expecting to see her watching him, waiting for him to get it.

She wasn't even looking at him.

She had paper in front of her. And a pen. Obviously taken from the open drawer of the single cupboard in the place.

With a flourish, she appeared to be signing her name at the bottom of whatever she'd written. And then, after turning the paper toward him, she slid it across the table. "You'll need my permission to get Carter's DNA," she told him. "It's on file with his pediatrician. Most hospitals are required to take newborn DNA at birth for certain screenings, and I requested that Carter's be kept. I'd read having DNA on file can actually save a child's life in certain circumstances…"

Stop talking.

Was she ever going to stop talking?

He wouldn't touch the paper. As if doing so would give any credibility at all to what she was saying. But he wasn't blind. He could see the words.

She'd just given him legal access to her son's DNA.

Why would she do that? Just to keep him going? To take her little game to the last possible play?

Okay, then, he had to keep up with her. "If you had my child, then you did so without my knowledge."

And he was the aggrieved party.

Though he couldn't be sure if he'd have been as adamantly gung ho about wanting to be a father five years ago…

He might have had misgivings.

Serious ones.

He still would have done the right thing—by her and for the child. He'd never have turned his back. He knew that as well as he knew that he would give his life to save another.

Again and again.

No matter what.

But if she hadn't told him… If the kid was his…

Holy hell. He jumped up from the table and went to the door. Knocked once, barely waiting for the response before yanking it open. "You'll need this," he told Bruce, handing the man the signed piece of paper through the wide-open door.

And then, closing out the world, he returned to the table.

Ready for Shelby to come clean. To let them both off their hooks.

"Two months after…what happened *happened* between us, I drove to your cabin in Payson. I told you I was pregnant. You called me a liar and shut the door in my face."

No way. She was lying. There was just no way he'd do such a thing.

He was not that guy. He never could have been.

He was ready to blurt out his disgust for her charade, but he stopped short of calling her a liar out loud.

That was his immediate reaction to her telling him that Carter was his: *he didn't believe her.* She was lying.

Was it so far inconceivable that he'd had the same reaction five years before?

A string of silent expletives filled his brain long enough for him to breathe.

How in the hell did he know what he'd thought? Or done?

She'd given him access to her son's DNA.

Would she really do that just to prove a point to him? That people could be cruel in how they played with each other's emotions?

He shook his head.

She wouldn't.

But the alternative…

He just couldn't take it on. Couldn't even fathom…

She was sitting there calmly. More calmly than he'd seen her since she'd shown up in his hospital room the morning before.

God, a lifetime had passed since then.

In less than forty-eight hours he'd…

When he met her gaze, she didn't look away. "Can we talk about this?"

She shrugged. "I'm not going to get into it with you, if that's what you mean."

He didn't know what he'd meant.

And then it dawned on him…

Horror sluiced through his pores. His veins. "My memory… The Marnell fire…"

She'd had a very definite reaction to the mention of his earlier injury…

"I told you the baby wasn't mine because I didn't remember us together…" Yes. It was the only thing that made sense. She had to see that.

Had to… He didn't know what.

They'd lost four years because he'd had a slight head injury?

Could life be that simple?

And that cruel?

"Maybe if you'd tried again…" He knew as soon as he said the words that they were wrong. Putting the blame on her was absolutely not what he'd intended.

But how could he have tried again when he had no memory of…

"You made it very clear there'd be no discussion, Luke. You shut the door in my face. It was clear to me at the time that you were entertaining. I heard a woman calling out to you from inside."

A woman? In his cabin?

That didn't feel right, either.

Tense, hot and tired—and so completely out of his element he wasn't sure of his next step—he put his hands to the back of his head. Held on.

What the hell did he know?

Really know?

He could see her hating him...if things played out as she was saying...

And no, they most definitely were not simple. This wasn't going to be fixed. Ever.

Carter.

He had a four-year-old son? His name was Carter?

And he'd missed...everything?

He'd been feeling such an incredible attachment to her. Had been hoping that when the would-be killer was caught, he could talk Shelby into continuing a relationship with him.

By whatever definition she'd allow.

He'd just wanted her in his life.

And now, was she playing some kind of sick game with him to teach him a lesson?

It was just... To believe what she was saying...

How could he, when he didn't believe? When he'd have to turn his back on his own sense of self to do so?

"I know you don't want to discuss what actually happened between us until I remember it all," he said then, weary beyond the hours he'd gone without sleep. "But can you tell me this? You said two months passed between when we were last together and you came to my door."

"That's right."

"So how did things end between us?"

From what he sensed, supported by what Bruce had told them during his report, he had women in his past, but he didn't leave them angry with him.

She shook her head.

He stared at her. "It ended badly."

"That's an understatement."

"Did we argue?"

"No."

"I just did whatever I did and that was it."

"Yes."

And yet, when she'd known she was pregnant, she'd done the decent thing—put the past aside and had gone to find him. Had told him about the baby.

And he, either knowingly or possibly not, had told her she was lying and shut the door on any possibility of conversation about it.

He just didn't get it.

Was pretty sure he never would.

Even if he remembered every single intimate detail from his past.

He'd paid her off before the injury. Shelby could not get by that one conscious choice that spoke to what he thought of her and their time together...

"Wait..." Luke slumped farther in his chair, looking over at her with a seriously grim expression. "Even if I didn't remember our...encounter...when you came to see me in Payson, I'd have known that I had memory issues... Would have known that there was a possibility I didn't remember..."

The man just didn't stop grabbing at her.

Which was exactly what had happened the week she spent interviewing him. And why she'd ended up in bed with him.

She knew how that had turned out. There was just no getting away from that fact.

And then there was Carter.

"And of course you already know all of that," Luke said as she sat there, saying nothing.

She was lost. Stuck in one room with him for the night. Missing her son. Afraid for her life. Scared of the things she was feeling for a man who'd already proven he wasn't good for her.

Being guarded by trained strangers.

And she'd never felt more alone.

Or unsure.

"Holy hell!" Luke sat up straight. Jumped up. "Carter... If he's mine...his life could be in..." He'd gone so pale she thought he might pass out. He'd just been released from the hospital. Could be...

"Luke." She stood, too. Reached for his hand, just to be there to steady him if he swayed, assessing distance to be able to lower him to his chair were he to lose consciousness. "It's okay," she said.

Surprised at the strength of his pull against her, his attempt to get to the door, she held on tighter. "No one knows he's yours," she said quickly. "No one."

Except now probably Bruce. And any Sierra's Web expert the man might already have contacted.

What had she done?

Luke shook his head, his look urgent, but he was no longer pulling away from her. "What about your mother?" He threw the question at her, his frown intense.

With a head shake right back at him, she said, "Not even my doctor knew. You and I. That's it. Ever."

It was like all life drained out of him as he glanced at her and then off toward a corner of the room. His jaw tight, she could see the muscles in his throat working. She could feel his struggle, like a physical weight beneath her ribs, and hated the fight she had to wage inside herself.

Wasn't it enough to have to defend herself from the rest of the world?

But from her own self?

How did she even have a chance at succeeding?

"I need to sit down." Luke moved toward the couch. He didn't really pull away from her that time, but she dropped his hand.

And then, like a lamb to slaughter, followed him to sit on the opposite end of the one piece of living room furniture.

"I can't believe this is real," he said, shaking his head. "Can I see pictures of him?"

She held up the unconnected electronic device she'd been given.

His chin hit his chest as though her inability to give him even that much was his last straw. And then he straightened, meeting her gaze head-on, no distress evident.

"I intend to be a part of his life."

Just like that, her world turned onto an axis she'd been avoiding—yet barreling toward. She couldn't accept his words. Not carte blanche.

Not until she knew more.

"You just gave me what I need to fight for the legal right," he said, reminding her of the man who'd shut the door in her face.

The one who did exactly what he wanted to do in spite of how it might affect anyone else around him.

"As soon as the DNA comes back as a match, I'm established as his father and—"

"Yeah, yeah, yeah," she said, cutting him off. Panicking.

Sierra's Web had expert attorneys, too. She had to hire one for herself before Luke bought them away from her...

"I have no intention of usurping your right to determine what's best for him." The voice came softly, reaching through her fog.

She glanced over at him. Saw the man she'd thought she'd known. Aware. Concerned. And not just for himself.

Throwing up his hands, he said, "I'll definitely provide back child support, as soon as we are physically able to make it happen," he told her, looking her straight in the eye. "And the rest... I leave it up to you to determine where and how I fit..."

The guy was killing her, one heartstring at a time. And before she could take a breath, she said, "He's been unhappy more lately because he doesn't have a father." She let the damning words fall out of that remote hiding place. "His best friend's dad takes him fishing and...you know, other things. I don't think the things matter, really, he just doesn't understand why he can't have a father, too."

Carter was his son. He deserved to know the little guy's state of mind. Didn't he?

"But...I can't give you access to him right now, Luke. Not until..."

What? Her feelings from the past were assuaged? Channeling her mom, again?

"I can't let you close the door in his face." The truth became clear to her.

She settled back into the corner of the couch. Stared him down without a flinch.

And found her peace again.

Chapter 11

Bare feet pushing against his own woke Luke. He wasn't sure of the time or how long he'd been asleep. The bare feet, though... He'd tangled with them before. In a hotel-room bed. Silky sheets. Bare breasts.

Eyes still closed, he lay there with the moment.

Skin to skin, from toes to head. Sliding, teasing... then not.

Wet with sweat.

With her.

Held captive by such explicit pleasure.

Knew he'd been changed.

And...

He moved his heel. Against rough tweed. Not cool, smooth softness.

And he opened his eyes to the dim light left on over by the small sink. In the tiny cabin, the past days came rolling back over him, flattening him.

The other foot—just one, not both—had barely touched

him. A heel to his arch. Enough to wake him up. His pull-back barely perceptible, he disconnected the contact.

He lay there on the end of the couch that had held him for much of the night. Aware that the mother of his child, still in the shorts and tank top from the morning before, had fallen asleep on the other end.

His child.

He had a son.

Carter.

He couldn't wrap his mind around this state of affairs. Didn't feel the truth of her words. But he no longer doubted her.

She'd been keeping track of him, had come to identify him, for Carter. He'd figured out that much.

Just as he knew she still wasn't sure if she'd dare let him around her little boy.

They'd fallen asleep talking. Him first? Her? He couldn't be sure. He'd had a million questions. The pregnancy, delivery, who'd been with her, had it been hard?

She'd been alone, other than medical personnel, for the twenty-seven hours it took their son to show his face to the world. Her choice.

She'd wanted the time for just her and Carter.

The family of two that they were going to be.

His son had rolled over at three months, pulled himself up on the side netting of a playpen at five months, had been walking by ten months. And hadn't spoken a legible word until he was almost eighteen months old. Then he'd talked in sentences.

A man after Luke's heart. Or rather, a son taking after his father. Luke had always been a guy who listened more than he spoke.

Who had no talent for small talk.

Lying there with a mind filled with the facts he was

certain meant more to him than any he'd remember, he flashed back to seconds before when he'd woken up.

He'd been in a hotel-room bed with Shelby.

Remembered undressing her, the leggings and long button-down blouse she'd had on. No underwire on the lightly padded bra. Black.

The matching bikini panties… He grew hard as the memory slammed into him.

Took a deep breath. Pushed forward…forward…forward…

The call. He'd pushed to answer before the first beep finished, not wanting to wake her. Had slid into his pants as he listened. There'd been a fire. A small desert community surrounded by flames.

He'd had to get out of the room so he could ask the questions burning on his tongue, give the orders he had to give. Had made his way out of the afterglow of a night of incredible physical pleasure as he entered his own room down the hall.

And had been on his way to the fire less than five minutes later.

It had been four thirty in the morning.

And he'd just left her there.

He had intended to call the first chance he got. Knew she'd understand. His career, his life of firefighting had been what had drawn her to him to begin with.

She of all people had seemed to understand how he rolled.

Had he called?

He didn't remember calling.

And…heard a gunshot.

There'd been a shot at the fire?

No. Senses sharpening, he lay perfectly still, listening. He heard another pop.

Felt a small movement against his foot. Pushing on him and not letting up.

Shelby.

She'd heard it, too.

Acting purely on instinct, when a third shot rang out, he tangled his half-bare legs with hers. Gently but determinedly, he rolled them both off the couch to the floor, and then, crawling up over her, holding his body above hers as a shield, gave a quick nudge toward the bathroom door. His legs moving against hers only enough to get her crawling, he kept pace with her. Across the floor.

Keeping her covered the entire time as a fourth shot sounded. If she noticed the residual hardness left from his thoughts just seconds before, he'd deal with it later.

Welcomed the possible distraction for her.

Neither Bruce nor Lorraine had come to the door or given any signal. He had to assume he and Shelby were alone.

Whether she'd figured that out or not, he didn't know. Couldn't worry on that one.

Lives needed saving.

The four-year-old son he'd never met would not be an orphan.

Shaking, praying, visions of Carter flashing before her eyes, Shelby sat crunched in the fetal position in a corner of the small bathroom.

Where were Bruce and Lorraine?

Had the shots come from their guns?

What was Luke doing?

He was supposed to have stayed in the bathroom with her. The protocols they'd been given were very clear.

He didn't have a gun.

No amount of determination and smarts was going to

win against flying bullets. Or get him close enough to the shooter to stop him without a weapon.

Afraid for him, panicked she'd never get a chance to tell him that she wanted him in Carter's life, needing him to know that...

A minute passed. Then five.

The knob turned, and her heart leapt to her throat. Blocking air. Butterflies the size of birds attacked her from the inside as she watched the door open.

"Shelby, let's go." Luke's voice, coming from the man's shadow she could see at the entrance to the unlit room.

She did as he told her, without consideration. Keeping her gaze on him, his knees visible beneath his shorts, she unfolded herself and moved toward him.

"We have to move fast," he said, his tone different than any she'd heard before. Commanding. And confident enough to offer hope.

As soon as she was in the room, she made out two other shapes.

Bruce and Lorraine, standing tall—seemingly uninjured—both by the door.

"Firebombs were shot into the brush on all four sides of us," Luke told her, taking her hand as he turned to include the other two. "Fire department's on its way. Smoke and flames are eating up the entire area, preventing any possible sighting of the perp for now, and that's our only chance for undetected escape. We have to act before this guy realizes that the cabin isn't going to burn. There's a fire block set up around this place, including a path to the creek that we can walk. An emergency vehicle will meet us somewhere upstream, with uniforms. We'll dress in them, complete with shields over our faces, and be positioned out on a perimeter of the fire. Stretchers will be carried out from the fire, looking like they came from here, and be taken up to the house to be loaded into ambulances. All four will have bodies posed on them, with sheets up over the heads. A news crew will be there and told specifically to film the sheet-covered bodies. The home's owner will be interviewed, and he'll identify me, two women and another man as the four people staying on his property. When we can be reasonably sure that the killer will be caught up in the drama, we'll be loaded into a fire truck and driven to safety."

The bodyguards nodded. Shelby didn't question how Luke knew who was coming.

"Take this and put it over your face. Hold it there while you walk," Luke said, handing her a cold wet piece of sheet before passing one to Lorraine, saying, "Signal when you see the creek."

Taking the wet cloth, Shelby slapped it up to her face and hurried through the open door as Luke motioned her forward behind Lorraine but in front of Bruce and Luke. A wave of Arizona-summer heat hit her before the acrid scent of smoke did. In her shorts, tank top and rubber-soled sandals, she moved through the night at a near run, without stumbling, just following Lorraine and focusing on what Luke needed her to do. The path was wide—raw soil kept clear of vegetation—and she realized the perimeter of the cabin had been landscaped in exactly the same way.

Something Luke would have recognized, she knew, as snippets from the past flashed in her brain: Luke telling her about fire blocks, digging perimeters around fires to prevent their spread. Raw soil didn't burn. The memories helped distract her from the process of breathing while engulfed in heavy smoke.

"In. Out. Deep enough but no deeper than absolutely

necessary," Luke's voice sounded from over her shoulder, just before she felt his body graze the right side of hers. He took her arm then, guiding her, almost as though they were in a choreographed dance—one of his legs between hers, the other on the outside of her right.

"You and the others are only being identified in the news by gender," he said, as he hurried her along yet seemed to be holding her steady, too.

In case smoke overtook her?

His next sentence came several seconds later. "Your families won't have any idea you'd even be in the area."

She nodded. Didn't dare take the second she'd need to turn for him to hear any verbal response.

"He knows where I am, which means he knows who I'm with. He hears that I'm one of the four dead, the gender IDs will make sense to him. Be enough for him."

And... Luke didn't have any family who would be devastated to hear about his death on the news.

No one who knew about him.

She couldn't see him, not really—just peripheral flashes when his head moved. He was clearly keeping watch—seeing things, she surmised, that she wouldn't catch had she been staring straight at them. Watching flame height, assessing spread speed... She didn't remember everything he'd taught her about hotshot firefighting, but she remembered a lot of it.

Mostly, she remembered being impressed by his mastery of the field. And of himself in times of crisis.

The wet cloth against her face was getting pasty, starting to itch. Her hand slipped, and she inhaled a puff of smoke. She coughed. But didn't miss a step.

"In and out." Luke leaned in closer. "Just keep it simple."

His tone, more than his words, put her in a different

place. A stronger, calmer moment. Lorraine moved in front of her without a hitch. She couldn't hear Bruce behind him, his big frame silent in the soil, but she assumed he was there.

She told herself the smoke was getting thinner as they moved away from its source, but she had no idea if the wish was fact. Didn't much matter. She needed it in that second, and so she went with it. Hurried along, determined to help in any way she could.

When Lorraine slowed and raised a hand, Shelby remembered hearing Luke tell the woman to signal when she reached the creek. And seconds later, Shelby was eagerly stepping into calf-high water that she couldn't see. Didn't matter what was in it.

Leeches, even snakes, were better than death.

Rattlers didn't live in the water.

No other poisonous snakes in Arizona.

Facts presented. And calmed her.

Water flowing through sandals wasn't pleasant or easily manageable. Most particularly when sliding atop loose rock. Each step was harder than the last as she slid, both her footwear against the rocks and her feet in the sandals. But she couldn't let it slow her down. Wouldn't be cause for any of them to be caught.

Or worse.

Putting her foot down quickly, she landed on a bigger-than-normal rock, slid down it, and her big toe hit something sharp. Drawing back was instinctual. And she fell sharply against Luke's torso.

Before she could right herself, he swung her up against him, all within one step of strong, steady wading.

"You don't have to—"

"It's faster this way," he said, cutting off her words, not missing a beat as he closed the distance between them and

Lorraine. She could see Bruce behind them. The body-guard didn't seem at all concerned with Luke carrying his other charge. His head kept moving from side to side, clearly keeping watch.

As was Lorraine.

Someone had just tried to kill them. Had they not been in a cabin purposely built to withstand attack, they'd have all been dead.

Tremors started within her as fear rose up. Luke's arms tightened.

As though he knew. Could feel her fright.

She didn't want that. Didn't want him to see any weakness in her.

To think that he had more of what it takes than she did.

She heard a bit of a splash ahead, like Lorraine was stepping over something. And in the next second, she felt Luke's thigh against her hip as his leg rose.

Another splash sounded, just beneath her this time, but she was too busy focusing on the pressure of his body against her butt to care. That touch… It sent her back to the cabin, to Luke an inch or two above her on the floor, keeping her covered as they slid to the bathroom door.

So close that she'd bumped into him. More than once. Had felt the unmistakable firmness in his groin grazing her body…

He'd been hard.

Because of the danger?

It would be safer to think so.

The steady rhythm of Luke's jostling lulled her, even as she pressed her cloth, grown warm, into her face.

They'd been lying on the couch, feet touching.

Had he remembered the love game they'd played? Did it matter?

Breathing, while labored, became easier as his chest

rose and fell against her. Her body became part of his rhythm, inhaling air as he did. Slowly, steadily. Taking time to exhale.

He'd remembered her breasts.

Did it mean something that he couldn't remember a single detail of his life, but he remembered having sex with her?

It had to mean something, didn't it?

Their sex had meant more to him than anything else. Including his disgusting actions afterward...

She tensed. Felt his arms tighten again.

No.

She wasn't going to give him any reason to doubt her strength. She forced herself to think smaller. Be in the second. His chest. Rising and falling.

His chest.

Covered with hair that tickled her nipples...

Inappropriate. They could die at any second and...

Wouldn't it be better to go out with pleasure on her mind? Better to enjoy the last breaths she took?

What was the matter with her? Thinking about sex with the man who'd abandoned her rather than going out with only Carter on her mind?

A flash of her son's sweet, smiling face nearly did her in. She couldn't die. Couldn't desert him.

Oh, God, she couldn't...

Think like that. Carter was safe. Sleeping securely, well loved, in his room at her mother's house.

Her mother...

Shelby was all Sylvia had...

And she'd make it back to her. To both of them.

After all, she was in the arms of the world's most accomplished danger fighter...

Another pressure of hard thigh against her butt, a

slight bump, and the arms holding Shelby changed, loosening her from Luke's chest, lowering her.

They'd left the creek.

And just as reality—the smoke, the darkness, the hot air—smacked her in the face again, Shelby's feet touched solid ground.

Barely waiting until she had her balance, Luke strode toward a big shape in the distance.

Leaving her without a word.

Again.

Chapter 12

With his mind drowning in a sudden blinding onslaught of memories, Luke didn't slow down. Pushing aside the mental breakthrough, he did what he always did. The only thing he knew how to do. Put the personal stuff in a box so he could get the job done.

Instinct drove him. He let it.

And didn't stop letting it until the door closed, locking him in the captain's living quarters with Bruce, Lorraine and Shelby at a Phoenix fire station. There were two rooms. One with a couch, television, mini kitchenette and a small table. The other, a bedroom with two twin beds. The bath was small, accessible only off the bedroom.

More close quarters.

It was what it was.

Captain McDonald had worked with Luke. Had been instantly agreeable to bunking with the crew for however long it took…

"Friday is shopping day," he announced to the room in general, avoiding all eye contact, as he'd been doing since setting up the fire rescue for the four of them. "Essentials and clothing changes will be brought in for us with the groceries."

The idea was for the four of them to remain hidden—no sign of coming or going, no sign of anything out of the ordinary—until the police found the would-be killer/arsonist who had it in for Luke. The guy wanted Luke dead for a reason.

"I appreciate you all going along with me here," he said, again to the air around him. Yeah, he was paying Sierra's Web. Didn't mean Bruce or Lorraine had to stay on the job.

And Shelby...

He couldn't go there. Not even a little bit.

Or venture beyond her to the little guy...

Not yet.

"Hopefully, he'll think he's succeeded and show his hand." Most likely by accessing Luke's money. Or his seventy-thousand-dollar truck. With the cabin in Payson burned, there were no other assets.

Something else he wasn't focusing on.

"In the meantime, as long as we're dead, we're safe." That was the thought, anyway.

As soon as he'd opened the door of the cabin to discover the fire burning and heard that the four shots had been firebombs, he'd taken control of Bruce's radio. Talking with Hudson from Sierra's Web, he had come up with the plan. On the spot.

It's what he did: assess and command.

The fire department had already been on the way. Luke's earlier assessment of the fire barriers around the cabin had filled in the blanks. The rest had been a no-brainer for him.

Who'd suspect firefighters at a fire?

Or follow the engines as they came and went?

Ambulances were what you'd watch for.

And his plan had delivered.

Four stretchers with dead bodies. Loaded into four buses.

They just had to stay dead long enough for the guy to show himself.

And that's where his wind tapered to less than a breeze.

Leaving the other three in the living area, Luke strode into the bedroom as though he had a plan. Something to do.

Standing in the small room, looking at McDonald's digital clock plugged into the wall, he fought to maintain homeostasis. Taking action was the only way he knew to do that.

Even a need to pee would be better than just…stagnating.

But the bodily function wasn't going to keep his brain at bay. Already, memories were swamping him. Peeing outside in the woods…

Hiking—the tougher the climb, the better—was how he coped.

His mother's funeral. And his father's.

The fiend had killed his father!

Shelby…

He'd just bought new living room furniture for the cabin.

Randy's wedding next month… He was his second-in-command's best man. And knew the man who was more brother to him than anything wouldn't give a rat's ass about Luke letting him down on his big day. He'd just need to know that Luke was okay.

He couldn't let Hudson get in touch with him. If anyone knew he was alive, acted in any way counterproductive to his death, the whole plan could be blown.

And Shelby would once again be in danger.

If there hadn't been a perimeter around that damned cabin, they'd all be dead. Another fire attempt.

A good one.

Made him think the guy after him knew fires. And had reason to want him to die in one.

Which gave him a plan. Silently apologizing to Captain McDonald for the intrusion, he pulled open drawers until he found paper and a pencil, and then, starting at the beginning of his career—his first training course— he started a list of anyone he'd encountered whom he might have pissed off.

And kept his mind off the woman he'd walked out on to go fight a fire. The woman he'd planned to see again. The first woman who'd ever given him the sense that, with her, he could have more than a career.

The woman who'd lied to him about coming to tell him about their son.

Dropping to the couch while the bodyguards, leaning on the counters on either side of the small kitchenette, conversed quietly, Shelby flipped on the television.

More as a distraction for them—a sound barrier to give them privacy for whatever it was they had to discuss— than because she had any hope of actually being able to pay attention to some show that she didn't give two hoots about.

In the ride back to Phoenix in the fire truck, she'd been

able to speak to Hudson on a private radio channel to record a message to Carter.

And was more grateful than ever that Luke had already arranged to have a Sierra's Web bodyguard stay with her mother and son until they apprehended whoever was trying to kill her and Luke. Her mother was now being told that the danger was over, that the guard was a formality required due to the story she was covering.

Hudson had told her. Not Luke.

The man who'd fathered her child, who'd crawled—with a hard-on—to the bathroom with her, who'd carried her in the stream, hadn't looked directly at her since he'd put her down on dry land.

Or spoken to her, personally, either.

He'd walked away.

And come back a changed man.

Albeit one who was still providing for the safety of her son and mother.

His son. And his son's caregiver.

The past was repeating itself with one huge difference.

Luke Dennison was no longer denying his son's existence. He was ensuring the boy's safety.

Because he'd ordered the DNA test and now believed that she'd told the truth?

His questions the night before, wanting to know every little thing about Carter—they'd been so sincere. So heartrending.

She'd babbled like a lovesick kid.

Maybe she'd gotten through to him.

As far as Carter was concerned.

And where Luke was involved, Carter was her only concern.

But...

The change in him...

From a man swearing he'd do anything to take accountability for what he'd done to her...to the stranger who'd set her on the ground outside the creek...

And it hit her... He'd been hard after their feet had touched... She wondered if he'd had another memory of them. Like his breast one.

But what if...it made sense that the traumatic events of the night before had triggered his brain?

He'd remembered.

And he wasn't...

Jumping up off the sofa, she left the television running, no idea what show was even on, and stormed into the bedroom, uncaring that the door had been closed.

Uncaring if the man happened to be just out of the shower, butt naked. He was not going to...

Luke sat on the floor, still in the tan shorts he'd had on two days before, writing in a wire-bound notebook.

Where he'd gotten it, she didn't know. But the man managed to make fire trucks with extra uniforms appear at will, so why not paper? And a pen, too, just because he could.

"You remembered," she proposed when, after a brief glance at the door, he returned to what he was doing.

How dare he think he was going to ignore her?

Everything she'd been through for him in the past couple of days—being in danger because of him, doing the right thing and telling him about his son, the promise he'd made to atone for the past...

And he was just going to sit there?

She'd exposed Carter to him!

And Luke was providing protection for him. Even after the danger was most likely gone and no one knew that Carter was his son.

Although…some Sierra's Web team members were privy to the test being conducted.

There hadn't been time yet to get results. Even Sierra's Web wasn't that good.

As her thoughts flew, she stood there, boring holes into him with her gaze. Not that he felt them. Clearly.

The man's pen hadn't faltered even for a second.

If he thought he was going to freeze her out, get her to turn around and leave him to his privacy, he'd underestimated her. She had all day, maybe even two, with nothing better to do but stand her ground.

Or lean into it, she decided, when five minutes had passed and the hotshot firefighter still hadn't said a word. Shoulder to the wall, she faced him.

"You were great last night." Apparently, her silence was too easy on him. She kept it nice, though. "Or rather, predawn this morning." They'd had a few hours' sleep on the couch prior to being forced to vacate.

The pen might have paused, briefly. She was pretty sure it did. Otherwise, her words garnered no response.

Which was just plain making her mad.

Had the man forgotten she was a reporter? Someone trained and with a real talent for getting information out of people?

Was he going to sit there and insult her further?

"Am I to assume that your desire to make up for the past vanished when you remembered what you did?"

He'd apparently thought paying her off served his purpose. She'd figured, as smart as he was, that once he'd remembered, he'd found his choice to be a good one.

And…maybe he hadn't remembered.

Could be that leaving and coming back a changed man was just who he was. Memory or not.

But he wasn't turning his back on his son.

That mattered.

And frustrated the hell out of her, too, as she had no way of knowing if, once he spent time with Carter—once Carter grew to love him, to need him—he'd turn his back on the boy.

She'd made the choice to sleep with the man. Had paid the price.

Carter didn't deserve to pay, too. That wasn't how it was supposed to work. The kid paying for the parents' choices. Her mother's decisions had shown her that first-hand.

Eventually, Shelby slid down the wall to sit on the floor. Eye level with him. Facing him across the small space.

She could stay there all night. She had no place else to be. Except in one of the two beds mere feet away from them, and that wasn't a choice she intended to make.

The bodyguards were going to take turns with watch and using the couch.

Of course, they hadn't even had lunch yet. There was dinner to get through after that, before it would be time for sleeping.

"Setting up a breakfast station for the entire crew was a nice touch," she said, remembering the semi-hot meal they'd had in the truck on the way back to Phoenix.

The pen didn't slow at all that time.

"Has anyone ever told you you're rude?"

"Many times."

Startled, she jerked when she heard his response. Stared at him. Waiting…

And got nothing but more silence.

So…if she criticized him, he'd respond? Because he didn't care what she or anyone else thought of him?

Leaning her head back against the wall, she thought

back to the interviews she'd done with him five years before. Drawing not so much on the information he'd given her but on the impressions she'd had.

Remembering for the sake of gaining real, honest insight into him, not to analyze or conclude. Not to hurt or hate.

But with a true need to reach the man. Whoever he was.

Because whatever he turned out to be, he was still her son's father.

He'd been hesitant about the interview at first, until he found out that she'd chosen him as a source to shed light on the dangerous and mostly underpaid teams of hotshots who risked their lives every day they went to work. Members of a crew had been lost in a fire, and not only had Luke prevented a much bigger loss but he'd also been trying to raise money for the families left behind.

Which showed compassion, caring, justice, brotherhood.

He'd been honest in his assessments, hadn't tried to sell her on anything or convince her that his beliefs were right. He'd only told his story from his point of view. As he saw it.

And he'd seen so much. Could look at people and see deeper than the surface.

"Last night…you knew what to do. It's because you see what others don't see…" Like she did.

That's what had drawn them into a personal sphere. The pain that came from seeing and sometimes being unable to help.

Like her mother. Try as she might, she'd never been able to get through to Sylvia.

And subjects whose stories she only got to tell after the fact—it had been too late for them. And their stories

would never have been told if she hadn't gone with her
instincts and dug deeper.

"I'm not looking for you to be someone you aren't,
Luke," she said then, softly, though she could still hear
the drone of the television on the other side of the wall.
"All I want is honesty."

She needed to know why. Not to judge. Or condemn.
Nothing was going to change the past. Or undo the mis-
takes either of them had made. She wanted to move on.
To make the right choices for her son's future.

She'd been playing with a string on her shorts, but at
his continued silence, she glanced up at him, wishing
she could take off her stream-ruined sandal and throw
it at him.

His pen wasn't moving.

He was staring right at her.

"Honestly," he said, "this isn't the time to do this."

Seriously? That's what he was giving her? What he
thought she deserved?

There'd be a better time when they were free from
captivity, off living their own lives? With him wanting
to see his son?

If he even still did.

The right time was right then. Where they could talk
it all out, figure out where they went from this point.

When they had nothing and no one else pulling at
them, nothing else they even *could* do.

"When is the time, Luke? What's more important than
figuring out where we go from here?" He'd said he was
going to be in his son's life. That her DNA test would
give him legal rights.

"More important is trying to figure out who's out to
kill us."

Oh. She glanced at his pad. The entire page was filled with notes.

"You've got your memory back," she said again.

He didn't look away. Just slowly nodded, then held up his pad. "I'm making lists, with notes."

Potential stalkers or attempted killers. Because he could remember who might have a grudge against him.

He'd been sitting there, living through every bad moment he'd just remembered, cataloguing them, in order to help set her—and himself—free.

Without another word, she stood and slipped silently out of the room.

Wishing there was some way she could help him.

Chapter 13

The room went stale the second the door closed behind Shelby. Luke noticed, pushed the sensation away and went back to work. He finished his list. Took it out to Bruce, who used interstation-landline paging to signal Captain McDonald to his quarters. None of the crew on shift knew the four of them were in the station. The firefighters had been told there was a clogged air-conditioning duct that had pushed McDonald down with them.

Shelby was in the small kitchenette, cleaning—walls, countertops, cupboards. In her same black shorts, she had to feel as desperate for a shower as he did, especially after being in the creek, but she didn't complain.

She cleaned.

He got it.

Keeping busy. Making something good out of tension-fueled adrenaline.

He didn't want to be aware of her. Couldn't not notice her. That long, wavy blond hair; the deep brown eyes that spoke without words; the curves in all the right places—they were captivating. But not nearly as much as the energy she exuded.

She'd lied to him.

And he couldn't walk away. She was the mother of his child.

Fully remembering their time together, he didn't doubt that they could have made a baby. He'd used condoms but had gone more than once without pulling out. Spillage was believable.

The lovemaking was what had been unbelievable.

"I'd like a word with you." He leaned over the counter to deliver his edict while Bruce was at the door of the quarters, conversing softly with McDonald. Lorraine was asleep on the couch, obviously used to catching sleep when and wherever she could.

Shelby held up a soapy rag. "I'm kind of in the middle of something."

He wasn't used to being argued with.

"Please."

Luke had no idea if his plea fell on deaf ears—if Shelby still had any desire to speak to him. She'd realized he'd regained his memory, that he knew she'd lied to him about coming to tell him about the baby, about his shutting the door in her face.

As soon as she'd figured it out, she'd come to him to talk it out and—being his usual blunt, focused self—he'd shunned her.

He'd been right to get the list made first; catching whoever was after him was paramount.

He could have been kinder in his delivery. Shelby wasn't someone who worked for him, part of his crew who knew him and understood the way he got right to the point to save lives. Including, on more than one occasion, their own.

And...her being able to deal with him mattered.

She finished wiping the shelves she'd been leaning on. Loaded goods stacked neatly in three piles on the counter back onto them. Rinsed the rag in the sink. Washed her hands.

And without even looking his way, walked back into the bedroom the two of them would be sharing. While still affording each other complete privacy.

A tall order, to be sure, but he didn't doubt either of their abilities to manage that one.

His confidence on the matter faltered as he walked into the room, saw how small it was with her standing there between the two beds, arms crossed and somehow looking...professional in spite of the two-day lack of grooming.

Or maybe the stance was pure defense. "You lied to me."

Dropping her arms, she pushed past him. Headed for the door.

His bluntness really paid off on that one.

"Shelby, wait," he said as she reached for the knob he'd just secured behind him in the latch. "I don't blame you." The words stuck in his throat. He'd lost the first four years of his son's life.

"Well..." He shrugged, facing her as she stood with her fist wrapped around the door handle. "I do, but...I understand, too."

Her stony expression remained right there, glaring at him. Not even a hint of softening.

Or caring.

But she was still there.

"I walked out on you after sex without a word," he allowed. "You grew up with a philandering father. Your mother constantly tried to force you to choose sides." He shrugged again. "I get it."

Who'd want to risk doing the same to their own kid?

Those soft, so-incredibly-kissable lips remained two thin lines. And her eyes—they were more like sharp points rather than the resting pools he'd found them to be in the past.

"You thought you were protecting your son."

His son. God have mercy, he had a son.

The idea just kept hitting him over the head. Seemingly brand new each time he thought about it.

Him being a father just wasn't taking shape. He had to see the boy, to listen to him, in order to believe having a son was real.

He had to make things right with the boy's mother first.

Even if he had some beef with how it had all gone down.

A full minute passed without words. Shelby was still there, more combative looking than not.

Unnerving him some, truth be told. He'd said his bit. Either she was going to meet him halfway or not.

Make peace or leave the room.

"That's it?" Her tone, much softer than he'd expected, fell into the silence. The words seemed to be laced with disappointment, not battle.

Maybe his good judgment wasn't in full force yet, still stifled by the blow to his head.

What more did she want?

All he had for her was another shrug.

"You sure you want to do this?" she asked next, still holding the doorknob.

"Yes." No doubt there. It was the first step toward his son.

And…toward maybe finding a place where he could talk to her again. As he had five years ago. Where they could be…friends. Or something.

"And you honestly think all you did was walk out after sex without saying a word?"

If possible, the slits in her eyes had narrowed further.

"Yes." He'd regained his memory; they'd established that. He was willing to get beyond her having lied to him about visiting him in Payson to tell him she was pregnant. Didn't that earn him some slack in the disappearing-without-a-word fiasco?

It wasn't like he'd just sauntered out to breakfast and then meandered through an easy day. He'd been called to a fire. And had suffered a minor injury on the job, too, resulting in brief memory loss. All of which she currently knew.

"So the money…" She shook her head. Her entire expression filled with disgust. Except that brief flash of hurt in her eyes before they sharpened right up again.

Money? "Did I leave you with a room service bill?" They'd had champagne. Chocolate. Filet mignon. He thought he'd charged it to his room, but maybe it had gone on hers since that was where they'd been…

"You left me with a thousand dollars…"

"I did not." Absolutely not.

Her expression flattened. It was as though all fight had gone out of her. But none of the warmth he'd found in her returned.

And he had to wonder…had she confused him with some other man?

Did that mean the boy wasn't his after all?

"You signed the thank-you card, Luke."

"What thank-you card?"

"The one that was sent up with the breakfast charged to your room."

The unmistakable accusation in her tone slowed him up.

Concerned him.

Had he sent breakfast? He didn't remember much after getting the call to report to Marnell. Lives had been at stake. He'd already been mentally assessing...

But...there'd been a huge flash of regret that he'd left Shelby to wake up alone in bed. Sending up breakfast sounded like something he'd have wanted to do, if he'd had the wherewithal to think of it.

But a card?

And a thousand bucks?

Shaken, he stared at her, needing to read her mind. Wishing she could see that the scene she described wasn't in his.

What possible reason could she have for lying to him?

If the boy wasn't his, she'd never have offered him access to her son's DNA. And he'd already let her off the hook over not having told him she was pregnant.

Money wouldn't have been an issue.

Well, not exactly accurate. Money was *part* of the issue.

The fact that he'd given it to her, not that she'd wanted to get it from him.

But even if she'd been after money, even if he'd done what she'd said—denied that the child was his—all she'd have had to do was sue him for child support.

And...another thought came tumbling on the top of the rest, a memory from the past couple of days, sitting there with his past. And not fitting.

When she'd told him that he'd denied that the baby was

his, she hadn't yet known about the memory loss he'd suffered in Marnell. She'd have been working under the assumption that when his memory returned, he would know she was lying.

Unless…were there still pieces missing? Had he never completely recovered memories after the Marnell injury? His doctor had said there could be blanks from the current injury. Ones that might never be filled.

How could he possibly trust himself if he didn't know what he knew was all there was?

While his thoughts stumbled along—tripping over each other, leaving him feeling weaker than he could ever remember feeling—Shelby just stood there.

Giving him time? Refusing to leave until he'd given her…some kind of closure? An apology?

And explanation.

He knew what she needed.

"I remember our night together," he told her, voice low because it was all he had in his current situation with her. "I remember the week of interviews. I remember feeling a connection to you like none other… Even considering for the first time in my life that there might be someone with whom I could partner and make a family…"

Nope. Wrong thing. She pursed her lips. Closed her eyes. And when those expressive brown orbs reopened, they were blank.

"I remember waking in your room to my phone beeping on your nightstand." He felt more like himself as he got back to his normal way of sticking to facts. "I didn't want to wake you. Left the room. Found out about the fire. And never went back."

And after the fire…had he not remembered their time together even after his memory returned the first time? He'd gotten the memories back. But how did he know if they'd just arrived back the night before with the rest of his past?

Could they have been missing during the entirety of the ensuing nearly five years?

"I don't remember breakfast, Shelby." He wasn't a liar. "It sounds like something I'd have liked to have done, but truthfully, being on a run to a fire, I'm finding it highly unlikely that I'd have done it. Except...you were so different..." He shrugged yet again. Then said, "But a card? Money?" He had nothing. Fell short of offering her...anything. Just shook his head.

Then, as she continued to stare at him, her silence like a nail in his coffin, he said, "It's just not something I'd do."

How did you convince someone that you didn't do something when you couldn't remember what you had done?

He knew he didn't.

"You slammed the door in my face when I drove up to Payson to tell you about the baby."

He just wouldn't have.

Ever.

"I have no memory of it."

A sense of acceptance seemed to come over her. Not in a joyful way.

"I can still remember the sound of the dead bolt as you slid it in place," she said. "It slid, seemed to catch. And then, as if to shoo me off, it squeaked as it fully locked."

No.

But, God, yes.

He remembered the catch, had chiseled at it—which caused the squeak—but didn't fix the original problem. He'd replaced the whole thing...

Everything inside him stilled. Hardened.

She'd been to his home.

A hard ball of nausea sat in his gut. Sick of not remembering, not knowing his own thought process, he felt equally undone at the thought of remembering that man. Of being him.

"I have no memory of ever paying anyone off for anything. Or of ever shirking my responsibilities or deliberately being an ass to anyone just to suit myself." He had nothing else to give her.

"What about the girls in the threesome?"

He'd forgotten that detail. Tried to bring up any pictures to go with what he'd been told.

Nothing.

Was it possible that he'd just chosen to lose that part of himself? Could the brain arbitrarily do that to a guy?

"So maybe your memory hasn't returned as completely as you thought."

Maybe.

He'd remembered himself pretty thoroughly.

It felt done.

As proven by the list he'd just turned over.

And none of it changed a very key fact. "I want to know my son."

He wanted to have the boy's mother in his life, too, as more than just a baby mama. But reaching for the stars was beyond him at the moment.

I want to know my son.

Standing with her back to the bedroom door, Shelby faced Luke and let go of her death grip on the handle of her escape to freedom.

She was never going to be free of the man.

Carter made that feat an impossibility.

"He needs to know you, too," she said, practically

choking the words out. Knowing, even as much as she hated letting them fly, that they were the right ones.

Regardless of why he'd refused to take accountability for what he'd done to her, whether he really didn't remember or just didn't want to own what he'd done, what mattered was whether he could fill the gaping void in Carter's life before her son started having issues she couldn't fix with a hug, a tickle or a bedtime story.

Her father had lied to her. So smoothly she'd believed him for a long time. But only about the affairs, the women who meant nothing to him.

Because he'd wanted them to mean nothing to her and Sylvia, too.

And he'd lied when he put sex with the current flavor over getting to a birthday party or dance recital on time. Or at all.

But he'd always shown up. With birthday presents, recital flowers, praise and support...whatever she'd needed. Just in his own time.

His love had given her confidence in herself.

His existence had given her identity...

Luke dropped to the edge of the bed. Sat there staring up at her, eyes wide, brow raised high. She could almost hear the questions racing through him. Felt as though some of the fear she was experiencing belonged to him, too.

But the elation she also read in his expression...took her breath away.

"There will be strict guidelines," she blurted out, panicking at the sudden impulse she had to hug him.

To hold on as they twirled together in a circle-dance of excitement. Or just stand together, body to body, absorbing life's goodness.

"I agree to them."

Nodding, she swallowed. Then said, "You haven't heard them yet."

"Doesn't matter. I agree."

For a second, she was transported back to the after-noon before they'd spent the night in bed together. Luke had been talking about disclaimers he had to sign for a side job he'd taken during the off-season. He'd agreed to help rescue all of the people from a small endangered community who were trapped in a valley built beneath a mountain ledge that had been compromised. And if anything happened to him, he'd be on his own. If the job went over budget, he was on his own.

It wasn't that he'd refused to consider the possible cost to himself. He'd been fully aware of his own poten-tial inconvenience, discomfort or loss. He'd simply been willing to deal with them if he was called upon to do so. The job had meant that much to him.

Did that mean being in Carter's life meant that much to him as well?

Meeting his gaze, she had her answer as silently as she'd had her understanding. He'd do what it took.

At least until she pushed him too far, and then he could always get a lawyer and sue for shared custody. The thought came with a dose of reality.

But even then, she couldn't...

A sharp knock on the door right behind her interrupted all thought. Swinging around, she was barely out of the way before the wood swung open.

"Did either of you order pizza?" Bruce's question, though seemingly bland, was issued in a harsh, urgent tone.

"Of course not," she said, her voice colliding with Luke's "No."

"We need to get you out of here," Bruce said, motioning them forward and then pushing behind them.

Lorraine waited by the outer door, holding two sets of fire gear, one over each arm, with a pair of boots on either side of her and head gear on the TV table to her right.

Shelby had no time to think. One quick look at Luke, his nod, was all it took for her to step back into the gear she'd recently vacated, listening as the fire sirens went off.

Figuring they were going out as they'd come in, as firefighters, she was surprised to reach the truck garage a quick staircase later and find an entire wall of uniformed men and women—dressed exactly like she, Luke, Bruce and Lorraine were—all lined up.

An engine roared out of the station, followed by an ambulance.

Three minutes later, another engine left, minus the sirens, with some of the firefighters inside. She and Luke and their bodyguards were crammed together in the back of the fifth ambulance to pull out of the station. And from what she'd seen, there'd be a sixth following right behind them out into the street.

All going in different directions.

All outfitted with cameras that would record anyone who was following them.

Because of a random pizza delivery to the fire station.

She caught the gist of what was happening through observation and a few hurried comments along the way. Luke's plan hadn't worked, was the assumption.

Not long-term.

He'd gotten them to safety.

But their killer knew he was alive.

And had already found him.

She understood what was going on and why.

What she didn't get was the way her hand found its way under Luke's bulkily outfitted thigh as she sat next to him on a gurney.

Or the way her panic calmed when she felt his fingers slide beneath hers.

They were two ships caught in a debilitating storm, she told herself. Banding together to fight the disaster attacking them.

They were an error in judgment she'd made years before. A soulmate mirage she'd created in her own mind.

They were the mother and father of the same child.

They were not a couple.

And they never would be.

Chapter 14

How in the hell had the killer found them?

If he'd found them.

Pizza-delivery mistakes happened.

He had to hope that was all they were dealing with.

But he wasn't taking any chances. Not with Shelby.

Luke owed her. She'd had his son alone. Raised him for four years.

Made sense that he couldn't stop feeling her.

Resolution reached, he allowed himself to stay connected with her as much as possible as they drove from one fire station to another, loaded into different vehicles and drove around the city. When Sierra's Web deemed it safe, they had quick showers at the last station, dressed in clothes that had been delivered to them as they'd been leaving the first one, and were driven in a firefighter's personal truck to a fancy hotel, where they climbed into the back of a swanky limousine.

They'd look conspicuous arriving at their destination—a six-thousand-square-foot home built into the bottom of a mountain on the beach of a popular lake dividing the Arizona and California borders—in anything less.

He'd been thoroughly briefed while Shelby had been in the shower. Had been given choices and made on-the-spot decisions.

The activities were overkill. So many people, so much effort to keep one man and woman alive. But he had the money to pay for it all. And nothing else he cared to spend it on.

More than ever, he was driven only to keep Shelby and himself alive to get them back to their son. Thoughts of meeting that small boy were more compelling than any he'd had while putting out flames. All assessment and planning went to that end.

The fire vehicle game of tag had come from him—as an escape route, if necessary—prior to occupying Mc-Donald's quarters.

The rest—the limo, the house on the beach—were all Sierra's Web's doing. The firm had former clients in high places who were only too happy to help out.

While Bruce kept watch, moving from one side of the long car to the other in various seats, Lorraine drove the nearly two hundred miles across the desert.

And Luke, in his clean black shorts and gray short-sleeved shirt, sat beside Shelby on the couch along the back of the vehicle. They'd each had three outfits from which to choose. She'd put on denim shorts and a white sleeveless blouse.

An outfit making it harder for him to not notice her as a woman. The shorts were no shorter than the ones she'd been wearing the past couple of days.

But his newly recalled memories filled in all the blanks.

Not that she seemed to notice.

Other than nodding where appropriate and thanking those helping them, Shelby had been quiet. He'd heard that she'd made another recorded call to Carter while he was in the shower.

"I apologize that I'm taking you farther from Carter," he said when Bruce answered a call from Hudson on his new burner phone.

"I travel all over for work. Distance isn't the issue. The time away is."

A sentiment he'd heard from various hotshot team members when they'd put in notice to take local jobs. One he fully understood for the first time. Although his brain had comprehended them before, his heart just now felt the emotion that had driven those choices.

He had nothing to say to that.

Bruce, hanging up the phone right then, turned toward Luke. Seeing the grim expression on the man's face, Luke braced himself.

"Sierra's Web, with the help of law enforcement, traced the pizza delivery to an online order from an internet café, one with no camera coverage..."

Of course. Tracing the order placer wasn't going to be easy. They'd probably need a warrant for payment information.

Which meant more time before they'd know for sure if the latest threat had just been a mistake...

"The order was paid for with a card connected to a Cayman Islands account."

As soon as he heard those last words, he tensed. Felt like Bruce and Shelby were staring straight at him.

"I wasn't at an internet café," Luke blurted out. So unlike him. To blurt. And to jump to his own defense.

He protected himself slowly. Methodically.

And why in hell would he order pizza and then lie about doing so?

"Of course not." Bruce nodded, holding Luke's gaze for a telling second.

The payment method made the chances of the delivery address being a mistake a bit less likely. Which meant Luke's overall plan had failed.

His killer knew he was still alive.

Luke didn't look at Shelby. He felt her move. Not away. Or closer. Just…move.

"That's proof that someone else is accessing the account, right?" she asked, still obviously on the Cayman thing. The anticipation in her voice… That's what he heard most.

"They don't know that it's Luke's account, just that the account originates there."

"But it's a pretty big coincidence, don't you think?" she asked.

And Luke wanted to preen like a little kid with a double-decker ice-cream cone. Dipped in chocolate. Shelby was coming to his defense.

Even if it was just a desperate attempt to convince herself that her son's father, the man who'd soon be meeting the boy, was not a complete creep—he liked hearing it.

For a second, until he remembered that they were likely still being hunted like animals.

"It's not my place to say." Bruce's response was job appropriate, until the man added, "But I agree—there's a whole lot going on here that's not fitting right."

With what sounded like a second man on board his

sinking boat, Luke needed a beer. "Are we getting a daily report sometime soon?"

"Later today. They're waiting on the pizza toxicology report. And Hudson said that the warrant for Gerard Michaels's financials came through. Winchester's on standby to go through them himself as soon as they arrive." Bruce named the financial expert.

So-so news, now that he had some of his memory back. Michaels was a good guy. Luke had trusted him implicitly.

As he would have if they'd been in cahoots together? Had Michaels helped him live a double life? Did the man know the side of Luke he couldn't seem to remember?

Or had Michaels been playing him for a fool? The man knew every time Luke was out of contact. Could the financial manager have orchestrated his own exploits on Luke's dime, making it appear as though Luke had done it all?

Paying off Shelby... She'd said she got cash in a card sent up at breakfast.

Anyone could have ordered that breakfast, signed his name to the card. But Michaels had Luke's electronic signature on file...

Didn't explain Luke slamming the door in her face when she'd visited him in Payson...

He didn't slam doors.

But that dead bolt—she'd described it spot-on.

Maybe he'd misunderstood who she was. If he hadn't remembered her...he could have assumed she was someone else. His phone could have rung, signaling an emergency, and he'd shut the door hard out of urgency, not rudeness...

"It could have just been a mistake." He hadn't meant

to say the words aloud. Not when he couldn't have the private conversation with Shelby they warranted.

"The pizza delivery?" she asked. "You think there's still a chance that someone just put in the wrong address? Or maybe a grateful homeowner was sending it to the station as a thank-you for helping remove a snake from the yard or something…"

Some local Phoenix-area fire departments went on rattler duty if they were available; he'd been on one such run himself.

"But who pays for pizza with a Cayman Islands account?" Shelby continued, and Luke knew she was reaching the same conclusion he had.

No one bothered to answer that one. They rode silently across acrid desert. But the tips of Shelby's fingers found the underneath of this thigh again.

No pressure.

Just…there.

Luke didn't move. Didn't reciprocate. But he wanted to hug her.

Just that. Hug her tight.

For as long as she'd let him hang on.

Shelby hadn't known until they were pulling into the circular drive of the lovely stucco home that she and Luke weren't going to be staying anywhere in the plethora of rooms.

He'd apparently known, though, based on his steady, sure movements.

Their destination was an underground shelter just to the left of the back door, a few feet along the tree line that bordered the beach.

They went through the house to get there—in case anyone had drone eyes on them somehow, she surmised by the way Bruce even had them under a big umbrella as they moved quickly from the car to the door. She caught a brief glimpse of the lake—gorgeous blue. Peaceful along that stretch of private beach. Felt the sun's warmth.

And the next thing she knew, she was climbing down a ladder just behind Bruce, with Luke following her.

Funny how the hotshot firefighter made her feel safer than a trained and proven bodyguard did. But there it was.

When it came to men…she was off-key.

A fact that hit her square in the face the second Bruce climbed back upstairs to relieve Lorraine of guard duty so she could rest from the drive and be prepared for a long night.

With both of their personal Sierra's Web experts gone, there was just her and Luke. Alone.

In a fully decorated—rather elegant—dungeon. It was all one long, skinny room. She figured a partition down at the far end marked off a toilet area but didn't ask.

And there was a sink set in a countertop at that end. She'd seen, coming in, that there were two other partitions with beds behind them. The rest was a living area, complete with bar, mounted flat-screen and some electronics.

"There's a generator in that cupboard," Luke told her, pointing toward where she'd been looking. "We won't have any reception down here—which is the point—but I'm told there's an ample selection of DVDs and a player. The refrigerator, also on generator, is kept fully stocked. And the toilet has a pump that runs along plumbing in the ground and empties into a cesspit."

So there she had it. The basics.

She was going to be sharing very intimate quarters with the only man she'd never been able to forget. The man who'd turned her on like no other.

And had hurt her like no other, too.

A man who was going to be in her life, part of her son's family, for the rest of her days.

And one with whom she'd wanted to lose herself in lovemaking in the early hours of that very morning, when the touch of his foot against hers had woken her from dreams of him.

The same guy who still claimed he hadn't paid her off and shut his door in her face.

It was all so messed up.

They'd had lunch on the way to the lake. A casserole had been prepared and left in the refrigerator for dinner.

If they were still there the next day, they'd be on their own.

Other than an electronic device that would be dropped in a little cage in the ceiling for message-passing, there'd be no more contact with the outside world until someone could prove that the pizza delivery had been a simple mistake.

That their cover of Luke's death hadn't been blown.

"All we need is the tox screen to come back clean," she said to the room at large, standing there with her hands clasping each other. Trying to keep a lid on the myriad of emotions roiling inside her. She wasn't claustrophobic… but she'd never been trapped underground before, either.

"And for the account to check out," Luke added. He was hunched down in front of a door he'd opened on the entertainment center that took up one whole wall. "If it's my account that paid for that pizza—and it was sent to the quarters in which we were staying—even if it's not poisoned, the warning is still clear. He knows I'm alive and where we were staying."

She'd already figured that out, of course. Just hadn't

wanted to think about it. Keeping panic at bay was key to a clear head.

Which was paramount to preventing her from contemplating the one thing she could think of that would momentarily wipe everything else from her mind. Every worry. Every fear. Every doubt. Gone.

For however many minutes the man would do to her body the things he'd done five years before.

"H-how could he have found us?" she blurted out. A question she didn't want answers to. Not while she was busy trying to maintain total control.

"Johnson. Maybe in league with Michaels at this point. Sierra's Web. The dozen or so firefighters involved in our escape from the fire this morning."

Not just the ones who'd given up their truck but the ones who'd posed as cadavers under sheets on stretchers. The ones who'd stood beside them in the line for the brief time they appeared to be working...

There was so much... Too much...

Fear engulfed her for a second, and she wanted nothing more than to walk over to Luke and beg him to hold her. Just until she got her grip back.

"National Lampoon's Christmas Vacation," Luke said, pulling out the case. "You want to watch it?"

"It's a Christmas movie." In the heat of summer.

The heat of him.

"It's a comedy," he pointed out, but he hadn't moved from in front of the collection or taken the disc out of the case.

She could demur.

She thought of a few scenes from the classic film and nodded. The movie was entertaining no matter how many times you watched it. It was filled with slapstick. Family ridiculousness.

And most importantly, there wasn't one sexy, tender moment in the entire reel.

Chapter 15

He sat on one end of the plush sectional sofa set after Shelby took the other. Far enough away that he could hardly see her in his peripheral vision. Couldn't feel the cushion move when she laughed out loud.

Not so far that he lost the feel of her. Even for a second.

Nor did he stop thinking about the news they were awaiting. The movie was only a third over when a clink sounded up in the ceiling.

Shelby's laugh cut off mid-guffaw. He stopped the movie as he stood, dropped the remote behind him on the sofa and raced to the ladder, taking the rungs two at a time.

The device was a phone with no SIM card. There were recorded videos to watch from Hudson and Winchester.

And one from Carter and then Sylvia, too. Luke had scrolled down the list by the time he reached the couch, reading aloud.

"Can we please save that one for last?" Shelby asked as he sat down. Busy casting the videos from the device to the television, he was ready to argue with her.

Was she kidding?

He was finally going to get to see and hear his son.

But she was right. They had much more urgent business than his emotional needs.

He could hardly believe *he'd* needed the reminder—the blunt guy whose job was giving out orders to handle life-threatening emergencies. That he hadn't been immediately keyed into the facts he had to assess to save his own life. Or Shelby's.

Sitting a full cushion's length away from her as the phone's contents came up on the flat-screen taking up the wall, he adjusted the volume up, and—leaning forward, arms resting on top of his knees—focused completely.

Winchester Holmes, the finance partner, was first. He'd found nothing unusual on a preliminary check through Gerard Michaels's financials, but he hadn't yet looked at tax reporting. He was going to spend the evening doing a much deeper dive to look for hidden accounts or expenditures that didn't fit. For instance, a car-maintenance bill on a vehicle for which there was no purchase record.

"Because he could have paid cash for an expensive car?" Shelby asked. "Spending money with no trail to its origin?"

Luke nodded. He'd assumed the same.

Winchester's last note was that the Cayman Islands account used to pay for the pizza was tied to the one owned by Luke. Either he had more than one account or someone was draining his account into another.

Most likely Gerard?

Either way, whoever was after him knew he was still

alive. That was the reason for the pizza delivery. To let him know his plan hadn't worked.

He wasn't surprised. He'd seen it coming since their forced evacuation earlier that day.

And sitting with a frustration that was becoming way too familiar, he clicked to the next video.

Hudson. The video was brief.

Toxicology had come back on the pizza. No poison. Not in the food.

But it had definitely been there in the message that pizza had delivered.

His killer not only knew he was alive—he'd found him in a matter of hours. Maybe he hadn't found a way to murder Luke at the fire station, but unless Luke intended to stay hidden forever, the man was going to get him eventually.

When he could have just laid low until everyone thought Luke was dead long enough to come back to life.

Whoever was after him didn't just want him dead. He wanted him to suffer. It was like with every failed murder attempt, the guy was finding some kind of fuel, more cruelty.

Making Luke doubt everything he knew about himself.

"Obviously, the guy isn't going to be accessing any of your assets, so that part of the plan is probably done," Hudson continued. "Johnson and his team are looking into every one of the firefighters, and both teams—Johnson's and ours—are scouring the list you gave us. I've got one investigator, Stan Busby—a man I trust with my family's lives—looking into the entire Sierra's Web team and into Johnson's team as well." Hudson paused, then added, "Johnson is also actively trying to trap any mole he might have in his department. We'll find this guy. But until we do—until we know where the leak is, how he's finding you—the two of you are going to have to stay underground."

"What about Bruce or Lorraine?" Shelby's tone held a hint of panic. "They were the only two who knew, at all times, where we were."

"If they wanted us dead, we would be," Luke said.

And without his hotshot training, they'd all have likely died in the bomb fire. If he hadn't recognized the slim control line perimeter leading to the creek, they'd have probably all hidden out in the steel building and been consumed by smoke inhalation.

There wasn't much else on Hudson's video. The team would be working through the night.

And he and Shelby would be spending it alone, together.

In an elegant underground prison where he couldn't be in charge of fixing any situations at all. Couldn't give orders or throw his body into danger, taxing it to the limit, to save lives.

He had to rely on others to save lives while he was forced to sit with a woman he knew he'd been drawn to, whom he'd apparently hurt and insulted beyond repair. A woman who was making him feel things he'd never known he could feel.

A woman who was the mother of the son he'd never met.

And he had to do it without a single screwup.

Lord help me.

She didn't want Carter's face plastered on the big screen, consuming the room. Or rather, out in the open in such a huge way for his father to consume.

She'd set the whole mess in motion by going to identify the man in the first place. And then going back a second time…

Part of her knew she'd done the right thing for her son. But damn…

Were they ever going to find the guy who wanted Luke dead? Who'd tried to kill her, too?

Would Luke ever fully regain his memory and at least tell her why he'd done what he'd done to her?

Like the reasons could somehow help her prevent Luke from hurting her son in the future?

Or…hurt her again?

"I'm sorry."

Her head jerked up at his apology. Were they so connected that the man could read her mind?

"I know you were hoping that the pizza was just a mistaken address…"

Right.

And maybe she should have been thinking on those lines, worrying about a fiend wanting them dead.

Maybe thinking about Luke, the past, her son's future, put life on the front burner instead of death.

"I don't blame you for any of this, Luke." How could she? The man didn't want to be dead any more than she wanted to be in danger.

"You just blame me for the past."

She wasn't going to feel bad about that. "You would, too, if you'd been in my shoes." He was a fact guy, and she had the facts.

"I'd like to watch the last two videos."

She understood. He needed to see what Carter looked like. Without her phone, she hadn't been able to show him.

Or comfort herself with the thousand or more photos

she kept on the card in her phone. Images she scrolled through frequently when she was away.

"They were meant for me, personally," she told him. "I'd like to see them first."

His expression hardly changed. Just went blank.

She'd hurt him. Hadn't meant to. Or even wanted to.

But...her family trusted that their messages were in her care.

Luke handed her the phone, got up and walked to the far end of the long room, disappearing behind the partition. She watched him the whole way with a hurting heart, but she didn't call him back.

Instead, with shaking fingers, she turned off casting from the device she held, turned down the volume low enough for just her to hear and hit Play on her mother's video first.

It was short. Just letting her know that everything was great and not to worry. It ended with the "Love you" that had been their standard goodbye forever. Always.

She watched the short clip a second time, feeling better. It wasn't the content of her mother's words that calmed her but the unlined expression on her face, the easy tone.

Her mom wasn't worried.

She figured that Sierra's Web, whoever they'd sent to her mother's home, had played a huge part in that situation.

And owed that one to Luke.

The video from Carter made her so lonely for her boy she teared up for a moment. And then, playing it a second and third time, she smiled.

And felt...a little less alone, too, for the first time since his birth. Because there was another person on Earth who shared the responsibility of being her precious boy's parent. Who wanted to take him on.

A man who would share the wonder of knowing they'd made such an incredible little human being.

Because, everything else aside, she knew in her deepest heart that if Luke said he'd be there for Carter—that he *wanted* to be there—he would be.

He'd done some things to her that were hard to accept, but he'd never lied to her. That week they'd spent together, the personal questions she'd asked, he made it very clear that he'd given his life to hotshot firefighting. In lieu of any kind of committed partner relationship. He'd made a clear, purposeful choice.

And in all the years she'd kept track of him since, she'd never once caught him out in any kind of lie. Not ever.

So while he was most definitely not a candidate for her heart, he did fit Carter's needs. Recasting the phone to the screen, she dropped it on the sectional and called out toward the kitchen portion of their odd-as-hell lodging.

"Luke?"

If he was…occupied in there with personal business, she didn't need to know. Or want to interrupt. But if he was waiting…

"Yeah?" Still fully dressed, hands in the pockets of his shorts, he stepped out to face her.

"You ready to meet your son?" She tried to sound excited. Like the moments ahead were going to be filled with all fun and happiness.

But, like Carter's birth—the first time *she'd* seen her son—there was a lot of pain and anguish mixed in with that happiness, too.

Moving slowly, hands still buried in fabric, Luke approached, holding her gaze the whole time. "You're sure?" he asked, that way he had of assessing—and determining—out in full force.

"I am." She didn't hesitate. The choice had already been made.

Right or wrong. Good or bad. Better or worse.

He studied her a moment longer but didn't ask again if she was sure. He must have seen what he was seeking. He seemed satisfied as he nodded.

And then walked right by her and off to the sectional as though she didn't exist.

He had a task. A job. Something he had to do.

A moment in life to experience that he knew, going in, he would never forget.

Knew, too, that it was going to change him forever.

She'd asked if he was ready.

How in the hell did he know? He had no answers for anything to do with parenting—or much about childhood, either.

His own had been cut short.

The glance she sent in his direction as he sat down seemed questioning. "Were you ready when you found out you were pregnant?" he asked.

"No."

Nodding, he felt a bit of vindication. And waited for her to pick up the phone and change his life.

He might not know what was ahead or have any solutions to problems that would present themselves, but there was not a single doubt that he was already on the Carter road for life.

She didn't turn on the video. He glanced her way. Noting that she'd chosen a seat a little closer to him on the couch than he'd chosen earlier.

Didn't matter.

Didn't mean anything.

He wanted it to.

"If you'd rather wait…" she started, turning those brown eyes he couldn't afford to get lost in his way.

He nodded toward the phone between them. "You're the one making the introduction." It was up to her to share her boy with him.

Not his right to take Carter from the mother who'd been there for him.

"Right." She picked up the phone. He tried not to notice that her hand was shaking. The moment ahead wasn't about her. Or him, either.

"So," she continued with a trembling smile. "Luke, meet Carter."

Just Carter. Not, *meet your son.*

Words didn't change facts.

It took two pushes for her to get the video up on the screen. A mostly black background, with some red and a white Play arrow.

Another bunch of unending seconds passed before she hit Play.

The black dissipated as the camera moved, and a small tennis shoe came into view with a blotch of red on the top. "I spilled paint, Mom, and it's alweady dwy," the voice came out loud and clear. And, as only the shoe was in view, the voice continued, "I hope yow coming home soon, and I miss you and guess what? We had macawoni and cheese for dinnaw!" The screen became a dizzying blur—or maybe it was his eyes, filling with moisture—and then, before he could do anything other than feel, the camera stopped moving. He saw a brown couch spread out before them, as though the phone was leaning against an armrest. And then a little body lay down. And…

There. Chubby cheeks. Light-colored hair, a little long. And…big blue eyes, filling the screen. "I ate a dough-nut." Hands came up to cup the little boy's chin, and the top half of his body, up on his elbows, came into view. "And when awe you coming to get me? Jason's dad took him fishing again. I love you, bye." And just like that, he was gone.

Seconds. He'd had mere seconds. Not enough for…

Not nearly enough.

Luke couldn't move. Couldn't assess or determine.

Frozen, he stared at the screen. Mostly black again, with the white arrow. The cover of the video.

His son. Carter. He had eyes that blinked, five fingers on each chubby little hand. He knew how to hold himself up on his elbows. He liked doughnuts and macaroni. Wasn't afraid to tell his mother he'd ruined his tennis shoe, but the fact was important enough that it was the first thing he'd told her.

And his friend had a dad who took him fishing…

The image on the screen changed, the camera moving out from the black to show a small tennis shoe…

She'd started the video over.

He absorbed…everything.

Again and again.

Hiding underground from someone who wanted him dead, he sat on a stranger's couch next to the mother of his child and watched the boy over and over again.

And then some more.

He had no words.

She didn't speak, either.

He had no plan. Just had to sit there. Getting to know every little thing he could about his son.

Carter struggled with his *r*'s. He licked his lips when he talked about food.

He loved his mother.

Who'd moved closer to Luke. Handing him the phone so he could watch and rewatch under his own control.

She didn't leave, though. Didn't move away.

They'd entered into a brand-new world together, and maybe neither of them knew what to do next.

Chapter 16

A need to pee finally forced Shelby off the couch. And a glance at her watch told her they'd missed dinner. Sitting underground, one kind of lost sense of time of day.

Or, maybe, watching a man gain a son did that to you.

Luke was still sitting with the video playing when she came back to the kitchen. Opened the refrigerator, found an unopened bottle of wine, along with the casserole—some kind of pasta—and heating instructions.

They had a convection oven. She'd never used one but got dinner going easily. Opened the wine and poured a glass for each of them.

He was more of a beer guy. But he'd had wine with dinner a time or two the week they'd been together. And the refrigerator had no beer.

If he didn't want the wine, he didn't have to drink it. She was making an executive order, pouring it and walking it over to him. They had nowhere to be. Most definitely wouldn't be driving. And the man looked like he needed a little nudge to help him chill.

"He's incredible." Luke looked straight at her as he took the wine. "Confident, secure and transparent with you. He trusts you." The long sip he took from the glass she'd handed him bore its own testimony.

"He has your biology." Carter needed his father. She had to share him.

But she didn't have to *want* to. So…why was she starting to?

A distant rumble sounded. Like thunder? They'd left blue skies and sunshine to descend underground.

Setting his glass down, Luke moved to a cupboard by the ladder, one she hadn't paid attention to. Set up at eye level and small, the thing was mostly inconspicuous. Luke's tight expression, the urgency in his deliberate movement were not.

Opening the cupboard, he reached his hand up and then stared. She had to go see what he was doing.

And why he suddenly looked not at all like a new dad. He'd completely transformed into the supervisor of a hotshot-firefighting team. He was the man who'd led them out of the fire before dawn that morning.

The CCTV screen behind the cupboard doors, reflecting the camera of the outside, was black and white. More black than white due to the darkness, but the moon's glow on the water was clear. Not so much the body she was pretty sure she was looking at on the sand directly behind the house.

"Is that Lorraine?" It looked too small to be Bruce.

"No idea."

Heart pounding, her throat so tight she could hardly swallow, Shelby moved closer to Luke. Made herself breathe. "He's found us *again*, hasn't he?"

Luke's gaze never left the screen. "The bunker isn't registered anywhere. Only our bodyguards, Hudson, the homeowner and the two of us know about it."

And if Lorraine was down, that left Bruce or their team leader at Sierra's Web as the possible moles?

"Who wants you gone so badly they'd pay off someone like Sierra's Web?" she asked, struck with chills, feeling the wobbles in her knees. "That wouldn't be cheap."

Someone would have to be paying more than Luke was...

He didn't speak. Just continued to study, as though he could see movement, change, on the mostly black screen.

Her question had been rhetorical, anyway. If he knew who was after him, they wouldn't be locked underground.

"The people who built it..."

"It was ten years ago, and again, not on record..."

She'd seen him in deep conversation with Bruce when she came out of the shower. Had assumed he'd be a part of determining whatever plan came next. He was footing the bill, after all.

Made sense, knowing Luke, that he'd be privy to every little detail.

About the bunker.

The camera hooked up to the screen in the cupboard.

He was the guy people called in extreme emergencies. For the worst fires, in season, and for any other life-threatening situation that came up when he *wasn't* fighting fires. The man had a reputation.

As she knew better than most people.

The intense concentration with which he was staring at the screen scared her. She hadn't even seen him blink.

And it hit her...

Oh, God. "Are we sitting ducks?" she blurted out.

"That's what I'm trying to find out."

She moved closer to him. She couldn't help it. Didn't touch him. She wasn't going to turn into some needy clinger. But she drew strength from his body warmth.

"We're safe down here," he said then. "From any kind of blast, flood or fire."

Relief coursed through her.

"But if he knows we're here, that the bunker is here— if he knows the codes to release the locks..."

Like if he was holding Bruce hostage and threatening to kill his family if...

She'd read too many suspense novels. Watched too many police shows.

"Does Bruce have a family?" she asked him, pretending she was just making conversation to try to keep a sense of calm between them.

"No idea."

Studying the live feed, growing more used to the grayish images, she pointed to the left corner of the screen. "That looks like the tree line just outside of here..."

"It is. There's vegetation over the door."

With their entrance and the small cage for supplies up in their ceiling both being flat in the ground, that made sense to her.

"So we'll know if anyone approaches."

He didn't answer that time, but she knew then why he wasn't taking his gaze off the screen. He was ready to take action if anyone got close to them.

Which gave Shelby hope. There was no one else she'd rather have down there with her.

Adrenaline racing through him, Luke fought against the frustration mounting alongside it. Fires didn't sit around and wait, and death didn't do surveillance; those were the entities he was used to doing battle with.

The ones he knew how to fight.

And he was no longer saving someone else's loved ones. He was saving his son's mother.

And…the boy's father.

Someone who could take him fishing and to ride in a fire truck. Or just…give him a dad, too, like Jason had. He'd felt, deep in his gut, the sorrow in the little guy's voice when he'd mentioned his friend going fishing with his dad.

It was one of those things he was never going to forget.

Shelby's warmth beside him was another. The woman unhinged parts of him that had been hanging on a hook, with chains around it, since his teens.

A good thing—or a very bad one, depending on the moment. Either way, it was a fact.

He wasn't going to be able to change it.

Eyes dry, he blinked quickly and then refocused. No movement yet. Didn't mean there wouldn't be. While he'd never heard a shot while encased underground in cement and steel, he'd bet his bank accounts that there'd been gunshots at the house.

There was a body on the beach.

And no one standing outside the bunker.

The plan had been to have Lorraine and Bruce taking turns patrolling the beach with their little bit of tree line in sight at all times. And for one or the other of them to be continuously visible via camera to Luke as well.

Failing that, he was to assume there was serious trouble unless he got an all clear through their message cage. Until he saw one of them approach and heard that rattle, he was standing guard.

Bruce and Lorraine could both be gone. Sierra's Web would know soon enough, when the bodyguards didn't signal their predetermined all-is-well. The firm would deploy law enforcement.

Who wouldn't know about the underground quarters.

A flash on the screen nearly blinded him.

"What's that?"

Shelby's question was like fog in the background as he moved in closer, staring intently. Powerful lights lit up the entire beach within his view. Uniforms moved in, all wearing guns, followed by two bodies in suits.

"Law enforcement," he said, mostly to distill the tension that could get in the way of him doing his best work. "Dealing with the body."

Not Lorraine. Or any name. Just a body. The time to grieve came when the work was done.

While he couldn't identify any of the living, either, he'd have been able to pick out Bruce. The man was taller than most.

Shelby moved to another part of the shelter. He didn't welcome the immediate chill that followed her departure, but he figured it was for the best that she not see whatever else might happen up above them.

Still: "Stay close," he said. He might need to grab and go. Already knew the direction through the trees he'd take before circling around to get her back to the beach. To a cove he'd seen off in the distance when they were heading in.

A cove offered protection, and the beach wouldn't burn.

From there, he'd figure it out as they went. His forte.

Officers had spread out. They were canvassing the perimeter of the beach as far as he could see, guns in hands stretched out in front of them. Ready to shoot.

Bruce had told him there was a loaded pistol in the small drawer beneath the cupboard he now stood before.

He had a carry license.

Wasn't going to worry about that, either way.

The body, covered with a sheet and on a stretcher, disappeared from view.

Shelby was back; he heard her before he caught a peripheral glimpse. "You need to eat," she said, holding a plate to him at chin level. Close enough that he could smell the onions, tomato sauce and cheese.

He took the plate, shoveled in food with his attention never leaving the screen. And when she lifted the empty plate from his hand, he nodded his thanks.

While the beach remained boldly lit, there were fewer bodies combing it. One group at the edge of his screen, standing closest to the house, had been in consultation for several minutes, with one member on the phone.

He'd still seen no sign of Bruce.

And not a clear-enough view to tell if Lorraine was among those walking around. She'd been wearing long black cotton pants and a dark short-sleeved shirt the last time he saw her. He wasn't seeing that attire on anyone, but she could have changed.

Without the bodyguards, it was unlikely anyone knew Luke and Shelby were on the premises.

Except their would-be killer.

Was he out there? Among those scouring the beach for clues?

A team with individual flashlights had entered the beach and were bent over, studying the sand. Forensics, he figured, by the way they appeared to pick up things and then put them in bags.

Shelby was back, standing just to his left and half a step behind him.

"Assuming we remain undetected, I'm planning to stay right here until morning," he told her.

"I'd have thought it would be best to move in the dark…" She didn't sound like she minded staying put. More like she was trying to be part of whatever was happening to her.

He got that.

"Ordinarily, yes, but because we don't have any idea what's happened, who's out there—even who the bad guys are—it would serve us best to be able to see."

"To assess our adversaries."

Luke almost glanced her way when she made the comment. "Yes," he confirmed. Proud of her for no reason whatsoever.

Because he didn't have any relationship with her that would give him the right to take pride in her accomplishments.

Except when it came to motherhood.

And he was damned proud of her there…

No.

Screen movement. The scene unfolding. That was all he could know until the coast was clear.

Pulling himself back wasn't easy. But he did it.

"If no one knows about us—most particularly, if the guy after us doesn't know where we are—we're safest right here. We've got more than a week's provisions. And with daylight, I'll have a much better view of our surroundings through here." He pointed to the camera.

She wasn't his crew. Didn't have to just do what he said without question. Her life was in danger, and she deserved to know everything he could tell her.

Unfortunately, he'd given her everything he had.

Another half hour passed as he stood there. And then an hour. Other than brief stints away, Shelby stood right there with him. Mostly silent. She asked a question or two, procedural things about the group, including the two suits, that crowded around the area where the body had been.

And then: "There he is!" she screamed, just as Luke saw a man who had to be Bruce come into view.

The bodyguard was alive.

And if Bruce wasn't the mole, Luke's chances of getting Shelby back home to Carter alive had just gotten better. The man knew where they were and hadn't pointed anyone in their direction.

The danger wasn't done. Not by a long shot. Clearly, their general location had been breached.

But not their exact one.

They still had a fighting chance.

As he stood there next to her in the small space, relief flooded him—and, acting completely like a guy he didn't even know, he reached down and took her hand.

Chapter 17

Shelby almost wept when she saw Bruce's face take over the screen. She'd been standing for more than half an hour, holding Luke's hand.

Not speaking about the connection.

Or questioning, either.

But she missed his touch, felt the cool air on her hand when, a few seconds later, he left her to climb up to the message cage.

They'd heard the thunk together.

She watched alone as Bruce stepped back out to the beach.

Luke came back with a memory card. She followed him to the couch and waited as he inserted the small plastic piece into the phone and then scrolled to find whatever was on it.

"It's a video," he said, coming over to her, standing close, huddling over the small screen with her.

"There was an intruder at the house," Bruce's voice

started when his face appeared on screen. "He briefly had Lorraine captive with a gun to her head, told her he'd let her go as soon as she told him where he could find Luke Dennison. She was able to throw him but not immediately contain him. He fled to the beach, where he saw me, pointed his gun—at which point, we both shot our weapons. After which, we immediately called the police. The intruder's prints came up. He's a known hit man working almost exclusively out of California. Unfortunately, he did not survive to be questioned. Law enforcement, with Sierra's Web's help, are combing through financials and phone records to determine who hired him. Lorraine and I have been interviewed, said that we were staying on the premises as guests of the owner, and have been let go. Sierra's Web cleared us to remain on duty.

"Local law enforcement do not know that the two of you, or the shelter, are here," Bruce's voice continued. "It's been determined that the two of you are safest right where you are, at least until morning. Sierra's Web has assigned a couple more bodyguards to the detail. The four of us will be taking turns throughout the night, resting and patrolling.

"Other members of the team will be working throughout the night to figure out how you're being tracked. There's been no evidence of any kind as to who a mole might be. Everyone is checking out with provable alibis. Our current burners weren't traced, and the car's tracking software had been physically removed before the car was put in service with us this morning. It's been gone over a second time, and there was no device found.

"If you have anything to report, send it up. Otherwise, get some rest."

Not likely, Shelby thought, glancing around their surroundings before Bruce's voice called her attention back to the phone.

"Oh…and Hudson said to tell you the DNA test came back as a match."

Her mind blanked for a second as the screen went black. She'd known, of course. There'd been absolutely no doubt.

But now there was official medical record… Carter was no longer just *her* son.

Legally, she was going to have to share him.

The thought scared her to death for the second it took her to glance up at Luke. Or rather, for her gaze to follow him as he took a few steps and fell to the couch.

"He's really my son."

She didn't think an *I told you so* was appropriate. But she moved over to sit beside him.

"I just…"

His gaze as intent as it had been on the screen for the past couple of hours, he studied her. Her eyes, her face, back to her eyes. "I have no idea why I'd ever have called you a liar and shut my door in your face," he said. "It's not me. I can't accept that I'd do such a thing. I'm many things, but I would never turn my back on my own child."

"If you didn't remember having sex with me…" She couldn't believe she was helping him make excuses.

But how did you hold someone accountable to something they couldn't remember—and therefore, couldn't explain or defend?

She'd never forget… Would always be on guard… But…

He shook his head without breaking eye contact. "I'd have asked for proof…"

"It's water under the bridge, Luke," she heard herself

say. There were so many more important things to figure out between them.

At the moment, they had to get through spending the night alone together in the small space. She was about to crawl out of her skin.

With fear.

Claustrophobia. Not so much of the closed space but of being trapped underground, with a killer believing they were in the area.

With wanting him.

The look in his eyes when'd found out he had a son...

The moisture she saw in them right then as he looked to her for answers neither of them had...as he slowly comprehended that he was really and truly a father...

She was sitting with the man she'd fallen head over heels for in one week's time.

Five years before.

The man whose child she'd borne.

Alone.

They were fighting for their lives.

The reality was too surreal to grasp.

"I lost the first four years of his life."

And there was nothing anyone could do about that. But: "Most of it, he's not even going to remember. Can you—" She broke off abruptly and then said, "I have very few memories from when I was that young."

"I don't have many, either," he said then, and she realized that he knew what she'd been about to say. Asking a man with memory issues to take comfort from what he couldn't remember—as though if he couldn't recall, no one else would be able to—wouldn't have been her best argument. "I do remember the first time my dad took me to play T-ball, though. I know I was four because that's how old you had to be to start the league, and I'm told I kept asking how many more days until my birthday so I could go play. I guess I was crushed that, with my actual birthday being out of season, I had to wait another two months for the league to start."

If she hadn't already figured out just how far Luke was from his normal self, his uncharacteristically long speech would have shown her. She ate up every word.

Smiled at him.

Grabbed his hand, squeezed and held on.

"I have videos from day one forward and thousands of pictures, too," she told him. "You'll know about every moment, will be able to picture them, to hear him say one of his first words—not as he's saying it but later that same day..."

And most importantly, Carter was going to have what he needed most.

A man in his life.

And her?

She dropped Luke's hand, under guise of reaching for the glass of wine she'd left on the table hours before, uncaring that it was warm.

Could memory have enhanced the lovemaking she'd shared with this guy? Had she built it into more than it had been to justify getting pregnant by a man she hardly knew? One who'd paid her off?

Had it been her way of not feeling...cheap? Pretending that she'd thought they'd had something out-of-this-world special?

She remembered his touch so clearly—when she let herself think about it at all. Remembered the couple of days before it had happened, how she couldn't stop thinking about going to bed with her interviewee. That had been a first for her, and she'd struggled with the ethics of it.

But was her mind playing tricks on her? Had she reframed it all to suit what her life had become?

How did she know?

Memory was a tenuous thing. Clouded by time and differing perspectives.

She'd never have slept with the man if she hadn't believed them to be mutually connecting on some deeper level.

Not *be a couple* or *get married* connected. Just...two people who were meant to meet and share something more.

Never in her life had she had sex with a man who didn't mean something to her.

And only knowing him a week? She'd known every other man she'd slept with more than a year before going to bed with him.

She was just weird that way.

Except when it came to Luke Dennison.

He'd been sitting there, watching the video again with the volume off. When he flipped it off, she tensed.

Told herself to relax. She wasn't going to do anything stupid.

Until the man reached for her hand again, taking it between both of his. "I need you to understand that I'm not a guy who uses women or takes sex lightly," he said, meeting her gaze. "You're letting me into your son's life. You have to know that I will teach him to respect and honor people, not take advantage of them."

She had to look away. Couldn't look away. Those vivid blue eyes—their look touched her.

Just as they had in the past. She hadn't imagined that part. Or enhanced it, either.

Had everything else been real, too, then? The lovemaking part?

The rest… Who knew? Maybe he'd left the money to cover her week's expenses? Because she'd expressed concern about mixing business with pleasure? He hadn't said, but he was a guy of few words…

She had to know.

Before they moved forward, she needed answers…

He couldn't tell her why he'd left the money, and only he knew. Same with shutting the door on her.

But the rest…

She leaned forward. Didn't think. Just did it.

When he didn't pull back, she leaned in more and…a little more.

Until her lips touched his.

And recognized him.

Oh, God.

Have mercy.

Those lips. Her scent. Her softness.

Just as he'd remembered. And then some.

Had to stop.

Couldn't take pleasure from her.

He owed her.

Had wronged her.

Was already hard with just their lips pressed together.

And couldn't reject her. Not ever again.

He waited for her to finish. Focused on maintaining control.

It was just mouths touching.

Her tongue slid between his lips. Torture.

Sweet, exquisite torture.

He had to respond. To ignore her would be like shutting a door in her face.

His tongue, his mouth, his arms—they knew what to

do without his direction. Free to not reject, they moved of their own accord.

Giving, and taking, too…

For her.

And—God help him—for him, too.

The woman was hungry and delicious. He kissed her, danced his tongue with hers, until he couldn't breathe.

And when he broke to gasp for air he couldn't draw in quickly enough, he planted his lips on her neck.

Moaning, she tilted her head back.

Moaned a second time.

A sound he remembered with more blood flow rushing straight to his penis, as he kissed his way down her neck.

She lay back, giving him easier access to more flesh, and his chin pushed the neckline of her shirt down as far as it would stretch.

He'd never known sex like it had been with her. As though his body knew exactly how to help her reach paradise.

He was a fire extinguisher, not a fire starter. Hadn't ever been particularly hot with women. But with Shelby…

"Don't stop," she half gasped when he raised his head.

"We should…"

Her hands up his shirt, she stopped moving them all over his chest. He missed them. They were still there, and he missed them. Their passion. On him.

"You don't want to?" she asked, looking him straight in the eye.

He couldn't lie to her.

"I want to more than just about anything I've ever wanted." Stupid, trite words. To show her what he meant, he lay back, pulling her down on top of him, and, holding both hands at her butt, ground his penis into her pelvis.

"I want to, too," she said, a Madonna-like smile

spreading over the lips pink and moist from his kisses. "We're here, locked in alone, no outside world for the entire night..."

The way her words drifted took him on a trail to what they could do with an entire night alone. Together.

He wasn't going to shut the door on her. Not ever again.

And he knew just how to please her. With his hands, his lips. Even his feet tangling with hers, holding them while he slid her legs apart.

Fully clothed, right then, and later, he spread them again, naked on the first partitioned bed they'd fallen onto.

He had a condom in his wallet. She carried a couple in her purse, too.

When the thought hit that her unexpected pregnancy had caused her to be more careful that way, he pushed it firmly away.

She wanted him to pleasure her, and he could do it.

As well as he fought fires.

So he did.

Over and over.

Until they finally fell asleep wrapped around each other.

Chapter 18

She wasn't sorry.

Waking up from what seemed like a long, deep, restful sleep, Shelby was immediately aware of the body snuggled up to hers. She knew who he was and that he was every bit as naked as she was. But in the partitioned space lit dimly by the small light they'd failed to turn off in the living area, she had no idea of the time.

She saw Luke's old-fashioned wristwatch on the arm wrapped around her. Was pretty sure it said it was just after seven.

She had to pee.

And to walk away from that bed and finally be able to leave the past behind. Reframed.

The lovemaking had been as incredible as she'd remembered. She hadn't fooled herself. Or been a fool.

The parts of Luke's personality, his spirit, that had drawn her were real. They connected in a deep unique way.

She'd found peace.

And this time, he wasn't leaving.

She was.

Not leaving him. She couldn't. Like it or not, the man was going to be in her life forever. Even if, after Carter was grown, she never saw Luke again, he'd still be there. The father of her child.

But she was leaving their bed.

And that was for good.

Sliding out from under the arm slung over her waist, she moved her leg slowly from beneath Luke's heavier weight, rolled over and off the edge of the bed, and quickly scooted around the partition closing them in. The bag of clothes and essentials that had been delivered was hanging from a hook behind the toilet partition right where she'd left it.

At some point, Luke had left his own there on the hook next to hers.

A practical necessity—not a sign. They weren't a couple. They were going to raise a child, not hang out together. Luke was…Luke.

Parts of him fit her. Parts did not.

Maybe if he could remember the way he'd treated her after the last time they'd had sex, if he could explain and there really had been different inferences, other circumstances and intentions…

No.

He'd called her a liar and then shut the door in her face. For a second there, she'd even thought he smiled as he did so, but she'd never been sure about that one.

And beyond the past, which she'd now put behind her, Luke Dennison would feel trapped by the needs of a woman, of a partner relationship. As a noncustodial father, he could come and go.

As a spouse, or even a monogamous long-term boyfriend, he'd feel obligations that warred with the man he needed to be.

She'd understood that from the beginning.

He'd even told her so during his interview, but only because she'd seen the battle inside him, had been fascinated and moved by his incredible commitment to what he did, and had wanted to be able to somehow express that part of him in her story. Luke was married to hotshot firefighting—a commitment that required him to drop everything at a moment's notice to rush off and put his life in danger. He'd said he couldn't, in good conscience, ask someone to be a life partner and then ditch the partnership on a constant basis.

And in the off-season, he was committed to overcoming other dangerous physical feats to save lives.

She'd gone to bed with him years ago, knowing that it wouldn't lead to any kind of coupling outside that hotel room. She'd made a conscious decision because she hadn't wanted to miss the experience of making love with him. Hadn't wanted to live the rest of her life never feeling him as intimately as she possibly could.

She'd wanted to know the real thing rather than risk carrying around a mirage of what she imagined being with Luke would be like, forever comparing every other man she met to the fantasy.

Instead, for once in her life, reality had been better than fantasy.

Until breakfast had arrived the next morning.

But no matter. She'd moved beyond all that. Doing her business, dressing quickly once she'd climbed out of her mental monologue, Shelby grabbed the travel toothbrush and paste she'd found in her bag. She went to the kitchen for some water and saw Luke standing, fully dressed in yesterday's clothes, in front of the open cupboard by their ladder up to the world.

"All's good," he said, smiling at her. "Lorraine's on duty right now. The beach is quiet. And I made coffee."

The look in his eye as he came toward her made her duck her head into the sink and shove a glob of toothpaste on her brush from down there, which was incredibly awkward. Then, with no water running yet, she started brushing.

No kissing.

The night was over.

Absolutely no kissing.

Resolve firmly strengthened, she turned the water on to rinse and spit. Didn't even attempt to be elegant about it.

He was Carter's father—period. And their son... There was nothing even halfway classy about his spitting tooth-paste at the mirror to see if he could make it stick.

Luke was gone by the time she'd finished brushing and had rinsed out the sink. From behind the back par-tition, she heard him bang what sounded like an elbow against the wood. She poured herself a cup of the cof-fee he'd made, deliberately leaving him to pour his own.

Not to be rude. At all.

But because she couldn't let herself pretend, even for a second, that they were...well...more than they were.

Pouring his wine the night before...that had been be-fore.

She heard the clank of a message dropping into the cage upstairs before she'd even had her first sip of the strong black brew.

"Luke? A message dropped," she called out. Two sec-onds later, he appeared from behind the partition, still getting dressed. His dark cargo shorts were on but unfastened, the orange T-shirt still in his hand.

Someone had picked green boxer briefs for him. They…um…molded to his… Yeah, he was hard.

But when she lifted her gaze—filled with intimate knowing—to meet his, Luke's eyes were not trained on her. He was focused on the ladder ahead of him, his head tilted up toward the cage she knew was there but, from her angle, couldn't see.

Had she been his girlfriend or even a woman who'd spent the night with him hoping they were starting a relationship, she'd have been hurt by his complete lack of awareness of her.

Of course he needed to get to the message. They needed to get out of the shelter and back to life. But he'd already said that everything up on the surface was peaceful.

The message in the cage was the briefing they'd known would be coming after all hands had been on deck during the night. A little eye contact could wait.

Maybe just a hint of regret that the night was through?

And, bing! Right there. Her hurt feelings. That was why she could never be in a relationship with Luke Dennison. Not that he was open to one. But even if he was, she couldn't be because of their son. It would be a recipe for disaster.

She knew that as clearly as she knew she'd give up her life for Carter's.

She couldn't give her heart to a man who would break it, making her defensive against him. Making others around her choose sides to keep her safe. Forcing people to feel horrible about loving the man who'd hurt her. She would not be her mother.

Because Carter didn't just need her in his life; he needed his father, too.

Just watching him glom on to the one video of Carter the night before, sitting through all his questions about the boy... Luke loved their son already.

Which thrilled her. More than she'd realized could happen. Made her teary-eyed with joy.

Her son came first, always.

So why, when her heart tried to tell her that having Luke in Carter's life would be enough, couldn't she believe it?

Not the least bit concerned about Shelby seeing his hard-on, actually thinking about his own personal future for the first time in a long while, Luke was eager to retrieve the electronic device—to find out who was after him, deal with the guy and go meet his son.

With his son's mother right by his side.

Where it all led, he had no idea. He was still him. Dedicated to firefighting. But most of his team members were married. Had families.

If they could do it, he could learn how, too.

Right?

With the right motivation, he could learn anything.

Shelby knew what he was. She'd come on to him with the same hunger she'd given him in the past—even knowing that, as a partner, he'd give her challenges and bumps in the road.

Not that they were going to be partners...other than in raising Carter. But they could at least look into the possibilities.

After climbing back down into the shelter, with thoughts of the work ahead shrinking his penis, Luke fastened his pants as he approached the sink, where Shelby still stood.

It had to be business first. For both of them.

Something they'd had in common in the past. An understanding that had made him lower his defenses around her from almost the beginning.

Wishing he could take charge, get the job done, just to wipe the concern off her face, he saw the video on the front screen and moved in close, needing to be there for her as much as they needed to huddle to see the screen at the same time, and tapped the Play arrow.

Hudson's face, needing a shave, filled the screen. The IT expert had obvious shadows under his eyes as he said, "The guy on the beach last night… He's suspected in several professional hits, but there's no sign of him getting paid for last night. No money connection at all between any of your possible enemies—or Michaels. But we did find an odd connection between the two of you, just not what we expected. You pulled his mother out of a fire a few years ago…"

Shelby's shocked indrawn breath echoed his own "What the hell?" He was being stalked by someone he'd helped?

What kind of world had he woken up in?

His expression grim, he stared at the screen.

"It's possible that he heard there was a price on your head, heard the job offer come through channels, knew where you were, and was there to warn you or get you to safety, but why threaten your bodyguard with a gun to her throat…and then pull that gun a second time on those keeping you safe? Surely, if he's at all connected, he'd know, as your killer does, that you've hired protection…and would find a way to warn us…"

So… Luke saves a life, and the woman's son thanks him by trying to kill him? It didn't make sense.

But then, so much about Luke's actions and activities didn't add up.

He could feel Shelby tense next to him. Could only imagine what doubts were raining down upon her.

Regrets from the night before?

"Moving on," Hudson continued, still staring straight at the camera, "nothing about Gerard Michaels looks fishy. Not anyplace. His books are meticulous. His bills are paid on the same date every month. Nothing at all unusual or noteworthy about his spending. There's no sign of any assets unaccounted for anywhere in his life. No numbers he calls, even, to people who might have such unaccounted-for assets..."

He was relieved about Michaels. For the time being.

Would be good to know that his trust in the guy wasn't misplaced. That he had the wherewithal he felt like he needed to judge people, situations, and get it right.

Still, while Sierra's Web was impressively thorough, if they'd found whoever wanted Luke dead, wouldn't Hudson have said so by then?

Which meant...

"We've been through the names on your list," Hudson went on. "Nothing suspicious stands out—no new gun license requests, nothing on social media that directs us anywhere in the direction of any of the locations where fires have been set..."

How much longer could the whole thing go on?

And if they couldn't find the guy, would it end only when he succeeded? Luke couldn't let that happen. Not to Shelby. And not to himself, either. He had a son who needed a father.

"With teams working together, side by side—comparing notes, dates, phone records, expenditures—we've discovered what we think is the key to solving the case." Hudson's voice dropped the news as though the guy were discussing dinner plans.

Stiffening, Luke felt Shelby's arm wrap through his, like he needed her to hold him up. And while he could stand perfectly fine on his own, it was…different, having someone stand with him. In a personal sense.

At the same time, he braced himself for her withdrawal, depending on what came next.

"Johnson's on his way over now, but our working theory is that you're a victim of identity theft," Hudson continued after a pause to take a sip from a water bottle. "A few timelines, phone calls to Michaels logged as you calling, but there's no record of you making the call from your phone… It's stuff no one would notice…"

Except Luke was paying for teams of experts in many fields…

"There's nothing linking Michaels to the Cayman accounts other than the deposits he made from the fake charity, but there was a call to the Caymans from a phone that called Michaels, at a time he'd logged a call from you. The other phone has been off since before you were found nearly dead in the desert."

And they weren't assuming it was Luke?

That didn't make sense, either. Not feeling Shelby's departure from him yet, he said, "I could have had a separate phone." He'd have said the words to Hudson, if the man could hear him. Instead, he just put them out there.

And got an arm squeeze for his effort.

"Which got us looking into that number and yours again," Hudson went on. "You were up in the mountains, having just finished a job, and made a call to Payson at the exact same time the other number made a call *from* Payson to Michaels. A few minutes' difference between beginning and end of calls, but you were both making calls during some of the same time."

Luke's entire body went limp for a second. And then

stood tall. They were getting somewhere. They just weren't there yet.

And still didn't know their destination.

Then, more than ever, he had to keep his mind on the immediate challenge in front of him. Shelby's presence, the knowledge of his son were constant pressures at his back to get them all safely through whatever demons his life had brought upon them.

"It's not the only call made from Payson from that phone, but there were only a few. Many more from Phoenix—and California, too—so not likely that this guy resides in Payson. And that's the bad news. We still have no idea who this guy is. We've checked his call locations against every single name on our list of people who've been privy to this case and on the list you gave us, and every single one of them has an alibi putting them someplace different than where the calls came from."

Seriously.

They had theories and no solid leads? Except a dead guy whose mother he'd helped?

How could anyone be that good? To know everything but leave behind only dead ends?

It was like he had a ghost out to kill him.

Luke had never believed in ghosts.

"Lastly, we believe we have a motive for wanting you dead."

The bombshell fell out, kind of pissing Luke off. Couldn't the man have led with that?

His gaze bore holes into the small screen as Hudson's image continued. "Say this guy started out using you as his mark for identity theft because you're absent for long periods of time and don't handle your own money. A simple hack into Michaels's business could have told him that."

He shared a glance with Shelby and felt his tension ease a small bit. Just because she was there.

"It's possible that this guy got so fully entrenched in your life, your assets, he believes they belong to him. Or, at the very least, is determined to have them all for himself."

Pulling himself away from Shelby at that, Luke focused fully on the screen. On the words he was hearing. Someone who was mentally ill was trying to kill him and Shelby? Not just someone with hatred for him or someone who was stealing from him...but someone who was so out of touch he believed he could *be* him?

"Right now we're combing through years of your records and whereabouts, comparing them to all withdrawals and hits on the Cayman accounts and this phone number. It's a burner phone, but we can see the calls and locations until a week or so ago, so that's a start. And anything you can give us, any memories of anything odd you might remember, send it up. We're going to pin this guy to the wall."

He'd possibly had someone stealing his identity for years? Without his total memory, how in the hell did he fill in the blanks to help the team? His whole life...this guy hadn't just wanted to rob him of property, money and belongings—he'd wanted to live his life? To take over and leave Luke for dead?

He didn't know what to do with that. How to take it down.

But he'd damn well figure it out. He had to.

"One last thing," Hudson was saying. "If either you or Shelby have anything on you that has been in your possession since the hospital, we need you to send it up. Every other avenue for figuring out how he's finding you is a dead end. Lorraine said something about Shelby's purse. Johnson's team ran a wand over it, but we've got to see it another time."

Hudson then told Luke and Shelby just to hang tight, assuring them that all agreed they were safest right where they were, and said he'd be in touch later in the morning. The video ended, returning to the start screen with the little white arrow.

He set the phone on the counter, frowning, but looked at her then, his gaze connecting with hers as it had done the night before when they'd been talking about Carter.

And later...

"Wait," she said, sounding tense, as the expression on her face hardened.

"The theory about this guy wanting me dead was because I identified you, right? Because he just wanted you gone, then he assumes your identity, empties your accounts and moves away, right? Maybe he sends a letter to the forestry division, resigning your position. Even saying that after your memory loss, a second one, you've determined to focus your life in another direction..."

"I can't imagine anyone there, higher-ups included, believing that one."

Everyone knew his career sustained him in ways nothing else could.

"Right, but say he doesn't know that part. Just go with me here a second. If I'm dead and can't identify you, assuming he doesn't know you've regained your memory, what's to stop a member of your team from coming forward now? I mean, if he kills us now, wouldn't he then need everyone who knew you dead? Anyone who could identify him as a fraud?"

She was right. He had to get a response to Hudson. Had to focus fully on the news he'd just heard.

His feelings for Shelby—what they'd done, who they'd

been or could be—didn't matter if they didn't have lives to live...

Shelby's gaze dropped. She turned away from him. Picked up her coffee cup as though that was what she'd been after but then put it back down again.

"What?"

She shook her head but didn't meet his gaze.

"Shelby."

Nothing. Had she remembered something else? Something he'd done that was no longer on his radar? No matter how hard he tried to bring everything back?

"Tell me what you were just thinking," he said in his supervisory voice. Then, hearing the tone, softened it with "Please."

Reaching out, he touched her shoulder, nudging her back around. The night they'd spent...they'd become something more. "Please."

Her glance met his, was gone and then back again. "It's nothing," she told him. "Just... I know how you work. You take the information you're given, and you do what you need to do with it to solve whatever problem is in front of you."

Yeah, but that didn't make sense because, "That was what made you turn away?"

Her chin lifted, she looked him straight in the eye and said, "It makes sense that someone who is planning to deal with you for the foreseeable future would need to find a way to communicate with you. You don't sit down and discuss things or have some heart-to-heart talk. You just state your facts, or hear others' facts, and move on. Meaning that those communicating with you need to move on also, out of the way, so you can solve the problems in the way you see fit."

He saw it. Clearly. Saw himself. Exactly as she described.

And, for the first time, he saw how his blunt, abrupt ways could make others feel...superfluous. He'd gotten so used to knowing what had to be done and getting it done in the most urgent ways possible...

He'd saved more lives than any other hotshot fire-fighter.

But...

"I'll be more aware," he told her.

For her—for Carter—he'd do better.

Or die trying.

Chapter 19

"We need to gather up our stuff," Shelby said, breaking eye contact with Luke before she drowned in what seemed like promises she'd love to have. She couldn't afford to hold on to them.

He wanted to be more aware. But Luke was Luke. You didn't get to change a person into being who you needed them to be just because you cared about them.

Her father—case in point.

She had to love him in spite of his flaws, not expect her love to fix him up into the package she wanted.

Her dad, she had to love.

Not Luke.

Her purse wasn't big. She'd given up the key fob, her phone, everything but the little bit of makeup she carried, the package of cleaning wipes she always had on her and her wallet, but she handed the whole thing over to Luke.

"It's never been out of my possession," she said. "Even

when they wanded it, I was right there. No way anyone could have bugged it."

But she didn't want it anywhere near her, either.

"If someone we're working with is a mole, it's possible they were close enough to your purse to inject something into the bottom of it."

They could do that with tracking devices?

"If someone we're working with is a mole, they wouldn't need a tracking device," she pointed out. "They'd know where we are."

"Not if it was someone at the hospital."

People had been in and out of his room. Had their killer posed as a doctor? A nurse? Or hired someone else to do so?

Was there no end to the possibilities?

Luke added his wallet to her purse.

"Your watch," she reminded him. It was ancient. Battery operated. Non-digital, and always on Luke's arm, but Hudson had said everything. Adding the time piece to the pile, Luke carried their meager items over to the ladder. He'd drop the things in the basket and push a button to have the conveyer belt move them through a pipe to a place farther down the beach, where Bruce or Lorraine would get them.

You didn't give up the location of your entryway by receiving goods through it.

Apparently, people in the bunker business thought of everything.

Something she was going to research when she got out of there. How many people in the country had places like this? Was there a whole society of them that people like her knew nothing about?

Or was their host just a guy who feared some huge threat might catch up to him?

Watching her only physical ties to the life that was currently not safe for her to live rise up that ladder, Shelby tried to keep her spirits in a healthy place.

They'd get past their days of running and hiding. Life would return to normal—a new normal with Carter having a father around sometimes—and she'd be home with her son, and all would be good again.

They were planning a trip to California's most famous amusement park later in the summer. It would be Carter's first, because she'd wanted to wait until he was old enough to know where he was. To maybe remember, as he got older, that initial feeling of magic and unending possibility...

So he could grow up and realize that it had all been make believe?

This intrusive thought was so unlike her that Shelby knew she was in trouble. And had to take back ownership of herself—the person who knew that the future always held a promise of possibility. Heartache, disappointment... If she let them, they'd rob her of that belief, just as they had her mother.

"About last night..." she said as soon as Luke descended the ladder.

His look—personal, warm. He didn't stop walking until he was standing right in front of her. He even cupped her cheek.

Surprised, unsure why he'd think he needed to make such an uncharacteristic move, she nonetheless kept her resolve but looked up at him, cupping his cheek, too, as she said, "I want to thank you. I had no right, coming on to you like I did. I just...needed... Well, it doesn't matter what I needed." How did he do it? Getting by with only facts. No feelings measured in.

He dropped his hand, so she dropped hers, too.

"Anyway, you have no worries that I'll make more into what we did than it was. And as a matter of fact, I need last night to be the only time…even if we do end up here another night."

How she'd pull that one off, she didn't know yet.

Just knew that she had to find a way.

He was watching her—listening, even she believed. But that personal look she'd thought she'd seen was nowhere in sight. Maybe she'd just imagined it.

Getting no reaction at all, she continued, giving him the honesty she wanted from him. "I just know me, Luke. The more we do stuff like…last night, the more my heart's going to get involved. I'm not someone who can just do the physical thing. And, frankly, I don't want to be…"

Still no response—other than apparent attentiveness.

"I'm going to need more than you can give or even want to give, which isn't fair to you at all. It would get messy, and there's too big a chance that Carter would be the one to suffer. Either from me being upset, us fighting or you not coming around as much…"

It wouldn't ever be about making Carter choose sides, though. That much she knew. Sylvia Harrington had made that mistake, and Shelby had been paying the price ever since her parents split up.

"So what was last night?" he asked her.

"Honestly?"

He nodded.

"My memories of us… I was afraid I'd embellished our time together in a subconscious attempt to explain to myself why I did what I did with you in the first place. It was so out of character for me, and ending up pregnant, my whole life was changed…" There she was, rattling on again when he'd just needed the facts. "Last night was me finding out that I hadn't been lying to myself. If I had to make the choice again, to have slept with you back then, I'd have done so." She stopped, then added, "Probably with more attention to condom care…" She stopped again. She tried to be more like him, keeping her stuff to herself, but ended up blurting, "But not really, because I don't begrudge Carter his life. Or in any way wish I hadn't had him." Her words tumbled over each other in their haste to get said. "My son is the best part of me. The happiest piece of my life."

Yeah, Carter had changed what she'd thought her life would be. But she wouldn't trade him for anything she'd thought she wanted.

"Anyway," she said, needing to get it done, "last night was me putting the past to rest."

He nodded.

Picked up the phone Hudson had sent down that morning.

He was going to walk away.

She knew it.

Knew she had to let him.

And said, "Are you mad?"

His blink, the raising of his brows, spoke surprise to her. "Of course not," he said. And then added, "I'm going to use this phone to message Hudson. I intend to keep the other until I can get a permanent copy of the video Carter made."

She figured, maybe, he intended to watch the video some more, too. Didn't want to be parted with it even long enough for the Sierra's Web team to get a permanent copy to him.

And she had to blink back tears.

Luke was going to make a great dad.

* * *

For such a skilled hotshot, he'd called that one all wrong.

During their lovemaking the night before, he'd thought they were saying hello. She'd been saying goodbye.

Wow.

And it wasn't because she wasn't drawn to him but because she knew him.

Knew, even more than he could remember, the lengths he would apparently go to in order to prevent himself from asking a woman to share his life.

And without knowing why he'd sent her a breakfast tray with an insane amount of cash in an envelope or, most importantly, why he'd shut his door in her face when she'd come to tell him about Carter...how in the hell could he even have a conversation with her about it?

One that would ring true to her?

He'd denied their child. Refusing to even speak with her about the pregnancy.

Watching the video the night before, he'd come back to that fact over and over, until it was driving him past the edge. That one choice—one he couldn't explain, didn't feel any affinity with and couldn't understand—had robbed him of the first four years of his son's life.

And robbed him of the trust and perhaps growing love of the one woman he'd ever cared enough for to even think about having a love of his own in his life.

The money on the tray... Anyone could have done that. For any number of reasons.

But she'd been to Luke's home. Knew that his dead bolt had had the catch and the squeak, because she'd stood on his doorstep, face-to-face with him, just before he'd shut her out and turned the lock into place.

No way there could be anyone else to blame but himself for that.

No one else for her to blame.

He couldn't just sit. Had done enough of nothing to last him a lifetime.

First thing he had to do was message Hudson and the rest of the team. Pacing the small living space, he held the phone up and hit Record.

"Question. If the guy wants to be me, how does simply killing Shelby and me serve his purpose? In the beginning, she was the only one who came forward, but everyone knows who I am now. My team, my boss have been notified. They'd all be able to say this new guy isn't me."

He hadn't asked Shelby to join him. But was glad to see her come sit on the sofa. She had good insights…

Right.

Pausing the video for a second, he looked straight at her. "I might not be good at the communication thing, but I listen," he told her. "I always want to hear your opinion. You notice things other people miss…"

The way her head turned a little and her brows rose, he figured he'd surprised her. Not in a bad way.

Good.

Back to the video, he said, "I could have exposed my weakness to identity theft to this guy. I recommended money managers to my crews in classes I taught, explaining that when we're in season, we aren't going to be able to watch our accounts or pay our bills. I recommended automatic deposit on paychecks, too. This opens up a whole plethora of possible suspects."

He paused once more, thought for a second and hit Record again. "And the things that seem most odd to me—the threesome, the house party—maybe this guy did those things in my name, but it wasn't me there." So maybe he was digging deep. He'd give much of his fortune to find out that he'd at least been cleared from those activities.

There might be more, but it was all he had at the moment. He hit the button to save the video. Named it.

And looked at Shelby. She had the phone with Carter's video in her hand, was watching something on it.

Missing her son?

The little smile she wore was...transforming.

And heartrending, too.

"Hey, what do you say we make a video to send back to Carter?" he blurted out. Selfishly, he knew, even as he heard himself, but he didn't retract the words.

What if things didn't turn out good with the investigation? What if he ended up not making it? Every single time he went to work, that possibility was right there. More for him than most. It was part of the life he'd opted to take on.

"We don't have to tell him who I am," he quickly asserted when Shelby's mouth dropped open and panic seemed to hit her eyes. "Just...say I'm an interview subject," he ad-libbed. "It wouldn't be a lie because I am. That's how you were able to identify me..."

"Interview subject is not something he'd understand," she said, but she seemed to be weighing his suggestion, as though it might have possibility, rather than outright rejecting it.

She hadn't said no. He stayed on that fact.

"He just knows I write stories about people."

So... "Can you introduce me as a person from one of your stories?"

She was looking at him, but he couldn't tell what she was thinking. Didn't want to push.

And wasn't used to waiting around to lose, either.

"I just want to tell him hello, Shelby. I want him to

see my face. To hear my voice. You can always delete the video if you decide you don't want to send it."

When her gaze narrowed, he felt caught. Like a fish on a hook. And he didn't know why.

"This is in case you don't make it, isn't it?"

She saw things others didn't. Could be a problem down the road for a guy who kept his private life strictly to himself.

And yet he kind of wanted to take on the challenge.

More than kind of.

She was done with him. He got that.

Understood it.

But they'd still be talking. Be in touch…

"Luke, it's in case you don't survive, isn't it?"

"Yes," he told her, looking her right in the eye. And didn't choke to death on the revelation.

She was making too big a deal of things. Luke was just a subject from an article saying hello to her son.

But…whether Carter knew it or not, she was introducing her son to his father for the first time. With a recording her son could watch for the rest of his life.

In the future—even with Luke sitting right there, watching the video with an eighteen-year-old Carter— the moment would mean something.

She wasn't going to think about the alternative.

That Luke wouldn't be around to sit with his son and do anything in the years to come.

Or that she wouldn't.

Bottom line, Luke was Carter's father. He had every right to his son, whether she wanted it that way or not. Which was why she'd gone to him when she'd found out she was pregnant—even after he'd served up that horrible breakfast—to tell him about the baby.

And why she'd stepped forward to identify him when she'd seen his picture in the news.

Apparently done with pacing, Luke sat down on the sofa, phone for Hudson still in his hand.

Ready to record one more video before sending the device back up to the surface.

It wasn't up to her to decide if Luke was good enough, if he was worthy of Carter. Unless he proved himself unhealthy for Carter's well-being, unless a court designated him as such, she had no right to keep him from his son.

And whether she brought Luke to Carter or not, her son was almost certainly going to find him on his own someday.

After Carter had been robbed of the possibility of growing up with a father's support and tutelage.

Luke bounced the phone a time or two in his hand.

She'd given up her purse. Had nothing with which to tie back her hair. "He's used to seeing me in a ponytail at home," she said inanely. Fighting back panic at how quickly life was moving forward. At how little control she seemed to have.

Even over her own body's wants. Or her wayward heart. She added the last silent lament as the man causing all the confusion in her life scooted a bit closer, revealing the video recorder up on the screen he was holding.

"I got used to putting it up when he was a baby," she said. "He was constantly grabbing at it—and I gotta tell you, that dude has a strong grip."

Luke raised a brow but otherwise just continued to watch her.

"And an even stronger pull," she went on. She swallowed, then said, "Plus, it's easier to clean the house without it falling all over my shoulders and blocking my view—you know, when I'm looking for toys under the television set. And yes, I hear myself rambling."

"Best just to do it, then, right?" Luke's calm tone stopped her.

"Why aren't you nervous?" He was the one making a first impression.

His shrug seemed to shove some of his calm over to settle upon her. "I'm me. Like it or not, it's what he gets."

Yes, but… She frowned. "Don't you want him to like you? Or think you're cool or something?" Didn't he want to impress his own son?

"I want him to know, eventually, that he can depend on me."

Holding his gaze, she felt her eyes fill with tears. Tried to blink away the evidence but couldn't move her eyelids fast enough. Oh, God, what was the man doing to her?

"He's not going to trust me if I try to be cool and then he finds out I'm not."

His gaze sharpened, seemed to jump right into hers with a message he wanted her to get. She received one. Just wasn't sure it was the right one.

"Like I can't trust you because sometimes you're a wonderful guy and other times you slam doors in people's faces." That look compelled her to be who she was. To say what she was thinking.

It wasn't just the door. Or even the money. He'd never contacted her again. Not in almost five years' time.

And if the threesome, the house party, all the other less-than-stellar moments in his life turned out to not be the result of identity theft…

The Cayman Islands account, financed with money he'd sent through a fake charity… What was that all about?

Michaels had seen him in person on that one. They

knew Luke was the one who'd mandated the entire setup...

As thoughts flew through her mind, Luke just sat there, watching her as though he was reading every single one of them.

"Do you blame me?" she asked, not even sure what the question encompassed. Just needing...words.

"No."

She needed more. Had just told him there'd be nothing between them other than co-parenting, so had given up any right to ask more of him.

"Okay, let's do this."

Picturing her son's grin as she'd just seen it on the phone still in her hand, she scooted her head next to Luke's and smiled at the camera he held in front of them.

"Hey, buddy! I miss you so much and wanted to show you my work! This man—his name's Luke, and he fights mountain fires and stuff. I told him about you, and he wanted to say hello!"

"Hey, Carter," Luke said, jumping right in as if they had cue cards or had practiced. "I hear you like to fish, and I do, too. I wish I had a doughnut right now. I think getting a dog someday would be cool. Dogs like to ride in trucks, and I have a truck. And I just want to thank you for letting your mom be away to work, because she tells stories that help a lot of people, and helping people is the best thing..."

Shelby picked up when Luke faltered. "Okay, buddy, we have to get back to work! You be good for Grandma, and make sure you both do what Charlie tells you to do because he's really smart, and you better be practicing at frogs, because we're going to have a long contest when I get home. I love you, buddy. Most and most."

Reaching out over Luke's phone-holding arm, Shelby

pushed the button to end recording. And then jumped up off the couch. Headed straight for the small partition in the back of the shelter. Sat on the stool.

And let the tears flow.

Chapter 20

He could hear her crying. Not that she made any sobbing sounds or moans. But the sniffles. The occasional nose-blowing.

Luke was definitely a single-focused guy—and right then, he was focused solely on Shelby. He delivered the message phone to the cage, pushed to send it along the conveyer for the slightly angled ride to the woods farther down the beach.

And then he paced until the monotony and lack of any accomplishment whatsoever drove him to the kitchen. There was fresh bread. A toaster oven. Packets of oatmeal and…a toaster oven to heat water for it. Moving without questioning decisions, he meandered around the small space, preparing nourishment. He peeled an orange, separated the sections and put them on plates, along with the toast on the outside of the bowls of oatmeal. He found some brown sugar, spooned dollops of that atop the cooked oats. And put both plates, with spoons and cups of coffee—and for her, a bottle of water—down on the small table for two along the wall at end of the counter.

He'd counted on the sounds, the obvious scents of food drawing Shelby out. It wasn't often that his plans failed. But he also didn't get deterred easily.

Standing halfway between the sink and the back partition, he called out, "Hey, Shelby, breakfast is ready. And there's water so you can rehydrate."

No response.

He stood there a second. Did he wait for her? Go eat, whether she did or not?

Communication. He'd said he'd do better.

"I'm, uh, not sure what to do here," he said then. And felt like a total ass. "You're an adult and have the right to not eat and also the right to some privacy, but if I eat without you, it seems rude, and…I don't really want to." The silence was acute. "So, in case you missed it, this was me, communicating."

With that, he turned and went to the table. Sat down. Tense. As though life and death would be determined by oatmeal and oranges.

Plan C hadn't yet formed when Shelby appeared. A bit red-eyed but otherwise seeming in complete control.

"I miss him," she said as she sat down.

He figured it was a lot more than that. From what she'd said, being away for a few days at a time wasn't uncommon, to the point that her son had his own room in her mother's home.

But welcoming a chance to be done with the whole communication thing while he ate, he let her excuse slide and asked, instead, "What's frogs?" He'd been wondering that on and off throughout breakfast preparation.

"A toddler video game," she said. She took a couple of bites of oatmeal as though she hadn't just eaten a hearty helping of pasta the night before, then continued. "Whenever I come back from a trip, I take half a day off just to be with him, and we have game marathons. I generally tell him which one I'm choosing a day or two before I get home so that he can practice. But mostly so that he has something to do to work toward me being home again. As though by playing, my being there gets closer."

He stared. "Did you read that in a book or something?" As soon as he was free, he was buying them all. Every parenting book he could find. He'd devour them multiple times if necessary.

"Read what? About the frog game?"

"No, about giving him something to work toward for your arrival, as though giving him some sense of control as he works toward the end date..."

Holding an orange piece between her lips, she pulled it back and said, "No. It just makes sense. Instead of hearing him ask me a million times when I'm coming home, give him something to distract him from the fact that I'm not there yet."

So maybe not books. Just common sense. He had a good supply of that.

And she was eating every bite of the food he'd prepared for her.

Two wins, right there together.

He was on a roll.

They cleaned up the dishes, working seamlessly, without words. And then watched a couple of movies—one her pick, one his—and discussed them both as though the fate of the world hinged on their opinions.

For a moment here and there, she forgot that their lives were at stake. Was able to ignore the fact that they were trapped in a tiny underground space and if they dared climb up to the beach above them, they'd likely be killed.

Or at least, he would.

The killer the night before had specifically asked for Luke's location. No mention of her.

If she left, now that the world knew that Luke wasn't dead, would she be safe?

Did she want to risk her life finding out?

Or tempt the fates that had allowed her to escape her own death once already that week? Had she not acted as quickly as she had, or found the exact space in which to move her vehicle, she'd have died, just like Luke's father had.

And until someone knew why the killer had taken out Luke's father over a year before attempting to kill Luke, she wasn't going to assume that she was no longer a target just because she didn't know why she would be.

They had canned chicken with crackers for lunch, watched another movie and were in the process of a half-hour workout, with Luke leading the regime, when the clang of a message arriving stopped them both. Turning down the music he'd had playing from the selection of compact discs, he took the rungs of the ladder steps two at a time while her heart thudded in her chest.

Did they have a response from Carter?

Would her son acknowledge the man she'd introduced him to? Would Luke be hurt if he didn't?

Not her business. Outside of her influence. Shouldn't be her concern.

There was only one new video.

From Hudson.

She stood with Luke at the bottom of the ladder, their shoulders touching as they watched the video together.

"Finally. A concrete answer," the man started, sending Shelby's nervous system into overdrive. Would Luke be vindicated? Or more enmeshed?

Were they getting out?

And going to be facing everything that meant in their personal lives?

"—found the—" Hudson was saying when she calmed the roaring in her ears enough to tune back in.

Lives were at stake, and she was freaking out?

"—tracker," Hudson said.

What now? They'd found the *tracker*? Which would lead to who'd been tracking them?

"It was in your watch, Luke," Hudson's voice continued, unaware that the man he'd spoken to had just stiffened against her. Every muscle and nerve was taut.

"Apparently, you weren't wearing it when Johnson's team ran the wand over you. Or the watch was somehow missed," Hudson continued, as he would since he was just a video.

Reaching over, she pushed Pause.

"In your watch?" she said, looking up at Luke. "How... When did anyone... It's not even electronic..."

"Bugs these days are so small they could be in your pocket and you wouldn't know it." Luke's response was impersonal. Cold, even. "And I have no idea how. Other than when I was unconscious in the hospital or in the shower, I've had the watch on."

She could attest to the fact that man slept with the watch on. At least, he had the previous night.

He hit Play again.

"We'll need to know every time you'd had it off," Hudson said then, as though, video or no, he'd been privy to their response. "The tracker itself isn't made or sold in the US, so it won't be as easy to trace as it might have been, though we have an expert working on it. It was too small for any hope of getting fingerprints off it, and there were none on your watch other than your own. It's being logged as evidence for now. We're looking at the Cayman Islands financials again, just in case we get lucky and find a purchase that fits, but in the meantime, we now have a solid plan."

She held on to Luke's elbow with both hands.

"We're driving the tracker, now implanted in another watch, to a cabin in a closed ski resort near Flagstaff. A fire perimeter is currently being dug around the old building and at the edge of the property, too. We'll have people all around the area, watching for anything or anyone around, and have drones set to send up as well, so we'll have eyes from all angles. Hopefully, we'll have good news for you before morning."

The screen went dead.

Not sure what to expect from Luke, Shelby stood still, looking at the white arrow on the video's starting frame.

"It was my father's watch," he said. "He gave it to me before I left for my first hotshot assignment. He told me that he hoped it would keep me on track and safe."

He walked away from her then, leaving her feeling inappropriately bereft, and she moved back to the couch. It wasn't like there were a lot of choices of places to be in the small space.

Or much to do, either.

Except try her best to ignore a cacophony of feelings for Luke.

And fight the thoughts that kept trying to run away with her.

Standing at the kitchen sink, he recorded his response to Hudson, telling the man what he'd just told Shelby. He'd had the watch on since waking in the hospital and

Detective Johnson returned it to him. Other than to bathe, at which time, it had been just outside the shower, which had had a glass door and had been fully visible to him.

This led him to believe that maybe Johnson had been the one out to get him all along. He paused recording when the thought struck him.

It didn't fit the team's theory.

Or make sense, when he considered how easily Johnson could have just done him in. A gunshot, claiming that Luke, in his suspended mental state, had gotten aggressive, taken his gun from him and tried to kill himself. Or any number of other scenarios.

Still, Johnson could be on the take. Apparently, Luke's life thief had no qualms about spending money in large quantities.

Tapping Record again, he sent a short message suggesting Hudson take another look at Johnson. Then hit Save and climbed up to send the recording on its way.

They were getting closer, which elated him. And bothered him a bit, too. When Shelby was safe, free, would he ever have a chance to speak one-on-one with her again?

Other than about their son?

What if he never remembered the day she'd come to tell him about her pregnancy? What if he couldn't ever explain, even to himself, why he'd done such a despicable thing to her?

Watching her as she sat on the couch—just sat there— he couldn't just let it all go without attempting to salvage some kind of friendship with her.

Saving things was his forte.

Taking a cue from her from the day before, he poured a couple of glasses of wine and carried them over to the couch, handing one to her.

She sipped and then said, "Thank you."

Reminding him of his own eagerness to consume the beverage when she'd brought it to him. How he'd welcomed the libation that might help him chill out a bit.

He hadn't consumed enough of it the previous night to feel any effect.

Shelby had been all he'd needed.

It felt like she was all he needed, still.

Which was so unlike anything he remembered himself to be…except that week she'd interviewed him…

"We did okay, talking about the movies, yeah?" he asked, sitting not quite a cushion's width away from her, lounging back as though there were no cares in the world. "What?"

"Discussing, giving out thoughts…the whole communication thing." He'd get it right eventually. Somehow, making a plan to save a burning mountain seemed easier.

And more likely to bring success.

She shook her head, took another sip of wine, sliding her knee up onto the couch as she turned some to face him. "This is what I'm talking about, Luke," she said, sounding to him more as if she were talking to her four-year-old than to a proven lifesaver.

The saver of a woman's life, a woman whose son later came to kill him?

He couldn't grasp it. So he let it go.

Figuring out how to make Shelby happy enough to have him in her life, not just her son's, was far more important than comprehending why a son would hunt down the guy who'd rescued his mother.

He'd been waiting for her to expand on exactly what she *was* talking about. When she didn't, he knew he was on the hot seat.

He was supposed to get it. Had missed some big emotional tell, apparently. "What?" he finally asked. All he had was honesty. And not even a full memory of that. "What are you talking about?"

"We just hear ground-shaking news, and you want to talk about a plebian conversation we had about movies?"

Relief flooded him. He grinned.

"You think this is funny?" Her tone certainly wasn't anywhere near laughter.

"No!" He got that out immediately. And with a completely open, totally sober expression, told her, "I think this is more a matter of life and death than funny," he said, and when she frowned, her lips pursing as though she didn't believe him, he added, "I was grinning because I'd thought I'd missed something big, and instead you just didn't like my way of using small talk to get the conversationing started."

Not a word, *conversationing*.

She didn't add a single syllable to it. But she was still facing him.

"So…to move on to the… Oh, hell…" He stopped. "I want my watch back." There. That was real.

Studying the shelves holding various media cases, he listened to the silence. Then started to fill it.

"After Mom died, my father and I… We just kind of became not just father and son but trusted help mates. Best friends, even."

He'd certainly never had a buddy he talked to about things. But his father had always understood, even without a lot of words.

"I think—no, I *know*—it scared him when I signed on with the hotshots. But he wanted me to do it almost as badly as I did. He took his watch off his wrist the day I left on my first call. It was like a continuation of our bond. A talisman to bring me out of the flames. And each and every time, it did."

And he didn't have it now, when he was fighting his biggest demon ever.

Shelby's fingers touched his arm. Light chills sailed through him as though on a breeze. A breath of fresh air. And when he couldn't quite look at her, he glanced down at them. Saw them moving along the white mark left in his tan by the watch's disappearance.

"You've still got it, Luke. Like a reverse tattoo, it's right here, branded into your skin. The talisman-part of it, anyway. And that's all that really mattered. By the time the tan fades, you'll have the watch back."

He'd seen the tan marks. Had viewed that white skin as a symbol of his loss.

Glancing over at her, he wanted to kiss her, to lose himself in her physically. Instead, he said, "Thank you." And acknowledged to himself that the whole *talking about stuff* thing…with Shelby…might not be as deplorable, as painful, as difficult as he'd thought it would be.

Chapter 21

She was falling for him all over again. There was no point in denying that Luke Dennison had a hold on her. The man's effect on her was different from any other guy she'd ever known. Not just sexually, though there was definitely that, but heart-to-heart...

As it turned out, she didn't need him to talk for her to feel as though she knew.

But listening to him, even the struggle he made to get words out to her... It all hit her in every single feel she had.

Right or wrong, she did herself no favors by denying the problem.

Neither of them mentioned the fact that with the trap being set for their would-be killer that very night, their time together was drawing to a close. They didn't talk about what the next day would bring or what the life ahead might look like.

They should have. Should be using the quiet alone time

allotted to them to discuss what shared parenting between them might look like. She didn't bring it up.

Neither did he.

He talked about his dad some. Maybe because he'd just become one? She told him a bit more about her mother. About the promise she'd extracted from Sylvia to never, ever bad-mouth Shelby's father in front of Carter or to ever make him feel bad for loving his grandfather.

Not that Carter saw the man all that much. Three times in his lifetime, to date.

But if Sylvia ever broke her word, if she ever tried to make Carter choose between family members, then Carter wouldn't stay with her again.

Maybe she told Luke about the promise to assure him that his son wasn't being hurt as she'd been growing up. A fact she'd told him about briefly when mentioning why, in the past, she hadn't seen herself ever marrying.

And maybe it was to let him know that no matter what he'd done to Shelby, Carter would never be privy to the information. Or asked to choose between his mother and his father.

"I just want you to know," she said as they started in on their second glasses of wine, "as far as I'm concerned, as long as you're a decent dad, you'll be a welcome part of Carter's life."

The hand raising his glass to his mouth stopped mid-air, and Shelby's stomach sank. Not because she was afraid of him or what he'd say, but because she hadn't wanted to ruin the mood between them. Just for those hours…she wanted to be able to enjoy his…friendship.

But when he put the glass down and turned to face her, knee to knee on the cushion, face-to-face, she met his gaze. Whatever he had to say, she'd handle.

"The other night, in the cabin, when I first woke up

and you were still asleep on the couch…my memories from our time together came back."

Oh, God. He was about to tell her about the money. Calling her a liar. And she didn't want to hear it. Didn't want to know.

But she wasn't going to start the future trying to pretend it hadn't happened. Or that he hadn't done those things. So she took a sip of wine. And waited.

Watching his obvious struggle to come up with the words he needed.

And knowing that she needed the truth.

To hear it.

And accept it.

Including why he'd been lying to her since that night, about shutting the door in her face.

"What I remember…" He looked her straight on, his vivid blue eyes filled with emotion that yanked at her, even as she fought to hold her distance.

"I wanted to come back for more."

What? Open-mouthed, she shook her head. But he continued to watch her, his gaze searching hers, until she could do nothing but stare right back at him.

"For the first time in my career, I understood why members of hotshot teams got married even though they had to be away so much. And knowingly and willingly risked their lives every single time they answered the call. To be honest, prior to…that week…I honestly thought they were all just either being selfish or had gotten married because they'd been raised to know it was expected of them…"

He broke eye contact then, straightened in his seat to reach for his wine without finishing what he'd started.

Leaving her hanging there.

Waiting.

For too long.

Until, not without a bit of ire, she said, "And?"

Looking over at her, he shrugged. "And I'm sorry that I brought it up, especially after your honesty this morning, but I thought this was what you wanted. Mutual honesty between us. Spoken out loud."

The walls that had begun rapidly erecting themselves around Shelby's heart disintegrated, and she took a full body-regenerating breath. And a small sip of wine, too. "I meant... And why is it that you think they get married now? What did you understand differently?"

"It's because they want to spend most—if not all—of their nonworking hours with that person. That they'd rather be with the one person than anyone else. Because they want to spend the rest of their lives doing what they can do to make that person happy."

She had to swallow. Her throat was a dry lump. Got her glass shakily to her lips.

"And you feel—*felt* that way?"

He didn't meet her gaze then. But he said, "I...remembered that I felt that way...the morning after..."

But the money...

"I remember that I was planning to reach out to you when I got back."

But he'd been injured. Had lost his memory.

"But you forgot me."

He glanced back at her. Shook his head. "No, after I got back, after I recovered what I believed was my full memory, I had second thoughts..."

Oh. Well, then.

"Not about how I felt but about how unfair it would be for me to ask you to take me on, because I knew I couldn't give up fighting wildfires. I'd been pretty clear that I wasn't a guy who could ever offer, or would ever ask for, a commitment and figured it was best just to leave it at that."

So when, a few months later, she'd come to tell him she was pregnant? He'd already moved on? Was afraid of what her being pregnant meant in light of what he'd thought their chances of making it would be?

"That's why you treated me so cruelly when I came to see you in Payson? You were trying to get rid of me for my own good?"

What was he, some God wannabe? Or a hero from a medieval romance novel? Seeking anger dulled the pain.

Elbows on his knees, Luke stared at the floor, shaking his head; then, turning, his eyes direct and open, he met her own had-to-be-pain-filled gaze. "I honestly and truly have no memory of that day, Shelby. Or of having breakfast sent up to your room, either, for that matter. But the day you came to Payson…if I was doing as you said and trying to do that kind thing for the long haul— saving you from me—I still can't see turning my back on my own child. Or, for that matter, leaving the mother of my child to cope alone, you or not. And I absolutely can't see turning you away if you'd come to me. Not for any reason. So maybe that's why I can't remember. Because I just plain don't want to live with that guy…"

Her eyes filled with tears. She didn't try to hide them. Or stop them.

And didn't stop him, either, when he took the wineglass from her hand, set it on the table, and then leaned over to cup her face and kiss her tears away.

Hard and aching with the need to crawl on top of her, Luke's hands shook as he pulled them from Shelby's face. Letting his thumbs trail last, he took the remaining moisture from her cheeks with him.

Being in completely new territory, he didn't immediately know what would happen next or how it would happen, but the one and only thing he could count on was his instinct. It told him not to push.

Unfortunately, from there, he was on his inept own where Shelby was concerned. And lacking in some confidence since he couldn't remember why he'd treated her the way he did in the past.

When she leaned forward, watching him with slumberous brown eyes, he stayed completely still. There for her and nothing more.

Her lips touched his, more tentatively than they had the night before. He responded, holding back the passion burning through him. He knew she wanted him. She'd shown him over and over the night before. And she'd as much as told him so that morning.

When she'd also told him why she couldn't be with him.

While her lips continued to move softly on his, he made himself think about how badly he needed her friendship.

And how friends had each other's backs.

Then her tongue slid through his lips, engaging his in a dance that was already completely familiar. Totally theirs.

Just like the night before, he couldn't reject her. And he wasn't made of stone. His penis was tormenting him for release.

But…they weren't just a man and a woman attracted to each other.

Breaking contact with her mouth, he buried his face in her neck. Kissing her lightly. And then, not. With a hand on the side of her neck, he looked at her and said, "The future."

He braced for her immediate withdrawal. Got a nod instead.

"I know."

So they were stopping, right?

That's what had to happen.

She seemed to be waiting. Again.

And it hit him. *Words, dude.*

Words.

"I don't know how it's going to look."

"Me, either."

But she was still turned toward him. When he dropped his hand from her neck, she slid her fingers through his. And his body flared to life all over again.

From a hand touch? What the hell!

Did not bode well for the picture they were trying to paint.

"I want to tell you that I'll quit the hotshots. There are a lot of other jobs I can do with the forestry division, but…"

Her shaking head stopped his words. They'd come to an end, anyway.

"You are who you are, Luke. Just as I am. You try to change for me, I try to change for you… Changing the way that's elemental to who we are…it's not right. It's not anything akin to love…"

Her expression went immediately deadpan. And she hurried on, "Not that I'm saying we're falling in love or anything…"

"Then why do I feel like I might be?" And, whoa, buddy. That was why he didn't say much. His getting-right-to-the-pointness didn't often fit well with normal human interaction.

Relief flooded him as Shelby dropped his hand and sat back against the couch. He wasn't sure how to gauge the way she leaned forward with stilted moves and grabbed her wine. Sipping before she'd even returned upright.

"I'm not asking for anything," he said. Needing to make his situation clear. "I have no confidence I'd be good at it. Can't see a way I would be."

She sipped again, nodded. Glanced his way and then back toward her wine.

"Where you and I are concerned," he said, clarifying some more. "As a dad, I'm good."

He wasn't. How could he be? He hadn't done it yet. But she'd be there to help him. Carter would help him. Memories of his own father would help him. Members of his team would help him. He'd get that one right.

"Kids grow up and away. They need their independence," he said, afraid that her silence would leave a gaping hole that would ultimately turn into another mess up on his scorecard.

But, hell, wasn't the communication thing supposed to work both ways?

"But partners... Yeah, they're independent, but they're together, too. An entity. In the same home, sharing life side by side forever..."

Now he was some kind of romance nerd?

Silence was better than this.

Even if it pissed her off.

He'd said he'd do better. He hadn't said he could become someone he wasn't.

As the thought hit, another fell right on top of it: her saying that it wasn't right for either of them to try to become someone they were not.

And she was right.

He was meant to be the person he'd been born as. He could do better. There was always room for improvement. But he couldn't be someone he was not.

"Life would be one big lie if we kid ourselves about what we're facing."

There.

He was done talking.

"I feel like I might be, too."

Shelby had tried hard to keep the words to herself. It wasn't her way.

Nor could she just let Luke hang out there. The man was trying. Honestly look-her-straight-in-the-eye trying.

Whatever name she gave it, she cared far too much to ignore his attempt to make things better between them.

He looked at her.

And she flooded. Down below. And in her emotional well, too.

Somehow, she had to stop getting turned on every single time his gaze met hers in that deep way it was doing.

"And I don't see a way for it to work, either." But she couldn't look away.

Wouldn't ever turn her back on him.

"Maybe there's something we can't see yet."

Always the problem solver. That was Luke.

"Maybe." She couldn't argue the point.

"Do you want to look for it?"

Her lower end was too wet, and her throat, her lips, too dry. Heart thudding, she sat at the precipice, aware that if she took a leap, she'd be changing her life all over again.

She took a sip of wine, instead, and asked, "What if we don't find it?"

"What if it's there and we don't look?" he countered back.

He'd be leaving with no notice, any time of the day or night, to rush off into out-of-control flames. Possibly to never return. Every single time.

Could she live with that?

The answer she sought wasn't in that question. Of course she could live with that. Memories of Luke were better than no Luke at all. That wasn't the problem.

"Do you see any possibility at all that you'd want to come home to me—not just Carter but me, too, even after he is grown—every single time you put the fire out?"

"I do."

Eyes flooding with tears, she threw herself at him.

And stilled completely when he held her back. "I can't promise, once I get out there on the mountain, how I'm going to feel. I don't know how I make both lives work."

His honesty nearly broke her heart. For the years they'd lost and the future they might not have.

"I can't promise that I'm ready to take it all on," she told him.

"This morning, you didn't want to try. Do you still feel that way?"

No. She didn't. Fear had her in its grip. He'd hurt her so badly she'd almost lost her ability to live with an open heart. For months, she'd been bitter…

He'd said that he remembered wanting to try in the past. But then he'd paid her off and denied their child.

The same child he was fighting for. Just as he fought every day he went to work. The lives he'd saved…the selflessness he engaged in…

Her head and heart battled while he sat there, close but not touching. Watching her and seeming to be ready to accept whatever answer she gave.

There was only one. The honest one.

"It's too late for me to pretend, even to myself, that I don't have to give it a shot," she told him. "Now that I know you feel something, too. That you felt it back then. That I'm not imagining our connection…"

She wasn't going to throw herself at him again. He could come for it.

Or not.

Maybe they had to figure out how it would work before…

"No matter if it works or not, I'll always be here for you," he said, melting her heart all over again. "You're the mother of my child. I'm a friend for life. One who will always have your back."

It was like their own private little ceremony—him saying his vows; her getting all weepy, listening to him giving her her heart's greatest desire. Becoming her dream come true.

With trembling lips, Shelby pressed her mouth to his, hard. Stopping him before he made more promises he didn't yet know he could keep.

Chapter 22

The sex was better than ever. Intensely physical. Ears to toes…they explored it all. Teased and tickled. For a time, he forgot everything but the sensations exploding through him.

But he remembered, each time, to pull out before emptying his seed inside her. It wasn't like they could send out for condoms. They'd used up what they had the night before.

And he absolutely was not going to trap her with another unplanned child. There were some things a guy didn't lose track of. No matter how mind-blowing it was to enter Shelby, she mattered more.

Lying on damp sheets a few hours after he'd poured their first glass of wine—remembering how he'd been hoping to somehow convince Shelby to be friends with him—he could hardly believe how far they'd come.

"If we find a way to make the rest of it work even half as good as this part does, we'll be home free," he told her, exhausted but revved up, too. Needing to know the next step. And the one after that.

Wanting solutions, not unanswered problems.

How in the hell could he approach a wildfire encroaching a thousand acres with no fear, knowing exactly what he had to do to contain it, but couldn't see himself getting it right when it came to keeping one woman happy?

"I see you in Carter."

Not the words he'd been expecting to hear. The boy was biologically his. Of course there'd be some resemblance.

"He gets so frustrated sometimes, when he's learning something new. And, with a baby growing into a toddler, everything is new. From learning to roll over, pull himself up, walk—the boy didn't seem to care how many times he fell down, bumped his head or landed on hard things. He'd just get right back up and try again."

He couldn't help but grin at that one, but he didn't see how being determined beyond logic, and somewhat hard-headed, helped their situation any.

Her head on his shoulder, her hair splayed out around them, she looped her leg over his midsection, causing his hips to automatically rise to press against her, but he didn't have the energy to take it any further.

She didn't seem to, either, just settled that way on top of him, as though bedding down for the night.

He loved having her there. And didn't feel at all ready for sleep.

"I'll tell you what I tell our son," she said then, which was when he realized they were still talking. About?

"You take things one step at a time. You're not always going to get it right the first time. You're not always going to know how to get it right. You can't expect to master something the first time you're presented with it. Or be an expert at everything you try. You aren't going to understand every aspect of every challenge when you're first faced with it…"

His grin had grown into a full-out smile. "I get it," he said, stopping her mid-flow. And: "'Aspect?' You use words like that with a four-year-old kid?"

"No."

"I get it," he said again, completely serious, afraid his teasing had stifled her.

"So…we're trying?" she asked.

"Yes." He'd passed that point already.

Just wasn't sure what the next one was. Tried to foresee the most immediate challenges that would be facing them when they got out of the hole in the ground. Couldn't land on just one.

How did he know what lay ahead when he didn't know how his current situation was going to end? It wasn't like a wildfire that would eventually die down, the only questions there being how many acres burnt, how much property, how many lives were lost before it ended.

What if he remembered all the things that were currently a blank to him? From party girls to paying off the most incredible woman he'd ever met. From inventing fake charities to drop money in foreign accounts to denying his own child…

What if he didn't?

"I should be out there, catching my so-called killer, not lying here, waiting for someone else to do it for me." He was a doer.

And if that was the only trait he'd passed on to his son, he could live with that. As long as Carter knew to focus on doing good works, not evil ones…

"You hired the people who are doing it," Shelby said,

her voice drowsy. "In the legal world, that makes you as culpable..."

Gotta love a woman who could talk law logic and fall asleep drooling on your chest at the same time.

Luke was still smiling, drifting off to sleep himself, when he heard the cage clang.

The lights were still on. They hadn't had dinner.

Raising his free arm to glance at the time, he was already out of bed when he saw the bare spot on his wrist.

"It's almost nine," Shelby said. She was out of bed, too, looking toward the digital plug-in clock among the electronics in the living area.

Back in his shorts within seconds, Luke ran barefoot up the wooden ladder rungs.

"You think it could be over already?" Shelby called out from just below him, hope filling her voice.

"Maybe." But he didn't dare hope. Couldn't lose focus on the facts by allowing his own personal wants to get in the way. Not when it came to battling death.

He pulled out what looked like the same phone he'd sent up hours before. Jumped to the ground from the third rung up and, still wearing only his shorts, joined Shelby, who was in her shorts and shirt, on the couch.

Her bra still lying on the floor in front of the right-side cushion, where he'd dropped it earlier. He liked knowing that she was still bare beneath the thin cotton shirt.

There for him to pleasure.

He liked knowing, because he wasn't sure what they were going to see on that tape. Their potential killer had apparently been stalking him for some time. Had stolen his identity and, even after a professional hit man had been killed, had still managed to escape without his identity being discovered. Didn't make sense that he'd be taken down within an hour or so of an operation getting underway. Because with the drive involved, that tracker would only have arrived at the ski resort sometime that evening.

There was only one video. From Hudson. Luke had figured that much already. With no phones being used to communicate between Sylvia Harrington and Charlie in Tucson, unless there was an emergency, all videos were being passed by Sierra's Web drivers.

Didn't mean he hadn't hoped he'd see his son again. Maybe even get a personal hello from the boy.

Shoulders touching, he and Shelby sat together while he called up the video and hit Play.

"An evening check-in to let you know that the team has arrived at the cabin near Flagstaff. Everything's in place as described. So far, all is quiet. I'll keep you posted, with as much immediacy as possible, if anything changes during the night."

Reaching over him, Shelby hit Pause.

"You feel good about that?" she asked him, sending off a surge of gratitude within him. Way more than anything he felt when his team turned to him for decisions and assignments.

She trusted him enough to want his judgment.

Who'd have thought the concept could be so heady?

"It's what I expected," he told her, pushing Play again. He wanted to kiss her in the worst way but needed to get the rest of the business out of the way first.

"Looking at specific dates and times of small purchases, fast food—that kind of thing—and comparing them against charges on the Cayman account, we've got a solid case for identity theft against this guy. He's careful to lay low when you're home but moved about pretty freely when you were off the grid with a fire, using the Cayman Islands account exclusively. We've been trying to figure out how he knew about the account when, by all traces, it should have been only you and Michaels who knew the account even existed. So we're looking into Michaels's associates but have to be aware that the guy might not be a US citizen and could have some link to the account in Cayman Islands himself. For all we know, he was a banker there who wanted to relocate in the US and is using you to do it…"

All of which just frustrated the fire out of him. He'd told Michaels to donate to charities. He remembered that part. But designating which ones? Choosing bogus ones? And the whole offshore account?

The account had been set up shortly after the Marnell injury. He had to admit that it was possible there were parts of his memory he'd never gotten back.

Which brought him right back to Shelby.

The things he'd done.

Would they always be there—unspoken, put to rest but still existing between them?

"From the phone records, we've been able to viably prove that this guy has been impersonating you for years. As smart as he appears to be, getting away with this for so long, eluding us now, he made the stupid mistake of using the same device—which lets us triangulate cell-tower locations using the International Mobile Equipment Identity number. He just updated the prepaid SIM cards."

Luke gladly took the small bit of good news. They were making progress. Not as quickly as he needed, but he had to remind himself that while it felt like it had been a lifetime since he'd woken up in the hospital, it had only been a matter of days.

"Nothing new on the hit man, Benjamin Garvey. We've talked to his mother, to friends, coworkers, and they all say that Benjamin held you in the highest esteem. To the point of letting people know that he was to be told when you were in danger. It's looking more likely that someone tipped him off to our guy, that he somehow didn't get the memo on Bruce and Lorraine and was just out to save you—"

Holy hell. Now a guy died specifically because of him? The complete opposite of his life's purpose?

Shelby hugged his arm holding the phone, pulling it between her breasts and holding it there. Bringing him home.

Didn't make the death right. But it made him hate himself for it a little less.

She hit Pause. "You remember his mother?" she asked.

And lead hit his gut again as he shook his head. The guy died for him, and he couldn't even remember the mother's name? He told her the truth: "I don't remember any of their names. Most of the time, I don't even know them. I get them to the medics, and I move on to the next…"

Always out to save humanity, just not to get too close to it.

Was he kidding himself that he could pull off a love thing?

Since there was no way he was walking away from Shelby or their son, ever, he was just going to have to find one.

He pushed Play again, needing to get the message over with so he could carry Shelby back to bed, cuddle her close and get some rest.

"—from danger," Hudson said, finishing the sentence Shelby had cut off. "That's it, other than something Charlie shared during private radio check-in a couple of hours ago. We aren't talking about the DNA test, as you said you wanted to know results, no questions asked; but I thought you'd want to know, Carter recognized you from the tape. He was quite excited, apparently, telling his grandmother about seeing you with the cat you rescued outside his day care. He said he saw the cat run out the door and chased it, and you caught it and gave it back to him but told him that he shouldn't ever, ever talk to strangers. You made him promise not to tell anyone he'd talked to you, and you wouldn't tell, either, as long as he didn't ever do it again. He said you called it a *buy*. He thought it was quite cool that he knew you before his mom picked you for her work..."

The words might have continued. If so, he didn't hear them.

While his ears roared inside his head, Shelby snatched the phone from him and disappeared to the tiny partitioned-off toilet area. He stood. He watched her go.

And knew that it was no mistake that she'd run to the farthest point she could get from him in what had just changed from an underground shelter to an underground prison.

Tears poured down her cheeks. Angry tears. Really, really angry tears.

How *could* he?

Had it all been lies? The not believing that he had a son? His not remembering sending her away? His emotional acceptance that he was really a father?

The insistence he was going to be in his son's life... Yeah, that had obviously been true. He'd just lied about not knowing about Carter.

And had probably known there was no way on earth he could compel her to give up her son's DNA to a man she'd known, briefly, five years before.

She could simply have denied having sex with him.

And without that proof, he couldn't force her to let him be part of his son's life.

He'd known better than to just approach her with an apparent change of heart, almost five years later, and simply ask her if he could see Carter.

Shaking so hard she couldn't hold the tissue to her nose, she tried for a third time to get a good blow in. Took some deep breaths.

Wiped her eyes with tight, furious fists.

She wasn't going to cry another tear for the man.

Nor was she going to hide on a toilet.

He was the one who'd behaved like sewage, not her.

Face clean, she waited until she was sure all moisture had stopped flowing and stepped out into the room, expecting Luke to be on the couch.

Or in bed asleep. And it better be the bed they'd had sex in because she most certainly wasn't going to be lying down in that bed again...

He wasn't asleep. Or lying down.

He stood, arms folded, leaning back against the kitchen sink. He'd put on his shirt.

"Why?"

He shook his head.

"And this is trying to do better in the communication department?" she snapped, uncaring if she sounded irrational.

"I don't know why." He threw up his hands, met her gaze head-on. Didn't even bother to blink with shame.

She didn't get it. Didn't get *him*.

How could one man be so giving—so selfless—and so disgustingly horrid, too?

"That's your story, then? You don't know why you just happened to be outside my son's day care when he let the cat out?"

His eyes widened a bit at that, which just pissed her off more. Anything he did right then, even evaporate into thin air, would make her mad. She just couldn't...

Couldn't...

"Yeah, I know about the cat," she snapped in a nasty tone she'd never heard come out of her own mouth before. Her mother's, yes... After her father had broken Sylvia's heart for the final time.

She didn't care. Luke wasn't her father. They weren't married and... "He didn't keep his word to you, so if you think you were something special—well, just forget it."

Luke stood up straight, surprise written all over him. "He told you about me?"

"No." She glanced away. "It wasn't about you." She wanted that part quite clear. "Carter told me he let it out. When I asked if they got it back, he said yes and then added that a man outside helped him, and he wasn't supposed to say that part because the man was a stranger."

So there. Carter had trusted his mother more than he'd feared being in trouble. For either of his wrongdoings: letting the cat out and talking to a stranger.

"You're doing a great job with him." Luke's gaze was completely serious, his tone even more so. She listened for defensiveness. For anger. For blame outside himself.

Heard none of it.

He was just doing it to confuse her. Acting like the man she'd first thought him to be.

And then thought him to be again.

"I'm warning you right now. You stay away from my son." She couldn't keep him away forever. But she could make him take her to court. And she had a whole lot to say about a man who denied his child for years and then waited outside his day care to approach him rather than contact her.

"He's my son, too."

Yeah, well, she'd see about that. No way…

Anger was getting her nowhere but sick to her stomach.

"Why?" she asked again.

"I don't know."

Another flare of anger shot through her. She let it pass. She would not become a bitter woman living with an angry heart. If for no other reason than because Carter deserved better.

She was off men, though.

Most definitely. Forever.

"How can you not know?"

"Because I don't remember any of it!" Luke didn't raise his voice. He didn't slam on the counter or do any of the things her father used to do when he'd been caught.

She heard the vehemence in his voice, though.

"I don't remember knowing I had a son. I don't remember turning my back on him, and I damned well don't remember sitting outside his day care—or ever seeing him before in my life."

For a second there, hope soared.

But sense knocked it out of the air to plop back down at her feet. Funny how the man could remember everything else about his life but just conveniently forgot the times that had to do with her and Carter. Other than an out-of-control house party, a threesome between strangers—both things which she found distasteful— the only other thing he'd apparently forgotten was the Cayman account.

And the house party, the threesome and use of the Cayman account Luke had set up could all be put down to his stolen identity.

Which left only things to do with her and Carter that

he was "forgetting." And that was far too coincidental for her to just have faith that he was telling her the truth.

Nor could she put those actions down to anyone else.

She'd seen the man before he'd shut the door in her face at his home address.

And her son had recognized him from a damned video.

He'd been watching Carter at day care? Every time the fact hit her, she lost her breath.

She couldn't keep hoping. Keep making excuses.

She couldn't do it again. Couldn't get sucked back in.

For some reason—maybe just maturity or, more likely, his own father's death—Luke had had a change of heart about being a father himself.

And her walking into that hospital room to identify him… He'd had to think the stars had aligned for him perfectly on that one.

She'd given him an opportunity too good to be true.

She fully believed that he hadn't remembered anything yet when she first saw him earlier in the week. But when his memory had come back…

He'd seen his chance.

"I don't remember, Shelby." His gaze implored her. And…no.

"I don't believe you." She knew how hurtful the words would be to him.

She said them anyway.

But wasn't 100 percent sure she believed them, either.

She just knew she couldn't trust him, no matter how much her heart cried out for him.

And without trust, she couldn't let him anywhere near her son, or her heart.

Chapter 23

Luke watched her turn her back on him. The slice he felt inside... Had that been what it felt like when he'd denied their child and shut his door in her face?

Frustrated beyond endurance, he forced himself to remain completely still, to breathe, to count until the first stab of loss passed.

He didn't even consider following her as she ducked behind the partition with the second bed in it. A space neither of them had occupied during the more than twenty-four hours they'd occupied the small shelter. He didn't blame her for being done with him. Given the circumstances, he'd walk away from himself if it was possible.

Pouring the rest of the unconsumed wine in the sink, he cleaned the glasses. Tended to his own nightly ablutions. And then, leaving on only a small light over the sink—still needing to see his surroundings even after Shelby had turned off the small light shining from behind her partition—he told the mother of his child a silent good night. He grabbed a pillow off the remaining bed—the unmade, love-mussed sheets mocking him—and dropped down to the couch.

They'd made love there, too.

He needed rest. And while he was used to bunking in unfamiliar places and had no trouble catching shut-eye when and where he could, he wasn't going to put himself through a night on the hard ground.

So, determined—and with an arm up over his face—Luke willed himself to sleep. He closed his eyes.

And waited.

Turned over and waited some more.

Repositioned. Waited.

And just kept seeing Shelby's face when she'd told him she didn't believe him. It was like the image was glued to the backs of his eyelids.

He wanted to make things right. And…couldn't.

How did he remember what he couldn't remember?

And yet…why did he just not remember things that mostly had to do with her? He didn't remember setting up the Cayman account, and according to Michaels, he'd done that in person. So there was that.

Sierra's Web had determined that the partying had been done by his identity thief.

But Carter?

He'd actually been stalking his own son? Sitting outside his day care?

He didn't see it. Not ever.

Still…the things Carter said he'd said to him—not to ever talk to strangers, even one returning a runaway cat—he could hear himself having a conversation like that. Not in memory but in imagination. It resonated with the person he felt himself to be.

But the rest…

He just kept coming back to what he knew but didn't remember. He wanted to believe in the man he felt he was. The man he wanted to know.

Facts weren't pointing him in that direction.

And he was nothing if not a fact guy.

One who made life-and-death decisions based on the speed and direction of wind, watching minute-to-minute reports to adjust plans over and over as needed.

He'd spent the past few days listening to report after report. The facts were speaking.

And as much as he'd like to change what he was hearing about himself, just like with the wind, he couldn't force his will on things that were out of his control.

No matter how determined he might be to make things right.

So maybe it was time to switch gears. To figure out what to do about the situation he was stuck in. Circumstances seemed to mostly center around Shelby.

But…

He sat up.

What if it wasn't Shelby specifically, but rather the timing? She'd definitely made him uneasy, with the emotional charges she'd lit inside him. He'd had a head injury shortly after leaving her with the situation completely unresolved. Had some part of his subconscious decided to suppress that which created conflict between who he knew himself to be and the man Shelby brought out in him?

Obviously, he'd remembered at some point, though. At least during her visit to tell him about the baby. How else would he have known to look the child up?

The first-known account of him acting in a way that he couldn't now believe…other than leaving her the money, which could have been meant to pay her expenses for the week since, technically, their association had turned personal…the first-known account was him denying her pregnancy as being his responsibility. Which had come after the first memory loss. Had that head injury unrooted something in him, giving him some kind of multiple personality dysfunction?

He'd heard that emotional trauma could cause severe conditions—but how different personalities were triggered in one guy, how they presented…

Sweating profusely, he jumped up off the couch.

As soon as Shelby's life was confirmed to be out of danger, he was going to see a therapist. He'd go through shock treatment, if they still did that kind of thing. Or whatever else it took.

He had a family to provide for. Even though they weren't going to be living like one.

He had to know he was still a guy who could be trusted.

Shelby woke with little light. She couldn't see the clock in the living area from behind her partition but felt rested.

She'd given up. Trapped underground, she'd had nowhere to go. There'd been nothing she could do, not even for her son, at the moment. Carter was safe. She was officially off duty from her entire life.

With the tracker found and nowhere near, she was physically safe.

Rest had been so turbulent during the past few days that she'd given up on trying to figure out anything and had just gone to sleep.

And then she was awake again.

Everything she'd escaped from was still there.

Including Luke Dennison.

She saw his feet propped up on the arm of the couch as she took a quick glance at the clock in the living area on her way to the back partition. Seven.

Had to be in the morning, right?

She hadn't slept through an entire day, had she?

Disoriented, lonely, she did her business, changed into clean clothes—a pair of blue shorts and a white sleeveless top—and thought about hand-washing the dirties…

No. She was not going to nest. To settle into life underground with Luke.

Her heart would never survive.

She was just finishing up at the sink in the kitchen, was putting her travel toothbrush back in its little holder, when she heard a message clang.

Luke must have sprung off the couch—leading her to believe he'd been awake, listening to her—as he was at the ladder by the time she'd turned her head in that direction.

In wrinkled beige shorts, he was up the ladder and then jumped down, barefoot, to the cement floor, already turning on the screen.

She was afraid for a second that he was going to cut her out of their briefing, but she gave him credit when he joined her by the sink, holding the phone so she could see it, too, before he pressed Play.

He didn't say a word. For once, she was glad.

Hudson's news shot at her the second the video started. "We didn't get him. There was infrared footage that showed a body in the area—six feet or so, at best guess, on foot—shortly after dark. But it looked up through what we believe were night goggles of some kind, seemed to pause on each drone we had in the air and, after a few more minutes of ground surveillance, it disappeared. Leaving no trail. Just vanished."

"How can someone just evaporate?" she cried out, so

done with…everything. "This isn't a cartoon here. It's real life!"

Luke's gaze met hers, seemingly concerned, but she couldn't take him in. The man was off-limits to her.

Period.

And she should be keeping her mouth shut so as to not invite his attention.

She stared at the X shapes in the overstitching on the pockets of his shorts. *X marks the spot.* Was the same stitching on his fly?

Hudson was going on about the details of the night, the plan having continued with no activity, the bodies on the ground searching for whoever had been in the perimeter of the infrared cameras they'd set up but then just seemed to no longer be visible to them.

"We're doubling up on the evidence we do have on this guy, following every lead on his five-year trail. We'll find him. And in the meantime, if you two need anything down there, let us know."

That was it? They'd just been told they were being subjected to another day of lost life in the dungeon?

Okay, way too dramatic, but…

"The guy's prepared, probably an outdoorsman," Luke said. "All he'd need was a foil-encased fabric to wrap in to avoid infrared detection."

"But he didn't stick around and attempt anything because he knew he was being watched?" she asked.

They were still fighting for their lives together. They could talk business.

She was making up the rules as she went along.

And it was ridiculous to think that they'd exist in the small space for what could be another twenty-four hours with a cold war between them.

Unhealthy, even…

Luke's silent shrug to her comment stopped her mental concession.

"You think he knew that it was a setup?" she asked next. "That'd be key, right? If he knows that his tracker is no longer of use to him, he'll change his method of operation..."

Luke glanced at her, almost as though he was seeing her but not. "Right," he said. Then took the phone with him as he put a few feet of distance between them.

Next thing she knew, he was speaking. To the phone. Recording.

Which was his right. He was paying for their detail...

And then, after agreeing with the teams continued attention to his identify thief's financial and phone trail—a phone that had been off since before the fire that had almost killed him—he said, "I need you to make a plan to get me up out of here without compromising the shelter's existence."

Her mouth fell open as, heart pounding, she stared at his back. Him? Not them?

"The one thing we know for sure, the guy wants me. Leaves us two choices. We can wait around for your teams to follow leads until you figure out who he is, then find him, then actually get him in custody—or, just as you were doing with the tracker, you use me as bait."

Her hissed intake of air was completely involuntary.

As was her heart's instant rejection of Luke's words.

Frozen, she listened as he continued. "It's been more than two days. I'm done letting others fight this battle for me. I'm making choice two. I'm coming out as bait. If you all want to quit me, that's your choice, but I'm coming up. I'm going to face off with this guy and get this done. I'd have a better chance of living through the experience with all of your professional assistance and connections, and am making a formal request that you stay on, while understanding completely if you determine you can't do so. I'm asking, either way, that whatever it costs, this shelter remain available to Shelby, as it's been proven safe, and that your teams continue to protect her and the boy and his grandmother in Tucson until this is done."

"No!" she cried out, every part of her aching. But he'd already turned off Record and was climbing the ladder to deliver his missive.

She couldn't believe it.

Being in the ground alone—she'd lose her mind.

Or not... she silently admitted, looking at the television set. To end this thing, to get home to Carter, to know that her son no longer needed a bodyguard—she'd sit in a much worse hole alone. For however long it took.

But... "Luke, you can't do this. No one knows who this guy is. He's already almost killed you. It's a suicide mission."

And...she cared. She heard it in her voice. Figured he did, too, when he turned to give her a long look. But all he said was, "I have to do this."

Oh, God. Please, no.

Was he doing this because of her? Because he knew, as she did, that the two of them trapped in a hole—albeit a luxurious one—was soon going to be untenable for both of them?

Or because her refusal to believe he wasn't lying had shown him the hopelessness of wanting a life where they got along and co-parented their son?

Did he figure out that she'd fight him in court and—given his rejection of his son from the outset, his lying since—likely win?

"This is who I am, Shelby," he said, standing almost directly in front of her. He held her gaze, no apology apparent, and went on, "We knew, going in, that there'd come a time when I had to take a risk that would be hard for you to accept…"

We. And *going in*.

Like they were still under the old regime.

Which…they were. Just because she couldn't sleep with him, or think about marrying him someday, they were still the two people who'd felt a connection and made a son who needed both of them.

Because, while she'd been beyond upset the night before, she knew that no court in the land was going to keep Luke Dennison from seeing his son. Most particularly not just because he'd lied to his kid's mother. Or had looked the boy up while keeping his distance. If he'd approached Carter, as opposed to just helping him save the cat the boy had inadvertently let out…

"I'm not going to try to keep you from seeing your son," she said, as though there was still hope that she'd be able to change his mind.

"I know." He was packing up his things, putting the meager pile back into the single plastic shopping bag that had been waiting in the shelter with his name on it.

Right next to the matching one bearing her name.

"And I'm not going to let either of you down," he said, but he turned his back before he'd finished the sentence.

He'd already let them both down. First with his rejection when she'd first been pregnant, and then by looking Carter up, hanging around outside Carter's day care and not contacting her.

That didn't mean she wanted him dead.

Or even out of her life. He just couldn't be the other half of her heart…

He'd moved to the couch. Put on a movie. A comedy

they'd talked about watching together. Frustrating her.
Scaring her.

But giving her a sense of closure, too. As he'd said,
they'd reached their impasse. The one that might have
broken them apart had they really tried to make a go of
things when they'd gotten back to real life.

She should be thankful they'd fast-tracked to that
point before Carter had gotten involved, she resolved as
she made oatmeal and toast; peeled another orange; and
served his up to him on the couch, while taking hers to
the table.

She could see the television from there, too.

And heard loud and clear when a clang, bigger than
any they'd had before, sounded in the cage at the top of
the shelter.

Sierra's Web had sent a map of a tunnel system,
through a hatch under the couch. And a wet suit. Luke
was to follow the map and end up in the lake, not far
from shore, half a mile down the beach. He'd stay in
his wet suit, walk up the beach to public parking and
get in a Jeep that would be waiting for him. He'd then
be transported to another location, where Sierra's Web
team members would go over a plan to use him to lure
out his would-be killer.

The whole thing made her sick to her stomach.

Sent panic racing through every vein in her body.

"Luke..."

He didn't so much as glance her way as he immediately stripped down, dressed in the suit he'd been
brought, shoved aside the couch, studied the map for
a good minute and then, leaving it on the table, pulled
open the hatch.

He was just going to go. Without...

"Luke!" She couldn't keep the despair out of her voice.

He glanced at her then, but he wasn't backing down.

"You let us down if you don't stay alive," she said, and watched through tear-filled eyes as he disappeared from sight.

Chapter 24

He had his mandate.

Stay alive.

Sitting at a table inside the mansion, Luke focused but couldn't buy into anything he was hearing. The plans were television quality, with all kinds of people putting their lives on the line to protect him, and that wasn't him.

Even sitting in that room with them all, he felt responsible for every single life around the table. Because being close to him put them in danger.

As much so as if he had some deadly and contagious disease.

Hudson talked. Bruce did as well. Winchester was there and half a dozen men and women he'd never met. Everyone throwing out ideas about how to draw out his stalker, where to do it, when to do it and how best to protect Luke as they did it. Suggestions flew, were bandied about by some while others moved on to explore different ideas.

And all Luke could think about was Shelby in the shelter, alone. Wanting to be out on the beach with Lorraine and the others, making certain that the area around the shelter wasn't breached. The guards never got too close. Never blatantly even looked in the shelter's direction. They weren't giving up the location.

If it were him out there, trying to find something no one wanted found, he'd pay attention to an area that no one accessed. To all the areas they left unwalked.

After an hour passed and midmorning approached, he was about ready to go walk the beach himself. To just work off some steam and let the fiend take a shot at him.

He had no death wish.

To the contrary—his mandate was to stay alive, and so he would.

But clearly, this guy was an outdoorsman. His knowledge of drones, his ability to escape infrared—to escape, period. Everyone had agreed the guy's knowledge of safety in the wilderness surpassed many. That certainty had already been discussed. Leading some members of the team to go diving back into anyone with firefighting experience, current or past, who'd crossed lines with Luke in a negative way. Hotshots were particularly well trained in all things outdoor survival.

Including knowing how to use fabric-wrapped foil to avoid infrared detection. Because you also used the method to protect against some radiation exposure...

Setting up a dummy of him in a boat was discussed. Perhaps the attacker would be exposed trying to take out the boat. Mentally vetoing that idea, Luke came back to the infrared disappearance the night before.

If he'd known he was being watched but had been certain his target had been in the cabin he'd been sighting, he'd have used the protection to get closer. Keeping himself undercover to avoid drones. It had been dark. Some kind of umbrella, maybe...

Hell, scooting on his belly could have worked, considering they'd been dealing with northern Arizona landscaping. Trees, brush, grass...

Getting to his subject would have been a challenge but a relatively easy one...

So why hadn't the guy attacked the cabin?

Because the infrared guy hadn't been their killer. Or he'd figured out somehow that Luke wasn't in that cabin, that Luke had been separated from his tracker.

Put that together with the fact that guards were still around the house, the beach...

One could surmise that perhaps the home's owners had hired security for their own protection after the break-in two nights before.

But more likely...

He'd heard a small plane flying overhead when he walked out of the lake earlier that morning. It had been so low that he glanced up to see it pulling a bannered advertising message for beachgoers.

But that early...who'd pay for advertising outside of prime beach times?

"Planes," he said. "Has anyone been watching for planes in the area?"

"Of course. Helicopters, too." Hudson stopped in the middle of a conversation to answer him. "It's a lake. There are a couple of companies up the beach that offer aerial-view excursions. And I can assure you that nothing and no one has dropped from one anywhere near here..."

He wasn't worried about what came down—more like, what could have been captured from above.

He had to get back to the shelter.

He was doing nothing but sitting in a chair, and there

was a remote possibility his stalker, if he was anywhere nearly as trained as Luke was, could know the shelter's location.

He had no proof. And without full memory, he wasn't even sure he trusted what he knew at the moment. Not enough to stop the team of experts from doing their jobs.

They could message him when they came up with their plan.

Shelby had been alone for hours…

He had to get back to her.

The fact that the guy hadn't hit the cabin last night, just in case, wasn't sitting right with him.

After excusing himself from the table, he pulled Hudson aside, telling the team leader that someone trained in outdoor safety would likely be fully versed on satellite technology and ground-penetrating radar. A plane flying over, with the proper equipment inside and in just the right spot, could find the shelter's location.

"Even if he knows it's there," Hudson pointed out, "he doesn't know where or how to access it, and I can guarantee you that any one of our people out there on the beach will see someone—anyone—out on this property."

He didn't doubt Hudson's words. "I still need to get back down there," he said. "The guy wants me. Shelby's just an aside to him, at best. I realize the shelter's proven to be safe, and I want her where I know that she's safest, but she's not trained to… I need to be down there with her."

He sounded paranoid even to himself. But he was paying the bills.

"I get it, Luke," Hudson said then, dropping his voice even lower. "You just found out she had your son…"

He tensed. He wasn't paying anyone to get into that personal hell. But before he could speak without biting the guy's head off, Hudson continued. "I've been there, actually. A thirteen-year-old girl had been kidnapped. I didn't know she was my daughter until I'd been called to the case…"

Luke felt his eyes widen. For a second there, he thought he was hallucinating. Did everyone have hidden nuances? Stuff going on no one else knew about?

Had Hudson's daughter been found? Safe?

Before he could ask, Bruce walked up, checking to see what was up, and Hudson explained as though Luke's desire to return to the shelter was all they'd been talking about, saying that he agreed with Luke's decision to go. The team leader assured him that they'd get a message down to Luke as soon as the team had signed off on a viable plan, and Luke hurried off beside his bodyguard.

Feeling like a lovesick fool.

And going anyway.

What had he done, really? He'd sent her away when she'd told him she was pregnant. He'd later looked her up, found out where her son went to day care and showed up there but hadn't sought Carter out. And he'd lied to Shelby about remembering both of those things.

Sending her away as he had had been hideous. She could kind of see why he'd wanted a glimpse of his son before he started the battle to be able to see him.

How long would it have been before she had legal communication from Luke if he hadn't been injured in the fire and lost his memory?

A day?

A month?

If he'd remembered her as soon as he'd seen her, would he have told her the truth from the beginning?

And…what if he *was* telling her the truth? What if he'd

been so emotionally conflicted by losing his son—enough so that he'd had to find him and get a look for himself—that he really had suppressed the memory?

She'd told him she didn't believe him, leaving him no choice but to move on. Because how would he ever be able to prove it to her?

Pacing the small shelter—television to toilet, again and again—she tried to think about other things. Recorded a message for her son, telling him all the things she loved about him, talking about his strengths and how happy she was being his mom.

She told herself the video was just to occupy her brain and keep her focused on things that would help her maintain her emotional strength.

In the back of her mind, she wondered if her fear for Luke was making her afraid for herself, too. If maybe the video was in case she didn't make it back to Carter.

Right after Luke had left, she'd finished watching the comedy he'd started during breakfast. Sitting on the couch, which was still askew. She hadn't wanted to cover the hatch in case Luke wanted to get back to her.

Video done, she left the phone on the counter, made a peanut butter sandwich and, after cleaning up the kitchen, had carried it over to the angled couch to eat.

Stupid of her to think Luke would be back.

About as ridiculous as making a final video for her son...

She'd been down in the ground too long. Was losing touch with reality.

She'd only been there two nights.

Wouldn't find a safer place to spend the night alone.

She'd only been apart from her son for three nights. It seemed like a lifetime.

Which was about as long as it seemed like since Luke had left. What was happening? The not knowing was…

What if she'd sent him out to die without telling him that she loved him?

Because of course she did, even if she didn't completely trust him. Didn't dare have him be her love.

Her lips fell open as she heard a noise at the top of the ladder, peanut butter and bread sticking to the roof of her mouth. It wasn't the cage.

The sound was louder.

A latch moved and…

The door in the ceiling at the top of the ladder was opening!

Please, God, let Luke come through it first.

Let her have conjured him back to her.

It was probably Lorraine.

She stood, swallowing her lump of soggy bread and peanut butter, tears in her eyes. *Please let Luke at least be alive…*

Legs descended, hairy. Just like Luke's…

The hem of beige shorts… He'd left in beige shorts. Holding her breath, she waited for the hem of his black shirt to appear and nearly cried out loud when it did.

Others would be waiting at the top. She knew that. It was over. They were free!

But oh, God, to have a minute with him first. To celebrate his living with the hug she'd wanted to give him when he left.

To hear him say it was over.

To tell him how sorry she was for turning her back on him.

Arms raised, ready to run to him, she got rubbery knees when she saw his face. Those blue eyes—they were intense but didn't meet her gaze.

She'd hoped, with him coming for her, that her harsh words would be forgiven. That he'd give her a chance to apologize, be open for conversation about a future for them...

"Luke?" She'd beg if she had to.

He glanced at her, as a stranger would when taking in another person, and her heart broke a little. Not just because of what she'd said, how she'd reacted to Carter knowing him already, but because of who he was.

The man who retreated.

Pulling her arms down to wrap around herself, taking back the hug she'd been about to throw at him, she watched as he quickly moved through the space, taking a long second to eye the hatch through which he'd left. His chin clenched, as though the sight didn't please him.

Because she hadn't put the couch back?

"Luke?" she asked again. "Is it over?"

He nodded. "Yeah, it's over," he said, sounding...determined more than elated. Like he was in the middle of getting the job done.

Yeah, she'd been upset, but she didn't deserve to be treated as though they were nothing to each other. If nothing else, they'd survived two days in an underground hole together.

They'd made love.

Multiple times.

Didn't that at least deserve a fond farewell?

And what about Carter? Wasn't he eager to go meet his son?

All he gave her was his back as he strode swiftly to the far end of the space, checking the back partition and then, coming back, going in the other two partitions as well. She made it over to the one closest to the couch—the bed they'd shared—in time to see him looking under it.

For what?

He was scaring her.

"Luke? Is there a tracker or something in here?"

When he didn't respond, she glanced toward the wooden ladder rungs, back at him and made her choice.

He'd do what he had to do, and if he came back to her, she'd...

At the ladder, her hands on the ropes running along both sides of the rungs, she started up. She needed to get back to her real life. To Carter.

She took the first step, still glancing toward the partition where she'd left Luke. As though giving him one last hope. And then, as she started for the second, she glanced up, ready for daylight.

Needing daylight.

There was no daylight.

The door was as closed as it had been the whole time they'd been down there. As though... She glanced at the inside latch, saw it clicked. Heart pounding, spines of fear poking her arms and legs, she lifted her leg higher—two steps' worth—and jerked when a death grip took hold of her hips.

He yanked her down so hard, so fast, her shoulders were nearly pulled from their sockets. Her hands stung with rope burn.

Luke wasn't a rough man.

He wasn't in his right mind.

Was he on something?

Or...dear God... Had his head injuries... Was he mentally ill?

He set her on the ground. Pushed her, hard, in the center of her back toward the couch. Caught her by her hair to stop her, and dragging her along with him, ripping some hair out by the roots, he used his free hand to slide the couch back over the escape hatch he'd gone down earlier.

What in the hell was going on?

"Luke, what happened?" she cried, her chin to her chest, face toward the floor due his grip on her hair.

He was beyond angry.

Letting go of her hair, he grabbed her throat. Scared out of her wits, she kneed him. Missed the groin she was going after and caught him in the stomach, just below his ribs. Winding him enough to get herself free.

Terrified, she didn't know what to do. There was nowhere to go… He'd haul her off the ladder before she could get the latch open…

Grabbing a kitchen knife, all she could think about was defending herself. For Carter.

Her son's face flashing in her brain, she blinked, could feel tears on her cheeks and sweat on her back.

If he came near her, she'd…

Staggering for a second, Luke approached, the look on his face menacing. Jeering.

He wanted her dead. She saw it on his face.

Horrified, she could hardly think…just knew she had to…

His shorts… Staring, she saw the stitching on the pockets of his shorts as he slowly came toward her.

There were no X's. *X marks the spot*, she remembered. From that morning.

And the hand raised toward her… A scar…on the forearm…

"Come any closer, and you're dead." She felt the words leave her throat, didn't recognize the voice as her own. And didn't doubt that she'd use the knife, either.

Grabbing a second one, she jabbed them both toward the figure that had stopped advancing for a second. He might win, whoever he was, but she wasn't going down without using up every ounce of fight in her.

"You aren't Luke."

He stood there, his gaze calmer, assessing...and still, not Luke.

"I will be," the man said, and the jeering look that came over his face...

She knew it.

Had seen it before.

In Payson. Outside Luke's house.

The day she'd gone to tell him she was pregnant.

Confused, disoriented, she faced the man.

Multiple personalities?

The shorts. No X's.

"Where is my dear brother?" the man asked then, as though he was suddenly, in the midst of evil, stopping to enjoy himself.

He wanted Luke. As soon as she gave him any information she had, she'd be of no use to him.

And he... Dear God, Carter!

He knew.

It had been him outside of her son's school. It had to have been.

Eyes hard with the intent to kill the man in her path, she calmed. Knowing what Luke would do. "Your brother?" she asked.

"Our darling mother... She had identical twins. Threw one away and kept the other for herself." The easy tone got lost in the sneer on his face. The content of his words.

Luke had an identical twin.

Who hated him.

For what Luke had and whoever he was had not.

"What's your name?"

She didn't want to know. Just had a sense that she had

to keep him talking. As long as he stood there spitting words at her, taking heinous pleasure from their stand-off, she was alive.

With time to figure out how she could knife the man before he used his greater height and far superior strength to overpower her and get the weapons out of her hands.

They'd land in her, she knew that.

"Larry," he told her. "Not by birth, of course. I grew up as Noah." The man took a step forward, as though to emphasize the name. As though it was all her fault.

Like she should have known...

"When did you become Larry?"

Keep him talking. Keep him talking. Keep him talking.

She didn't retreat. The counter was already at her back. It could help her. Steady her while she used her foot...

"Six years ago. When I got the DNA test back and found out that while I grew up in a system that didn't give a damn about me, my *identical* brother had known nothing but privilege."

Some of his spittle dropped to the floor. Shelby swallowed back bile.

"Well, now it's my turn." Larry stepped forward, his lip curled with hate.

"Wait!" she called out, completely out of thoughts. "It was you, wasn't it? Who slammed the door in my face."

"Hell yes, it was me! You think I was going to let some whore and her kid take away what was mine?"

If she died, she'd do so knowing that her son's father was a decent man. The best.

And that she'd loved him rightly.

"And that's why you need me dead," she said, seeing the writing on the wall. She wasn't getting out of there alive.

Did the man realize that Sierra's Web now knew that Luke was Carter's father?

"That's why I'm not going to fail this time."

Larry's hand came out so swiftly she almost lost her life. She slashed his hand instead. He growled, bunched his shoulders, bowed his head and came toward her.

Both knives ready, she braced for the onslaught. And heard a loud splintering sound coming from just beyond Larry.

The fiend paused, turned, and Luke came flying. Both feet off the ground, he landed on Larry, tackling him to the ground, pinning him down with a knee between his shoulders, just below the base of his neck.

Shelby stared in shock, unable to comprehend what had just happened.

Larry's expletives filled the room. He bucked, his arms swinging as far behind him as they could; he grabbed Luke's arm, twisted.

She held her knives ready. To use them, hand them over—and when Larry grunted, twisting Luke's arm again, she lunged forward.

The knife didn't penetrate. She wasn't that good. But the graze was enough for Larry's grip to loosen for the second it took Luke to free himself and grab the arm. Twisting it up Larry's back, close to Luke's knee.

She jumped when sounds came from behind Luke, but he didn't seem to budge. She stared, afraid of what else was coming, and then saw Bruce jump down from the ceiling entrance, forgoing the ladder altogether, followed by Lorraine.

Activities swirled around her. While Lorraine held a gun pointed at Larry's temple, Bruce used a belt to secure the man's arms behind him. Luke grabbed rope from a drawer in the living room and secured the man's—his brother's—feet.

Did he know? Had they all figured it out?

She had no idea what might have happened, if she and Luke would have killed his brother together, or if, God forbid, they'd have died together.

She was just glad it was over.

Chapter 25

Luke had never killed a man. But if Bruce and Lorraine had been any later, he would have done so. He was still burning, adrenaline pouring through him, to make the bastard pay for having hurt Shelby, for what the man would surely have done if Luke hadn't gotten there in time, as he jerked the last knot tight on his would-be killer's feet.

Breathing hard, not ready to be done making the guy suffer, he sat back, hard, on the guy's tennis shoes, cramming the man's ankles toward the ground, hearing the new rash of expletives, and stood up.

As badly as he wanted the guy dead, he needed him alive long enough to get some answers. Like...what had Luke ever done to him?

And how had he breached Sierra's Web security to get to the shelter's entrance?

If Luke hadn't been in the tunnel... If he hadn't heard...

That's why you need me dead.

That's why I'm not going to fail this time.

Words he was never, ever going to forget. He'd practically come out of his skin finding the hatch closed, had probably broken a hand getting it open with the couch on top of it.

He couldn't even feel the pain.

The prisoner was swishing his body back and forth like a fish, trying to get up.

"Stay down," Bruce ordered. "The police are on their way."

The man's body went limp for a moment, but then he lifted his head, got his weight on one shoulder and turned to look right at Luke.

What the hell? Luke staggered back a step.

The man had had surgery to make himself look like… It was a mask. Had to be a mask…

Or Luke had just lost the last hold he had on his sanity.

The thief hadn't just stolen his identity. His money. He'd also stolen his looks?

"That's how he got past the guard in the yard," Bruce said. "They knew you'd come up and thought you were getting some fresh air…"

"Good to see you again, too, brother," the man said, his lips curled in a way that made Luke want to punch him in the face.

"'Brother?'" he hollered, his voice echoing off the walls in the small space. So much so that Shelby jumped, hitting her back on the edge of the counter.

Shelby.

He hadn't let himself fully look at her yet. Not while the man who'd wanted her dead was still within his reach.

Just enough to know she was fully dressed. And standing guard like a banshee…

"Yeah, *brother*," the man on the floor said. And then spit in his direction.

He would have stomped the guy's face at the lie, at the insult, except that Shelby had moved, was standing next to him.

As though she'd known what he was about to do and was there to save him from himself. She didn't touch him.

Just stood there.

He wanted to tell her how great she was. How proud he was to know her.

And that he didn't need saving.

While he hadn't been able to hear what she'd been saying until he'd reached the hatch, he'd heard her voice as he'd slithered his way through the tunnel, knew she was in trouble and had radioed his bodyguard to get to the shelter just before he'd heard the fiend tell Shelby he wasn't going to fail. That's when he'd plowed through the hatch.

If she hadn't stood up to the intruder...

The man on the floor continued to taunt him. "What, Lukey boy, you speechless now?" He didn't get it.

Reached down to pull the man's mask off.

If he was doing this, it was happening man to man.

He didn't get any further than a hand to the prisoner's throat, ready to push down into his shirt to find the edge of the mask, before Shelby screamed and Bruce grabbed Luke by the arm, pulling him back.

"Get the damned mask off!" he shouted. To the world in general. Then said, "I'm not talking to this...this..."

"There's no mask," Bruce told him.

Of course there was a mask. No amount of plastic surgery was that good.

"He's your brother, man," Bruce said, still holding on to him.

Shelby was there again, threading her arm through his free one, as he faltered back.

What he noticed was that she wasn't exclaiming any shock.

What the hell?

He had a…

Something else he'd forgotten?

Would his mind ever return his life to him?

For a second there, he flashed back to being in the tunnel. First hearing Shelby's voice and then a male one in response. He saw himself, lying there on his belly, crawling like a snake. Saw his life pass before his eyes as he filled with rage, and didn't like the image that stayed. Him—a man who lived to make his parents proud but not to ever…*ever* let himself care enough individually to hurt like he did when his mother had died.

He'd known in that moment in the tunnel, as he radioed Bruce, that it was too late for him. He'd already fallen in love. With a woman who hated him.

Didn't get much more painful than that.

Until he'd considered that woman's life being snuffed out of her.

His parents… "No way this man's my brother," he said as his vision cleared and he stood up straight.

Bruce dropped his arm but stayed close.

Shelby hung on. He didn't let himself pay attention to her arm in his. But didn't move away yet, either.

"Actually, he is," Lorraine, standing guard at the prisoner's bound feet, spoke up. "Just before you radioed up to get to the shelter, the team had heard from Dorian, one of the Sierra's Web partners. She's a doctor, and they'd run DNA on you and your father once his death had been determined to be connected to see if anything popped… turning over every rock…"

He heard the calm tone. Heard the words.

Shook his head.

"The person who was killed in that car crash wasn't your biological father, man," Bruce said.

Luke. His name was Luke.

Not *man*.

And…

He stared down at the prisoner, who was still staring up at him.

Like he was looking in a mirror.

Except not.

The eyes.

They weren't his…didn't have the same…

"What…" he started but couldn't come up with a question that would give him an answer he wanted.

"Your mother had identical twins. She kept you," Shelby said, her voice soft.

His mother had kept him. But not…not…whoever this was.

"He named himself Larry," Lorraine said. "Six years ago. He was raised as Noah Fisher."

"And my father?" He looked only at Lorraine. The calm voice in a storm that didn't end.

"Died in jail fifteen years ago," Noah-Larry said. "Yeah, you think you're so pure and privileged, but you come from the same dirt as me."

His mother was not dirt.

And his father—the man whom he'd thought was his father, his adopted father—had raised him, not with privilege but with a sense of honor. With the knowledge that he had to work his hardest every single day to be worthy of the life he'd been given.

Just as his dad—not his biological father, his *dad*—had done.

And just as Luke would teach his son.

Somehow.

* * *

Lorraine took Shelby upstairs when the police arrived. Hudson Warner met her on the surface, and because he strongly advised that she be seen by a paramedic, in spite of her assertion that she was fine, she went along with Lorraine to a waiting ambulance.

Sitting on a stretcher inside the open vehicle, she saw a handcuffed Larry being led across the yard toward a bevy of vehicles parked in the circular drive in front of the mansion. And a few minutes later, she saw Luke and Hudson, head-to-head, as they disappeared out of sight.

Probably getting him medical attention as well.

Just in case.

It was over.

They'd both survived.

She could hardly believe it.

And yet she'd never let herself believe anything but that they'd make it back to Carter.

They.

She and Luke had to talk.

Now that the danger was gone, their future had arrived.

Minus any lies between them.

Luke Dennison had been the man her heart had known him to be from the very beginning. She could hardly believe it.

Was still wrapping her mind around the ramifications of all that Larry had put in motion.

Most particularly, the losses Luke had suffered for a choice made when he'd been a newborn baby.

As though Luke's mother keeping him had been his fault.

Why she hadn't kept both boys, they'd probably never know. Just as it was unlikely they'd ever know if Luke's adopted father had known he had a twin. Lorraine had told her that Luke's birth certificate listed his adopted father as his father.

Noah Fisher's had said *father unknown*.

Shelby's vitals were checked over the course of an hour, and her hands were treated with salve and wrapped lightly with gauze.

She hadn't seen Luke.

And just assumed that he'd appear at some point. But when Lorraine told her that she was ready to take Shelby back to Phoenix, she couldn't very well refuse to get in the car.

Luke was paying for the service, not her.

Lorraine handed her phone to her as they got in the car, and, telling herself that Luke would call, she held on to the device long after she'd hung up from a lengthy video call with her mom and Carter. Sylvia was bringing Carter home so that they'd be there when Shelby arrived.

And in spite of a heart full of tears where Luke was concerned, she was overjoyed when she climbed out of Lorraine's car just before dusk that night and saw her little guy's lit-up face as he raced toward her.

Sylvia had dinner made—Carter's favorite, macaroni and cheese—but left before they sat down to eat, saying she wanted to get back to Tucson before night set in.

And two hours later, freshly showered and in an old, short denim skirt and T-shirt, Shelby was sitting in the full dark, alone.

She'd put Carter to bed. At his request, she'd lain with him, cuddled up to his little body, until he was sound asleep.

And then, out on her own couch—in her own living room—she just sat. She wanted to call Luke.

But knew she wouldn't.

She hadn't trusted that he really didn't remember the things he'd done. Understandable, since she'd seen him, and he'd remembered pretty much everything else about his life. But still, she'd done to him what she'd accused him of doing to her.

She'd turned her back on him.

And, sitting there in the dark, she finally admitted to herself that Luke hadn't been the only one shying away from a relationship that first time they were together.

The strength of her feelings for him, the speed with which it had all happened… She'd been scared to death she'd end up like her mother.

In love with a man she didn't know well enough.

A man who, in the long run, wouldn't fit her.

Eventually, knowing she had to pick up the reins of her life, with or without Luke contacting her, she went to the kitchen for a bottle of beer.

Uncapped it. Sipped.

And felt her phone vibrate against her butt.

She had it out of her pocket in a split second, staring at the screen, and almost dropped it when she saw the newly programmed number on her screen. Lorraine had given it to her. Just in case, she'd said. Shelby had been hoping she'd done so at Luke's request.

"Hey," she said softly. Not because their son was asleep, but because…she was filled with soft places for him.

"You got a minute to talk?"

"Of course."

"In person?"

"I can't leave, Luke. Carter's in bed asleep…"

"I'm at your front door."

That's when she dropped her phone.

Luke kept his right arm behind his back when Shelby opened the door. He held her tight, though, with his left arm as she flung herself at him, hugging him so close he was fine to just meld right in forever.

And then she let go.

As he'd known she would.

"Come in," she said, turning around as though embarrassed, and led him through a spotless, spacious entryway past a living room and into a family room and kitchen that ran the entire length of the house. Where she flipped on a light.

And he about wept at the sight of her. All gorgeous thigh and leg under denim, topped by a short white thing that was pretty much see-through. Enough so that he knew she wasn't wearing a bra.

Her hair—long, blond and silky-looking—teased against her nipples.

"You want a beer?" she asked, burying her head in the open refrigerator.

"Yeah." Thinking of the day—the week—he'd had. He'd take ten.

Or...just her.

Reappearing, she uncapped his beer and then, turning to hand it to him, saw his arm.

"A cast, Luke? What happened?" He'd break his hand all over again if it meant he got to hear that soft concern in her voice directed at him.

He shrugged. Saw a couch that looked comfortable. Made his way toward it.

"Luke?" She followed him, as he'd hoped she would. Wanted nothing more than to wrap his good arm around her, hold her close, love her slowly and then sleep for twenty-four hours.

But...he'd learned a thing or two. If you didn't communicate, others didn't know.

"I broke my hand breaking through the hatch in the

floor." He brushed through that part quickly. Didn't want to spend any more time there.

Ever. He rushed on, "The hit man on the beach," he blurted out. Then, swallowing a long swig of needed sustenance, he paused.

Even her frown endeared her to him. "He's dead," she said.

Luke nodded. Then took a deep breath. He had a job to do, and his way was to get it done.

"Larry had approached him, told him he was me, asked him to kill the man staying at his house impersonating me. The guy had seen pictures of me. And owed me. He died thinking he was protecting me."

Shelby scooted closer to him. He wanted to lose himself in her.

Instead, he got lost in the things he had yet to say. Had to find the exact right words…

"I'm sorry, Luke, for not believing in you."

What? Glancing at her, frowning, he shook his head again. "You… Even when you had doubts, you were always open…" he started, and then the words rushed forward. "Don't you get it, Shelby? You reach out to me, pull me in, and I want to stay. I don't understand. I don't see how I be me and live that way, but… What I know now… I don't ever want to come home again if you and Carter aren't there waiting for me. Or…at least living there and coming home at some point, too."

He ran out of air. Out of words. She seemed to know. Ran the back of her hand against his cheek, and he took her by the wrists, turning both open palms to him.

They were raw and glistening with what he guessed was more of the salve Lorraine had told him she'd been sent home with.

"I want to kill him for doing this to you."

"No," she said, putting her finger to his lips. "You're a lifesaver, Luke. And I don't have a complete picture of what our future looks like, either, but I know that I don't want to live anywhere but the place you call home."

"As soon as this cast comes off, I'm going to be back on duty." He had to be honest. Had to communicate.

And trust that it would be enough.

Better that than live like his twin had—a lifetime without love. His parents had taught him better than that.

"I fell in love with a hotshot firefighter once," she said. He assumed she was talking about him. Wasn't sure if she was telling him she'd try to do it again... "And I've loved him ever since," she finished.

She loved him.

Him. The guy who left home and stood up to wildfires.

"I do have a good bit of free time in the off-season I could spare," he told her. He'd always signed on with local fire departments, but nothing said he had to. And he grew completely serious. "We don't know how we're going to make this work, but...today...we kind of did, didn't we? You kept yourself alive. Safe. I knew you needed me, and I made it there. And you with your knives and me with my brute anger...we took danger down."

Her eyes filled with tears.

"I love you, Shelby." The words didn't choke him. Or scare him. Ironically, they freed him. "I..."

"Mom!" The young cry split the night, and Luke was up, heading straight for it without thought, down a hall, running into a small form that buried its head in his thighs, just above his knees, wrapping both arms around his legs.

"I'm right here, sweetie." Shelby stood beside Luke, her hand on his back and on Carter's, too.

Luke was man enough to admit he was glad she was right there. He might need her help.

"You have a bad dream?" she asked.

"No!" Carter glanced up. "I had to go pee, and I saw a spidaw!" The boy's wide-eyed look of horror turned to a frown of confusion. He'd already dropped his hands, had backed around toward his mother and was looking up at Luke. "You aren't my mom."

"No," he said. More words were there. He tried to get them out. Stood there staring at the most incredible creature he'd ever seen and had…no sound.

"He's your father, Carter." Shelby's words came softly as she kneeled down to the boy.

Carter didn't seem to react much. Luke felt poleaxed. Afraid to fail.

And so in love he knew he could be hit over the head a thousand times and not forget either one of them.

"Huh?" Carter's nose scrunched after a few seconds, his brows almost together, as he stared up at Luke.

Taking his cue from Shelby, Luke kneeled and then said, "I didn't know about you, buddy, not until this week. I was gone, fighting wildfires a lot. But I'm here now."

"You saved the cat."

He couldn't lie to the boy. But there were some things a little guy just didn't need to know. "You need to remember always not to talk to strangers, right?" he said. Knowing that as evil as his twin was, he also had a decent bone in his body. He'd taught Carter a good lesson.

"You said you fish," Carter said next, holding on to his mom's arm as he faced Luke. Shelby had dropped to rest her butt on her calves, and Luke followed suit.

"I do. And I'm planning to teach you, too, if you want to learn."

"Okay."

The boy rubbed his eyes, and Luke remembered he'd been asleep. Standing, he reached out a hand to the boy. "How about if we go kill that spider and get you back to bed?"

He was amazing himself, as if he'd been around kids forever.

Pulling back his hand, Carter reached for Shelby's as she stood. "Mom and I will wait wight heah, huh, Mom?"

The glance Shelby sent Luke was filled with humor. And a message, too.

He'd just been given a chance to be his son's hero.

Without another word, he headed down the hall, looking for a child's room, but had to stop before he got there.

Once he became a hero, he wasn't turning back, not even for a night. "Just one question," he said, spinning around, surprised to find Shelby and Carter only a couple of steps behind him.

"What?" they said in unison.

He stood there, forgetting what he'd been about to say as he got lost in the view. The woman who took his breath, the little guy who had eyes the same color blue as his own—eyes that were looking up at him expectantly.

Eyes he would fight every day to live up to.

"Will the two of you marry me?"

He heard the words. Started to die a thousand deaths. Would he *ever* learn finesse?

"I will," Carter, said. "S'long as you take me fishing. How 'bout you, Mom?"

Carter glanced at Shelby, as did Luke. Her eyes brimming with tears, she was smiling, too.

"Yes." She said it calmly.

"Oh, and…" Carter piped in and, slightly lost in euphoria, Luke glanced at the boy. "You have to sleep in Mom's woom, not mine. Her bed's biggaw."

Luke could hardly contain himself as he looked at Shelby. "How about it, *Mom*?"

"Yes," she said again. And then, with more tears, she threw her arms around Luke's neck and whispered, "Oh, yes," right by his ear.

He held on tight.

With no idea how he was going to keep her happy but knowing he'd do better every single day they were together.

"Hey, guys, what about the spidaw?" Carter was tugging at Luke's shirt, and when he looked down, he saw the little guy had a hold of his mother's skirt, too.

And that's when he knew.

With or without all the answers, or the right words, they'd just become a family.

* * * * *

You'll love other books in Tara Taylor Quinn's
Sierra's Web miniseries:

His Lost and Found Family
Reluctant Roommates
Tracking His Secret Child
Her Best Friend's Baby
Cold Case Sheriff
The Bounty Hunter's Baby Search
On the Run with His Bodyguard
Their Secret Twins
Not Without Her Child
Old Dogs, New Tricks

Available now from Harlequin Romantic Suspense
and Harlequin Special Edition!

Get 3 FREE REWARDS!

We'll send you 2 FREE Books <u>plus</u> a FREE Mystery Gift.

FREE Value Over **$20**

Both the **Harlequin Intrigue®** and **Harlequin® Romantic Suspense** series feature compelling novels filled with heart-racing action-packed romance that will keep you on the edge of your seat.

HARLEQUIN PLUS

Try the best multimedia
subscription service for romance
readers like you!

Read, Watch and Play.

Experience the easiest way to get
the romance content you crave.

Start your **FREE TRIAL** at
www.harlequinplus.com/freetrial.